A KISS BEFORE SLEEP

"Go to sleep, *chérie*." Dominic cupped Abigail's chin in his hand and brought her mouth against his briefly.

"Yes." Her voice quavered on that single word, but she was glad he had seen sense.

"No," he murmured when she moved away. "Here in my arms."

"Are you out of your mind?"

He shook his head. " 'Tis chilly. If one of us sickens, we may lose our only chance to get out of England."

"Do you promise not to . . . that is . . ."

"I promise to hold you in my arms and nothing else." He winced as he shifted his leg. "And, Abigail, I keep my promises as well as you do."

"All right."

He drew her back against him as he rested on the ground. His hard chest was the perfect pillow. "You are beginning to trust me, *chérie*. Could it be that you are no longer afraid of me?"

"I have not been afraid of you for a long time, Dominic."

He leaned his head against hers. "You can trust me on this one thing if on nothing else. If I had thought I could woo you to do as I wished with a few kisses, I would have done that long ago."

"Which you could never do," Abigail protested.

"Which I will never be able to do." As he sealed those words into her lips, Abigail let sleep take her. That way she did not have to guess which one of them was still lying.

Dear Romance Reader,

In July, we launched the Ballad line with four new series, and each month we'll present both new and continuing stories set everywhere from medieval England to the American West—the kind of passionate, romantic stories you love best, written by the most gifted authors. At the back of each book, we'll tell you when you can find subsequent books in the series that has captured your heart.

Beloved author Jo Ann Ferguson continues her *Shadow of the Bastille* series with **A Brother's Honor,** as a French privateer and the spirited daughter of an American ship captain brave Napoleon's blockade and discover the legacy that will shape their passionate destiny. Next, rising star Cynthia Sterling invites us back to the dusty Texas Panhandle as the second of her *Titled Texans* learns the ropes of ranching from an independent—and irresistibly attractive—woman who wants to become a lady in **Last Chance Ranch.**

Beginning this month is newcomer Tammy Hilz's breathtaking *Jewels of the Sea* series, a trilogy of three sisters who take their futures in their own hands—as pirates! In the first installment, a stubborn earl wonders if the fearless woman who was **Once A Pirate** will decide to become his bride. Finally, fresh talent Kelly McClymer introduces the unconquerably romantic Fenster family in her *Once Upon A Wedding* series, starting with a woman whose faith in happy endings is challenged as a man who refuses to believe in love asks her to become **The Fairy Tale Bride.** Enjoy!

Kate Duffy
Editorial Director

Shadow of the Bastille

A BROTHER'S HONOR

Jo Ann Ferguson

ZEBRA BOOKS
KENSINGTON PUBLISHING CORP.
http://www.zebrabooks.com

ZEBRA BOOKS are published by

Kensington Publishing Corp.
850 Third Avenue
New York, NY 10022

Copyright © 2000 by Jo Ann Ferguson

All rights reserved. No part of this book may be reproduced
in any form or by any means without the prior written consent
of the Publisher, excepting brief quotes used in reviews.

If you purchased this book without a cover you should be aware
that this book is stolen property. It was reported as "unsold
and destroyed" to the Publisher and neither the Author nor the
Publisher has received any payment for this "stripped book."

Zebra and the Z logo Reg. U.S. Pat. & TM Off.

First Printing: October, 2000
10 9 8 7 6 5 4 3 2 1

Printed in the United States of America

For Sunni,
Thanks for your sense of humor and all your hard work . . . and, most importantly, your friendship

Also look for these books by Jo Ann Ferguson

Lady Captain
A Daughter's Destiny
(Book #1 of Shadow of the Bastille)
Sweet Temptations
The Captain's Pearl
Anything for You
An Unexpected Husband
Her Only Hero
Mistletoe Kittens
An Offer of Marriage
Lord Radcliffe's Season
No Price Too High
The Jewel Palace
O'Neal's Daughter
The Convenient Arrangement
Just Her Type
Destiny's Kiss
Raven Quest
A Model Marriage
Rhyme and Reason
Spellbound Hearts
The Counterfeit Count
A Winter Kiss
A Phantom Affair
Miss Charity's Kiss
Valentine Love
The Wolfe Wager
An Undomesticated Wife
A Mother's Joy
The Smithfield Bargain
The Fortune Hunter

And writing as Rebecca North
A June Betrothal

Chapter One

Republic, 1813

"I will see you hang, you French pirate!"

A hint of a smile curled along Dominic St. Clair's lips. Such threats had been shot at him before, and he still lived. He watched as manacles lashed together the American captain and his officers. "I think I shall, instead, have the pleasure of watching you hang, Captain Fitzgerald."

"You will be stopped!" Fitzgerald raised his hand, then cursed as the chains rattled.

"But not by you and not today." He chuckled. "Mayhap, on your next voyage, Captain Fitzgerald, if you have another, you will be wise to command a ship that moves through the water like a bird instead of a sea cow."

He ignored the American captain's curses and turned to his first mate. Speaking in French, which he suspected none of the Americans understood, he ordered, "Ogier, keep them shackled during the voyage. Put them in one of the crew's bunkrooms.''

"Not the brig?'' Ogier's eyes widened, even as he wiped blood from a cut on his arm.

"They are officers, and manacles are enough.''

"*Oui, mon capitaine.*'' His grin twisted with devilment. "I would that I could gag them as well.''

Dominic laughed again. "The reward we will receive for bringing this crew to France will be worth having your ears battered. Think of how your share will buy you the time of a pretty miss who will tease your ears much more delightfully.''

As Ogier and the rest of his men aboard the American ship *Republic* chuckled, Dominic turned back to his enemy. What a fool Fitzgerald was to ply these waters with such a cargo! Fitzgerald's men had been barbaric in battle, and they would be dangerous in defeat. By separating the captain from his men, Dominic hoped to bring both ships intact to France.

"Captain Fitzgerald,'' he said, switching back to English, "you and your officers will be transferred to *La Chanson de la Mer.* If there is anything aboard the *Republic* you need to have conveyed to my ship for your journey to France, ask now.''

"You will grant me what I ask?'' Fitzgerald spat on the deck. "That is what I think of your benevolence, pirate.''

"I have been benevolent enough to grant you and your officers safe passage on *La Chanson de la Mer.*''

"As prisoners.''

"True, but my other choice would be to hang you and your officers in front of your men as an example of how we treat those who aid the emperor's enemies.''

The men surrounding Fitzgerald grew pale, but Dominic simply spoke the facts. No quarter could be given to those who tried to slip past Napoleon's blockade.

"Captain Fitzgerald, I ask you again. Are you satisfied with the arrangements I have offered you?"

"Cap'n!"

Dominic looked over his shoulder, shocked that one of Fitzgerald's men dared to interrupt. He frowned at the scrawny man who, he recalled, was the ship's cook.

The cook took a step forward, but halted when one of Dominic's men held up a bare sword. Gulping so loudly Dominic could hear him, he called, "Cap'n, you can't go without—"

"Silence!" roared Fitzgerald, his eyes burning with fury and frustration. "There is nothing I wish to take, for nothing remaining here shall have any value to me by the time we reach land."

"Cap'n," the cook began again.

"Silence!" Fitzgerald motioned toward the sleek ship rocking to starboard. "I vow to you, St. Clair, that I shall see your neck stretched for boarding my ship."

Dominic scowled as he saw fear on the cook's face. The man was so terrified that he could do no more than choke as Fitzgerald and his officers crossed the plank between the two ships. Did the cook fear Dominic planned to hang the crew? No, they were needed to sail this ship to Calais. It must be something else, but what?

"I do not like this, *mon capitaine*," Ogier mumbled. "Fitzgerald cannot be trusted."

"Make best speed, so you can be swiftly rid of him." He clapped his mate on the shoulder. "Guard my ship well."

Watching as his officers shouted orders on both ships, Dominic strode toward the captain's quarters at the stern of the ship. Fitzgerald had refused to reveal the *Republic*'s destination. Mayhap the American captain had not had time to destroy the logs. They should explain why this ship was here months after the United States had declared war on England.

He threw open the door and smiled. This ship had no speed, but she did have luxury. The captain's saloon was big enough to hold a table that would seat six or more men for a conference or to share a bottle of Jamaica rum. Overhead a lamp hooked to a rafter rocked. A porthole let in light to splash on a cabinet that was topped with bottles.

Two doors were on the opposite side of the room. One was open and led to the captain's quarters. The other? Something stroked his ankle. With a curse, he jumped back. He pulled his pistol, then laughed as he saw a calico cat reappearing from beneath the table.

"Take care, puss," he said as the cat tilted its head beneath his outstretched fingers. "You may find yourself short more of your lives than you can afford to lose. If—"

A scream froze him. The cat skittered away.

He tightened his grip on his pistol and opened the door. A pair of shapely legs kicked at the man leaning over the bed built against the stern.

Without raising his voice, Dominic snapped, "Enough!"

The man jumped away from the bed.

Dominic ignored him as he looked at the young woman scrambling to sit on the bed. Her hair was the red-gold of a sunrise sky, and her eyes the bluish gray of the sea after sunset. Fear glistened in them, but she held her head high as she tried to pull a blanket over her tattered dress.

"You need not stare," she said with a decidedly American accent.

What in God's name was a woman doing here?

Dominic intended to get an answer. But first . . . He pulled a gold wrapper from a hook by the door and flung it to the woman. As she drew it around her, he said, "Boleyn, report to me on deck at sundown."

Boleyn's face blanched, but he nodded. He edged toward the door.

"No!" cried the woman. She stood and winced. "Do not let him go! He tried—"

"Be silent." His next command sent Boleyn scurrying out of the cabin.

Dominic stepped inside and surveyed the room. The bed was built beneath a bank of windows. Drawers under the platform holding the mattress were the only storage. A table and a single chair took most of the floor. Overhead, an unlit lamp matching the one in the saloon swayed with the motion of the sluggish ship.

"Who are you?" Fear heightened the woman's voice.

"I would ask the same of you."

"Abigail Fitzgerald."

"Fitzgerald?" The cook's horror burst from Dominic's memory. Was this woman what the cook had wanted his captain to take with him? Yet Fitzgerald had left her behind. Why? "Impossible! What is your real name?"

"I told you. My name is Abigail Fitzgerald."

"The captain's wife?"

Abigail shook her head, then winced again. How dare these pirates abuse her like this! Even if she had not seen how that brute obeyed this man, she would have known that he must be an officer on the ship that had attacked them. His midnight eyes, in a face as sharply carved as the beams framing the ship, drilled her. He was barefoot and wore no stockings beneath his torn breeches, which were stained with gunpowder. A loose shirt opened to reveal the muscles across his chest. Sunlight glinted off his raven hair that drifted to his broad shoulders, and she saw the flash of a small gold ring in his left ear.

"No, I'm not the captain's wife," she replied, fighting to keep her voice steady. Unlike that other disgusting brute, there was only curiosity in his eyes.

"His mistress?"

"No!" she gasped, shocked at his vulgar question.

"Then who are you?"

She whispered, "Captain Fitzgerald is my father."

"You are Fitzgerald's *daughter?*"

"If you doubt me, ask my father," she retorted. "I demand that you take me to him immediately."

"You demand?" He closed the distance between them. When she did not move away, surprise appeared and vanished from his eyes. "You will demand nothing, Mademoiselle Fitzgerald. You will listen to my orders and follow them. Or . . ."

His threat remained unspoken as he spun on his heel. The door slammed behind him. She ran to it, but heard the table from the saloon being shoved across it.

This was worse than she had feared, and this might be only the beginning of the hell she faced as the prisoner of a French pirate.

Morning dawned with no relief from the terror. No one came near Abigail's door. Hunger stalked her, and she wondered if anyone remembered that she had not eaten yesterday.

This was not how her first voyage with Father was supposed to be. Aunt Velma had not wanted Abigail to sail on the *Republic*, but Abigail had thrown aside caution. She barely knew her father, for Arthur Fitzgerald had been only an occasional visitor. Raised by her beloved aunt and uncle in Massachusetts after her mother died shortly after Abigail's birth, she had waited anxiously for each visit from her father.

When Father had offered her a chance to sail with him, she could not have imagined refusing. For once, she ignored Aunt Velma's words of caution and hurried to pack the few things she could bring. She had been warned of the danger awaiting any ship that left an American port. Both the English and the French preyed on American ships, stealing their cargoes and impress-

ing their crews . . . or worse. Her breath caught. Her
grief had not lessened in the two months since the arrival
of the news that her uncle's ship, the *Arcot*, had been
sunk with every officer and crewman.

Was her father the latest victim of the war? The Frenchman had refused to tell her anything yesterday, not even
the courtesy of his name.

Hearing voices, she rushed to the door. It opened only
far enough for Cookie to hold out a covered dish and a
cup. Thank God! Cookie was alive!

"Cookie, what—?"

He shook his head. "Cap'n's compliments, Abigail."

"Captain? Father?" she asked, although she knew her
hopes were foolish.

"No, the other one. The Frenchie one. He—"

The door was shoved closed. She jumped back, spilling
soup on her wrapper. With a grimace, she set the dish
on the table and opened a drawer under her bed. She
drew on her other dress, arranging the limp, green muslin
sleeves and gold ribbons at the high bodice.

She would make the French pirates pay for this. She
would find her father, and together they would—

The table on the other side of the door was pushed
aside again. As the door opened, she held her breath.

She stared at the tall man who had rescued her yesterday. His gaze swept along her, his eyes burning holes
into her with their dusky fires. A restrained smile tilted
his lips.

"Good day, Mademoiselle Fitzgerald," he said as if
he were a welcome caller. He closed the door and sat on
a corner of the small table. "Now is your opportunity to
ask me the questions you wanted to last night."

"And you shall answer me? Very amusing."

"I am being, as always, honest, Mademoiselle Fitzgerald."

She tried to edge away, but he took her hand, and the thick, gold ring on his left hand cut into her.

Again his gaze captured hers. All her retorts vanished as she fought her fear. If she let him control her, she was lost. She straightened her shoulders. "I assume you are the captain of these pirates."

He smiled. "You assume correctly about my rank, but we are not pirates. We sail at the pleasure of Napoleon."

She walked toward the door. When he did not halt her, she hid her surprise. Then the truth fell on her shoulders as heavily as a mast crashing to the deck. She had no way to escape unless she jumped over the side. Locking her fingers together, she said, "I do not know your name."

"Dominic St. Clair, captain of *La Chanson de la Mer.*"

"A French pirate ship!"

"Privateer is the word your countrymen prefer."

"Whatever you call it, you have attacked our ship without provocation. The United States has not declared war on your country, nor yours on ours."

"Officially, no."

His serenity irritated like a burr in her stocking. "What have you done with my father?" Her voice broke. "He is still alive, isn't he?"

"Yes." A strange expression stole across his face, leaving it vulnerable. Just as swiftly, his lips grew tight again. "Your affection for Captain Fitzgerald is exemplary."

"He is my father! Why shouldn't I be anxious for him?"

"An interesting question, albeit one we do not have time to pursue now. Your father and his officers were transferred to my ship. Because this ship is slower, I expect they will reach landfall in Calais nearly a week before us."

"You are taking us all the way to France?"

Puzzlement drew lines in his forehead. "Of course. Once we are there, you can be returned to your *père's* loving arms. However, that will happen only if you wish to share his jail cell.''

"And then what?''

"And then I shall be rewarded for capturing this ship.'' He glanced around. "I shall get a good price for it, although it does not have the speed of my *La Chanson*.''

"But what will happen to Father and me?''

He clasped his hands around one knee as he put his foot on the chair. "In war, Mademoiselle Fitzgerald, there are victors and there are the vanquished. I fear you are the latter.''

"Not for long!''

"Be that as it may, for now, you are my guest.''

"Guest? Do you imprison your guests?''

His icy eyes cut through her like the prow slicing the waves. Standing, he said, "After what I interrupted here, I thought you understood keeping you here was for your protection. Or mayhap you didn't want me to halt Boleyn?'' He seized her shoulders and tugged her to his hard chest. "Is this how American women enjoy being wooed?''

She struck his cheek. Horror strangled her as his eyes narrowed. What a fool she was! He could kill her for less.

"Forgive me, Mademoiselle Fitzgerald,'' he murmured, releasing her. "I should not have said such a thing.''

Stunned that he would apologize, she hesitated. Could it be that he was not simply a rapacious pirate like that beast who had followed his commands?

"You must be upset,'' he continued. "I trust you were wise enough to remain here during the battle.''

She nodded.

"But you heard it.''

"All of it,'' she whispered. "My grandfather spoke of

fighting the English in the War of Independence, but . . ."
She shuddered. "I had no idea how men could scream."

"If it makes you feel better, only two men died."

She almost laughed, although not with amusement.
"That does not make me feel better. I cannot understand
why you had to attack us."

He opened his mouth, then closed it. A smile returned
to his lips. "I regret you had to be a witness to yesterday's
fighting. You have my assurance that our journey from
here will be peaceful."

"I doubt that. I am your prisoner."

"Yes, you are, but I have no intentions of confining
you to the brig."

"Not confining me?" She was being bold, but she had
so little to lose now. "Captain St. Clair, may I leave my
room?"

"When we are finished."

"Finished?" Cold sifted across her face. Moments ago,
he had been speaking about her safety. Now . . .

"You should sit before you swoon," said Captain St.
Clair.

"I'm not going to swoon!"

He smiled while he sat her in the chair and put his
hand on its back so she could not rise. "I suspect I know
what is wrong. My grasp of your language is not perfect.
What I intended to say was that, if I have satisfied your
curiosity, I have a few questions."

Embarrassment sent fire through her. When Captain St.
Clair chuckled, she knew her cheeks were scarlet. "I
doubt if I have answers for you," she replied.

"Let me judge that. First, tell me where your father
kept his log."

"I don't know."

"No?" His eyes became ebony slits again. "Where is
this ship bound?"

"I don't know exactly."

"You don't know exactly? Pardon me if I find that hard to believe, Mademoiselle Fitzgerald."

"But it is the truth. Our destination is . . ." She swallowed the fear clinging to her throat. "Our destination was somewhere in the Caribbean. That is all Father told me."

"The Caribbean?" He stared at her, shaking his head as a smile tipped his lips. "I had thought you would be honest with me about your destination if nothing else."

"I am."

"How can you ask me to swallow such a ludicrous tale?"

" 'Tis the truth!"

"Mademoiselle Fitzgerald, you must think me a complete fool to believe that you do not know that you are only a few hundred miles from England."

"England?" She groped for the edge of the table, sure the whole ship was spinning. "No, that cannot be true! You are lying to me."

"I am being honest with you."

"But Father told me—"

"A lie."

"Why should I believe you?"

"Because I am telling you the truth, while your father plied you with falsehoods." Leaning forward so his nose was only inches from hers, he demanded, "And you don't find that odd?"

"No." This must have been Father's way of protecting her in case something like this happened. But if Captain St. Clair was being honest with her, what was the *Republic* doing so close to England? Father had told her how he wanted to introduce her to the best of society. How she had anticipated the chance to take part in balls and masquerades and rides along the sandy beaches! She had planned that the half-finished dress in her cupboard would be ready in time for their arrival at the first island. But now . . .

Her terse answer seemed to have startled him. He drew back, then pulled a pistol from behind him. Her mind screamed for her to run. She could not, for she was frozen as if she stood in the midst of a New England blizzard.

"I bid you good day, Mademoiselle Fitzgerald." His smile again belonged to a rakish pirate. "You have answered my questions, but others have not. I ask that you stay here until I have finished those interrogations."

"But you said I could leave my room."

"I changed my mind."

She looked away from his smile that dared her to protest. What a beast he was!

He opened the door and tapped the other side. "I shall have a bolt put on here."

"For my protection?" she fired back. He was insolent and insulting.

"You are a lovely woman, Mademoiselle Fitzgerald, and my men have been at sea many months. Neither I nor Jourdan, who is serving as my first mate aboard this ship, will be able to keep an eye on the crew every minute of the day."

"But you are putting the bolt on the *outside!* That will not protect me from anyone."

He chuckled and, taking her hand, lifted it to his lips. A flurry of fire flew up her arm and caught in her throat. His thumb teased her palm as he raised her hand again to his mouth. A soft breath drifted from her parted lips when the warm moistness of his kiss oozed through her skin, adding to the flame. His gaze held her, but, for the first time, she did not want to look away. The unexpected warmth in his eyes urged her to delve further into the secrets glowing there.

He whispered lowly, so lowly she had to strain to hear him. "You need worry about no one . . . but me."

Abigail drew back as he laughed. He was playing her for a fool, and she was letting him do it. As the door closed, she shuddered. She would have to deal with Captain St. Clair until they reached . . . wherever, and she must find a way to best him. If only she had some idea how.

Chapter Two

Abigail paced her tiny room, three steps each way. How long before she wore through the boards? Another day with no answers. Another day of sailing toward the mock justice which could leave her father dead before she had a chance to know him.

Her door swung open. Seeing Captain St. Clair's smile, she tightened her hands into fists. No, she would not say it. She would not remind him that a gentleman knocked and asked permission before entering a lady's room. He was sure to find that amusing.

"I suspect this is yours." He dropped the calico cat on her bed.

"Yes, Captain." She turned away and patted Dandy's head. She did not want Captain St. Clair to see her tears of relief. Dear Dandy! She was so glad he had not been hurt or killed in the battle. She should have known better than to worry. The cat hunted through the lower decks every night and would have known where to hide.

Her eyes widened when Captain St. Clair reached past her and stroked the cat. Betrayal scorched her when Dandy began to purr. How could her cat welcome this French pirate who wanted to see Father dead?

"Why don't we let your cat sleep while you join me for dinner, Mademoiselle Fitzgerald?"

She stared at Captain St. Clair, noting for the first time his black velvet coat and white breeches. The style was better suited to a fine drawing room than the *Republic*. With his hair brushed behind the collar that reached his cleanly shaven jaw, the twinkle of his earring matched his gold waistcoat.

"Mademoiselle Fitzgerald?" he repeated.

"Yes . . . I mean, if you wish me to." She was flustered by his metamorphosis from pirate to gentleman.

"I would not have asked otherwise." Captain St. Clair led her into the saloon. Seating her graciously on one bench by the table, he poured a glass of white wine. "Compliments of *La Chanson de la Mer*." He smiled. "Your father's taste in wine is as poor as his judgment in sailing into my waters."

Abigail took a sip so she could avoid answering. When he sat on the bench facing her and the door to the deck, she wondered if he feared being attacked. With her father's crew aboard, he was wise to be cautious.

He spooned a generous portion from each dish onto a plate and set it in front of her. "Not hungry?" he asked as he folded his arms on the table.

"Not particularly." When she saw that his food was as untouched as hers, she asked, "And you, Captain?"

He picked up her fork. Dipping it in the fish stew, he ordered, "Eat."

"Captain, I am quite capable of deciding when or if—"

"Eat!" His laugh was cold. "*I* am hungry, Mademoiselle Fitzgerald."

Instantly she understood. Captain St. Clair had invited her to join him so Cookie would not poison the food. She thought about defying him, but she must pick her battles with care. Although she almost choked, she swallowed.

"You appear to be enjoying good health still," he said, dropping her fork and picking up his own.

"Mayhap your enemies chose a slow-acting poison."

He smiled. "They know better than to give me a chance to cut out their cowardly hearts before I die."

"Then have you given thought to the idea that I might consider it worth my life to rid the world of you?"

Taking a piece of bread, he offered it to her. She ignored it. With a shrug, he took a bite. "No, for how could you satisfy your desire for vengeance if you are dead?"

Abigail stared at him. She must never allow herself to forget, not even for a moment, his power over all of them.

When she did not answer, Captain St. Clair said, "You will like France. I suspect Paris is like nothing you have ever seen." His hand covered hers, pinning it to the table. As she stared at him, unsure if she should believe his smile, he lifted his glass with his other hand. Taking a sip, he said, "If you wish, I can give you a tour while we await the disposition of your father's case and while this cargo is sold for a great profit."

She drew her hand away, but did not lower her eyes. "Profit? You have halted the wrong ship if you wished to get a chest of gold for your troubles."

"I expect to sell the weapons at a tremendous profit."

"Weapons?" She laughed icily. "Captain St. Clair, you are sadly mistaken. We carry foodstuffs."

"Who eats gunpowder?"

"No one, but I saw what was going in the holds."

"Did you?" Laughing, he stood. "You are a charming innocent. Come with me."

"Captain, I—"

All gentleness vanished from his voice. "I said, come with me."

"And I wish to know why."

"Mademoiselle Fitzgerald, after you have refused to answer my questions, why do you expect me to answer yours?"

Despising his reasonableness, she said nothing as he took down the lamp and opened the door to the deck. He offered his arm. In disbelief, she looked from it to his face. So many emotions flashed through his eyes. She did not know if she was in more danger when he taunted her or when he eyed her boldly.

Her fingers rose to his velvet sleeve. His firm muscles warned that his strength was no illusion. As he drew her closer, she pulled away. With a smile, he recaptured her hand and held it on his arm.

"I do not bite, Mademoiselle Fitzgerald," he murmured. "Unless you request me to."

Heat seared her face, and he chuckled. If only her face did not betray every thought . . .

Abigail was aware of the men watching as she crossed the deck at Captain St. Clair's side. Grumbles of rage came from her father's crew. They should realize that she was not a traitor for consorting with the enemy. She had no choice. She was Captain St. Clair's prisoner.

The captain led her to the bowels of the ship, which her father had forbidden her to enter. Father had warned of dampness and rats and darkness. The stench twisted in her stomach.

Captain St. Clair paused and withdrew a ring of keys from his pocket. "From your father."

"Father *gave* you the keys?"

"He knew it was the only way to keep my crew from battering down every door. On the small chance he might regain his ship, he did not want her damaged. 'Tis a shame he did not worry as much about his daughter."

Abigail tried to hide her flinch. She must not let him poison her mind with his lies. *But why did Father leave me here with these pirates?* She could not silence the perfidious thought. "My father knows he can depend on me to take care of myself. I am not a child."

"That I have noticed." His grin was as frigid as a Massachusetts winter. "I simply find it odd that a man—" The lock clicked open. "This should help you understand our interest in this ship."

As light pushed back the darkness and Abigail saw the crates and iron-bound barrels, her eyes widened in disbelief. "This is all wrong! Where are the bales I saw on the wharf in New Bedford?"

Captain St. Clair shouldered her aside. She started to protest, then saw he held a crowbar.

"I knew you would refuse to believe the truth until you pried your charming nose into every corner," he said through clenched teeth as he popped a lid open. A nail spun through the air, and he lifted the top. *"Voilà!"*

Abigail reached in. Slime coated her fingers as she stared at guns covered with grease to prevent them from corroding. As Captain St. Clair raised the lamp, she saw the word *gunpowder* stenciled on barrels.

"The war between France and England has gone on for many years," he said. "Even England may need more weapons than they can produce, so the government would be eager to buy more."

"My father would not do that! He ... he ..." She took a deep breath, but could not calm her horror. "He would not sell weapons to the English! His father was wounded in the War for Independence."

"Then who was to receive these weapons?"

"I do not know."

"Mademoiselle Fitzgerald—"

"I am telling the truth. I do not know!" She gazed at the boxes. What *had* Father planned? Turning, she saw one of the guns in Captain St. Clair's hands. She fought to keep from blanching. "And what will happen now, Captain?"

"Selling weapons to our enemies is a very serious crime." He looked along the barrel before putting the gun back in the crate and wiping his hands on his breeches. He hammered the top of the crate into place. "If a man is convicted of that, he hangs."

"You will send my father to hang?"

"Wouldn't he do the same to me?"

Abigail knew her father would be delighted to see Captain St. Clair at the end of a hemp noose. When Captain St. Clair picked up the lantern, she asked, "And what will happen to me?"

He cupped her chin and tilted her face toward him. His voice dropped to a husky whisper, "*Chérie*, I told you that you need not worry about anyone harming you."

"Except you!"

With a laugh, he strode away. Abigail had no choice but to follow, because she did not want to be left in the dank, dark hold. She did not look away from the angry stares of her father's crew on deck. They had known. Her father could not have hidden the truth from them as easily as he had from her.

Why had Father lied to her? *And how could Father have left me here with these French pirates?* He should have taken her with him. Or were things worse on the other ship? Mayhap he had been trying to protect her the best way he could. She had to believe that.

Captain St. Clair ushered her into the saloon. As she sat, he shoved a glass into her hand. "Drink."

"Are you afraid someone poisoned the wine?" she snarled back.

"I think only of you. If you get any paler, your freckles are going to jump off your face."

Putting her fingers up to her cheek, she ignored his

grin. Although she hated obeying, she took a sip. Its warmth oozed through her, easing the tight bands around her heart.

He sat beside her. "You must, of course, stay in France until your father's trial is over."

She held the goblet with both hands, for she did not trust her quivering fingers. "I assumed that."

"If your father is found guilty as I expect, it will not be easy for you there alone."

"I assumed that, as well, Captain." She refused to let him see how scared she was. If Captain St. Clair had a heart, he kept it well hidden.

Reaching across the table, he snagged his own wine. "Mayhap you could find work teaching English. That might serve you better than working at a harbor tavern."

A tavern? Father had promised her the chance to meet the highest of society on this voyage, not its dregs. "If you think I would—"

He laughed. "No, I did not think you would be interested in such a position. Mayhap you might wish to return to America."

"Yes." She watched him. What was he thinking now? She wished she could guess . . . even once. "My aunt lives in Massachusetts."

He leaned toward her as his arm slid along the table behind her. She started to rise, but his fingers around her shoulder became a clamp. His other hand tipped her face toward him. "A message can be taken to her."

"For a price?"

His dark eyes twinkled. She did not know whether to believe the merriment in his eyes or the threat displayed on his wind-roughened face. "You are learning very, very quickly."

"And what is your price, Captain, for delivering that message?"

"I will let you guess." His gaze touched her face, leaving its heat as one finger stroked her cheek.

"Your price is too high." Her voice was breathless, a mere whisper. With fear, she told herself sternly, not with delight at this pirate's touch.

"How do you know when I have not spoken it?"

"You speak it well without words."

"Sometimes words are unnecessary." He tipped her mouth toward his.

With a cry, Abigail leaped to her feet and away from the enchantment he spun with the ease of a master sorcerer. "Captain St. Clair, I didn't want your crewman touching me. I do not wish to have you paw me either!"

He stood, his face hardening as she put the table between them. "You would prefer to work for a man who will expect more from you than lessons for his children?"

"Good night. I have no appetite for either dinner or your company." She faltered when she saw the shiny lock which had been set on her door.

"I am not trying to scare you needlessly."

"Why should my future concern you?" she asked, facing him. "Rest assured, I can take care of myself."

"True." He leaned one shoulder against the wall and crossed his arms over his chest. Even his fine feathers could not hide the truth. He was a vile pirate who was enjoying her fear. "But it is just as true that it may be impossible for you to live as you planned."

"If I decide to sell myself for passage home, it shall not be to you." She slammed the door behind her.

It cut off the sound of his laugh, but she knew, as he did, how futile her courage was. With a shudder, she feared he soon would tire of playing with her as Dandy quickly tired of playing with a mouse. Then he would destroy her.

* * *

Dominic St. Clair stared at the sails. They bulged with the wind that flipped hair into his face. Brushing it aside, he sighed. This ship was not as poorly made as he had feared. Still, it would need all his skills to gauge its passage. On his own ship, he could determine the height of each wave by the way *La Chanson*'s bow dipped and danced.

He pushed away from the rail. *La Chanson* would be his again as soon as he delivered this American ship to France. That hour would be delayed if they were caught in the blow threatened by the dark line along the western horizon.

He snarled a curse as he almost stumbled into someone. His smile returned when he took a deep breath of sweet perfume. "Mademoiselle Fitzgerald, I do not recall telling you that you may take a stroll about the deck."

"No, Captain, you did not." When she frowned, it ruined her gentle loveliness. The green dress with its gold lace flattered her coloring, for the sun set on fire the few wisps of her russet hair that had escaped from beneath her prim bonnet. Keeping her hair hidden was, in his opinion, a crime. Those ruddy curls should cascade along her slender shoulders and over her soft breasts. "I wish to go to the galley."

He chuckled. Abigail Fitzgerald was as fiery as her hair, but she must accept the truth. She belonged to Dominic St. Clair by right of capture. Her wit had made last evening interesting, but he wanted more than conversation with her. He imagined her slim arms wrapped around him and those inviting lips soft with eager breaths of passion. No doubt, she would be as vicious as her cat, but he would enjoy taming her until she purred.

"Captain St. Clair, if you have nothing to say, would you be kind enough to step aside?"

Again he chuckled. If she had any idea of the course of his thoughts, she would be even more outraged. "Why do you want to go to the galley?"

"I wish to speak with Cookie."

"Speak of what? Some conspiracy against me?"

Her laugh was sharp. "Which of Father's men would trust me when they think . . . ?"

He cupped her chin and drew her closer. Her perfume was beguiling for a man who had been at sea for so long, but the downy brush of her skin against his finger was even more intoxicating. "When they think you are my mistress? Is that what you wish to say?"

The blush climbing her cheeks gave him his answer. She had, it was clear, more wit than her father, for somehow, even in her quarters, she had sensed the rage boiling among the *Republic*'s crew. He glanced across the sun-swept deck. Would Fitzgerald's men turn that frustration on her? He must remind Jourdan, who was serving as first mate on this American tub, to keep a closer watch on Fitzgerald's crew. Especially Woolcott, he noted, when he saw the onetime bo'sun scowl at Abigail before turning to mutter to one of his cronies.

"If you are so bored in your quarters that you dare to disobey my orders," he said, "I can suggest something to fill the afternoon."

Sparks burned in her blue eyes. "I am sure you can. However, I am interested in something more worthwhile."

"What could be more worthwhile than pleasure?"

Abigail considered retorting, but anything she said would be used to insult her anew. She walked away. During her three days in his captivity, Captain St. Clair had allowed no one else in the captain's quarters, save for Cookie. But Cookie had been granted no time to talk to her.

She needed to ask Cookie about the guns in the hold.

She needed to ask him why the crew had surrendered instead of taking the ship to the bottom as her uncle had when attacked. She needed to know, most of all, why her father had left her here as Captain St. Clair's prisoner.

As her eyes adjusted to the companionway's darkness, Abigail saw several men in the lower passage. One man, thin and wiry, stepped forward. She pretended to be unaware of his leer. The only thing more disgusting than Captain St. Clair must be his crew.

The man put out an arm to block her way. "Come closer," he taunted in a thick French accent. "Come closer, and share with us what you share with the *capitaine*."

"You are mad!" she retorted, then wished she had remained silent when the men edged closer.

"I speak only of business." His friends laughed as he continued, "Our reward for capturing this scow will be grand. Why not earn yourself some gold instead of just giving yourself to the *capitaine* for nothing?"

She tried to slide away. "Leave me alone!"

"Jourdan!" cried one of the men. She could not understand the rest of his words.

Her eyes widened. *This* was Captain St. Clair's first mate? The man who was supposed to help protect her from his salacious crew?

Jourdan cursed as another shout rumbled along the passage. She recognized that voice. Captain St. Clair! She opened her mouth to answer, but, as the other men scurried to answer the command, Jourdan snarled, "Tell the *capitaine* of this and you will die."

Leaning her head on the wall, Abigail shivered. A hand touched her arm. She whirled and screamed.

" 'Tis me, my girl." Cookie's face was taut with fury. "They tried—"

"To frighten you, but you are a Fitzgerald. You will not let them scare you."

"I will try to be brave," she whispered.

"Good. Come with me." He led her to the galley.

The heat from the stove reached out to suck them in, but Abigail did not notice as she continued to shake.

Cookie sat her on the nearest barrel. "Ye shouldn't be down here alone, my girl." He pulled a cup from a shelf and opened a canister. Filling the tin cup, he held it to her lips. "Drink."

A flame rolled along her throat with the rum. Tears blurred her eyes, and she choked. Pressing her hands to her chest, she fought the fire. Cookie slapped her on the back.

"Thanks," she gasped. "If thanks is the proper word."

"Ain't nothing like rum to cut to the quick of the problem."

"To the quick, anyway." She rested her head against the uneven wall. Gazing up at the greasy ceiling, she mused, "Mayhap we should cut our throats and be done with it. If the French hangman does not have us, it will only be because these pirates have murdered us."

Cookie took a gulp of rum and smacked his lips. "Ye don't believe that."

"I do not know what to believe any longer." Leaning forward, she whispered, "Cookie, there are weapons in the hold."

"Yer father wasn't breaking no law."

"Are you sure? Will you testify to that under oath?"

"Abigail!"

"Cookie, I know you would do anything for Father." *Even lie*, she thought, but could not say the words aloud.

"Aye," he breathed as he stared into his cup. "But what good will it do? Those accursed Frenchies won't believe an honest American sailor."

She grasped his arm. "But why are there guns in the hold? Who was Father planning to sell them to?"

"What ye don't know, Abigail, that French cur can't seduce out of ye."

"Cookie! The only one who shares my bed is Dandy."

His wrinkled face brightened as he smiled. "I'm right pleased to hear that. If yer father were to learn ye were bedding down with that Frenchie, he'd be furious."

"If he cares . . ." She glanced away. She could not let Captain St. Clair taint her thoughts with lies. But why had Father left her behind on the *Republic?* That one thing she could not understand. Not at all.

"He cares," Cookie retorted.

"But he left me here!"

"He must have had his reasons."

"What could they possibly be?"

Cookie put his hands on her arms. "Can't know 'til we ask him. Go back to yer quarters and stay there."

"Until we reach Calais?"

"Is that where they be taking us?"

"You didn't know?"

He smiled. "Now I know, Abigail, and so shall the rest of our lads." Putting his gnarled hands on her shoulders, he said, "If ye want to help, and I know ye do, listen well to what that Frenchie cap'n has to say. Anything ye think might be helpful, let me know."

"I shall come right—"

"No!" He lowered his voice. "Don't come here again. I shall find a way to talk with ye. But heed his words well, Abigail. What ye learn may be our salvation." His lips tightened into a straight line. "Our only salvation."

Chapter Three

Thunder obliterated the high-pitched scream of the wind through the rigging. The ship rocked wildly. Flashes of lightning danced through the sky, coming closer to the mast. Rain splattered on the windows.

With each crack of thunder, Abigail flinched. She bent to pick up the pillow that had been knocked off her bed. Clutching it, she clung to the bed as the ship pitched. She shivered beneath her paisley shawl. If Captain St. Clair was not the captain he boasted he was, they could be sunk.

She knelt to stare out the window. Although it was mid-afternoon, the sky was black. With a moan, she pressed her face into the pillow as lightning struck the sea. She knew it was silly to be terrified of storms. When she had been a child, her aunt had eased her fear by taking Abigail into her arms and singing lullabies until the storm passed. Now she was alone. A voice—any voice—would help mute the noise overhead. When she heard the door to the saloon open, she ran out. It took all her strength not to fling herself into Captain St. Clair's arms.

He gave her no more than a glance as he rushed into her father's room. She followed, glad it was only a pair of steps across the pitching deck. When she gasped at another peal of thunder, he looked up.

"I hope your face's gray hue does not mean you suffer from seasickness when the sea is a bit rough," he said.

"No, I am not seasick. 'Tis the storm."

Selecting a map, he turned. "Frightened of thunder and lightning?" He smiled before crossing the saloon. Over his shoulder, he threw, "Hope we endure only this noisy show. If the heart of the storm catches us, we shall have more to worry about."

Rain shot into the saloon as he closed the door. She huddled by the table until the lamp hooked to a rafter flickered and went out.

The door crashed open. A man blew into the room. "Is the captain here?" he shouted.

"No." She swallowed harshly when he faced her. Jourdan!

He snickered as he walked toward her. Although the wind screeched through the open door, her heart thudded even more loudly.

"Captain St. Clair is on deck," she said, backing toward her room. "If your message is urgent—"

"Let the message wait." His voice was hoarse with lust. "You owe me for the reprimand I got from Captain St. Clair."

"Reprimand?"

"For the lies you told him." He caught her arm. When she screamed, he smiled. "Screech all you want, woman. No one will hear you but me."

She grabbed a wine bottle from the cabinet and broke

it over his head. He dropped to one knee, but reached for her skirt.

She ran to her bedroom door. He lurched to his feet and blocked her way. She raced the other way, fighting the deck, which seemed alive beneath her feet. He followed. She pushed the bench toward him. He crashed to the floor. His murderous scowl nearly paralyzed her. He threw himself forward.

With a cry, she stumbled back against the open door. The wind thrashed her skirt in the wild melody singing through the rigging. Sea spray burned her face. She raised her arm to cover her mouth and nose as she clung to the door.

Jourdan reached for her. She tried to push him away. She shrieked as she was flung onto the deck. Water crashed over her. Struggling to her feet, she slipped on the wet deck, which arched and flowed like Dandy. The ship dropped into a deep trough. She gripped the railing. Her eyes widened as she saw the other railing dip toward the water. Glancing over her shoulder, she stared at a black mountain of water about to pounce on the *Republic*.

Crouching, she pressed her face to the rail as water crashed over her. Then the ship righted itself. Could Captain St. Clair steer the *Republic* through this? She had to get below before she was washed away.

With her shawl over her face, she ran to the nearest companionway. She kicked the covering, but could not loosen it. She must go back. If Jourdan was still there . . . Water struck her, forcing her to her knees. She had to go back.

She took one step, then cried out as she was knocked off her feet. Waves ground her under gray paws. If she was washed overboard, she never would be found.

Rising, she lurched to a mast. A rope flailed in the wind. She tried to grab it, but it spun away. She pressed her face to the mast as a wave broke over the ship. Her cry for help was lost in the roar of the water. She kept a death grip on the mast. As the water flowed through the scuppers, she fought to breathe.

A strong arm caught her. She gasped as water slammed her and her rescuer against the mast. Opening her eyes, which burned from salt and wind, she gazed up at Captain St. Clair's stern face. His chest was as hard and unyielding as the mast. The iron bar of his arm encircled her waist. His tattered shirt blew about his shoulders. She winced as it struck her.

His mouth moved, but the sound was swallowed by the storm.

She shouted, "I cannot hear you!"

He lowered his head. She leaned toward him. His mouth brushed hers. She pulled back and stared in astonishment. The ship rocked violently, and he released her.

"Captain . . . Dominic!" she cried. "Don't—"

He swept his arm around her again. With one hand against the mast, he balanced himself on the heaving deck. "Make up your mind, *chérie*. Do you stay in my arms or no?"

He did not wait for her answer. He shouted something across the deck, then pulled her away from the mast. She would have fallen if his strong hands had not guided her into the cabin.

Abigail leaned on the table and gulped deep breaths of air. The door closed, and the wind's scream was stifled.

Hands stroked her shoulders. She closed her eyes, letting the pleasure of Dominic's caress consume her. As he brushed aside her soaked hair, his mouth teased the damp skin beneath her ear. A shiver flowed along her, urging her to lean back against him.

Gently he turned her to face him. His dark gaze roved along her face, branding her with its power. He wanted her. She could see that in his eyes and sense it all along his strong body as the motion of the deck pressed them

even closer. His mouth lowered toward hers; then he
released her with a curse.

She stared in amazement as he strode to the door. She
had thought . . . hadn't he wanted to . . .

"Wait right here, *chérie*." He grinned. "I look forward
to the reward you owe me for saving your life."

"Reward?"

Regret deepened his voice. "Something I shall discuss
with you later, for I must go. I am needed on deck. When
the storm is past," he added sharply, "you can explain
exactly why you decided to take a stroll along the deck
now."

Abigail recoiled. How could she have been so stupid?
She had fled Jourdan only to fall prey to Dominic's seductive wiles. She could imagine the two men laughing over
her idiocy.

Dominic St. Clair was her enemy. Worse, he wore a
wedding ring on his left hand. But still she yearned for
him to hold her again, his mouth on hers as their bodies
strained against the storm of passion swirling through
them. She must forget that pleasure, or it would betray
her again.

Abigail yawned and pinned her hair in place. Opening
her door, she went into the sunny saloon. Most of the
cups had shattered during the storm, but she found one
that was not cracked and poured herself some of the strong
coffee.

The door to the deck opened. Dominic said to someone
she could not see, "We shall convene here."

Abigail turned to go back to her room as a half-dozen
men followed him into the room.

Dominic grasped her arm. "Stay, *chérie*."

"I am not properly dressed." She closed the top button
on her wrapper.

"I do not care if you are naked. Stay here, and say nothing." He picked up her cup and carried it to the table.

Abigail was unsure whether to be insulted or irritated as he sat at the table and sipped her coffee. When he nodded, the man closest to the door opened it. She gripped her wrapper as Jourdan inched forward. The first mate fired a scowl in her direction. What was happening?

When Dominic spoke, it was in French. The first mate started to reply, but Dominic cut him off. Again he snapped something at Jourdan.

This time Jourdan said, "*Oui*, Capitaine St. Clair."

Dominic fired more questions, but nothing on his taut face gave her a clue to what he said.

The first mate snarled and took a step toward her. Dominic's order halted him. Jourdan stormed out.

Standing, Dominic leaned his fingertips on the table. He spoke quietly, then dismissed the others. He motioned for Abigail to come to the table.

"What happened?" she asked.

"I have dismissed Jourdan as my first mate."

"Why?"

His laugh was honed with anger. "You know why. Although you think I am a fool, Abigail, it was clear to me, once the storm was past, that your trip onto the deck matched the moment when Jourdan should have been giving me his report."

"You know what he tried to do?"

"Only what he would admit to, but that was enough." He pulled a pin from her hair and dropped it onto the table. When she gasped, he did the same with another. Her hair fell down her back and over his arm as he drew her to him. "I made my orders clear. Like the *Republic*, you are mine."

"I am not—"

He bit back a curse as the door opened again. Giving orders to Jourdan's replacement, he said when the door closed again, "You will find Normand is wise enough to leave you alone."

"I hope so," she whispered.

"I should throw Jourdan in the brig with a diet of hard biscuit and water." Sitting, he said, "I cannot, because we have no water."

"No water?"

"Every barrel was washed overboard or ruptured."

"We still have the rum."

"'Tis gone, too, save for one small keg."

"The wine—"

"Every bottle has been smashed."

"Oh," she whispered, not sure what else to say as she looked at the broken cups on the sideboard.

"Just 'oh'? You have been asea long enough to know how desperate our situation is." He leaned toward her. "More desperate, because it was not an accident. Someone among your father's crew took an axe to the barrels and split the tops. The roll of the ship toppled them. Not a drop remains beyond the half barrel of rum in the galley. It will not be enough, even if we ration it, to reach France. Off course amid the English waters as we are . . ."

At her soft cry of alarm, Dominic drew Abigail to sit beside him. He brushed his hand along her loosened hair. She smelled as fragrant as a summer meadow, and her swift breaths grazed his skin. If only he could find the time to lean her back on her bed as her breath grew even swifter . . .

"Are we lost?" she asked.

"The stars tell me the storm blew us north." He smiled. "We are not lost. Just off course."

"But we have no water!" She started to pull away, but he tightened his hold on her. "You should concentrate on our problems, Captain."

"You are my problem, chérie. I think of you when I should be thinking of punishing those responsible for this crime." He ran his finger around the top button of her wrapper and murmured, "You burn like a flame when I hold you in my arms."

"I believe you are mistaken." She stood and picked up her cat, holding it as a shield. "Consider the kisses a reward for saving my life. Nothing more."

"That is where *you* are mistaken." He plucked the cat from her arms and tossed it onto the deck. Gripping her chin, he brought her eyes up to his. "*Chérie*, I have grown accustomed to you lying to me. Must I become accustomed to you lying to yourself?"

Her eyes sparked with fury. "You are accustomed to getting what you want, Captain, aren't you?"

"Always."

"If not by charm, then by coercion."

He smiled. "Exactly."

"If not by coercion, then by force."

"If necessary." He brushed his lips against her cheek.

Her voice was unsteady as she murmured, "I hate to disillusion you, Captain, but you finally have encountered someone you cannot have by charm or by coercion."

"Do you mean I should not waste my time on the first two? You prefer, I take it, that I go directly to force?" He laughed. "I assure you, *chérie*, I shall not have to resort to force. You have already proven you are more than willing."

"Captain—" Her breath exploded out of her as he bent to run his tongue along her lower lip.

"My name is Dominic, *chérie*," he whispered. "You used it before."

"This is a mistake."

"Is it? I think not." His arms tightened around her as every muscle responded. She was just what he needed, a balm for a man thirsting for satiation.

He cursed. Thirst! Sweet water was close by, but it was English water. To go ashore here would mean hanging for everyone on this ship, French and American alike. Treachery reeked throughout the ship. She might be part of it. What better way to distract him than by pretending to be reluctant and then to surrender? Mayhap she was right. This was a mistake.

"Stay here," he ordered.

"Captain—"

"Stay here, or you will wish you had." He slammed the door behind him. Nothing eased his frustration. Only having Abigail Fitzgerald in his bed would, but now he had to think about the water situation and deal with those responsible. *Merde!*

They would replenish the water. Then he would turn his attention to her until he had satisfied his craving for her.

Chapter Four

Abigail leaned on her elbow on the pillow and watched the moonlight dust the waves with its cool glow. The ship was moving again. She was both pleased and horrified. Would it have been better to die of thirst on the ship or to arrive in France as a prisoner and watch her father hanged?

All day, the *Republic* had drifted with the motion of the current and the waves. The storm had damaged the rudder. At least that was what Dominic told her, but she suspected that Father's men had had a hand in jamming it. She was not sure how, but something in the way Cookie had avoided answering her questions warned her that she was getting close to the truth.

If she knew that, so did Dominic. He had lied to her. To soothe her? Unlikely. She grimaced. 'Twas more likely that he did not want her to share his opinions with her father's crew.

"Not that they would ask me," she mumbled as she dropped back into the musty pillow. When she had gone out on deck to view the repair work, she had been met with only grumbles and curses. She had wanted to remind her father's men that Dominic St. Clair was her enemy, too, but she doubted that they would heed her. Since Dominic had replaced Jourdan as first mate, even Cookie had treated her with distrust.

Where was Dandy? She wished her cat would come and curl up against her back. Then she would not be so alone with this unending ache of fear.

Abigail turned away from the window and sat as the door opened. She pulled her wrapper around her, buttoning it in place as Dominic rested his shoulder against the door frame.

"Were you sleeping?" he asked.

"No."

He held out a tin cup to her. "Your evening's ration of water."

Looking into the cup, she saw that the water barely covered the bottom. She sighed. Her lips tasted salty when she tried to dampen them. This was not enough water to wash away her thirst, but she tilted back the cup savoring every drop.

"Thank you," she said, handing back the cup.

He set it on the table. "Tomorrow we may have enough for only the evening's ration."

"We cannot be far from France."

"The length of England and the Channel, and the winds are fickle."

"Mayhap they are tired after that storm."

He smiled. "I wish the rest of the crew had your sense of humor, Abigail."

"I have the privilege of not having to work in the sun all day." She stared at the cup so she could avoid the dark fires in his eyes. "I might not be so willing to jest if I suffered what they are suffering."

"So that is why you have stayed in your room since the storm?"

"Yes." That was a lie. She did not want to go on deck and see her father's crew regarding her with the hatred that had increased since the storm. Someone must have seen, even through the high winds and lashing rains, how Dominic had kissed her by the mast. That single kiss had damned her as Dominic's mistress, a woman who had betrayed her father and her country in exchange for his touch. If they guessed that kiss had not been the only one . . .

"I believe we shall put in at the Channel Islands for water before continuing to France," Dominic said, interrupting her uneasy thoughts.

"But aren't those islands British?"

His smile grew sly. "I have ways of confusing even the most diligent port master."

"I am sure you do." She reached for the blanket at the foot of her bed. "I bid you good night, Captain."

"I thought you were going to call me Dominic."

She frowned. "What I would like to call you is not appropriate for a lady to say."

Dominic laughed, not with the arrogance she had heard from the moment he had captured the ship, but with honest amusement. "Finally I am getting to see the true Abigail. I was certain there was more to you than the puritanical daughter of a traitor."

"You have no proof my father is a traitor."

"Now you sound like your father's men. They cannot see sense until it is forced upon them."

"Mayhap we would see sense if there were any about why you attacked this ship."

He laughed again. "A weak argument, now that you

know what cargo this ship carries.'' He stepped in and closed the door behind him.

"Dominic, I was planning on sleeping.''

"Were you?''

Taking a deep breath to slow her pulse as she gazed up into his eyes as he crossed the room, she stood. "What is it that you want to talk about tonight?''

"I thought I had made that obvious, *chérie*.''

At his husky answer, his broad hands caught hers and brought her against his firm chest. When he bent toward her, the odor of rum swept over her. Was he drunk or simply mad? He could not be drunk. There was too little to drink.

"Stop!'' she cried.

"*Chérie*, we have not yet started.''

His lips covered hers in a kiss which was as savage as the sea. No, she would not surrender to him or to her body which was aching for his touch! She turned her face away as his hands slid up her back as he teased the curve of her neck with gentle nibbles.

"No,'' she whispered as he reached for the top button of her wrapper.

When it opened, his questing mouth followed the lace along the top of her nightdress. "Do not be scared, *chérie*,'' he murmured. "It is time to stop pretending.''

"I am not pretending. Release me!'' She tugged away and held her wrapper closed over her breasts. "You are drunk!''

"Drunk?'' He shook his head. "Only with the thoughts of the rapture awaiting us.''

"You reek of rum.''

"I drink rum, so you might have my share of the water.'' He slipped his hands over hers, peeling her fingers, one by one, away from her wrapper. "I have had only a dram, for I would not want too much rum to dull my chance to relish what we shall share.''

"We cannot share anything but enmity."

"You wish this as much as I," he whispered. "I taste the hunger on your lips. Together we can satisfy it."

"I mustn't. This is wrong." She needed to remember that. "This is all wrong. I shan't be just another way you avenge yourself against your enemies."

"Do you think that is why I want you?" His eyes became ebony nuggets, hard and faceted. He captured her lips, all tenderness gone, as his tongue delved to caress hers.

She moaned against his mouth. She did not want to be swallowed by this incredible delight. She must not melt into the pool of heated fire surging through her. Clenching her hands at her sides, she fought her own body that urged her to surrender. It was impossible to deny the truth. She wanted this ecstasy.

A man shouted on deck. Fists pounded on her door.

"Wait here," Dominic murmured against her ear. When she quivered as his breath became a sweet caress, his hushed laugh warmed her skin.

Abigail pulled her wrapper around her again as Dominic opened the door. Her eyes met the shock in Normand's, and she looked hastily away. Now everyone aboard the *Republic* would know without question that she had been in Dominic's arms. If Father learned the truth, he would despise her for shaming him with his enemy. How could she have been so foolish? Dominic may not have been drunk, but she had been intoxicated with his touch.

She looked up when she heard Dominic curse. She could not understand what he said in French, but there was no mistaking his fury. Normand raced across the saloon and out onto the deck.

"What is wrong?" she cried.

Dominic did not answer as he stormed out of her quarters. She ran after him and saw him go into her father's room. She froze in the door as he threw open a drawer in her father's desk and pulled out a pistol. He grasped her arm and shoved her back into her room.

"Are we under attack?" she cried.

"Stay here! Once we halt the Americans' mutiny, I shall deal with you."

"Mutiny?"

He slammed the door. The bolt snapped into place.

Abigail gripped the chair. *Mutiny!* The ugly word riveted her to the deck.

She moaned as a gun fired. In quick succession, many others answered. Her father's crew must have stolen weapons from the hold while Dominic's men worked to repair the rudder. Now she understood why Cookie had avoided answering her questions.

She cringed when something brushed her leg. Realizing it was her cat, she closed her eyes and shuddered. "Dandy, you are scaring years off my life."

The cat jumped up on the bed, preening. He adjusted the covers to his satisfaction and put his nose against his paws before falling asleep.

Abigail wondered how Dandy could be so oblivious to the noise from the deck. A man shrieked. Just as one had when *La Chanson* had captured this ship. Sweet heavens, someone had to halt this before more people were killed.

She struck the door with her fists, but it did not give. Her shout got no answer. If anyone was in the saloon, they were too busy with the fighting.

The ship halted to rock with the motion of the waves. Were they out of their minds? The ship must get somewhere where they could obtain more water, or they all would die.

Although the room was stifling, she shivered, wrapping her arms around herself. Father's crew would die whether by thirst or the hangman's noose. They had nothing to lose, so they were willing to risk their lives now to see that Dominic and his crew died with them. The fighting could last for days before the losers surrendered or were killed to the final man. Only the moon inching across the sky told her that time still moved as guns fired again and again.

Who was winning? She shivered. If her father's men defeated the Frenchmen, they would kill her as a traitor who had warmed their enemy's bed. If Dominic's men won, he would see her father hanged.

She heard furtive footsteps in the saloon. She flattened herself against the wall by the door. If she could rush past when the door opened, she might be able to escape. *But to where?* She silenced that fearful thought as the latch lifted.

Abigail jumped forward, then gasped, "Cookie!"

The short man waved her to silence as he looked fearfully over his shoulder. Wiping blood from a cut on his face, he whispered, "Abigail, can you swim?"

"Swim?"

"Answer me!"

"Yes, but why? Are Father's men losing?"

"We ain't winning or losing, but we gotta lose. Most of our lads are cornered below." He cursed vividly. "St. Clair is smarter than any of us guessed."

"You should have asked me," she said tautly. "If just one of you had dared to trust me, I could have told you that Dominic is no fool."

"I thought Woolcott was the wiser of the two."

"Woolcott?" She stared at him in disbelief. "Even Father said more than once that Woolcott thinks himself far better a sailor than he truly is."

"Cap'n Fitzgerald said that?" He cursed.

"Why didn't you trust me? Now the French will kill all of us."

Cookie shook his head. "They won't get a chance. They've gone mad!"

"They? The French?"

"Our lads. Woolcott is gonna destroy the *Republic*."
He seized her shoulders. "Get off the ship."

"Off the ship? How?"

"Swim!" He ran out the door.

Abigail called out his name as she heard him bolt the
door again. Was *he* mad? He had ordered her to leave,
then relocked the door.

She looked at the bank of windows over her bed. Climbing onto the bed, she peered out, not at the water, but at
an unmoving line on the horizon. Land! Land was no
more than a half mile away.

But that land must be England. If she tried to swim
ashore here, she would be among enemies. She shivered
again. She might not have to worry about reaching England. In the water, she would be a tempting target for
every sharpshooter on the deck. Then she remembered
what Cookie had said. The fight was belowdecks. Cookie
had risked his life to bring her this warning. She could
not ignore it.

The deck shuddered as an explosion shook the ship.
She fell, hitting her knees hard on the floor. Jumping to
her feet, she grabbed the chair. She flung it through the
windows. Clambering onto the bed, she used her pillow
to clear away the claws of glass.

Gingerly, she put her foot on the sill. She stared at the
black waters below. As she tensed to jump, she heard a
yowl behind her.

"Dandy!"

He skittered away to hide between the wall and the
floorboards, frightened.

Taking a calming breath, she knelt. "Dandy! Come
here, boy. Good kitty. Pretty kitty."

Slowly, too slowly, the gray cat eased out, pulling back
as another blast resonated through the ship. She could
not leave Dandy to be killed. She grabbed his front paws

and pulled him into her arms. He snarled his outrage, but she ignored him as she scrambled onto the bed.

The ship quaked violently again, and her shoulder slammed into the wall. Spitting a curse that would have reddened her aunt's face, she knelt and leaned out the window. If she dropped the cat too close to the ship, he could strike the stern.

Her sleeve ripped, and fire ran along her arm. When Dandy's teeth clamped on her thumb, she yelped with pain and shouted, "This is for your own good!" She tossed him into the night. It seemed to take forever until he splashed into the water, although these windows were not far above the waves.

Praying the soft sound had not been heard, Abigail took a deep breath. Now it was her turn. She would—

Her arm was seized, jerking her back from the window. "Dominic, let me go!"

"So you call for that Frenchie from your bed?" growled a voice she did not recognize.

But she recognized the man's face, even though blood ran from several cuts on his forehead. Woolcott! The leader of this mutiny!

Trying to tug away, she cried, "Let me go!"

"So you can run back to your Frenchie lover?"

"He is not my lover!"

"You can explain that to him and the devil while you burn in hell!" He raised his sword.

It was knocked aside with a crash of steel. Abigail struck the bed as Woolcott whirled to face Dominic. She recoiled as the swords came together again. She could not keep from staring at the blood on Dominic's shirt. Was it his or someone else's? Had everyone on this ship gone crazy?

Woolcott screeched as Dominic's sword found its mark. Abigail closed her eyes and fought not to be sick as Dominic pulled his sword back out of the sailor. She heard a thump and saw Woolcott's corpse on the floor beside her. With a moan, she scrambled away. Her stomach heaved as the deck had in the storm.

Dominic smoothed her hair back from her face while she gave in to her sickness. As soon as she could breathe without retching, he put his hand on her arm and whispered, "You must come with me, Abigail."

Sitting back on her heels, she leaned her head on his shoulder. She could not go anywhere. Her knees would not hold her now. "Where? Where can we go?"

"Somewhere where you can be safe. I was a fool not to think that your father's men would aim their vengeance at you."

"Are you saying you made a mistake, Captain St. Clair?" she asked softly.

"It happens on occasion." He pulled her to her feet. "Now to make sure it is not the last one you shall ever see . . ."

"Where are we going?" Abigail asked as she tried to keep up with him as he led her through the saloon toward the door to the open deck.

Another explosion from deep within the ship slammed them into the sideboard. Dominic groaned an oath as his sword fell to the floor. He grasped his right arm and cursed again. His fingers were numb, but pain raced up to his shoulder.

"Get my sword, Abigail," he ordered through clenched teeth.

Her face was gray as she picked up the sword. She balanced it in her hand, then grasped the hilt with both hands. Slowly her gaze rose to his. He did not need to hear her speak. Her thoughts were as clear as if her freckles spelled out the words across her cheeks. She now had the means to slay him.

When she shoved the sword into his left hand, he heard, through the rumble of agony, footsteps running toward the saloon door. He pushed himself away from the side-board and balanced the sword awkwardly in his left hand.

"Back into your room, Abigail," he shouted as the door burst open.

He had no time to see if she obeyed. Two men came at him. He parried their thrusts, but he was too off balance to take advantage of any openings. Backing toward the cabins, he tried to lead the men away from Abigail's door.

One man rushed forward. Dominic groaned as he jumped back and hit his right arm against the wall. Hearing laughter, he cursed all the mutinous Americans to the deep. He fought to make his eyes focus through the haze of pain. Had more men joined the battle against him, or were his eyes betraying him?

A shriek brought a curse from one of his attackers. In disbelief, Dominic saw Abigail rush out of her room. She was carrying a chair. She dashed it against the head of one of the men. He collapsed, bumping into his comrade as if they were a stack of cards. Before the American could regain his balance, Dominic drove his blade into the man.

The motion undid Dominic. He fell to his knees on the deck. Abigail grasped his left arm and helped him to his feet.

"*Merci*," he muttered as he reached for his sword. It skittered away when the ship lurched with another discharge of the gunpowder stored below.

"Forget it!" she cried. She tugged him toward her bedchamber.

"Abigail, we must go."

"We are." She put her arm around his waist and steered him through the door. "The only way we can." She faltered. "Can you swim?"

"Swim?" He frowned. "I am not leaving this ship while it is still afloat. I have won—"

More men rushed into the saloon with triumphant

shouts. Dominic swore viciously as he picked up his sword and raised it. He had to give Abigail time to flee. He was not sure how much longer he could protect her from her father's insane crew.

"Go!" he shouted. "Get off this ship any way you can."

Abigail did not hesitate as she climbed onto the sill. The ship lurched as something rumbled through it. She teetered on the edge. Her arms windmilled. She screamed as her feet slipped from the sill.

Falling, falling, falling, she shrieked again. The wooden stern became a blur. She tucked her feet beneath her at the last second. When she crashed into the water, its salty maw swallowed her.

Down, down, farther down she went. She tried to fight her way to the surface, but she could not halt the momentum carrying her toward the bottom. Her chest burned. Her soaked clothes pulled her downward. She pulled off her shoes. As they fell away into the murky mist, she struggled upward. She had to breathe.

As her head came above water, Abigail heard gunfire and more explosions. Debris crashed around her. They *were* going to destroy the *Republic!* She did not look back as she struck out for shore with a clumsy stroke.

Where was Dominic? Had he followed her, or was he staying to fight? She did not believe that he would relinquish the ship, but he could be killed easily when his right arm was useless. She choked back a gasp of horror. If he had jumped, he might not be able to swim.

Scanning the water, she saw nothing but the ship and the endless rise and fall of the waves. She could search the night away and never find Dominic.

Abigail took a steadying breath and started for the shore. Again and again, she raised her head to look toward land. It never appeared any closer. Her heart pounded against her chest, and she gasped for breath as her arms and legs grew exhausted. The gentle waves broke in her face, choking her.

Rolling over onto her back, she stared at the *Republic*. Her eyes widened. A small flicker of scarlet erupted from a porthole on the lower decks. Fire!

She swam furiously. The pull of the waves toward the shore helped. As the water became shallow, she waded, fighting to escape the water. Her fingers clenched the small pebbles on the beach as she dropped, panting, to the ground.

An explosion ripped the air. Abigail jumped to her feet as a fireball climbed from where the *Republic* had been. She raced for the trees at the edge of the beach as sparks soared toward her. Another crash rang through her head.

Clutching a tree, she watched as the fire seemed to feed directly off the water. The cloud of smoke took the shape of the ship, with fingers of fire outlining the masts. The center one dissolved into the flames. Another explosion crashed over her seconds after she saw a flash on the starboard side of the ship.

Wood splashed into the sea. Each piece was alight with fire, burning as ferociously as her horror. She stared at the blaze. As flames crackled wildly against the smoke-filled sky, she knew she had never been so scared. The crew was mad.

Or following orders, whispered a soft voice inside her head. Father! Father could have ordered this, and the crew would have followed his orders, but surely her father had hoped to save his ship and crew . . . and her. Yet now he would be free. The French could not hold him and the rest of the crew without the evidence destroyed with the *Republic*.

"But why did you leave me to die, too?" she whispered as she slid down to sit beneath the tree. She feared that was a question she would never get an answer to.

Chapter Five

Abigail scrambled over a mound of the rocks that cut through the strand, dividing one cove from the next. Behind her she heard excited voices. Englishmen! She could not let them find her here.

Spies died on the gallows, and she doubted that anyone would heed her tale of being a prisoner on the ship. Then these people would ask the same questions Dominic had—that she had. What had the *Republic* been doing so close to England with a load of weapons? Her very lack of an answer could condemn her to hang.

She scurried like a child from one huge stone to the next, watching carefully because the moon was slipping beneath the bank of clouds rising out of the sea. When she reached the top, she clung close to the boulders and looked back toward where she had come ashore. Several forms were coming out of the trees, not more than a stone's throw from where she had paused to catch her breath. If she had remained there, they might have seen her.

Staying low and thankful for the concealing darkness, she slipped down the other side of the rocks. She winced when she scraped her hand on a sharp stone, but did not slow until she reached the sand piled up on this side of the break.

Abigail crouched in the shadow of the boulders. She wondered why the Englishmen had not come to this beach first. It was already littered with charred boards from the ship. In horror, she realized those were not boards. They were bodies. No wonder the English were not coming here. They were more interested in the ship's cargo than in corpses. Those they could rob later.

She swallowed her desperate yearning to flee from the carnage that had washed up onto the shore. Mayhap someone was still alive. She refused to admit that she was the only survivor. If someone else had washed ashore, she would have an ally against the English.

Inching toward the bodies, she submerged the disgust swelling into her throat when she discovered the corpses were burned beyond recognition. There was nothing left to suggest they had been alive. She saw knife blades that were twisted out of shape, their hafts gone. The stench rising from them was worse than belowdecks.

Her toe hit something half-buried in the sand. She bent and picked up a pistol. A loaded pistol, she saw when she tilted it. Carefully, she slid it through the sash of her wrapper. She did not want it to misfire, but she might need it.

A mournful yowl resonated along the strand, and Abigail whirled. She laughed weakly when she saw her cat nosing around a corpse. Dandy gave a low cry.

"It is horrid, isn't it?" Abigail whispered.

The cat prowled back and forth before settling to clean his whiskers in a very self-satisfied manner. He had survived, so that was all he cared about. She sighed. Dandy would take care of himself. She did not doubt he soon would be feasting on the birds that lived among the trees lining the strand. She must become as ruthless.

She froze as she heard a strange sound. Were the English coming here to steal from the corpses? Looking back over her shoulder, she saw no one. No one alive. She gasped as she heard the sound again. Was it from a corpse?

Dandy inched past her, but that did not ease her superstitious fear. Aunt Velma often said cats could hear and see unearthly things. The cat nosed the sand by one of the corpses and wandered away, disinterested.

The soft sound came once more. It sounded like a man moaning.

Abigail gasped again. That sound did not come from a ghost, but from another survivor off the *Republic*. If the English heard the groan, they would surely come to investigate. She had to help the man before the English could find him and her.

She ran to a pair of bodies farther along the beach. She started to touch the first, but pulled back in horror when she saw that his face had been ripped away by one of the explosions. Her stomach threatened to betray her, but there was nothing in it. She knelt next to the other body on the sand.

"Dominic!" she breathed in shock.

His shirt was shredded and his breeches torn to reveal scorched skin on his legs. Other burns were an angry red on his chest and arms. With his eyes closed, she was spared his powerful glare.

Her fingers trembled. He had been her captor. Looking past him, she saw a stone that would fit perfectly in her hand. If she crashed it against his head, he would never awaken. He was a French pirate. He deserved no mercy. At his command, his men had murdered her father's crew. Because of him, the *Republic* was gone.

Her fingers closed on the rock, but, instead, she thought of how he had rescued her in the middle of the storm. Closing her eyes, she recalled the haven of his arms. No, it had not been safe. There had been nothing safe about the passions he aroused in her.

When another sigh of pain oozed from his lips, Abigail knew she must help him, for he had saved her life more than once. She suspected the French were even more hated than Americans here in England. She must hide him.

Straining, she rolled him over on his back, taking care not to touch his right arm. She brushed sand from his face. The stickiness of blood caught her fingers, and he groaned. She pushed aside his matted hair and found blood, but no wound. She tore a long strip from his ripped shirt, then cringed as the sound was like a scream in the darkness.

She held her breath, but no one climbed over the rocks. As more shouts came from the other beach, she guessed the scavengers were finding whatever had washed ashore from the ship. She hoped it would keep them busy until she could get Dominic off the beach.

Rinsing sand from the material she had torn off his shirt, she carefully wrapped it around his head. As she tied it in place, she saw that some of his hair had been singed away. His dark eyebrows were as full as ever. The wound was over his left ear, she found. That surprised her, because she had guessed he always would confront danger face to face. She wondered how many of her father's crew he had fought alone in the moment before the ship exploded.

A flush darkened her cheeks as she ran her hands along his body. To be embarrassed to touch an unconscious man was ridiculous, but the heat on her face burned hotter as she cautiously touched his ribs, seeking to discover if any were fractured. As she moved her fingers across his chest, she could not keep from remembering how it had been so strong against her as he held her. She glanced at his face, but the only expression he wore was of pain. Suddenly she wished for the irreverent smile she had detested.

She looked at his legs, which remained half in the water. Like hers, his feet were bare. She noticed a swelling in his right ankle and did not dare to touch it. If it had been broken, she feared he might never walk again. As her fingers slid along his breeches, which were ripped and flapped at his knees, she shivered with sensations she did not want to acknowledge. Even in senselessness, his sensual power continued to exert its beguiling control over her.

Abigail shook those thoughts from her head and looked over her shoulder again. Still no one on the stones. If the English remained in the other cove, she might be able to save him.

As she reached to grab Dominic's left arm, she heard another sound. This low grumble had not been a moan, but the distant drumbeat of thunder. In horror, she saw clouds had swallowed the moon completely.

"No, not now," she whispered. Just thinking of a storm terrified her, urging her to race into the shelter of the trees.

She must not leave Dominic here. He had saved her from the last storm. To abandon him to the waves would make her worse than a French pirate.

Stooping, Abigail put her hands under his arms. She tugged. She collapsed to the sand. Dominic was tall, past six feet, and he carried no extra flesh on his muscular body, but in spite of that, she could not budge him.

She glanced upward. The sky was laced with lightning, revealing the contortions of the storm clouds. Thunder sent fear rumbling through her, and she gripped his arm again. She braced her feet against the sand. Taking a deep breath, she took one step backward, then another. She wanted to shout with joy when his senseless body shifted.

Each excruciatingly slow step demanded all her strength. Sweat lacquered her nightdress to her back. She did not dare to stop, fearing he would sink into the sand. She might never get him moving again.

"Wake up, Dominic," she repeated over and over. If he woke, then he could help her save him.

Although her breath seared beneath her ribs, Abigail kept moving until the grass at the edge of the strand slipped beneath her feet. She pulled Dominic beneath the trees and sat, cradling his head in her lap as she panted with exhaustion. Pressing her hand to her side, she kneaded it to ease the pain. An ache ran from her shoulders along her spine.

Dominic did not react when she lowered his head to the ground. Jumping to her feet, she plucked some ferns and ran back onto the beach. She swept away any signs that someone had been dragged off the sand.

More thunder cracked as she ran back to where he was lying. When lightning played across the sky, she pulled him toward some fallen trees that were piled atop one another. A legacy from another storm, she guessed, and hoped the trees would protect them now. With a tired groan, she wondered if he had gained weight since she had pulled him from the water. A crack of thunder spurred her.

Dragging him beneath the overhang of dead branches, she wished he would wake. All her hopes were useless. He was still senseless.

A few drops of rain struck her as she collected two pieces of wood from under the trees. She looked up, but no more rain fell. It must have been spray sent ashore by the rising wind. She bent her head and ignored it as she placed the wood along both sides of Dominic's ankle to keep it immobilized and bound them together with another strip from his shirt.

Abigail froze with renewed horror when she heard voices not far from her. Was someone searching for survivors?

"The storm will wash it all back out to sea before we get a chance to gather it." The man's disgust was clear.

"Don't fret," said another man. "What the sea takes away tonight, she'll wash back on the morrow."

"But if 'twas one of the king's ships, his men will be here to lay claim to every morsel."

"Who's going to tell the king's men about this?" The second man's laugh was swept away by thunder.

As the men's voices vanished into the distance, Abigail fought not to scratch the itchy spot on the tip of her nose. It was harder to ignore than the burning along her arm where salt had gotten into the scratches left by Dandy when she had tossed her cat out of the ship's window. She wondered where Dandy was now.

She could not look for him. She could only cower in the shadows and watch as dark forms hurried away from the strand. Their voices continued to drift to her as the men went along a path on the far side of the fallen trees. They were curious about why a ship had exploded just off their shore, but were more eager to discover what of her cargo would wash to them.

She shifted, then froze again when the branches around her rubbed together at her motion. No one slowed along the path. Shouts of excitement announced that some of the debris had reached shore and been gathered to take back to the village that must be farther inland.

How long had she been crouching here? Every muscle protested, and that blasted itch threatened to undo her.

Leaves rattled beside her. Just the wind or . . . ?

"Dandy?" she whispered.

Abigail got no answer, but she saw his small prints in

the mud beneath the trees. She flinched when a weak explosion tossed more debris across the water. One of the barrels of gunpowder must have washed away from the ship before detonating.

Inching back more deeply into the shadows, she could not halt her sneeze. Not moving, she waited for someone to follow the sound. Then she realized that the people were too interested in getting their prizes back to their homes before the rain fell in earnest. Now anyone else who reached shore from the ship had a chance to hide, too.

But what if you and Dominic and Dandy are the only survivors?

She sighed, wishing that thought had remained silent. Hanging her head over her knees, she stared out at the sea that was now the same black as the night sky. So many had died. She was not sure for what purpose.

The wind wheezed at Abigail, spinning the hem of her nightdress about her legs. When the wind rose to a shriek, she huddled under the branches and pulled them closer to her and Dominic. Her cat slipped in to sit behind her to escape the storm.

Dominic moaned.

"Are you awake?" she whispered.

She got no answer. Tearing another strip from his shirt, she wrapped it around his head. The other one was already stained crimson. She did not know how much blood he had lost, but she doubted that he would live if it continued to seep out of him at this rate.

"Please wake up," she whispered.

Lightning seared the sky. Abigail moaned and, hiding her face in her hands, huddled next to him.

When Dandy curled up near her chest, she put her arms around him. How she wished someone was holding her. "Please wake up, Dominic," she whispered again, more desperately.

Why didn't he open his eyes? The thunder was loud enough to wake the dead. In horror, she stared at the shore.

Waves, which had been gentle strokes on the beach, began to crash with a vengeance. She did not know what would happen to the unburied bodies. Fearfully she prayed they would not rise to haunt her. She closed her eyes as she imagined the faceless man crossing the sand.

She flinched at a tap on the leaves overhead, but it was only rain. Her shaky laugh filled the rough shelter. The worst of the thunder's fury soon would be past.

She had survived it!

A drop striking her head cut short her celebration. When she looked upward, another fell on her nose. She glanced at Dominic. The rain was taking no pity on his helpless condition. Reaching beneath her, she grasped some green ferns. She held them over his head like an umbrella.

Drawing her knees up, she balanced her elbow on them. She frowned when her elbow struck something in the sash of her wrapper. She pulled out the pistol. Sweet heavens! She had forgotten it while rescuing Dominic and facing the tempest's fury.

"You continue to be trouble, Dominic," she said, although he could not hear her words. "But when you wake up, it will be different. I promise you that. I am not your captive any longer." She laughed again as she ran her finger along the pistol's barrel. "You shall be mine."

Chapter Six

Dominic St. Clair's first thought when his senses returned after an infinite eternity of darkness was an oath that did not reach his lips. Pain cut through him. He was not sure where he was injured, because his agony was too powerful and too pervasive. Every bit of his body ached. The anguish began in his head and radiated down him. His right arm was on fire, and his right ankle throbbed.

He cursed again, although the sound never left his mind. The last time he had ached like this was when he and his then partner Evan Somerset had nearly died while smuggling an early Renaissance painting out of Florence. His only consolation as he had spent a month healing was that those who had attempted to halt them had suffered more.

Had they been jumped again? He dismissed that thought. He and Evan had parted ways several years ago

when they had disagreed about accepting a commission
to steal another piece of art. Evan had warned it was a
trap, and it had been. Dominic had escaped with his life
and his crew's, but his ship had been sunk. His despair
at losing that ship had been eased when he obtained *La
Chanson de la Mer* after he promised to serve Napoleon
as a privateer near the English coast.

It had not been as interesting a life as smuggling art.
Yet he had vowed to serve Napoleon, and he would not
break that vow for anything or anyone, not even to save
himself from his own boredom.

As his eyes creaked open, Dominic stared at the green
and brown blur over his head. *Trees*, his slow mind suggested, but trees at a very odd angle. Then he realized
the tree trunks must be lying on their sides with their
branches spread across the earth. But how had he gotten
from *La Chanson* to whatever this place was?

Not *La Chanson*, he reminded himself grimly, but the
American merchant ship. Memory burst into his mind
with renewed agony, and he cursed. Only a dull croak
sounded in his ears. Damn, crazy Americans! When they
learned that they had no choice but jail or a noose, they
tried to destroy the ship and themselves. Apparently, they
had succeeded in achieving the martyrdom they wanted.

Dominic St. Clair was no saint ready to die so worth-
lessly for his country. No one loved France more than he
did, but he would have served Napoleon poorly by getting
himself killed by a crew of American zealots. If he had
suspected that Fitzgerald had left such orders behind him,
he would have slain every man on the ship. If . . .

There was no time to think of "ifs." He had to discover
what this place was and how he had gotten here. It must
be the English shore, because they had not sailed far
enough toward France before the mutiny began for him
to reach landfall there.

He tried to focus his eyes to ease the blur into something

that would give him a clue to what had happened since his last memory. Even that memory was uncertain, but it was clear that someone had brought him to this place. As resourceful as his enemies considered him, he knew his own limitations. In his obviously pitiful condition, he could not have dragged himself from the beach without help.

Hands appeared out of the fog surrounding him. Compassionate hands which made every effort not to hurt him as they gently placed a cool cloth on his head. He moaned as a swift pulse of pain almost stripped away his senses again.

"Who is it?" To his ears, his voice sounded as wobbly as an old man walking along a cobbled street with his cane.

When he received no answer, he wondered which one of his enemies had survived the ship's sinking. But why would any of his enemies keep him alive? Mayhap he had been rescued by one of the English. Again he dismissed that thought instantly. They were as much his enemies as the Americans and would have killed him before he could regain his senses. Then who was tending to him? He repeated his question.

"Hush, Dominic. You should not strain yourself."

In disbelief, he listened to the softly husky voice which was undeniably feminine. Only one woman had been aboard the *Republic.* "Abigail?"

"You are exerting yourself when you should be resting. Please stay calm."

Frustration fired him, giving him strength he had not expected he could find. He pushed against the sand as he struggled to sit, although it was an effort simply to keep his unfocused eyes open. "I demand that you tell me—"

"Stay still. You have a head wound, and you should remain quiet for as long as you can," she ordered.

When her slender hands on his shoulder kept him pinned

to the ground, he realized that he did not have the strength to fight her. Moving slightly, she reached for something just beyond the range of his vision.

Dominic stared at her profile. Why was she tending to him? She had cursed him when he had tried to persuade her that she wanted him as much as he wanted her. He had guessed she would be happy to see him dead. But, she was caring for him instead of leaving him to die on the beach.

He did not realize he had spoken her name aloud until she turned and asked in a whisper, "What is it, Dominic? You must be quiet."

"Quiet?"

"The English are not far from here."

An oath reached his lips. He snarled it again, but nothing eased his fury. "How many others?"

"From the ship?"

"Yes!"

In the gray of what he was beginning to realize was a rainy dawn, he saw her glance away. Toward the sea, he guessed when she murmured, "As far as I can tell, you and I and Dandy are the only ones who survived the explosion on the *Republic*."

Dominic collapsed back against the ground. Just the two of them and the cat? *Incroyable!* Was she jesting with him? No—her face was serious in the dim light. "No one else?"

"Not that I have seen. Your enemies outnumber you, Dominic."

"They always have."

"You like long odds?"

"Always."

Arranging her wrapper around her, she said, "Then you have your wish, Dominic. As far as I can tell, we and the cat are the lone survivors of the *Republic*. No one who might rescue us knows where we are. You have several bad burns, a useless right arm, and possibly a broken ankle. If those odds are not long enough for you, I am sure I can think of other reasons why our situation is appalling.''

"Those are quite enough for now." He reached up and put his finger against her cheek to turn her gaze back toward him. "Are you hurt, Abigail?"

"Other than a few scratches and bruises, no." A smile tipped her lips. "I survived in much better condition than you."

He raised his right arm and wiggled his fingers. A tingling warned that sensation was returning to them. The pain was muted along his shoulder. Mayhap he had not broken his arm. With a grimace, he pushed himself up to sit.

His head spun, and he cradled it in his hands. When a cool cloth was held to his brow, he drew his fingers away to see Abigail leaning toward him. What he had thought was a shadow was a bruise across her left cheek.

"It seems I owe you my life," he whispered.

"You do." She let him keep the cloth in place as she tended to the fabric wrapped around his aching skull. "If I had left you out on the strand, you would have come to your senses in time to face the hangman."

"If they had not taken care of me right here."

"Don't be so barbaric!"

He caught her wrist when she was about to turn away. "Abigail, this is not your aunt's house in New Bedford. You are in the middle of a war."

"I know."

"Do you?" He ignored the pulse of pain ricocheting through his head as he drew her toward him. "If you truly had, you would have killed me out there by the water."

"I considered it."

Dominic laughed softly. "Good."

"You would not have thought so if I had rammed that rock into you."

"As bad as my head aches now, I'm not sure what difference it would have made." Before she could retort, he added, "You cannot be so fainthearted. You are among your enemies here. Among *our* enemies."

"I know." She eased her hand out of his grip. "That is one of the reasons I did not kill you. You know more about England than I do."

"And what were the other reasons?"

"You know them."

"Do I?" Again he tilted her face back toward him. "Could it be that you were unable to bring yourself to slay me because you were thinking of how you react when I hold you in my arms?"

"You saved my life. I could not take yours."

"And that is the only reason?"

"Of course."

He laughed again when her fiery blush belied her answer. Running his crooked finger along her cheek, he said, "Then I shall say again that I am grateful." He frowned as he pushed a branch away from his head. "What is this place?"

"The closest shelter I could find when I pulled you off the beach. These trees must have fallen in a recent storm."

"We cannot stay here. We could be seen by anyone on the beach."

She nodded. "I know. There is what looks to be an abandoned hut on the next cove. As soon as you can walk, we can go there."

"Walk?" Dominic did not hold back his curse when he saw the splint around his right ankle. That explained why his leg thundered with agony. Stretching, he touched his swollen ankle and winced. "I cannot feel any broken bones, so I should be able to hobble there, if you help me."

"And then what?"

For a long moment, he did not answer. He tried to make his cobweb-infested brain work. If only his head would cease aching ... "We find a way to get out of England."

"*That* I know. But how?"

His blurred gaze moved along her. As if for the first time, he admired her brilliant blue eyes and the warmth of her red hair. He had to acknowledge what had been easy to ignore on the ship. Abigail Fitzgerald was not simply a pawn in her father's lust for wealth. Although she seemed to have a blind spot in regard to Captain Fitzgerald's activities, she was an intelligent woman who had managed to survive what her father's crew and his own had not. He owed his life to her, and he was sure she expected a generous payment in return.

"I think it would be better to discuss what we must do after we are somewhere where the English will not find us." He hesitated, then asked, "Do you have anything to drink?"

"Are you thirsty?" she asked.

"Very."

Abigail smiled at the sincerity in Dominic's voice. When he was not in pain, she guessed that he would regain his arrogance, but he seemed grateful for her kindness. And he should be.

Reaching behind her, she picked up the tin cup she had left out in the rain. She had guessed he would be craving water when he awoke.

He took the cup and downed the water in one gulp. "*Merci*," he murmured, then frowned. "Where did you get this cup?"

"The English should not be the only ones to scavenge what is left of the *Republic*." Backing out of the shelter, she was careful not to bang the pistol against the trunk.

She had hidden it in her pocket, because she did not want Dominic to guess she had it.

When she held out her hands, Dominic grasped them. He edged out of the shadows slowly. As soon as his head cleared the lowest branches, he jerked on her hands. She gasped as she fell toward him. His arms surrounded her when she struck his chest.

"What are you doing?" she choked. As close as they were, she was unsure if the shivers were only hers or his, too.

"Nothing yet, *chérie*." He laughed as his fingers twisted through her snarled hair. A lightning bolt seared her when his gaze explored her face with yearning. Only when his other hand caressed her waist, outlining it with a warmth that sparked to her very center, did she start to pull away. His hands tightened on her as he whispered, "Now I am doing something."

His mouth slanted across hers. Everything she wanted was in his kiss, for it offered her as much rapture as it demanded. His fingers stroked her back, sending tremors up her spine. As her hand curved along his nape, his thick hair caressed it.

When Dominic pulled back with a curse, Abigail blinked, still lost in pleasure. She saw him touch his shoulder and grimace.

"Be careful," she said in a whisper, not daring to speak louder in case the English villagers were near. "You were burned when the ship exploded."

She was amazed when he grinned. "That explosion was not as fiery as your lips, *chérie*."

"You should not be thinking of that now."

"Why not?" He chuckled as he clambered to his feet, leaning against the tree trunks. "We may be captured at any moment, and I can think of nothing I would rather have as my last sensation than the taste of your lips. Well, mayhap a few other sensations we might enjoy, but you would slap my face if I were to list them.''

At his roguish laugh, she looked away. With the white bandage twisted like a turban around his forehead, he could have been one of the legendary pirates who sailed the Caribbean over one hundred years ago. She refused to let his enticing gaze daunt her. She was no longer his captive.

Abigail stiffened as she heard a sound from beyond the trees. Voices! The villagers must be returning with the first light to discover what had washed ashore. ''You may get your chance for that last thought pretty soon,'' she muttered as she motioned for him to follow her.

He took a single step, then dropped to one knee. She hoped the hiss of his bitten-off curse did not reach English ears. Bending, she put her shoulder under his left arm and helped him back to his feet. As his arm draped over her, she feared her frantic heartbeat would betray them to their enemies. She should not be affected by him like this. She did not even like this pirate.

His breath scorched her skin as he leaned heavily on her with each unsteady step through the undergrowth. She glanced again and again in the direction of the path that paralleled the beach. A parade continued along it as more and more villagers joined the others by the water's edge.

Abigail swallowed her gasp as Dominic suddenly pressed her back against a tree. She looked up at his face, which was as sharp as the trunk behind her. Nodding when he put a finger to her lips, she held her breath as she heard someone crashing through the underbrush. She tensed when the noise grew closer. Slipping her hand into her pocket, she gripped the butt of the pistol. Firing it would alert everyone on the beach, but she would not be captured without a fight.

Her breath slipped past her tight lips when a dog ran

past them, not pausing as it headed for the strand. Sagging against the tree, she smiled when Dominic did. There was nothing amusing about being spooked by a dog, but she was so relieved she could not help grinning.

By the time they reached the battered hut that was set in a thick stand of trees, Abigail was fighting for every step. Dominic's arm ground down into her shoulder. She wanted to tell him to lessen his weight on her, but she knew from his gray pallor that she had been fooled by the passion in his kiss into believing that he was as strong as he had been on the ship.

"How did you find this?" Dominic asked as Abigail helped him through the door and out of the rain.

"As soon as the thunderstorm passed—"

Compassion blossomed in his eloquent eyes. "That must have frightened you greatly."

"Yes, and I was determined not to be outside in another." She sat him on the uneven floor, for there was no furniture in the room that was so short he could not extend his legs fully. "I was scared and hungry and thirsty, so I went a short distance along the beach and found this."

Dominic leaned his head back against the wall, struggling to hold on to his senses. He needed to stay awake, because she could not fight alone if the English came here. He almost laughed bitterly at that thought. He would be of little use when he could not walk without her help.

His head spun, and he knew he was fading. He had to keep her talking. That might keep him alert. "You have proven your skills are many, Abigail."

"At least I knew enough to get off the *Republic* before it exploded instead of vowing to go down with the ship."

"I assume from what I saw in your cabin that you had warning of what they planned."

She nodded. "Cookie told me."

"When?"

"If you think I knew of their plans before last night, I assure you I did not. Of course, even if I had, I would not have told you." She laughed tersely. "Not that they would have shared their plans with me when they were sure I told you every secret during the nights we shared a bed." She folded her arms in front of her, then frowned as water coursed down the front of her nightdress. Moving to a spot where the roof was not leaking, she added, "Shows how wrong everyone was, doesn't it?"

"So you had no clue?"

Anger tainted her voice. "I said so, didn't I?"

"You have to be the first to admit you have not had a history of being honest with me, Abigail."

"Or you with me."

"True." He smiled as he drew up his uninjured leg and leaned his elbow on the knee.

The rising sun glistened on her face and sent a flame of gold along her wet hair. He recalled how it had been drenched like this when he had held her on the *Republic*'s deck during the storm.

When the colors wavered before him, Dominic forced another question from his lips. "Was that warning why the windows in your cabin were shattered?"

"I had just tossed Dandy out of the window when Woolcott came in." Holding up her arm, she revealed the scratches running the length of her forearms. "Dandy was not pleased."

"I can see that." He reached out a finger to touch her swollen thumb. "Did he do this, too?"

"He bit me." She winced as he turned her hand slightly. "Be careful. It still hurts."

When he kissed it, she pulled her hand out of his. "Don't be offended," he said when she glowered. "I was only offering my sympathy."

"I think it would be better if you do not touch me,

Dominic. I had to suffer your attentions on the *Republic*. I will not suffer them here.''

He regarded her tight lips before his gaze rose to her sapphire eyes. That she continued to be afraid of him when he could not walk without her assistance astounded him. "It was never my intention that you would suffer, *chérie*."

"The very fact that you paid attention to me would have guaranteed that if my father's crew had won the ship back I would die."

"Did you think that your father's men would succeed?"

"I was afraid they would fail. Then I would be your prisoner again, and you would . . ."

"Do this?" He hooked an arm around her waist and drew her toward him. Her soft lips were beneath his for only a moment before she pulled away.

"Exactly!"

"Then you should know, *chérie*, that that was not *exactly* what I had in mind." He ran a finger along the soaked sleeve of her wrapper which clung to her so appealingly.

She shrugged his hand away, but he smiled. Since he had seen her lithe legs and snapping eyes, he had wanted her. He would not force her as his men had, but Fitzgerald's unruly and uncooperative crew had left him no time to seduce her as he had wished. He wanted to take the time to learn the enchanting secrets she hid beneath her modest frocks.

A smile teased the corners of his mouth. Time was a commodity he suspected they would have more of than they wanted. Traveling to where he could get a message to *La Chanson* would not be quick, because they must be constantly wary of the English. His gaze moved along her again. She resembled a lost waif, urging him to take her in his arms.

When Dominic started to ask another question, he

swayed. Abigail's slender hands caught him before he could topple onto his face. Although he was tempted to make some light comment, he could only groan as she lowered him back onto the floor. She turned away, but he caught her hand.

"Don't go, *chérie*. I need you."

For a long minute, she did not reply. Then, so softly he was not sure if he had heard her or only the words he had hoped she would whisper, she said, "I will not leave you."

He took her promise with him into the never-ending maze of pain. Abigail Fitzgerald might remain his enemy, but he suspected she never would break such a vow.

At least, he hoped so. His life was, most literally, in her hands now.

Chapter Seven

Abigail bit her lip, holding her breath and hoping the shadows would conceal her. The heat from the animals in the byre surrounded her as she knelt by the wall behind a mound of hay.

She had not expected the farmer to come in here now because she had seen him going toward the field behind the cottage and byre. When he walked toward the cow that was chewing contentedly, she eased closer to the floor. She froze when she heard a click from the eggs she held in the long shirt she had stolen yesterday from another cottage closer to the village. That household was also missing a set of boys' breeches and a man's shirt. She wore the breeches beneath her shirt, and the second shirt had replaced Dominic's ruined one.

A week ago, she would have been racked with guilt at her thievery. How furious Aunt Velma would be to dis-

cover Abigail skulking about as she stole what she needed
for herself and Dominic!

But this is not New Bedford, she argued silently.

Her first foray had been the day after she had helped
Dominic to the hut. With so many of the villagers down
on the shore scavenging what was left of the *Republic*,
it had been simple to slip among the stone cottages and
help herself to a meat pie from one house and a small
loaf of bread from another. She took a cup and two plates
from a third house, not wanting to steal everything from
one family.

You have too many ethics for a thief. She frowned as
Dominic's voice intruded into her mind. She did not need
his opinion. He could barely walk, so he could not take
over this disgusting task, but . . .

Abigail held her breath again as the farmer turned
toward where she was hiding. If he came closer, he was
certain to see her. She put her hand on the knife she wore
at her waist. She had taken the blade from another farm
yesterday.

The gray-haired farmer stabbed the mound of hay with
his pitchfork, and she drew back closer to the wall as he
turned to drop the hay in front of the cow. Doing the
same for the horse, he went back out of the byre as he
called to someone to come and help him in the field.

She released her breath. Even though she wanted to
sag against the floor, she stood and slipped out of the
byre. She saw no one in the barnyard, so she raced into
the woods edging the path that led in one direction to the
sea and in the other to the village. She did not dare to
walk on the path, because she might meet someone who
was suspicious of a stranger among them when so many
items were disappearing.

Abigail hurried through the trees to the abandoned hut,
but was careful that the trio of eggs in her shirt did not

break. Entering, she closed her eyes and leaned back against the warped door that refused to shut completely.

"Abigail?"

Although she did not want to open her eyes, because then she would be caught up again in the horror of being cast upon this enemy shore, she looked at Dominic, who was struggling to his feet. His ankle was still swollen, but the deep bruises were easing to a lighter shade. The wrinkled shirt refused to button across his chest, revealing a breadth of muscular flesh that drew her eyes far too often. Around his head, the strip of cloth from his old shirt added to his raffish appearance.

He took the three eggs from her and smiled. "You are becoming skilled at this skulduggery."

"I hate it."

"That is because you are looking at your excursions as if you were a thief."

"That is what I am."

"No. It is your chance to even the odds we face with our enemies."

She laughed in spite of herself. "I thought you preferred long odds."

"It is difficult to consider farmers and villagers worthy adversaries."

"You can say that because you are not the one sneaking about."

"No, I am the one sitting here with nothing to do." He sighed. "When I am able to walk, I intend to try my hand at fishing in the stream where you get sweet water for us." His frown became a grin. "It has been many years since my childhood summers of fishing along the Loire. I hope I have not forgotten how."

"As I do. I am tired of purloined pies and stale bread."

"Until I can walk around enough to slip away if one of the English comes near, I am afraid the taste of fish will remain only a fantasy. I shall remain cooped up in this hut, going mad with boredom.''

"Can you whittle?" she asked slowly.

He sat back on the floor. "Not without a knife."

"True, and I would be a fool to steal you one." Abigail smoothed her tangled hair back from her face. Every day she longed more for the comb she had had on the *Republic*. Her braid was thickened with snarls she could not loosen with her fingers.

He scowled and folded his arm on his drawn-up knee. The other leg remained stretched out so he did not put any extra pressure on the splint. "You don't trust me, do you?"

"Why should I?" She met his gaze evenly, so he could not suspect she had both the knife at her waist and the pistol which was hidden beneath her wrapper in the far corner. He thought she used the wrapper and her night-dress only as pillows, not suspecting what she concealed under them. "Why should I trust you when we are enemies?"

"Because we are not enemies any longer."

"Oh? Has Napoleon apologized to President Madison for his pirates preying on honest American sailors and ships?"

He snorted loudly. "*Honest* and *American* are two terms that do not go together. You preach your frontier idealism to anyone foolish enough to listen, but your father's cargo proves that you care only about trading your so-called virtues for gold as if you were the cheapest streetwalker."

Abigail flushed. "That language is not necessary."

"No?" He grasped her wrist, pulling her toward him.

"Let me go!" she cried as she tried to tug away.

"Not until you prove you have more sense than your witless father."

"If you think I will steal a knife for you . . ." Her eyes widened as he held the blade near her face. Touching her waist, she discovered that he had disarmed her without her realizing it.

His smile broadened as he placed the flat of the knife against her cheek. His arm encircled her waist. "*Chérie*, you look quite pale. Could it be that you fear I will kill you?"

"No. Then you would starve to death. You cannot get your own food now."

"I suspect I would find a way."

She did not answer. Applying the slightest pressure of the knife to her cheek, he tightened his arm around her waist and leaned her down toward the floor. When she held up her hands to halt him, he turned the blade so the edge brushed her chin. In horror, she drew her fingers back. She stared up at him as he leaned over her.

"Do you think I will force you to submit to me?" With a quick motion, he made the knife disappear beneath his shirt. "Have you forgotten? I told you I would not need force to seduce you."

"Dominic!"

He sat up and chuckled. When she scrambled to her knees, she knew she wanted him out of her hut and out of her life. Immediately would not be soon enough.

"That blade is not very sharp," she said, "but it might be enough for you to make us some utensils to eat with. I am tired of using my fingers all the time."

" 'Twas sharp enough for you to fear I would slice into your throat." Dominic withdrew the knife and ran his thumb cautiously along the blade. He grimaced. "I think my fingers might do better than this dull knife."

"Stop complaining!"

Taking her hand, he said, "*Chérie*, forgive me."

"Forgive you? You are apologizing?" She stared into his dark eyes with amazement.

"I always apologize when I am wrong." He caressed

her cheek and chuckled. "When I know I am wrong, not when others think I am."

"I will keep that in mind."

His hand splayed across her cheek, sending tendrils of yearning deep within her. "I like the idea that you keep anything about me in mind, *chérie*."

Abigail stood, not wanting to be caught up in his seductive web again. "It is not easy to forget something as irritating as a toothache."

"Where are you going?" he called as she reached for the door.

"To get some kindling and down to the stream to find a flat stone to cook those eggs on."

"You should wait until darkness."

She scowled. He was right, but she did not want to admit that when her only other choice would be to remain here. "You did not seem too distressed that I was sneaking to that farm and stealing your supper."

"The farm would be nearly deserted at midday. The stream may not be. Stay here until dark, Abigail."

Facing him, she fisted her hands on her hips. "I do not take orders from you any longer."

"You never did!"

She smiled coldly. "But now you take orders from me. Sit still," she said when he started to stand. "The swelling is going down in your ankle, but if you start hopping around like a one-legged rooster, you will be sure to injure it again."

"I promise I will behave as long as you promise to stay away from the stream until twilight sends the English back to their homes."

"Dominic—"

He caught her hand and kept her from turning away from him. When she looked from her fingers to his smile, she waited for him to speak. If she pulled too hard, she might tip him over and hurt his ankle worse. She doubted that even the blows that had left cuts beneath his hair could reach through his thick skull, which seemed impervious to good sense.

"Promise, Abigail," he ordered in a deceptively calm tone.

"Very well. I promise I will not go to the stream until dark."

"Good." He released her and leaned back against the wall. Folding his arms across his chest, he smiled at her like a benevolent king meeting with his least important subject.

As she went out the door to gather some wood for him to carve and for a fire to cook those stolen eggs, she heard him laughing. A smile edged along her lips. He was the most exasperating man she had ever met, but she knew once his ankle could support him, he might be her best chance of escaping from here alive.

As soon as the stone Abigail used to cook their supper cooled, Dominic used it to hone the knife. It took hours until it was sharp enough for his use. Whittling wooden forks and spoons kept him busy. As he worked, he sat in the doorway, looking through the trees to scan the horizon, but the ship he sought never came.

The lure of the sea haunted him. Every night he went to sleep listening to the sound of the waves stroking the sand, whispering soft secrets only a sailor could comprehend. The same song woke him and taunted him.

"You look pensive," Abigail said as she came out of the woods and put some berries in one of the chipped cups. Holding it out to him, she added, "They are not quite ripe, so do not eat too many."

"I am not hungry."

"Not hungry?"

He smiled at her astonishment, then sighed. "All I can think of is how long it may be until I can be asea again."

"I know how this must be so difficult for you."

"You know?" he asked irritably as she clasped her arms around her knees and stared at the leaves rocking gently with the breeze. "How could you know? You are a landswoman."

"No one who lives in New Bedford can be indifferent to the sea." She smiled. "And it is not a crime to be born to a life on the land."

"Did I say that? I simply said that a landswoman cannot begin to understand the lure of the ocean."

"I know its call well. My aunt's house overlooks the harbor, and the rhythms of the sea were bred in me. My father is a sailor. My uncle was, also. His ship was sunk just over a year ago."

"Did he survive?"

"No." Her face became a mask of sorrow, and he regretted asking the question. "His ship went down with every hand. I know how seldom anyone is rescued."

"I was."

"You?"

He tapped the gold ring in his ear. "Didn't you know what this means? A sailor wears an earring to show that he has survived the loss of his ship at sea."

"I did not know that."

"You thought it was just an affectation?"

She shook her head, and her silken hair that she wore pulled back in a braid brushed his arm. "I thought it was what all pirates wear."

"Privateer, *chérie.*"

"The difference is very slight."

"The difference between being hanged and having your throat cut is very slight, too, but the latter is much quicker." He started to add more, then snarled, *"ventre bleu!"*

Abigail glanced at him with sudden concern. She began

to laugh when she reached for the bandage around his head. It was drooping across his face. She pushed aside his hands, which were trying futilely to fix it. She knelt as she retied the cloth around his head.

"There," she said after she had adjusted it to her satisfaction. "How is that?"

"Marvelous."

Her gaze lowered to meet his. When he ran his finger along the skin bared along the top of her shirt, she pulled away. "You could have some gratitude for what I do for you."

"I do. Trust me. I do appreciate *everything* you do for me."

"You are incorrigible!"

She stood and went out the door, walking toward the stream. Dominic did not call after her to remind her that she had promised not to go there during the day. His very shout could be what betrayed them to their neighbors. When she turned toward the strand, he cursed. He envied her her ability to wander about the countryside, while he was imprisoned in this tumbledown hut.

"Damn!" he muttered when a chip of wood popped out of his hands to roll across the floor to land on her wrapper. If Abigail stepped on it, she could cut her foot. Then both of them would be unable to walk. Then both of them might starve.

He stretched his hand out as far as he was able. When his shoulder was seared by pain, he sat upright again. The burned skin allowed him too little motion. Concentrating on not putting any weight on his ankle, he shifted himself along the floor.

When his fingers touched something hard beneath her wrapper, he scowled. Slipping his hand under her castoff clothes, he withdrew a pistol. She must have hidden it there. When? Had she had this ever since she came ashore?

Glancing from the pistol to see Abigail returning to the hut, he checked the gun. He cursed. It was useless. It had been ruined by the seawater. Mayhap if she had cleaned it immediately, the mechanism might have been saved, but rust dotted the metal and the hammer refused to pull back.

He lowered it to his lap. Damn! It would have made the situation easier if they had had some weapon other than his knife.

A shadow crossed Dominic. Raising the gun in a swift motion that he had practiced as a boy until it was instinctive, he heard Abigail's sharp intake of breath. That she did not scream and race away like a frightened child showed him again that she was not given to swoons.

He tossed the gun across the floor. When she choked out a warning, he said, "Don't worry. It is useless."

"Can it be repaired?" she asked, her face regaining some color.

"If we had access to a gunsmith's shop, possibly. Here, no."

"I was afraid the gun had been ruined, but I did not want to fire it and waste the only ball in it."

He laughed bitterly. "Were you saving it for a special occasion?"

"Mayhap I was."

"You should have told me that you had it. What else have you hidden from me?"

"Nothing."

"An easy answer."

Her sapphire eyes sparked like his knife on the honing stone. "The truth is always easy, Dominic. You might know that if you spoke it more often."

"You are accusing *me* of lying when—"

"I did not lie to you. I simply did not tell you about the pistol. I was saving it for an emergency."

He scooped it up again and shook his head in regret.

"Then you would have faced an enemy and been unable to fire it. This little pistol would have guaranteed your death, *chérie*."

"I could have thrown it!"

Although he guessed she expected him to smile at her half jest, he continued in the same somber tone, "Whether the gun worked or not is hardly the issue. What is the issue is that you hid it from me."

"Yes." She took a deep breath, then released it slowly. "You are right. I should have told you about it."

"Abigail Fitzgerald is admitting she was wrong?"

Her smile appeared and vanished so quickly he could have believed he had not seen it. "I do admit I am wrong when *I* think I am wrong, not when others think I am."

"*Touché.*" He leaned toward her, capturing her gaze with his. How he wished he could lose himself in those crystal blue depths that were as changeable as the sea. "*Chérie*, you must be honest with me as long as we are in England."

"If you will be with me."

"For as long as we are here, which should not be much longer."

"We are leaving England?" Her eyes grew round.

"Of course."

"When?"

"That I cannot answer as quickly."

"Oh." Her shoulders slumped, and he put his arm around them. He had thought she would pull away, but she rested her head against him. That warned him how high he had raised her hopes and how hard he had dashed them.

Dominic was startled at the regret racing through him. Being less than honest with her would be stupid. Yet he wished he could ease that lost expression that stole every bit of glitter from her eyes.

Tilting her chin up so he could look down at her, he

whispered, "By now we have been missed in Calais, but Ogier will not—"

"Ogier? Who is that?"

"Ogier Broulier is my first mate. He is mastering *La Chanson de la Mer* until I return. He will search for us as long as he can."

"As long as he can? You are his captain. Why would he stop?"

"They have other things to do, *chérie*."

Abigail shivered involuntarily. Dominic's words were like a slap across the face. This man holding her was her enemy. He wanted to see Father hang, and he had had no sympathy for what she would have endured in France.

Trying to keep her voice steady, she said, "I already have faced the fact that I may not get back to New Bedford for a very long time."

"And that does not frighten you?"

She started to reply with bravado, but halted her sharp answer. Meeting his gaze steadily, she said in an even tone, "It scares me almost as much as being captured and being put to death as a spy. I do not want to die here in England all alone."

"You are not alone." He stroked her hands gently.

Withdrawing her fingers from his, she pulled away from him and shook her head. "In many ways, Dominic, I am more alone than I ever have been. Unlike you, I am accustomed to being with my family."

"The crew of *La Chanson* is my family."

She glanced at the wedding ring on his left hand and stood. "If we want to eat tonight, I should find us something."

"*Chérie?*"

"I am sorry I did not tell you about the pistol, Dominic, but it does not matter, does it?"

"No, it does not matter." Sorrow filled his voice.

"Nothing matters but getting out of England before we are discovered."

"It will not be easy."

"True, but we must try."

She dampened her abruptly arid lips, then whispered, "Do you think we will succeed?"

"I am not sure." His eyes met hers as his voice grew cold. "The only thing I am sure of is that, if we must, we will die trying."

Chapter Eight

Hearing someone outside the hut, Dominic woke and reached for the knife. He clenched and unclenched his hands. Yes, he could beat back an intruder.

He lowered the knife as Abigail peeked in and asked, "Awake?"

"Yes." He growled a French curse as he rubbed his aching shoulder.

"Are you hurting worse?" she asked as she held out a cup of water to him.

He was about to chide her for risking her life, then realized that the sun was just rising. In the past ten days, Abigail had kept the promise she had made not to go near the stream during the daylight. He hoped she would hold as dear other vows that he must ask of her.

"Dominic?"

Giving her a wry smile so she could not guess the course of his thoughts, he said, "Yes, I am hurting, but 'tis my fault. All night I was careful not to lie on the burned skin across my left shoulder. So I woke with my right shoulder all cramped from sleeping on it.'' Stretching, he winced again. He scratched his cheek, which itched with unshaven whiskers. ''Why are you smiling?''

Abigail chuckled. ''Because you are in such a charming mood this morning.''

He glared at her, then relented. Her continual attempts to cheer him must be as difficult on her as on him.

He tried to move his ankle, and the ruts in his forehead eased. The pain was almost gone. Cautiously he stretched his left arm, then his right, and grinned. Only his head continued to ache. The wounds there would take a few more days to heal. It was time to find his way back to *La Chanson*.

As Abigail handed him a slice of stale bread for breakfast, he appraised her. She had tended to him tirelessly. Every day, she crept into the village to find something to eat. She had been an excellent ally, but would that change when he told her what he had planned?

He smiled as he took a sip of the fresh water and looked over the cup to admire Abigail. In her loose shirt and breeches that accented her lovely legs, she urged him to forget about the dangers of crossing England and think only of making love with her.

Abigail lowered her eyes from Dominic's smile. If he thought she was unaware of his gaze, he was a fool. And she knew he was no fool. As soon as he was well enough to travel, they must be on their way, so she could say good-bye to England and this intriguing French pirate. The uneasy truce between them must not be broken until then, but she feared that was impossible.

''The villagers were speaking about attending a fair day,'' she said as she took another sip.

''When?''

''Tomorrow.''

He laughed. "The timing could not be better. They will be exhausted by dark."

"And we can be on our way?"

"Yes."

"Where?"

"London."

Abigail stared at him. "Are you mad?"

"Mayhap, because, if I am not wrong, we are near the region the English call Dartmoor."

"Where is that?"

He smiled. "Almost the full breadth of England away from London. We were swept by the storm north almost to Caernarvon in Wales. As soon as the rudder was repaired, I headed the *Republic* south to go around Cornwall. We had not gotten far when your father's crew decided to destroy the ship rather than face their fate in France."

Abigail frowned, waving aside his words that did not matter now. "That is not what I meant. You must be mad to go to London."

"Mayhap, but London offers us our best chance to flee this island, because so many ships come there."

"Not French or American ships."

He chuckled. "You would be surprised, *chérie*. It is not difficult to hide a ship's origins when there is money to be made." He put his cup on the floor. "*La Chanson* has sailed into the Pool at least a half-dozen times in the past two years. It sometimes is easier to buy supplies in London than to return to France."

"But your accent must give you away."

"Men who are interested in profits seldom care about their government's policies. If we can reach London, I know of several people I can get to help us."

"Help us or just you?"

He smiled tightly. "I hope they will help both of us."

"You want me to base my life on a hope?" She toyed

with the hem of her long shirt. "And even if they are willing to help, I am no better off than I am now. I will be among my enemies in France instead of in England."

"I have thought of that." All amusement disappeared from his face as he took her hands. "*Chérie*, help me get to London, and I shall see that you are sent back to your aunt in New Bedford."

Abigail knew she should agree before he changed his mind, but she could not. "What of my father?"

"Once Ogier has turned him over to the authorities, I can do nothing." He put his finger to her lips to halt her next question. "My debt is to you, Abigail. You saved my life, and I will do all I can to return you to yours."

She nodded, not knowing what to say. Dominic St. Clair would not unbend enough to break the laws of his country, but he possessed a certain sense of honor. She did not want to admit that, because then she might have to admit as well that she had come to enjoy his wit and his efforts to save her from the dismals . . . and she had enjoyed his kisses.

She looked at the ring on his left hand. Mayhap he did not intend to be as honorable about his wedding vows as he was about helping her, but she must be.

"All right," she said in little more than a whisper. "I will help you if you help me."

"Is that a promise, Abigail?"

"Yes."

"And 'tis a promise from me as well." He lifted her right hand to his lips and kissed it swiftly. "A promise sealed with a kiss, *chérie*, is one that neither of us can break."

She laughed, unable to halt herself when he sounded so serious. When a smile warmed his stern face, she was certain of one thing. The trip ahead of them would not be boring.

* * *

Night trailed out of the trees to throw itself across the shore. In the distance, the lights from the village looked like earthbound stars. A lantern from a small ship bounced with the waves.

Abigail shoved her ruined clothes beneath a loose floorboard. Nothing must suggest that anyone had been living here. She glanced toward the shore. The bodies there had vanished. Had the sea reclaimed them, or had the villagers taken them away and buried them? Even if the villagers had shown that kindness to the corpses, she doubted that their clemency would extend to a living American and Frenchman.

She brushed dirt back over the board, satisfied that it would not catch anyone's attention. Coming to her feet, she wondered who else had taken shelter here and then disguised any signs of their stay. She took one last look around before going to the door. This moonless night was perfect for beginning their journey.

A darker shadow passed in front of the door, lurching with every step. Abigail picked up the dark lantern she had taken from a shop in the village. She went out and watched as Dominic struggled to walk. He leaned on the hut with each step. When he turned at the end of the hut, he hobbled back toward her.

"It will not be easy, *chérie*," he said. "This ankle will not support me completely."

"Then we will go slower." She forced a laugh. "It is not as if we need to be anywhere by a specific time." She hesitated, then asked, "Dominic, will you be all right?"

He slid her hand across his cheek that was turning black with whiskers. When it was against his lips, he kissed her palm.

She yanked her hand away, fearful of the luscious fire

that surged along her arm. She must not surrender to his easy seduction. "I can see you are quite yourself! I do not know why I waste time worrying about you. Let's go."

"Have you been worrying about me?" Astonishment filled his obsidian eyes.

"As I would about any wounded beast. If you delay any longer, we shall not be on our way before the sun rises."

When he frowned at her, she refused to be intimidated by his black brows beneath the dingy bandage across his forehead. "I will match you step for step," he said.

"If you don't, you may find yourself sitting by the side of the road at daybreak."

He nodded, surprising her, for she had thought he would argue further. Then she realized that he knew, as she did, that they must put a few miles between them and the village before dawn forced them again into hiding.

"Have you found your cat?" he asked.

"Yes."

"Are you bringing him with us?"

She shook her head. "He has found himself a home at a dairy near the village. He will be happy there."

"He is wise. I wish you would be as wise. This would be much easier if you were more cooperative."

"Me? I am cooperating."

"As your father did. When he saw it was useless to fight any longer, he accepted surrender to *La Chanson*." He laughed quietly. "In fact, he surrendered before I was certain we would win."

She closed the dark lantern. "I think it would be for the best if you refrained from flaunting your victory over the *Republic* all the time."

"I am not flaunting our victory as much as I am stating how curious I am that such a brave woman could have such a spineless father."

Abigail did not answer. How could she? She still did not understand why Father had capitulated to the French, or why the *Republic* had been sailing in English waters, or, the thing that bothered her most, why Father had left her aboard to become Dominic's prisoner. No matter how many ways she tried to explain Father's actions to herself, she could not. There must be a good reason why he had done what he did, but she could not guess what it was. She hoped she would have a chance to ask him.

Taking Dominic's arm, she drew it around her shoulder. In the thin light from the stars, she saw how his lips were clamped closed as he took a step, putting some weight on his right ankle. Pain raced through her as his fingers dug into her shoulder.

"Forgive me," he whispered. "Damn, that hurts!"

"I can support you if you do not grind your fingers through my skin."

His answer was lost in a groan as they took another step together. When they took a third, he said, "Thank you, *chérie*, for not dressing me down."

"For what?" she asked as she led him toward the thicker trees.

"For not bearing this in silence."

"I wouldn't."

His chuckle brushed her ear, and she fought the quiver that raced through her. "But you are quite wrong," he said.

"I am?"

"You endured all sorts of abuse from me and my crew in silence."

"I complained."

"When I touched you, yes, but you never spoke to me of Jourdan accosting you belowdecks."

"You knew of that?"

Again he laughed, then moaned as they skirted a tree. "As captain, I needed to know everything that happened on my ship. I forgive a man one mistake. Two, no.'' His side strained against her as they reached the path. ''It can be quite galling when I can barely walk to recall how brave you are.''

His amusement disappeared as another pang cut through him. When he cursed, she eased him to the ground. He winced, and she adjusted his ankle quickly.

She knelt beside him. ''It should be easier from this point forward.''

''If we use the road.''

''I fear we have no other choice. I cannot carry you through the woods all the way across England.''

He kneaded his ankle gently. ''It is healing well. Within a day or two, I should be able to walk on it.''

''I hope so.'' She touched the darkest bruise.

''Ventre bleu!'' he spat. ''Take care!''

''I am.'' Her brow furrowed. ''If you were wise, you would stay off it until the sprain heals.''

''But I am neither wise nor patient.''

She laughed. ''Undoubtedly, you are the most impatient patient in the world.''

He stood when she did. Slipping his arm around her again, he cautioned as she put her arm around his waist, ''Take care. The burns back there still hurt.''

''You should have let me check them before we left. If they fester, you could be in real trouble.''

''Then check them.'' He took the lantern from her and opened it slightly. As the glow washed along them on the deserted path, he loosened the few buttons on his shirt.

''What are you doing?'' she asked.

''Don't you want me to take this off?''

''Not here. Not now. Wait until daybreak when we stop. Then I will check your back.''

He redid the few buttons that would close on his shirt

and smiled. "That gives me something to look forward
to, a reward for the miles we put behind us tonight."

"First, we have to make those miles disappear."

Abigail had expected him to make a retort, for he
enjoyed having the final word in any conversation, but
Dominic remained silent as they went along the path. She
noted how he scanned the road ahead of them as well as
looking over his shoulder every few minutes. When her
fingers brushed the haft of the knife at his waist, she knew
he would not hesitate to use it. She began to believe they
might just do the impossible and escape from England.

Never had Abigail been happier to see the night fade
into the thick gray of the moments before dawn. Fog had
come ashore to keep them from seeing more than a few
feet ahead on the road. It was chilly and clammy, but she
was grateful, because she knew that no one would want
to be out on such a night.

Every muscle along her back and legs ached, threatening to give out if she took another step. She ignored the
cramps. She had said they would continue until daybreak,
and she would, even if the very next step was her last.
Beside her, Dominic was silent. She did not need to look
at his face to sense how he strained for each step. His
fingers drove into her shoulder, and he panted on every
breath. His lighthearted jesting had vanished.

" 'Tis sunrise," he murmured.

"It is still gray."

She was amazed when he chuckled. "You are letting
the fog baffle you." He drew his arm off her shoulder
and pointed to the east. "See? The light is much stronger
in that direction. The sun has come up out of the sea."

"Thank heavens," she whispered.

"My thoughts exactly." Instead of putting his arm
around her again, he grasped her hand. He limped to the

side of the road where a dark wall became a line of trees. " 'Tis time to stop and rest."

"After I find us some water."

"No, rest first, *chérie*. You don't need to encounter one of our new neighbors by a stream."

Abigail acquiesced to his good sense. After all, she was not thirsty. She had been swallowing gulps of the fog all night.

With more stability than she had expected, Dominic led the way into the trees. "The walking seems to have loosened my tight muscles," he said, warning her that he had noted her surprise.

"You will want to massage your ankle before we begin walking tonight. Your muscles may tighten up while we are resting."

He sat near some briars. Taking care, she lowered herself to the ground. She sighed, wanting to fall instantly asleep. She was not sure where they had walked for the past hour, because she had been half asleep.

"Before you rest, Abigail . . ." Dominic put his hand on her arm as she was about to curl up on the damp ground. "You wanted to check my back."

"Can't it wait?"

"For tonight?" His laugh was hushed. "Then you will be so anxious to be on your way that you will be furious at yourself for not doing this now."

She sighed. She hated it when he was right. "All right," she murmured, then swallowed harshly as he slid the sleeves along his arms. Although she had cared for him since they were washed ashore, the motion of the muscles between his bronzed skin mesmerized her.

She leaned forward to check the puckered skin where he had been burned by flying debris from the ship. She tried to ignore the expanse of bare skin before her eyes. It was futile, but she strove to concentrate on her task. Without his shirt, she could not overlook the sinews knotted along his arms and across his chest. He must have helped with all aspects of sailing his ship, for he appeared as strong as the crewmen who hauled in the sails and worked as stevedores in port.

Telling herself the pleasure simmering within her was from discovering his burns were getting better, she loosened the sweaty cloth around his head and smiled. His cuts were healing well, too.

"I don't think you will need to bandage your head any longer," she said, sitting back on her heels. "I do believe you are going to survive."

"You need not stop, *chérie*." Taking her fingers, he drew her forward until her face was only an inch from his. He held her hand between his as he said, "I like your touch." Pressing her fingers to his bare chest that was softened so slightly by dark, curling hair, he chuckled when she gasped. "Can I hope that your eyes are wide because you are pleased by this, too?"

She jerked her hand away. "I find no pleasure in being seduced by a married man."

"Married? What are you babbling about now?"

She pointed to the ring on his left hand. "That."

He laughed.

"What is so funny?" she asked.

He touched her cheek. "The only one I am wedded to is *La Chanson de la Mer*. I have no wife mourning my reported demise. This ring is a family heirloom which fits on that finger. Nothing more." His eyes twinkled mischievously as he pulled her against him. "If you do not make it a practice to be seduced by married men, would you consider being seduced by an unmarried one?"

"Dominic, I do not intend to be seduced by you or anyone else today."

"Why do you insist on using that precise tone when you are frightened of me?"

"I am not frightened of you!" She started to rise, but

he put his hand on her shoulder, keeping her on the ground beside him.

When she gasped in astonishment, he laughed. He might be hobbling, but he had recovered the strength he had on the ship. She should have guessed when he matched her, as he had promised, step for step all night.

As his fingers moved along her shoulder to the curve of her neck, he tilted her face toward him. She knew she should tell him to stop, but she could not deny the delight oozing through her at his gentle caress.

"I think we should go to sleep," she whispered.

"Why?" he asked reasonably as his finger moved along the line of her pulse to the responsive skin behind her ear. "We have no reason to hurry anywhere, *chérie.*"

A thousand words burned on her tongue. Insults and retorts she wanted to shout at him. She was not going to cede herself to him now. Whether he was married or not did not change her mind. He was her enemy, and she was with him still only because she needed his help to flee England, not because she was fascinated with his touch. She intended to say that and more, but instead she swayed nearer to him as his tender touch brought back memories of the night of the storm when he had held her so sweetly.

His fingertip teased the curve of her ear, sending strange, wonderful sensations cascading through her. When her hand rested on his shoulder, he smiled. It was the only warning she received as he pressed her back onto the earth beneath him at the same moment his lips found hers.

She softened as he snatched her breath from her with the tempest-strong power of his kisses. Under her fingers, his strong muscles responded to her touch. He raised his head to gaze down at her, and she wondered why she had denied herself this pleasure for so long.

She did not speak as she stared up at his midnight-dark eyes. The glitter in their mysterious depths could mean anything, but she did not care. Slowly her fingers rose to touch the coarse texture of his fiercely sculptured face. She closed her eyes as his tongue traced her lips before seeking within for secret rapture.

Turning her head away, she whispered, "No, Dominic." Anguish filled her voice. She could not forget the last time he had kissed her like this. Then he had been ready to force his way into her bed.

"Abigail?" When she refused to look at him, he cupped her chin and brought her face up toward his again. "Abigail, that was a mistake."

"Today or that evening on the ship?"

He laughed lowly, but there was only regret in the sound. "How can you ask that?"

Pushing him away, but taking care not to hurt his injured leg, she sat and brushed the dirt off her shirt. He caught her hand again. She glanced at him quickly and away. That he refused to release her until she answered his question should not have been a surprise. Dominic St. Clair was a man accustomed to having his way.

"You have hurt me, Dominic," she whispered, "any time I have lowered my defenses in the slightest."

"Hurt you? I did not think holding you in my arms and kissing your luscious mouth would hurt you."

"You know what I mean."

"*Oui*, I do. But do you know what this means?" He tugged her back into his arms. Her protest against his lips was halfhearted. Cradled against him, she was aware of every inch of his skin. His mouth moved along her neck as his fingers had, and her arms arched up his back. While she stroked his skin, sparks burned into her with his eager kisses.

When he raised his head to look down into her eyes that were blurred with passion, his gaze moved along her. "You fit so perfectly in my arms, *chérie*."

"Dominic . . ." She sighed eagerly as his tongue teased her ear.

"You are always a puzzle. I never know if I shall find a wildcat or a temptress in my arms." He whispered against her ear, "Now do you know what my kisses mean?"

Pushing against his chest was the most difficult thing she had ever done, but she could not remain in his arms. The craving within her demanded satisfaction. But she must not. She had to remember who he was and who she was. "You are a fool!"

"Mayhap, but even a fool craves happiness." He cupped her chin in his hand again and brought her mouth against his for the shortest second. "Go to sleep, *chérie*."

"Yes." Her voice quivered on that single word, but she was glad he had seen sense.

"No," he murmured when she moved away. "Here in my arms."

"Are you out of your mind?"

He shook his head. " 'Tis chilly. If one of us sickens, we may lose our only chance to get out of England."

"Do you promise not to . . . that is . . ."

"I promise to hold you in my arms and nothing else." He winced as he shifted his leg. "And, Abigail, I keep my promises as well as you do."

"All right."

He drew her back against him as he rested on the ground. His hard chest was the perfect pillow. "You are beginning to trust me, *chérie*. Could it be that you no longer are afraid of me?"

"I have not been afraid of you for a long time, Dominic."

"Then what frightens you when you are in my arms?"

Abigail saw no reason to lie as she nestled her cheek against his chest so his heartbeat thundered beneath her ear. "Of being your prisoner again."

"My prisoner?"

"Forced to do as you wish."

He leaned his head against her hair. "Trust me on this one thing if on nothing else, *chérie*. If I had thought I could woo you to do as I wished with a few kisses, I would have done that long ago."

"Which you could never do."

"Which I will never be able to do." As he sealed those words into her lips, she let sleep take her. That way she did not have to guess which one of them was still lying.

Chapter Nine

A carriage burst from the darkness along the country road. Dominic shoved Abigail out of the way. She winced when she fell onto the grass beside the thick hedgerow. The carriage was swallowed by the night before she could stand.

"Are you hurt?" he asked as she rubbed her hip.

"Just another bruise to add to my collection."

He laughed and took her hand as they continued along the dark road. In the three days since they had left the hut, his ankle had strengthened, and he now used a heavy branch as a cane instead of leaning on her.

"Mayhap, Abigail," he mused, "you should have stolen a carriage for us instead of that delicious meat pie you purloined from a windowsill."

"I suspect a carriage would be missed a bit more quickly, and we would have been arrested in no time."

"And why would we want to travel so swiftly along the road in such comfort when we can enjoy this walk?"

Abigail laughed. She had not guessed that Dominic St. Clair would have such a honed sense of humor or that she would come to appreciate it. Whenever she was exhausted or irritable, he found a way to make her smile. She glanced at him as she recalled her favorite way. That was when his lips brushed hers while he drew her into his arms.

With a shout, he leaped out onto the road before she could answer his silly question. What was he about? She gave chase.

She skidded to a halt when she saw the carriage that had nearly run them down stopped in the middle of the road. A single man stood by the door, silhouetted by the lanterns hanging off each side of the carriage.

Dominic did not slow. She wanted to shout after him to take care, for she could not miss the way the dim light glinted off the barrel of a pistol in the man's hand. Dominic was not armed. He could be killed.

"Now!" the man by the carriage snarled. "Give the baubles to me now, m'lady, or you shall be wearing them in your coffin. If—"

Dominic jumped from the shadows and wrapped his arm around the highwayman's throat. Abigail took another step forward, then froze when she saw something glitter in Dominic's hand. The knife!

"*Donnez-moi le pistolet,*" Dominic shouted.

Abigail stared in horror. Why was he speaking French? She understood when the highwayman froze, shocked.

With a growl, Dominic repeated in English, "Give me the gun." He chuckled as the highwayman threw down his pistol. "A very wise move, *mon ami.*" Shoving the thief toward his horse, he added, "Begone before I do the king's work and put an end to your useless life."

The thief swung up onto his horse and raced into the

darkness. Motioning for Abigail to join him, Dominic picked up the highwayman's gun and hid it somewhere among his tattered clothes. He took her hand as voices burst from the carriage. .

"Are you all right?" he asked.

"Other than having my wits scared away, yes," Abigail said.

"Good." He turned to the carriage and peered inside. "And you?"

Abigail could not help staring at the elegant vehicle and its two occupants, who were dressed to match. The woman, whose hair was as dark as Dominic's, appeared to be younger by a few years than Abigail. A boy sitting next to her had a similar aristocratic nose set in the middle of his narrow face. His face was pale, emphasizing the splash of freckles that were more numerous than Abigail's. Their clothes were fashionable, even to her uneducated eyes, and were elaborately decorated with lace and glittering gold buttons.

"We are unhurt," the young woman said, fluttering a lacy handkerchief in front of her face. "Thanks to your valiant efforts, sir."

"It was my honor to be able to assist . . ."

"Lady Clarissa Sudley," she said in a whisper.

"My pleasure, Lady Sudley." He bowed toward her with as much grace as if he stood in Napoleon's court instead of in rags by the side of this narrow country road.

"Are you—?" Lady Sudley gulped. "Are you French?"

"Not all the French are from France, my lady. There are many in Quebec," he said with a smile that was so genuine that Abigail would not have guessed he was creating a story for the lady to swallow. "In Canada, my lady," he continued when Lady Sudley's brow ruffled, "I am Dominic St. Clair, and this is Abigail."

"Abigail is not a French name," the little boy said.

"No." Dominic gave him another broad smile. "But remember that most of the people in Canada are not French. Many came from England or the colonies before the War of American Independence."

"Forgive us for being so questioning," Lady Sudley said.

"You have reason to be flustered, my lady."

"But we are safe, for you saved us, Mr. St. Clair."

Abigail could not keep from flinching at what Lady Sudley called him. When Dominic looked at her, Abigail knew he had sensed her reaction, even though the darkness had not been battered back far by the pair of carriage lanterns. Nothing must hint to Lady Sudley that Dominic was accustomed to another title, because addressing him as *Captain* would bring forth dangerous questions.

"I am pleased I could be here to be at your service, my lady," he said with another gracious bow.

"You must allow me to reward you." She smiled. "I have just the dandy. You must allow Sudley Hall to host you and your lovely wife tonight."

Dominic's hand squeezing Abigail's arm silenced her gasp. *Wife?* She realized that Dominic had allowed Lady Sudley to believe that by not using her last name. No wonder Lady Sudley had this mistaken assumption. To disabuse her of her misconceptions now might topple the stack of lies Dominic had devised. That could be fatal for both of them.

"That is very generous, my lady," Abigail somehow said. Dominic's hand gave her arm another quick squeeze. She drew away. Being false with this kind lady sickened her.

"Edgar?" called the lady.

Abigail glanced into the carriage. Was that the child's name? No, she realized when a man jumped down from the top of the carriage. The name must belong to the coachman.

"Yes, my lady?" he asked, tipping his tall hat to her. His voice trembled with residual fear, and Abigail was sure that if the night had been a bit more quiet, she would have heard his quivering knees knocking together.

"Will you have Mr. and Mrs. St. Clair's things put in the boot?" Lady Sudley smiled, clearly delighted to offer this benevolence.

"His help is not necessary," Dominic replied. "We have no bags with us."

"Nothing?" asked the boy.

"Hush, Newton," chided the lady. Her smile grew strained. "You will have to excuse my little brother. He seldom thinks before he speaks. Do come and sit while we are on our way to Sudley Hall."

Abigail's answer vanished when Dominic wobbled as he was about to step back to assist her into the carriage. She grabbed his arms. He still would have fallen if the coachman had not helped keep him on his feet.

"My ankle," Dominic said with a moan. "I fear playing the hero has a high price."

As Lady Sudley gave orders and her brother squealed with excitement, Abigail helped Edgar guide Dominic into the carriage. The coachman was stronger than he appeared, and with his help, Dominic managed to hop up on one foot and sit on the green leather seat facing Lady Sudley. Newton edged toward his sister as Dominic set his right foot on the seat beside the boy.

"Thank you," Abigail whispered when the coachman offered his hand. She sat next to Dominic.

Lady Sudley's eyes were wide with dismay as she stared at them. Abigail could not fault her. Even though Dominic spoke like a gentleman, both he and Abigail looked like the lowest of vagabonds. Lady Sudley gripped the little boy's hand tightly and blanched when the coachman closed the door.

When Dominic did not make a comment to assuage

the lady's qualms, Abigail turned and gasped. His face was nearly as colorless as Lady Sudley's. When the carriage lurched into motion, a soft groan bubbled past his lips.

"Is he ill?" Lady Sudley asked, her handkerchief now pressed to her face.

"No. He was injured when the ship we were sailing on was sunk." Abigail was glad to be able to speak the truth.

"Sunk?" Newton nearly jumped off his seat with his enthusiasm. "By the French?"

She shuddered, hating what she had to say, but fearing that if she lied, she would make a mistake and betray them later. "The Americans sank the ship."

When Lady Sudley and her brother asked for more details, Abigail tried to give them answers without revealing the truth. She must not allow them to find out that her father had been the captain of the ship or that Dominic had captured it.

Lady Sudley pulled a small vial from the beaded bag on her lap, the very bag Abigail suspected the highwayman had been interested in stealing. She gave Abigail the bottle.

Opening it, Abigail smiled as the sweet scent of flowers rose from it. The perfumed water would be perfect to dab on Dominic's temples to ease his pain. Thanking the lady, Abigail was curious why Lady Sudley carried this with her, but did not ask. She was glad that Newton kept the carriage from becoming silent as he prattled on and on about how exciting it must have been when the ship sank.

Bending toward Dominic, Abigail placed the dampened handkerchief against his forehead. "How are you faring?" she murmured beneath Newton's enthusiastic chatter.

"Not as bad as you think, but not as good as I wish when you are touching me like this." His voice was not much louder than a breath, but his provocative smile spoke volumes.

"You should remember we are not alone," she replied as quietly.

"Odd that I have been wishing we would chance upon such help, but now that we have, I am sorry to lose our time alone." Before she could retort, he smiled. "You spin an intriguing tale, *chérie*. It causes me to wonder how many falsehoods you have plied me with."

"Me?" She quickly lowered her voice when she saw Lady Sudley's amazement. "I have not been the one to spin all sorts of stories to obtain what I want."

"When have I lied to you?" He closed his eyes and smiled as she put the cool handkerchief over his forehead. "That is heavenly, *chérie*."

She wanted to fire back an answer, but she had none. Dominic St. Clair might be arrogant and overbearing and too handsome for *her* good, but she could not recall a single time when he had not been starkly honest with her.

More honest than Father was with me.

Abigail bit her lip and sat back against the carriage's lush seat. She could not deny that truth, but she did not want to think of it. Father must have an explanation for why he had done what he had. But what? What reason could he have had for leaving her with French pirates?

Dominic answered a question from Lady Sudley, but Abigail was lost in her uneasy thoughts and paid neither the question nor the answer any mind. Whether Lady Sudley spoke to her or not, she could not recall when the carriage came to a stop in front of a doorway that was swathed in light.

When Abigail reached for the door, Dominic's hand on her wrist halted her. The merest motion of his head warned her to remain where she was. She understood when the door was opened with a flourish.

A lad in dark green livery bowed. His smile wavered

when he straightened and saw the extra passengers in the
carriage.

Lady Sudley said, "Henry, run and let Richards know
we have guests."

"Richards is the butler," Dominic whispered.

"I know that!" Abigail scowled at him. To be honest,
she had *guessed* that, but she would not tell him that.

With the coachman's help, Dominic got out of the
carriage. Dominic had to lean on the door, but he handed
out Lady Sudley and then Abigail. Putting one arm over
her shoulder, he draped the other on Edgar's as the coachman helped them to the pair of steps leading to the carved
front door.

The door opened, and Abigail was sure they had been
ushered into a castle out of a book of fairy tales. She had
not been able to see Sudley Hall as they approached,
because it had been swathed in darkness. The foyer was
bright with lamplight, and she could not keep from staring.

The floor was an intricate pattern of different types of
wood that reminded her of the chessboard her uncle had
kept ready in the front parlor for his return. A skilled
artist had painted a mural in which people were gathered
in groups as if for an outing, but over their heads, instead
of a sunny sky, were swags of gold and green topped
with a crest that must belong to this family.

Doors were closed, giving no hint of what might await
beyond them, but a double staircase curved up in boastful
grandeur. At the landing where the stairs split to go to
either side of a balconied gallery above, a life-size marble
statue of a naked man caught her eyes.

She knew she was flushing when Dominic laughed
lowly and asked, "Do you have no appreciation for
ancient art, *chérie?* Or mayhap you have a great appreciation for it."

"Richards," Lady Sudley said, saving Abigail from
having to answer the unanswerable, "have Mr. and Mrs.

St. Clair taken to where they will be staying." She smiled.
"I shall have a tray sent up to you, if you will forgive
the informality. The hour is so late."

"We appreciate your kindness deeply," Dominic said,
winning a broadening smile from her.

"I hope you will join me and the rest of the family for
breakfast on the morrow. You need only ring, and you
will be shown the way to the breakfast-parlor."

"Thank you," Abigail murmured. "Lady Sudley, this
is an amazing house."

"I hope you will find it comfortable. I owe you a
debt that I can never repay." Taking off her befeathered
bonnet, she handed it to a footman who appeared as if
upon her silent command. "I shall have some clothing
delivered to you as well, if you will accept it."

Abigail looked down at her bedraggled shirt. "More
than you could guess, my lady."

"No, no. You must call me Clarissa. Your kindness
has made you a part of our family." Lady Sudley put her
hands on her brother's shoulders. "Now you must be off
to bed, Newton."

The little boy grumbled but went with her up the magnificent staircase. With the help of two footmen, Dominic
followed, Abigail trailing after them like a tired duckling.

She ran her fingers along the banister that was wider
than her hand. As she climbed, she saw even more incredible pieces of art set on elegant tables between the curved
doors on the upper floor. The floors were covered with
soft rugs that muted the sounds of their footfalls as they
went up another set of stairs.

Abigail forgot the splendor when she heard Dominic's
breath strain as he fought for every step. He must have
injured his ankle again even worse than she had guessed.
Mayhap he had been honest with her before, but she
feared he had been lying about how bad his ankle was.

One of the footmen opened a door and helped Dominic

through it. Dominic waved aside the men's help as he leaned on the door frame to enter the room. He smiled when Abigail drew his arm around her shoulder again. Closing the door, he limped with her across the large room.

"You played your part perfectly," he said as he eased himself down into a chair.

"My part?"

"You appeared completely awestruck by this house."

"I am!" She went to look out the curved window to the lawns that were lost in the shadows. That let her avoid looking at the large bed that would be perfect for a husband and a wife. Yet its reflection in the window taunted her. She tried to glance away at the collection of chairs and full-length glass, but her eyes kept shifting back to the bed with its ruffled coverlet and thick pillows.

A knock came at the door.

Abigail went to open it and realized two other doors were set in the wall on either side of the bed. One was ajar to reveal what she suspected was a dressing room.

A woman in a gown of the same dark green as the other servants said, "Madam, my lady asked me to bring you and Mr. St. Clair these things."

"Thank you," Abigail said, holding out her hands for the clothing.

"I will be glad to bring them in for you, madam."

"Of course." She waited for Dominic's laugh, but it did not come. Mayhap because he knew the danger of showing his amusement at how she was overmastered by all of this. Stepping back, she added, "You can put them on the chaise longue."

"As you wish, madam." The maid set the clothes on the pale gold chaise longue before unfolding them.

Abigail was unable to keep her fingers from brushing the soft fabric of the nightdress that the maid placed over the arm of the chaise longue. Jerking her hand back, she glanced to where Dominic was sitting in odd silence. A single raised eyebrow and a quirk of his lips warned her that he was fascinated with her discomfort at being here with him.

The maid hesitated, then asked, "Do you wish help dressing, Mrs. St. Clair?"

For the first time, Abigail kept from flinching at the name. Mayhap it was because she was so shocked at the idea of having a maid help her. "No, thank you. I shall be fine."

"If you are certain . . ."

"Yes, but thank you." She did not glance at Dominic, for she refused to have him give her a glare to warn that she had spoken thoughtlessly again.

"I shall be glad," he said with his disarming smile that brought a glow to the maid's eyes, "to give Mrs. St. Clair any assistance she requires."

"Of course, sir." As the maid hurried out of the room, Abigail was certain she heard a muffled giggle.

Picking up a clean shirt, Abigail flung it at Dominic. He laughed loudly when he caught it. "A shirt will not ease the fury that I see in your eyes, *chérie.*"

"How can you say things like what you said to that maid?"

"For two reasons. One, it is what a husband might say, and two, because I want to keep my neck the same length it is rather than let a hangman stretch it." Abruptly somber, he pushed himself to his feet and reached for the few remaining buttons on his shirt.

She whirled to go into the dressing room. Although she could not wait to put on the lovely nightdress and the matching wrapper, that longing was not what sped her feet. It was another craving, one that frightened her, one she could not erase from her mind. If she stayed to watch as Dominic undressed, she feared she could not control this craving to be in his arms and against his skin that had been burnished by salt and the sea winds.

Abigail closed the door and folded her arm against the wall. Leaning her head on her forearm, she struggled to ease the swift pace of her breathing. What was wrong with her? He had not even touched her or given her one of his seductive grins, but still her skin was atingle with anticipation and her heart thudded against her breast like a wave crashing on the shore.

She raised her head when she heard Dominic curse in French, then in English. She could not mistake the raw edge of pain in his voice. Dressing hastily, she brushed her hair back and tied it with the ragged ribbon from her old wrapper. With care, she opened the dressing room door.

"I am not going to ruffle your sensibilities," Dominic said, his voice still strained. "You need not lurk in the dressing room."

Abigail took a quick glance to assure herself he was being honest with her. He was tucking the tail of his shirt into the black breeches that emphasized his bronzed skin and lean strength. Forcing her gaze up to his face, she inched out of the dressing room.

"You look much better," he added.

"As you do."

He gave her a bow that was a mocking caricature of his courtesy to Clarissa Sudley. "I am pleased that you approve."

"Why are you taking that cold tone with me?"

"Because I do not like being dressed down each time you open your mouth. You have chided me like a chaperon who has learned her young charge has been kissing a rogue. Why are you so disquieted when I did nothing more than save the lady and her brother from a fate worse than death?"

"There is no need to resort to theatrics." Abigail went back to stand by the window. "If you want the truth—"

"Always."

She scowled at him. "I was not raised to use people for my own ends."

"Nor was I." Dominic tossed his ruined shirt on the chair, then pushed it aside as he sat with a wince. Looking up at her, he said, "But I do not intend to let this opportunity pass me by."

"It must be highly convenient to be able to pick and choose when you wish to be honest or not and never suffer any guilt."

"Why are you judging me with such a heavy hand? After all, you accepted Lady Sudley's invitation, too."

Abigail faltered. She was unsure how to tell him the truth that she had feared betraying him and that she wanted him to have a doctor check his ankle. Nor could she admit that she yearned to sleep in a bed with clean linens, a bed that did not rock with the motion of the sea, a bed that was wide enough for both of them.

She stared out the window again as she clasped her hands until her knuckles were pale. Where had *that* thought come from?

"Do not worry, *chérie*." Dominic patted the arm of the chair and set his right foot on a wide stool that he must have found while she was in the dressing room. "I will not be sharing your bed tonight." His enticing smile increased the pace of her furiously beating heart. "Unless you wish me to."

"You cannot sleep in that chair."

"I have no plans to do so."

Abigail sighed as she went to the chaise longue. It was too short for her to lie down on, but it would have to do. "I am so tired it shall not matter," she said as she sat.

"What shall not matter?"

"Sleeping here."

He laughed, the sound as boisterous as when he had stood on the deck in command of the *Republic*. "I keep forgetting how egalitarian your country is. Here, as in France, the wealthy enjoy all the prerogatives of their privileged lives."

"What are you babbling about?"

Coming carefully to his feet, he took her hand and led her to the door on the far side of the bed. It was almost hidden by the drapes. He swept the door open with a grand gesture.

Abigail stared as she had in the foyer. This room was magnificent, with light gold silk on the walls and sweeping up to the center of the ceiling to wrap around a medallion with a raised relief of cherubs and flowers. Against the far wall, a huge tester bed was draped in forest green brocade threaded with gold. When she took a single step into the room, the carpet threatened to swallow her toes.

"Impressed, I see," Dominic said with another chuckle. "Aren't you?"

"Of course." He limped to the bed and patted the covers. "Here a fine gentleman can savor the charms of his favorite mistress while his wife is cozily tucked away in her own rooms."

"With a single door between them?" She sniffed. "The English are obviously different from Americans."

His arm swept around her waist, tugging her up to his chest. As his lips brushed her ear to send sweet heat deep within her, he whispered, "You speak with such authority, *chérie*. Is it because you know that if you were to lie here in my arms you would cry out with joy?"

"You flatter yourself!"

"Quite to the contrary. I flatter you and the passion you cannot restrain." He etched that fire into her skin as his mouth glided along her neck. When she gasped at the very moment his tongue laved the curve of her breast above her wrapper, he chuckled and captured her lips.

His kiss was swift and sapped her knees until she feared she could not stand.

With a hushed chuckle, he bent to slip his arm beneath her knees. He did not heed her warning to take care as he swept her up into his arms. He laughed again as he dropped her on the bed. Eagerly, he pressed her back into it.

His hands framed her face as he rested his arms on either side of her. She gazed up at him. She wanted him to hold her like this, but she should not. He was her enemy, her father's most savage foe. Would he be gentle or fierce when he held her here?

He leaned toward her, and she closed her eyes as her fingers sifted up through his hair. She wanted to be in that magic place where the only loyalties were those of two hearts seeking joy.

When he did not kiss her, she opened her eyes to look up at him. "Is something wrong?" she whispered.

"Only that I am unmanned by the strength of this passion I wish to share with you, *chérie.*"

"You do not seem the least unmanly to me." When she laughed, she saw the passion in his ebony eyes flare even hotter.

She gasped when his mouth tasted the skin at the base of her throat. Sending far from her all thoughts of the world beyond his arms, she reveled in the ripples of sensation that rolled along her as he explored her with lips and fingers.

He pinned her to the bed, but she could not be still. The craving rippled through her like an unheard song, inviting her to be a part of this dance she had yet to learn.

Drawing his mouth back to hers, she heard his breath strain with hers. He pulled the ribbon from her hair and tossed it aside. He twisted his fingers through her hair, bringing her even closer to him as he buried his face in it. He groaned, and she reached for him.

With a curse, Dominic pushed her hands away. Abigail sat, then slid off the bed to kneel beside it. She peeled his fingers from around his ankle and repeated his curse.

"Oh, no!" she whispered. The swelling across his ankle had returned, distending it far beyond its customary shape.

"I believe I am a bad influence on you, *chérie*," he said, his attempt at a jovial tone falling flat.

"I believe you should stop playing the hero until you are better." She rose and went to the bell pull. Giving it a tug, she turned. "I shall insist that Clarissa send for the doctor in the morning."

"And tonight?"

"The only thing you shall have to warm you in bed will be some damp cloths around that ankle."

"You are cruel, *chérie*." He held out his hand. When she could not halt her fingers from settling on his, he smiled. "And you are bewitching when you stand there with your hair falling about your shoulders."

At a knock on the door, Abigail went to it and asked the maid to have warm cloths brought for Dominic's ankle. She closed the door. Turning back to the bed, she said, "You would be wise to ask for replacements every hour until the swelling goes down."

"Me?" He smiled, although his lips were still puckered with pain. "I thought you would stay to oversee my care."

"I shall leave that to the maid." She chuckled. "Tonight, *Mr. St. Clair*, I shall be the understanding wife and sleep in oblivion in my private chamber while a parade of maids wait upon you."

Dominic caught her arm as she started to leave. "*Chérie*, if you were mine, you would never sleep alone." He ran the back of his hand along her cheek. "You need not sleep alone tonight."

She took his hand in hers and lowered it from her face. "Yes, I must. Be as honest with me, Dominic, as you claim you are with everyone else. Nothing has changed.

You are my enemy, and I am yours. Even if I were not, your life is your ship. There is no place for me there, only in your bed tonight and for every night until we leave England.''

"My life is *La Chanson de la Mer*. That is true, but it is also true that I want you.''

"I know.'' She lowered her gaze from his eyes that seared her with their ebony fires. She added nothing else as she hurried out of the room before he asked her to be as honest. Then she might have to admit that she wanted him, too, but not just for a night. She feared her heart wanted to belong to this French pirate for a lifetime.

Chapter Ten

"Oh, you are busy . . ."

Dominic lowered the towel he had been using to dry his hair. Looking over his shoulder, he started to smile, then realized Abigail did not stand there. The thick towel had betrayed his ears, because the woman's voice did not belong to Abigail.

This woman was older than Abigail by a decade. The first hints of silver frosted her black hair around her face, giving it a bright glow. Her gown was a sedate cream, but the fabric flowed with elegance as she did not wait for his invitation to sit. Raising her quizzing glass, she peered through it.

He closed his robe over his breeches. He had not intended to receive callers here. *Receive callers.* He laughed silently at the thought. This elegant house was having a decidedly civilizing effect on him. No doubt, Abigail would be amused to see this. However, his work in the past had taken him from the highest reaches of society to the lowest, and he had to learn to blend in so completely that nobody would take more note of him than he wished.

"Never too busy," Dominic said, bowing his head toward the woman, "to stop and speak with a lovely lady."

"Bah!" She waved her hand at him. "Save your nothing-sayings for your wife, Mr. St. Clair."

"You seem to have the better of me, madam, for I do not have the privilege of knowing your name when you seem well-acquainted with mine."

She held out her hand, which was decorated with only a single ring. That told him she came from a wealthy family that had been in control of its riches for many generations. She did not need the pretensions of the *nouveau riche*.

He was glad she had chosen a chair close to where he stood. That way, he did not have to lurch across the room like a new crewman who had not yet gotten his sea legs. His ankle was not as swollen this morning, but he wanted no sign of his weakness to betray him to this woman who, no matter what she had to say, was his enemy.

Dominic bowed over her hand as she said, "I am Lady Herbert Sudley, Mr. St. Clair. You have met my daughter and son, I believe."

"I have had the honor." He hoped his smile hid his amazement that the younger lady had failed to mention that her mother was alive and had not corrected their mistake in addressing her as "Lady Sudley." The urge to smile grew. Mayhap the young woman had enjoyed being treated with the deference due a peer's wife instead of his daughter.

"I would say, Mr. St. Clair, that the honor was theirs." She folded her hands in her lap and regarded him with brown eyes that suggested she would endure no flummery.

"This family is greatly indebted to you for your bravery in stepping forward and halting that knight of the pad from relieving Clarissa and Newton of their valuables and mayhap even their lives."

"I was there."

Lady Sudley nodded, and he knew the matter would not be spoken of again today. It was the honor of a gentleman to risk his life for a lady, even if she was not of his acquaintance. He suspected Lady Sudley would expect nothing less from those of her class. If so, he knew from his past relations with the *ton* that she was due for disappointment. He had discovered more honor among his men on *La Chanson de la Mer* than among the Polite World.

"Clarissa did do one thing correctly, Mr. St. Clair. I want you to know that you and your wife are welcome to be our guests for as long as you wish." A flush showed through the rice powder on Lady Sudley's cheeks. "She hinted that your circumstances were not the best."

"An understatement." Glad that Abigail was not here, he let his smile uncurl along his lips. "When the ship we were on went down, so did everything but the clothes we were wearing. I have contacts in London who can provide what we need to continue on our journey."

"London?" Lady Sudley's smile was as cool as her exterior. "We leave for there at the end of the week to join my husband at our house in Town. You and your wife must allow us to take you there."

"You are too kind, my lady."

"On the contrary, Mr. St. Clair, it is little in exchange for saving my wayward children."

"Wayward?" he asked, unable to halt himself.

Lady Sudley rose gracefully. Her smile contained a hint more warmth. "Neither Clarissa nor Newton had permission to be out so late last night. Their father will tend to the task of giving them a punishment commensurate with their absentmindedness. 'Tis my pleasure to have the task of making you and Mrs. St. Clair welcome.'' She glanced about the room. "Where is Mrs. St. Clair?''

Dominic knew he could not hesitate in his answer. "She is still asleep. When I woke, I came in here so I would not disturb her. This has all been most traumatic for her, as I am sure you can understand.''

"You prove your kindness over and over, Mr. St. Clair.''

He gave her a smile, not sure if there was a deeper meaning to her words. Discovering what this woman was thinking was almost as difficult as trying to determine what was on Abigail's mind. Yet, with Abigail, he could taste the truth on her soft lips and know that she hungered, as he did, for more than a kiss.

The connecting door between the rooms opened slowly. Dominic's smile became more comfortable on his face as Abigail stepped in. She must have heard their voices from the other room and known better than to knock or peer around the door like a fearful child.

In spite of himself, he could not silence the sharp intake of breath as he stared at her when she stood in front of a tall window. The morning sunshine set her hair to blazing. In her dress of the palest green, she possessed a cool serenity that contrasted with the fire he knew burned within her.

"Good morning,'' Abigail said as she crossed the room to stand beside him.

He kissed her cheek, for to do more in front of their hostess would be considered rude. Again the temptation to laugh taunted him. How offended the lady would be if he whirled Abigail into his arms and claimed her mouth and the pleasure waiting there for him! Again his breath caught as he raised his head and saw the silver glitter of yearning in her blue eyes.

Dominic looked at Lady Sudley before he could no

longer resist his craving to have Abigail in his arms. "Abigail, *chérie*, this is our hostess, Lady Sudley."

"Lady Sudley?" Abigail's forehead threaded with confusion. "But—"

"We met Lady Sudley's daughter last night." He watched the puzzlement in her eyes become understanding and let the breath he had been holding hiss past his lips as Abigail greeted Lady Sudley prettily. He could not have asked for a better conspirator in this masquerade than Abigail. Her naïveté might be her best asset in dealing with the Sudley family, because she had to depend on him instead of arguing with him as she usually did.

"Lady Sudley has offered," Dominic added when the women had completed their greetings, "to let us travel with the family when they visit London at the week's end." He laughed. "That saves our tired feet the rest of the journey."

"How is your ankle today?" Abigail asked.

"Ankle?" Lady Sudley repeated before Dominic could reply.

He wished Abigail had waited to ask that question. Then he let his shoulders ease from their stiffness. Yes, he was among his enemies, but he must not act as if he were. Quietly he said, "I hurt it when the ship went down."

"And exacerbated it when you saved my unthinking children." Lady Sudley tapped her finger against her lips, then said, "I shall have several of Lord Sudley's favorite walking sticks delivered to you posthaste. Then you can use one when you join us in the breakfast-parlor."

"Thank you, my lady." He recognized her words as the order they were. "I appreciate your unending kindness."

"As I said, we are in *your* debt." She went to the door and, opening it, said, "Cook's biscuits are best eaten warm."

Dominic restrained his laugh until Lady Sudley had

closed the door and her footfalls had vanished along the hallway. Sitting, he grimaced. He balanced his aching ankle on his other knee.

"Your pride will keep that from healing," Abigail said, folding her arms in front of her.

"Do not chide me, *chérie*."

"Why not? You have wasted no time in reminding me of my shortcomings any time I did something you consider foolish." She went to the ewer and dampened a cloth. The water was no longer hot, but even a tepid cloth might ease the swelling. Kneeling, she placed the cloth on his ankle that was still an ominous collection of colors.

"But you were foolish not to heed me on the ship." He put his hand over hers holding the cloth in place.

She looked up at him. "You were my enemy."

"Were?"

"Don't try to trip me the double because of a simple word." She rose.

"I missed you last night, *chérie*," he murmured. "I have grown accustomed to listening to your soft breathing during the night and, in the morning, discovering your pretty face so close to me and waking you with a kiss."

"I missed that, too."

"You did?" He had not guessed she would say this. He had thought she would demur as she usually did when he spoke of the ache within him to be within her.

"Yes." Her fingers curved along his face.

The cloth struck the floor with an odd sound as he stood and slipped his arm around her. Her soft moan as he found her lips sent a fierce need through him. Pulling her up against him, he deepened the kiss, wanting to possess every inch of her mouth. The fiery flush flowed over him as, with a tender, demanding pressure, he urged her to cede herself to their craving. When her tongue brushed his, a lightning thrill of ecstasy cut through him. It teased his, daring him to give free rein to his longings.

Although she was soft against him, he exulted in his leisurely exploration of the moist recesses of her mouth. Her fingers sifted up through his hair as her breath burned fast into his mouth. He sought the source of that heat as he peppered her neck with eager longing.

A sound intruded. Dominic tried to ignore it, but the knocking at the door grew rapid and loud, warning him that he had not noticed it right away.

Abigail drew out of his arms and went to the door. She looked back at him before she opened it. Again he savored the sheen of her gaze that caressed him as eagerly as her fingers had.

When she opened the door to allow a maid to bring in a half-dozen walking sticks, Dominic knew he had not been wrong about Abigail longing for him as he longed for her. He did not intend to wait much longer to persuade her that, at last, she was making the right decision.

"Why are we stopping here?" Abigail asked, looking out of the carriage window. She recognized the village with its small collection of houses on either side of a church. It was the village near where the *Republic* had been destroyed. More than one of these houses had been her target when she had stolen food so she and Dominic would not starve. If someone had seen her and she was now recognized . . . She shuddered. Why had Dominic asked her to come with him here today in the carriage he had borrowed from the Sudleys? "Let's keep going."

"No, I have an errand that needs to be done." Dominic did not wait for the footman to open the door. He pushed it aside and stepped out, striding away. He looked every inch a gentleman from his well-made black coat to his embroidered vest to his carved walking stick.

Abigail followed until he went through an iron gate around the churchyard. She hesitated. Why was he going to the church? Wrapping her arms around herself, although the day was warm and the breeze off the sea was as gentle as a child's caress, she looked around the village. Two women were standing in front of a cottage at the end of the village closer to the sea. Their heads were bent toward each other, and she could hear their excited voices, although not the specific words. She guessed they were simply curious why such a grand carriage was in their simple village.

Hearing Dominic mutter something inappropriate for a churchyard, Abigail looked back at him. She put her hand on the iron gate as she watched him pause and rotate his right foot as if trying to ease a cramp. He hobbled toward the church, his walking stick accenting each step. When he turned toward the cemetery beside the church, she tightened her grip on the gate until the uneven paint cut into her palm.

The cemetery? His errand was *there?*

He opened the smaller gate and looked at her. It did not matter that they were not standing face-to-face. The fires in his determined eyes seared her. This was the expression worn by the inimitable Captain St. Clair when he commanded the *Republic* and the seas. He would not be defeated by anything. Not by his enemies, not by the storm, not by the ship exploding.

Slowly he raised his hand. She said nothing as she went to place her fingers in it. He might have vowed not to be defeated, but she sensed his disquiet. Was it the same as what flooded her to be in this place again when they had struggled so hard to flee from it?

"Thank you," Dominic said quietly.

"Thank you? For what?"

"For standing beside me now, *chérie.*" He took a deep breath and released it as he gazed at the stones that were being scoured by the sea wind's constant battering. "It takes a braver man than I to face what waits within this stone wall.''

"You are afraid of graves?"

"Afraid that I shall never forgive myself for not foreseeing the disaster that left my men dead." He sighed as he went to where the grass had been shoveled aside. Dropping to his knee, he patted the overturned earth and sighed. "Now they lie here beneath English soil, unmarked and unmourned, save by me."

Abigail's eyes grew wide as she looked from his stern face to the newest graves in the cemetery. Biting her lip, she wondered if her father's crew was buried here, too. Her heart cramped as she thought of Cookie and how he had saved her life by giving her warning to leave the ship. In the past few days, she had not thought of him at all as she struggled to help Dominic reach London and to keep Dominic from luring her into his arms.

"How did you know they were here?" she whispered.

He put his hand on her shoulder as he heaved himself to his feet. Leaning on the silver-tipped walking stick, he sighed. "Where else would they be? The villagers took the bodies from the sand. You saw that, too, although you said nothing to me of it at the time."

"I did not want to distress you." She shivered. "I had feared that the sea had reclaimed them."

"No. The villagers were kind enough to take them and bring them here for a decent burial. Of course, they had no idea where the corpses belonged."

"Do you?" asked a deeper voice from behind them.

Abigail whirled to see a tall man who appeared as broad as the church. His clothes and hair were the same funereal shade, save for his reversed, white collar. When Dominic put his hand on her arm, she wanted to tell him that he need not warn her about speaking carelessly. She had no idea what to say.

"Do we what?" Dominic smiled and held out his other hand. "Are you the reverend here?"

"Yes. I am Mr. Hallock," he said, shaking Dominic's hand. "Do you know where these corpses belong?"

"They belong to the crew of the ship that we sailed on." Dominic glanced at Abigail, then back at the minister. "We may have been the only survivors when it exploded offshore here after we were sent far off course by a storm."

"It was horrible," Abigail said, knowing she must say something. "As you can see, Dominic was hurt. He has to depend on a cane to help him walk now, but both of us are healing." She did not have to feign the sob that bubbled up from her heart as she looked at the unmarked graves, wondering again which one held Cookie's corpse. "We are so grateful for what was done here, Mr. Hallock."

"Yes." Dominic drew a small bag from beneath his coat and pressed it into the minister's hand. "Please see that those who helped with the burials are compensated for their work."

"You are very generous, sir," the minister said, clearly amazed at the offer.

"We are simply very grateful to be alive." He smiled at Abigail.

She could not smile in return. Where had Dominic gotten that bag that clicked with coins? She wanted to ask him, but she could not when the minister would hear the question.

"Would you like to join me in the parsonage?" Mr. Hallock asked. "It is nearly time for tea."

"Thank you, but no," Abigail replied quickly. This was too uncomfortable, and she did not want Dominic agreeing simply to gather more information about the coast. "We need to return to Sudley Hall posthaste."

"Sudley Hall?" The minister appraised them anew.

"We are Lady Sudley's guests," Dominic said, his smile never wavering.

"Are you the gentleman who rescued Lady Sudley's youngsters from that highwayman?" He did not give Dominic a chance to answer. "I pray that you have persuaded him to perpetrate his crimes elsewhere. We have had a rash of robberies here lately. Small things missing. A pie or a few eggs. It appears the cur has taken to greater crimes than what he had before."

Abigail hoped her wide-brimmed bonnet would hide any hint of the color she knew must be flashing up her cheeks. When Dominic drew her hand within his arm and bade the minister a good day, she was sure she said something, but she could not recall the words after they had left her lips.

As Dominic handed her into the carriage, Abigail sat and stared straight ahead. She did not shift her eyes even when he sat beside her, closed the door, and slapped the carriage to signal the coachman to return them to Sudley Hall.

His arm around her shoulders turned her toward him. "I borrowed the money in that bag from Lady Sudley."

"Oh."

"To pay for markers for the graves. I did not want them to go unnoted in this land they hated so desperately." He sighed as he had by the graves.

"But you told Mr. Hallock to give the money—"

"I thought dividing it among the villagers would ease your distress in the wake of your brief career as a thief." He cocked an eyebrow at her. "And neither your father's crew nor mine cares if there is a stone over their heads."

Abigail opened her mouth to reply, but a sob erupted from her. She buried her face against his waistcoat. The tears she had not cried in the cemetery raced down her face.

"*Chérie*, do not weep," he whispered against her bonnet.

"How can I not?" she answered as softly. "Cookie saved my life, and now he is dead."

"He did not die because of you, but because of his loyalty to a man who did not deserve it."

She raised her head. "What do you know of my father or of Cookie or of anything? Cookie was a gentle, amusing man who was my friend. He was no adventurer, seeking great wealth on the sea." Her voice broke. "He went to sea as a youngster, but this was supposed to be his last voyage before he retired and married his sweetheart whom he always called Widow White."

"You cared for him more than you do for your father, didn't you?"

"I came to know Cookie much better. Father was always busy with sailing the ship." She stared at a button in the middle of Dominic's waistcoat. "Cookie took time to listen to my concerns, no matter how trivial. I shall miss him for as long as I live."

"As I shall my men. They were good men. Loyal as your Cookie was. Brave and unwilling to back down even when death faced them." His finger tipped her chin back. "Like you, *chérie*."

"Like you, Dominic."

"Who would have guessed that we could find something in common when we have so much that is at odds?"

She was amazed when she could smile. "That is not the only thing we have in common."

"No, it isn't." He circled her face with his hands, tilting her head back so her bonnet slipped off her hair.

He drew her to him as his mouth claimed hers. She gripped his arms, yearning for them around her as she softened against him. When he lifted his lips from hers, she murmured a protest.

He needed no further invitation, and she tasted sweet,

desperate passion on his mouth. Her pulse throbbed with the yearning to be a part of him, to melt to him like a wax candle in the midday sun. His mouth touched her hair, her cheeks, her mouth, bringing each to life with the magic of his touch. She lost herself in the powerful heat of his embrace. Combing her fingers up through his hair, she ceded herself to her longing to be in his arms.

Splaying her hands across his back, she whispered, "By week's end, we shall be in London. Then we can leave England."

"It may not be quite that quick." He chuckled. "I have to get word to *La Chanson* and work out a place to meet."

"And then we will leave."

"We?"

Abigail slid out of his arms as a sudden icy flood surged through her. "Nothing has changed, has it? You are still Dominic St. Clair, pirate and freebooter who cares only for his ship. You can barely wait to return to your life of killing my countrymen."

"I have told you that my life is my ship."

"How simple it is to complicate your life only with something that will never have a chance to ask more of you than you wish to give."

He clasped her shoulders and scowled. "You know that is not true, *chérie*. You have complicated my life in so many ways." His tongue traced her lips before he whispered against her ear, "I might have halted your father's crew from committing suicide if I had paid more attention to the battle and less to my anxiety about what would happen to you if we were defeated."

"I am sorry to be so intrusive in your heinous life on the sea." She wrenched herself away from him. Settling her bonnet back on her mussed hair, she folded her hands primly in her lap.

"*Chérie*."

When she did not answer, his finger gently turned her

face back toward him. She knew he could see the tears filling her eyes anew because he shook his head before saying, "Mayhap it would be better if we concentrated on what we do not have in common rather than what we do."

"Yes," she answered, although she feared he would not hear her answer over the crystalline shattering of her heart.

"Enemies who must work together to escape a mutual enemy," he said, his gaze not releasing hers.

"Yes."

"Enemies and comrades."

"Yes."

He turned to look out the other window, and she clenched her hands until her fingers ached. Everything he had said made sense. Everything he said she knew was the right thing to do. Nothing had changed, so why had her mind amended his words to *enemies and lovers?*

Chapter Eleven

The sound would have woken Dominic even if he had been sleeping. He had been lying in his dark room, staring at the underside of the wooden canopy of his bed, and trying to sleep when the thunderstorm first rumbled up out of the west.

Then he heard the scream.

He leaped from the bed, paying no attention to the twinge in his ankle on his first step and how it grew into a serrated knife by the time he reached the connecting door between his room and Abigail's. He threw it open.

From out of the darkness, something flung itself at him. He recoiled, then realized the slender arms were Abigail's. He reached for her, but she slid to the floor, her arms about his waist, her face pressed to his bare abdomen. The heat of her tears washed along his skin, but he could only think of the soft warmth of her ragged breath and how she pressed so enticingly against him. Above the modest neckline of her linen nightgown, the curve of her breasts brushed his legs. Each of his muscles grew taut as she turned her face against his stomach, her moist mouth and cheeks sending liquid flame to every inch of his body.

He struggled not to press her back onto the rug and lose himself deep within her softness. His fingers trembled as he stroked her hair that had fallen free to drape across her shoulders.

"Abigail?" he whispered.

"The darkness!" she moaned. "It is smothering me. Help me escape the darkness."

When he turned to light a lamp, her arms tightened on him.

"Do not leave me," she begged.

As he looked down at Abigail, who still clung to him, he wondered if he would ever be able to breathe again. In the thin light pouring through the windows, her hair flowed in a river along her back, pooling on the pristine white of her unadorned nightgown. Intriguing shadows of her slim legs drew his gaze toward her bare toes. Knowing what he risked, he stroked her silken hair again.

She tilted her face back, and he was mesmerized by the raw desire in her eyes. Her fingers glided along him in an eager invitation to share that passion. He struggled to bridle his reaction to her bewitching touch. To take advantage of this situation when she was so obviously distressed . . .

He captured her face in his hands and brushed his mouth over hers. The luscious pulse of her uneven breath swirled into him. A low moan floated from her when he took her earlobe between his teeth before the tip of his tongue traced each whorl. Fire flared within him, an uncontrollable blaze. As he found her mouth once more, the flame cascaded along him, scorching away every thought but of her bewitching touch.

He gasped when she came to her feet and her lips swept across his cheek, his nose, his chin, the swift throb in his throat, leaving scintillating sparks. When her tongue teased the shockingly sensitive skin of his eyelids, he twisted his fingers through her hair. He sizzled with a craving to taste her soft skin.

With a groan, he brought her mouth back to his. This time, he threw aside gentleness as he gave himself to the craving to sample each pleasure waiting for him. His tongue sought to explore every shadowed secret of her mouth. Its slick warmth seared him to his very soul.

Lightning flashed, and thunder resonated through the room.

Through Abigail's head, sweeping away every bit of rapture with the power of the storm's winds, came a memory from her childhood. "Aunt Velma!" she had screamed with every ounce of her terror. Then her aunt had come to comfort her. Where was that comfort now?

Another peal of thunder rang through the night's black blanket. It threatened to consume her in inescapable fear. Hands caught her shoulders. Lightning burned into her eyes, blinding her.

"Abigail?"

In her panic, she did not recognize the voice. She did not care who held her. She only wanted someone between her and the savage storm. "Help me," she whispered, clinging to the strong body that was her only bastion against the storm's wrath.

"Come here, *chérie*."

"Dominic!" She pulled back. "What are you doing here? You should—"

Thunder cracked like a branch being snapped over a knee. Abigail closed her eyes. A shiver coursed through her, and she pressed her hands to her face.

"Abigail?"

She opened her eyes and stared up into Dominic's face.

Even in the faint light of the single lamp he had lit, she could see concern and bafflement rutting his forehead. "Dominic?" she whispered.

"Are you all right?"

"I am fine. I—" She gasped as he lifted her to sit on her bed. Pulling away from him, she groped for her wrapper and struggled to push her arms through the sleeves. "What are you doing here?"

"I came when you screamed."

She faltered, no longer certain of anything. "I screamed?"

"Yes. I came in here, and you cried out something about the dark smothering you."

She shivered. "Yes. It is dark in here. Mayhap if we lit a few more lamps."

"That is simple enough. If you are frightened of the dark, you should leave on more than just one turned low." He lit the other lamps in the room.

"Afraid of the dark? I am not afraid of the dark. It is the storm . . ." Lightning flashed, making the trees ebony against the white sky.

When Abigail sobbed and buried her face against his chest, Dominic enfolded her to him. "I recalled you saying how frightened you are of storms. I guessed you would be upset by this one." He sat on the edge of the bed, and she nestled against him.

The sky glowed with more lightning, and she moaned.

"It is all right," he murmured. "Hush, it is all right."

"Don't leave me, Dominic. Please don't leave me." She hated her own weakness, but she could not help her fear as thunder crashed overhead.

He tipped her face back. When her hands slowly rose to his shoulders, he captured her lips. The storm's power flowed through her as his kisses became more demanding. She forgot the tempest overhead as she was swept away

by the thunderous pulse of his desire. When his lips
brushed a ticklish spot along her neck, she began to laugh.

He drew away. "What is so funny? I must say, this is
the first time a woman has laughed when I kissed her."

"Oh, Dominic," she said through her chuckles, "forgive me. It is just . . . just . . ."

"Just what?"

" 'Tis just that I could begin to love storms if you
spent them with me like this." Her laughter eased as she
stroked his cheek. Her voice thickened with desire. "You
make me feel so safe."

With a scowl, he pressed her back against the rumpled
covers. "I do not want you to be safe with me, *chérie*.
I want you to fear that your mind will be stripped away
by the madness of ecstasy."

Just as his lips touched hers, thunder cracked overhead.
She cringed and hid her face on his shoulder. "I am trying
not to be scared," she whispered.

"Do not be ashamed. We all fear something." He
smoothed her hair back from her face.

"What are you afraid of, Dominic?"

He smiled. "Of being away from the sea. Of being
unable to delight in the wind on my face and feel my
ship dancing with the rhythms of the water."

"I had no idea."

"How could you?" He tweaked her nose. "After all,
have we ever spoken of the fears deep in our hearts?
Usually we spit at each other."

"I am sorry that you are so far from your *La Chanson*."

"Give me no sympathy, *chérie*, for soon I shall be
sailing *La Chanson* again."

"Do you believe that?"

"I must."

Lightning flashed. Despite her efforts, Abigail quailed
from the thunder that ached through her head. She was
glad to have Dominic's arms around her.

When he gathered the pillows against the headboard, she smiled as he leaned against them. She rested her cheek against his chest. Rain struck the window, and she sighed with relief. The arrival of rain usually signaled the end of the lightning and thunder.

Amusement tinged Dominic's voice. "Have you always been so afraid of storms?"

"Always. Aunt Velma tried to cure my fear with stories she invented about the thunderstones where lightning was born."

"Thunderstones?"

At his shocked gasp, she looked up. She could see his eyes' shadowed depths, but could not guess what hid there. "You know about thunderstones?"

"Yes, but I have never heard anyone use that term in English."

" 'Tis an old word my aunt learned from her grandmother. She told me tales of magic elves who brought the sun's power to the thunderstones, which crashed to earth in the midst of a storm." She sat and leaned her chin on her knees. "Even that did not help ease my terror."

He stroked her hair. "I was scared of storms when I was a child, too." He wrapped his arms around her. "My *maman* held me like this and sang French lullabies."

"I cannot imagine you frightened of anything." She laughed softly. "How your mother must worry about her son the pirate."

"The privateer." When she laughed again, he squeezed her shoulders. "*Maman* long ago learned that her son was born to a life of adventure. In that way, she says I am much like my father. Apparently, he found it as hard as I do to compromise his ideals. She is pleased that I serve my country this way. The other choice would be to find myself in the infantry marching across Europe."

Her laugh disappeared as another boom of thunder invaded the room. "Isn't that storm ever going to leave?"

"Hush, *chérie*." Putting his finger under her chin, he brought her lips to his. Her arms encircled his shoulders as he lowered her back to the pillows and leaned over her. "Don't think of the storm, *chérie*. That is not part of our lives anymore. We are apart from the rest of the world, for how else could a lovely American lady be kissed by the captain of a French privateer and not be filled with hatred?"

"Mayhap this night is a magic one."

"Aye, and you are the sorceress who drives me crazy with her spells."

As the thunder vanished into the distance, Abigail did not hear the last rumbles. His kisses rained against her skin as fiercely as the storm threw itself at the windows. His fingers stroked her eagerly, as did his lips. Through her rose a heated wave which threatened to drown her in desire. She touched him, learning the shapes of his body which were so different from her own.

When his fingers moved along the upsweep of her breast, she gasped against his mouth. Trembling with the need as compelling as the man who invoked it, she tangled her hands in his hair. Her ragged breath was loud in her own ears when his lips explored the skin above her nightgown's neckline. Deep in her, an aching emptiness beseeched her to press closer to him.

Suddenly something moved along Abigail's leg. She cried out in horror.

Dominic pulled away and put his hand over his ear. "What in hell are you screeching about now?"

"I thought . . . But 'tis just rain. It is blowing through the window. I must not have closed it completely."

"Then close it now, *chérie*, and come back to my arms."

"No," she whispered. "Give me time, Dominic."

Holding her face between his hands, he murmured, "I do not know how much time we have."

"No one seems to suspect the truth."

"But the truth has a way of becoming known." He ran a finger along her arm and whispered, "But it is not just that. I want you, Abigail. I want to touch you without anything between us. I long to taste every inch of your slender beauty. When I pulse within you, you will understand how you seduced me to heed the longing on your lips instead of the words you speak."

Unsure how to answer, she whispered a good night. He stood and gazed down at her. All she needed to do was reach out to him and he would stay. She could not— not when she recalled the words spoken in the carriage. Her fingers rose to touch his face.

He caught her wrist in a tight grip. His voice was as taut. "*Chérie*, be certain of your choice."

A knock sounded on the door.

Abigail slowly drew her hand out of his. Going to the door, she opened it to see a maid.

"Lady Sudley wished to ascertain that nothing is amiss," the maid said with a quick curtsy.

"You may inform her that everything is as it should be." As she closed the door, Abigail turned to see Dominic by the door to his room. "That is the biggest lie I have ever spoken."

"Mayhap it is just as well, for it is clear that our hostess is being most attentive." A whisper of a smile tilted one side of his mouth. "She would be quite shocked if you were no longer my oblivious wife who sleeps here alone, but my lover who expresses our pleasure with her not-so-soft sighs."

She was not sure how his words managed to crawl beneath her skin to quiver there like a bolt of lightning. They stirred through her, whetting her longing until it became an ache she could not ignore. She gripped the latch on the door to keep her feet from carrying her into his arms.

He must have mistaken her silence for anger, because he said, "Good night, *chérie*. If another storm sweeps down on us, you need only to come to me."

And if a storm does not arrive, I still can go to you. She could not silence that thought, but replied, "Good night, Dominic. Thank you."

He was gone, the door clicking closed behind him, before she could be stupid and say what she really wished to. She climbed into her bed, which seemed so empty. She loved how he made her feel when his gaze roved along her. Then she forgot the eye-scorching color of her hair and the freckles that dotted her nose. When his finger traced the planes of her face in the seconds before his lips touched hers, she believed she was as lovely in his eyes as he whispered against her ear.

If the rain had not interrupted, she might have succumbed to Dominic's promise of delight. What scared her more than even the thunderstorm was how undecided she was if falling in love with her father's most hated enemy was right or wrong.

Chapter Twelve

Watching Clarissa arrange the flowers in a bowl on the table in the sitting room, Abigail tried not to let her boredom show. She was accustomed to the busy life in her aunt's house where there were always chores to be done. Even on the ship, she had helped her father with some of the tasks he despised.

She made some excuse to Clarissa and went outside. The fine house seemed too close, although she had expected to delight in the comfort of four strong walls and a roof after days of sleeping in the thin shadows and nights of walking along a country lane.

"Escaped?"

Abigail whirled to see Dominic rising from a chair on the terrace. She smiled when he walked more easily than he had since the *Republic* was sunk.

"I should not say yes." She laughed.

"But that is the answer."

She nodded, admiring how the sun danced with blue
fire off his hair. In the fine clothes that Lady Sudley had
taken from her husband's dressing room, he could have
been a country squire himself, enjoying this sunny day
as he kept an eye on his estate.

Walking to the edge of the terrace, Abigail leaned her
hands on the stone rail. She was silly to have such
thoughts. There would be only one place where Dominic
St. Clair belonged, and that was on his ship.

"You seem aimless," Dominic said as he sat on the
rail beside her.

"I am."

"Mayhap it is wiser to look at this time and this place
as an opportunity to give ourselves a chance to catch our
breaths before . . ."

She faced him. "My breath is well caught. Several
days ago. Now I am at wits' end trying to keep from
losing them."

Dominic laughed. "Is that your very polite way of
saying you are suffering from ennui?"

"You are assuming the vocabulary of the Polite World
with incredible speed."

"As you are." He laughed again. "A few days ago,
you would not have known what the term Polite World
meant. Now listen to you. You could be a miss about to
enjoy her first Season."

"I fear I am too old."

"You?"

"When her mother is not about, Clarissa laments endlessly that she will be left on the shelf because Lord
Sudley insists that she wait another year before she is
fired-off." Abigail sat next to him and let her feet rock
against the wall. "You are right. Listen to me."

"I am, and I am glad you have such a quick ear for
the language that may be our best guise in London." He

paused as a bird shrieked overhead, then added, "Such skulduggery is not easy for an honest man like me."

"You seem to be as quick at learning that as I am with the cant of the *ton*."

"Fortunately for both of us."

Abigail gazed up at the trees where two birds seemed to be having an argument. She listened to their squawks, which ended when they flew away in opposite directions. With a sigh, she ran her fingers along the uneven stones.

Dominic's hand lightly settled over hers, following the sinuous motion her fingers made across the edges of the stones. She looked at him and knew she did not want to look away. The enticing curve of his mouth, the heated sparks in his eyes, the gentle caress of his rough skin on her hand, all offered an invitation that echoed within her heart.

His other hand came up to cup her cheek as he whispered, "I could not ask for a better partner in this adventure."

Abruptly he stood and looked toward the road that wound from the gate to the house. Several riders were coming at top speed in front of a carriage.

"Who do you think that is?" Abigail asked, coming to her feet, too.

"I have no idea, and I shall not complicate matters by jumping to conclusions." He chuckled. "We have enough to do without making matters worse."

"Mayhap you have enough to do."

Dominic turned back to Abigail. Although she was watching the riders, her fingers were clenched by her sides. He recognized that pose. She was distressed about something that she feared she could not escape.

Putting his hands on her shoulders, he asked, "What is that supposed to mean?"

"It means I am bored." She shrugged off his hands and walked along the wall to where the rosebushes framed a view of the pond. "It is a hateful feeling for someone accustomed to being busy."

"I do recall you mentioning that you were bored on the ship."

"When you were captaining it, yes."

"Do you mean your father gave you work to do?" His laugh was terse. "None of his crew mentioned that you had been climbing the sheets or raising the sails."

Facing him, she scowled. "Of course not, but there were things I could help with. I kept his log for him."

"His log?" He closed the distance between them and saw her face grow gray. "I thought you said you did not know where it was."

"I lied."

"That is clear. Did you lie as well about not knowing where the *Republic* was bound for and what was in its holds?" He ignored the sensation that reminded him of a fist in the gut. He had not trusted this American woman when he first took control of her father's ship, but that distrust had been eroded away by her concern for his well-being . . . and her kisses. Had he been the greatest fool to be seduced by those luscious kisses and her tentative touch?

She shook her head, her eyes wide with dismay, as he stepped even closer. He caught her face between his hands, keeping her from edging away.

"I did not know what was in the holds or where we sailed," she whispered. "I swear that, Dominic. The information Father gave me for the log was usually only numbers. I had no idea what they meant, but I could copy them neatly into his log."

"Which you kept safe for him when the ship came under attack?"

"Yes." She closed her eyes, but opened them to meet his gaze evenly as she whispered, "The log book was in the drawer under my bed."

"He left his daughter to guard over the ship's most vital information?"

"It worked, didn't it?" She squared her shoulders. "Mayhap that is why he left me behind."

Dominic snorted. "I do not believe that, and neither do you."

Abigail wanted to retort that she did, but she would not lie to Dominic again about this. If Father had truly worried about the log books being discovered, he would have destroyed them as soon as *La Chanson de la Mer* came over the horizon and it was clear the *Republic* would be forced to surrender.

"Can we speak of something else?" she asked.

"Whatever you wish, *chérie*."

A quiver rippled through her at the name that softened his voice to a husky yearning. Her fingers rose to frame his face as his did hers. His smile broadened as she brought his mouth toward hers. She tasted its warmth while his arms enfolded her to him.

"Sometimes not talking about anything else," he murmured against her ear, "is what we do best."

She laughed in the moment before he captured her lips again. Sifting her fingers up into his hair, she pressed closer to him. She wanted to savor him with every inch of herself. Her uneven breath rang in her ears as his mouth glided along her neck even as his fingers were sweeping up over her breast. The quivers became a storm within her.

Whispering his name with the insistent craving, she steered his mouth back to hers. Her lips were jealous of any other part of her, wanting all of his kisses for themselves.

He released her.

Abigail stared at him as she banged a hip against the stone wall. Was he out of his mind? He never had treated her so roughly before.

"I am sorry. I did not mean to cause you harm, *chérie*," Dominic said, then turned away.

Her answer dried up in her throat when she saw at least a half-dozen strange men crossing the terrace toward them. Only because Lady Sudley was with them could Abigail keep her feet from fleeing.

Lady Sudley smiled warmly as she came forward and took Abigail's hand. "My dear friends, these gentlemen from the admiralty would like to ask you some questions about your interrupted voyage."

One man stepped forward. His dark hair fell into his eyes as he bowed and said, "Good afternoon. I am Harold Kiley, and it is my duty to investigate the sinking of what appears to be an American ship along the shore south of Dartmoor."

"An American ship?" Lady Sudley asked, glancing at Dominic with a baffled expression.

"My lady," he replied with the gracious tone he always used with her, "any captain from North America would be proud to set sail in a ship constructed by the Americans. They have some of the finest oak that has ever been found."

Mr. Kiley smiled coolly. "That is a lament heard often in the halls of the Admiralty since the end of the Americans' war for independence. You seem very familiar with the ways of ships, Mr.—"

"Dominic St. Clair." As he held out his hand to shake the other man's, Abigail saw no sign of anything but curiosity and goodwill on Dominic's face. Again she wished he had given the Sudleys a name other than his own.

Mayhap her worries were groundless, because Mr. Kiley shook his hand and motioned for them all to sit in the chairs the other men gathered from the sunnier sections of the terrace. When refreshments were brought while Dominic and Mr. Kiley discussed the ship design, Abigail hoped no one took note of how she clutched on to her glass of lemonade to conceal her shaking hands.

"We would be glad to help in any way we can," Dominic said after taking a sip of his lemonade. "However, you must understand that my knowledge of shipbuilding comes from what I have read and what I have observed on my own voyages before this first opportunity to sail on an American-made ship. I do not know how much we can tell you, because Abigail and I were quite lost at sea, if you will pardon the pun."

"Of course. You must have been witness to whomever attacked the ship." Mr. Kiley motioned to one of his companions, who pulled out a lap desk and writing materials and poised to take down their answers.

"It would be difficult . . . no, I would say it would be impossible not to take note of a battle at sea when one is on board one of the ships involved." He glanced at Abigail. Although he did not jostle her elbow, she knew he wanted her to take part in this conversation, because he thought it would draw more attention to her if she remained silent.

Her voice shook, but she did not try to calm it as she said, "The attack on our ship was horrible, Mr. Kiley. The noise, the screams of the wounded men, the clatter of swords as well as guns firing. I will never forget one moment of it."

"You speak only of sounds," Mr. Kiley said. "Can you tell me what you were able to *see*, madam?"

"Nothing." She put her glass on the table and wrapped her arms around herself. She quickly folded her icy hands in her lap, because she was already shivering as she recalled those horrible hours on the *Republic* when she had been unsure if her father was dead or alive. "I could see nothing. I was told to remain in my quarters, Mr. Kiley. I did. Mayhap it would have been less horrendous if I had seen the actual battle instead of allowing my imagination to paint such a wretched picture of what must have happened on deck. Now, I fear, those scenes from my imagination will remain imprinted on my mind forever.''

Dominic's hand slid over hers, his fingers closing gently. ''I had no idea,'' he said softly.

''I know.'' Again she found herself lost in his eyes. The sympathy in them was as solacing as an embrace, but she wanted his arms around her. She did not want them giving her compassion, but passion.

Mr. Kiley cleared his throat as a flush climbed his thin cheeks. ''A few more questions, if we may.''

''Of course,'' Dominic replied, but continued to hold Abigail's hand.

She held tightly to his fingers, glad to let him answer Mr. Kiley's questions. Listening in growing amazement, she realized Dominic had not been jesting when he said he tried always to speak the truth. Not a word that he told Mr. Kiley was false, but allowed no hint that Dominic had been commanding a French ship that had halted an American ship trying to slip through the blockade.

Mr. Kiley seemed pleased with the information that Dominic had provided, because he pumped Dominic's hand heartily and thanked both of them when he rose to take his leave. Lady Sudley stood to escort them to the door.

Dominic sat again when the others had gone into the house. Folding Abigail's cold fingers between his hands, he sighed. ''I am so sorry, *chérie*.''

''You already apologized.'' She set herself on her feet and went to stand by the wall again.

''I did? When?''

''When you bumped me against this wall when Mr. Kiley arrived.''

His smile was gentle as he limped toward her. ''I was not speaking of that, *chérie*, but of the fear I instilled in you during the attack on the ship.''

"You had no idea I was on the ship when . . ." She glanced anxiously toward the house.

He tipped her face back toward him. "I was not speaking of that, either. I was speaking of when I found you in your quarters."

"You enjoyed taunting me!" She pulled herself away from him.

His hand on her arm halted her. She knew, if she shook it off, he would not hold her against her will. If she had an ounce of sense, she would end this conversation now and recall that they were enemies, that he had captured her father's ship and had sent her father to hang, that he could betray her in an effort to save himself and his ship.

But her heart thudded as she faced him again. His fingers stroked her cheek, luring her back to him without a single word. When her hand rose, he caught it by the wrist and pressed his mouth against her palm. A thrill pierced her, fiery hot and unrelenting.

Not letting her hand go, he raised his head and whispered, "Mayhap I did, but there is one thing I would enjoy with you more now, *chérie*. One very dangerous thing that could rip your very soul from you as you give yourself to me."

"You should not speak so. If someone were to hear—"

"We are alone."

A shout contradicted him, and footsteps pounded the stones as Newton rushed up to them. Somehow the boy inveigled his way between them, squirming like the snake he carried in his hands. Holding it up for Dominic to see, he chattered like one of the birds scolding them from the trees.

Abigail backed away, knowing she must make her escape now before her lack of sense betrayed her into Dominic's arms. She had not gone more than two steps before her elbows were grasped and she was spun back to face the fierce fires in his eyes.

154

"*Chérie?*"

"I think I should go now while you and Newton enjoy his snake."

"That is not what I wish to enjoy," he growled lowly so the boy would not hear. "This house is too crowded. Even in our private rooms, there is always a parade of maids and footmen passing through."

"Mayhap that is for the best, Dominic."

His kiss was deep and hard, leaving her breathless.

"If you think so," he whispered, "then it is my duty to change your mind for you as soon as possible."

She slid out of his grip and backed away one step, then another. She whirled and ran into the house, but she knew there was no escape from the truth. She wanted the rapture he could give her, even if that desire made her a traitor to everything she had ever believed in.

Chapter Thirteen

"We never go inside this building." Clarissa gave a shiver as she pointed with her parasol toward the stone barn that was set along the edge of the pond in the very center of the garden.

"Why not?" Abigail asked, coming down the garden steps to stand beside the younger woman.

Abigail hid a yawn behind her hand. She was not bored, just sleepy. For the past two nights, there had been thunderstorms rumbling overhead. She had huddled beneath her blankets, biting her lip to keep from crying out in horror. If she did, Dominic might come into her room. She knew she would not be strong enough to ignore again her desire to be in his arms. But that desire frightened her even more than the storms crashing overhead.

"Mama says it is dangerous. There is a spring inside it, and someone might have drowned there." Clarissa's eyes sparkled with mischief. "Do you want to see inside?"

"I thought you said—"

"Mama says not to *go* inside. She said nothing about looking inside."

"And," Dominic's voice interjected, "it is too tempting not to peek into."

Clarissa's cheeks flushed an enticing pink. When she fluttered her eyelashes at Dominic, Abigail did not smile. She was not bothered by Clarissa's childlike flirting with him, but by the thought of how Lady Sudley would react if she discovered the truth about Dominic St. Clair. He might look elegant in his fashionably cut coat and unpatched breeches, so Clarissa could be excused for practicing her fascinating arts on him. Yet, even when he was dressed like this, Abigail always saw him as the pirate, standing with arrogant pride on the ship, looking into the wind and past the horizon.

"Yes, it is most tempting, although I am sure it is dangerous within," Clarissa said, her voice softening. "Of course, Mama would not mind us going in if you were with us, Mr. St. Clair."

Newton popped out from behind a tree, a piece of long grass hanging from his mouth like a country bumpkin's pipe. "Mama said no one was supposed to go in there. Not even Mr. St. Clair." He giggled as he squinted at his sister. "You need not worry. Clarissa won't go in there anyhow, because it is full of spiders."

"I will too go in there," Clarissa argued.

Abigail now had to struggle to hide her smile. Seeing how Dominic's eyes twinkled, she fought that impulse even harder. Clarissa might be close to her own age, but her pampered life as an earl's daughter made her seem much younger. The only worry she had was which dress to pick for tea. Had Abigail been so immature before Dominic and his pirates were thrust into her life? Mayhap she had, because, then, she could not have imagined her father abandoning her on the *Republic*.

Holding out his arm to Abigail, Dominic asked, "Shall we peek within, Newton, and see if there is a reason for your mother's anxiety?"

Newton ran toward the door with a squeal of excitement. Clarissa followed closely in pursuit of him. Drawing Abigail's hand onto his arm, Dominic led her after them, no longer limping as he had even yesterday.

"You are walking much better," Abigail said.

"Newton believes that a tour of the grounds was just the thing I needed to work out any residual strain." Dominic chuckled.

"You are spoiling that boy."

"He is a good boy, and he misses his father. Lord Sudley has been in Town for more than three months on business for the estate, and apparently for the government."

"At least the family will be together once more by week's end." She stared across the pond that glittered in the sunlight.

Pausing, he said, "If all goes as I hope, you will see your father again."

"As the noose is being slipped over his head?" She yanked her hand off his arm. "How kind of you to remind me of that."

He caught her hand, folding her fingers between his. "His fate is yet to be seen. All evidence of his crimes is gone, which may have been the real reason the *Republic* was sunk."

Her eyes widened. "That is true, but if you testify against him, the judge is sure to heed the word of a Frenchman over an American."

"Mayhap. You cannot tell." He picked up a stone and skipped it across the water. "I must admit that I envy both you and young Newton your hopes of being reunited with your fathers."

Abigail was kept from replying when Newton ran back to them and tugged on Dominic's sleeve. "C'mon!" the boy cried. "You can give her moony looks later. I want to see inside the barn." He raced to where his sister was waiting with as little patience.

Dominic chuckled. "He seems bent on finding as much trouble as possible to crowd into each day. If I ever were to have a son, I would want one who was as curious and mischievous as Newton."

"Be careful what you ask for, Dominic. You might just get it."

His grin became rakish. "I find that hard to believe when I have not gotten what I asked for with you, *chérie*."

"How do you know that I have not asked for just the opposite?"

"Because of what these tell me." He grazed her lips with his fingertip.

"Mr. St. Clair!" Newton's voice was sharp with frustration.

Dominic laughed again as Abigail walked with him to where the boy waited. The barn was not large. Scents of damp and the sound of running water came from within, and she suspected it might be simply a springhouse.

Giving Clarissa a wink, Dominic lifted the latch and swung open the plank door. Thicker odors of clammy shadows oozed out, but Abigail smiled. It had the same aromas as her aunt's root cellar. That hole in the ground had been populated by a vast collection of spiders and crawly bugs and the occasional worm, but she had loved seeking its coolness on a humid day when even the breeze off the sea did not ease the heat.

Newton peeked in and scowled. "I thought there would be something exciting in here."

"Like buried treasure?" his sister asked.

"Or something or *someone else* buried in there."

Clarissa shuddered. "How horrible!" Then her eyes twinkled. "Do you think so, Mr. St. Clair?"

"I suspect," Dominic replied with a chuckle, "that your mother might have noticed one of her servants going missing if foul play had taken place here."

"Oh," Clarissa said as Newton grumbled something under his breath.

Abigail wondered how someone as prosaic as Lady Sudley could have given birth to two such fanciful children. As they walked away, clearly disappointed, Abigail paid their conversation no mind. She watched as Dominic went into the barn. Edging past the door, she waited for her eyes to adjust to the darkness.

"Take care," he said. "There is a spring in the center here, and the floor is slippery. It may rise and fall with the tides."

"We are too far inland for that."

"Mayhap, but it is clear that the spring bubbles up over the floor at least part of the time. Take care," he said as he held out his hand to take hers. "I know better than to suggest you might want to go outside and wait. You are as eager as Newton to stick your freckled nose into everything." The humor left his voice. "I recall saying that before. In the *Republic*'s hold. Curse your father, whose greed has destroyed so many."

Abigail whirled and went back out into the sunshine. She blinked in the bright light as she struggled to swallow the pain clogging her throat. How could she defend Father when she could not comprehend why he had been bringing those guns to England?

Dominic's hands on her shoulders were gentle and asked for nothing, save that he could offer her solace.

When she leaned back against him, his arms folded over her. His cheek rested on her borrowed bonnet, but he said nothing.

"I do not pretend to understand this hatred among those who used to be friends," she said as she smiled sadly. "Among those who used to be family. Somewhere in England, I have distant cousins who occasionally sent a letter to my aunt and uncle. I believe my uncle once visited them."

"But you do not know where they are?"

"No. They could be anywhere in England." She turned to face him. "Yet my family in America would be glad to see the family here defeated."

"And both septs want to see France brought to its knees."

"Yes." She sighed. "It was so much simpler to share that determination for victory at any cost before I took this voyage."

His fingers moved to caress her ear. "Does it disappoint you that we Frenchmen are not the beasts you expected?"

"You can be beastly, but so can Americans be."

"You speak of your father's crew."

"They would not have been forgiving if they had recaptured the *Republic*."

"Which was why I refused to let them have that opportunity."

She laughed. "Your gallantry would be more believable, Dominic, if I did not know already how much you wanted to bring your prize to France."

"You know me too well, *chérie*. 'Tis a dangerous enemy who knows me so well."

"Mayhap someday our countries will be allies again."

His laughter boomed. "I hope not."

"Dominic, that is horrid! Just because you hate the English—"

SPECIAL INTRODUCTORY OFFER!!

A $22.00 value absolutely FREE!

4 Free Ballad Historical Romance Novels

Passion – Adventure – Excitement – Romance

Ballad Historical Romances...

INTRODUCING *BALLAD*,
A BRAND NEW LINE OF HISTORICAL ROMANCES

As a lover of historical romance, you'll adore Ballad Romances. Written by today's most popular romance authors, every book in the Ballad line is not only an individual story, but part of a two to six book series as well. You can look forward to four new titles a month each taking place at a different time and place in history.

But don't take our word for how wonderful these stories are! Accept our introductory shipment of 4 Ballad Romance novels – a $22.00 value – ABSOLUTELY FREE – and see for yourself!

Once you've experienced your first four Ballad Romances, we're sure you'll want to continue receiving these wonderful historical romance novels each month – without ever having to leave your home – using our convenient and inexpensive home subscription service. Here's what you get for joining:

- 4 BRAND NEW Ballad Romances delivered to your door each month
- 25% off the cover price of $5.50 with your home subscription
- a FREE monthly newsletter filled with author interviews, book previews, special offers, and more!
- No risks or obligations…you're free to cancel whenever you wish… no questions asked.

To start your membership, simply complete and return the card provided. You'll receive your Introductory Shipment of 4 FREE Ballad Romances. Then, each month, as long as your account is in good standing, you will receive the 4 newest Ballad Romances. Each shipment will be yours to examine for 10 days. If you decide to keep the books, you'll pay the preferred home subscriber's price of $16.50 – a savings of 25% off the cover price! (Plus $1.50 shipping and handling.) If you want us to stop sending books, just say the word… it's that simple.

If the certificate is missing below, write to:
Ballad Romances, c/o Zebra Home Subscription Service, Inc.,
P.O. Box 5214, Clifton, New Jersey 07015-5214
OR call TOLL FREE 1-888-345-BOOK (2665)
Visit our website at www.kensingtonbooks.com

FREE BOOK CERTIFICATE

Yes! Please send me 4 Ballad Romances ABSOLUTELY FREE! After my introductory shipment, I will receive 4 new Ballad Romances each month to preview FREE for 10 days (as long as my account is in good standing). If I decide to keep the books, I will pay the money-saving preferred publisher's price of $16.50 plus $1.50 shipping and handling. That's 25% off the cover price. I may return the shipment within 10 days and owe nothing, and I may cancel my subscription at any time.

The 4 FREE books will be mine to keep in any case.

DN100A

Name _____

Address _____

City _____ State _____ Zip _____

Telephone ( ) _____

Signature _____

(If under 18, parent or guardian must sign.)

Orders subject to acceptance by Zebra Home Subscription Service. Terms and Prices subject to change.
Offer valid only in the U.S.

Get 4 Ballad
Historical Romance Novel
FREE!

BALLAD ROMANCES
Zebra Home Subscription Service, Inc.
P.O. Box 5214
Clifton NJ 07015-5214

PLACE
STAMP
HERE

"You misunderstand, *chérie*. My most trusted friend is English."

Abigail stared at him. What tale was he spinning for her now? "You are joking!"

"Hardly." He walked closer to the pond and bent to stir it with a short stick. Mud rose to cloud the water. Tossing the stick into the water, he said, "I cannot believe how many years it has been since I last saw Evan Somerset. Three? No, more than that. Back then, we ran a very profitable smuggling enterprise across the Channel."

Abigail stared at him. "Smuggling? Is that how you knew to suspect the *Republic* of carrying contraband?"

"Partly, although I never carried guns to help my enemies slay my countrymen."

"I have heard of the smuggling across the English Channel." She would not be baited into changing the subject by his insult to her father. That Father was bringing those guns to England was something she wanted to avoid talking about until she had a chance to talk to him. If she ever did . . . Dominic's words had suggested that French justice would be swift and brutal. Despite her efforts to calm her voice, it trembled when she added, "Smugglers bring brandy and silk and wine to England."

"That is not what we smuggled." He stood and faced her, grinning. "We dealt with slightly more exotic items. Fine art and antiquities usually."

Shocked, Abigail tried to guess how many more amazing facets of this enigmatic man waited to be discovered. "Did you smuggle art to or from England?"

"Whichever direction it needed to go." He shrugged. "I am not a connoisseur of art. I left that in Evan's hands. My ship served as a mode of transportation." With a laugh softened by memory, he added, "We had some grand times and some very close escapes. I wonder if he still is in the same business."

"You don't know where he is?"

"The war has made it impossible for us to find a shore-side tavern and share a few lies over a pint. As an Englishman, he could not send a message to me in the blockade. It could send us both to the gallows, but we both know that if we ever have a need for each other, somehow we will meet up again."

"If he is in England now . . ."

He chuckled. "Now you are privy to my plan, *chérie*. Evan might be in London. If not, one of my other allies will be. I know one or two who will help us get out of England. I would rather have Evan's help, because I know he would do whatever he must to help, as I would for him."

"Do you realize how lucky you are to have a friend like that?"

"As lucky as I am to have found you?"

"You are charming today, Dominic."

As his arms tightened around her, he drew her against him again. "I warned you a long time ago that I intended to charm you out of your hatred."

"You have." She had no chance to say anything else as his lips found hers. When the banked waves of desire surged out to surround her, she savored the warmth of his embrace. Her hands eagerly stroked his back.

Suddenly he released her. She wanted to ask him what was wrong, but she already knew the answer. Nothing she had said suggested she had changed her mind about what they had discussed in her room the night of the first storm. Reaching out to take his hand, she whispered, "Be patient, Dominic. Give me some more time."

"Time I may have little of." He whirled her back into his arms and against the strength of his chest. "Patience I have even less of. Do not forget that, *chérie*."

His kiss burned against her lips, swift and fiery, but he released her and walked back toward the house. She started to call after him, then paused.

Whirling, she looked back at the pond. Even its muddy waters were less opaque than her mind. Her heart knew what it wanted her to do, but if her father had betrayed her, how could she trust Dominic?

She wished she knew the answer to that.

Chapter Fourteen

"No," said Lady Sudley as she set her cup down on the tray with the remnants of their luncheon, "you need not stop first at the modiste, Clarissa."

The young woman's lower lip jutted with her vexation. "But, Mama, I need the gown I ordered for the *soirée* Papa is hosting the night we arrive." Her face brightened as she turned to Abigail. "You will attend, won't you?"

Abigail glanced at Dominic, who was sitting beside them on the terrace near the rose garden, but he was staring at the low hills that were the only thing between him and the sea. His regret at being so far from his beloved ship radiated from him like the sun's heat, stealing his smile. Grief crushed her heart in mid beat. This delay at Sudley Hall, although it had given his ankle a chance to heal, whetted his longing to return to his *La Chanson*. She had seen a similar craving in her uncle's eyes when he went down the wharves to oversee the reloading of his ship before he set sail again.

Stretching, Abigail put her fingers on Dominic's arm. He turned toward her, his gaze slowly focusing outward again. As if oblivious to his sorrow, she said in a light tone, "We would be delighted to accept an invitation to Lord Sudley's *soirée*, wouldn't we, Dominic?"

"Delighted," he answered quickly, although the slight narrowing of his eyes warned that his answer was not exactly the truth. "That is, if you wish us to attend, my lady."

"Most certainly." Lady Sudley's smile was genuine. "I shall be thrilled to introduce to my friends the man who saved my children's lives."

"I must insist that matter be kept quiet."

Her smile faltered. "But why, Mr. St. Clair? I cannot imagine any reason why you would not want your heroics known throughout the Polite World."

"Dominic is," Abigail said with a quick grin toward him as if this were a longstanding jest, "surprisingly shy about such things. He prefers to keep such things to himself."

Newton bounced to his feet, slashing an imaginary sword. "Like Robin Hood."

"A bit." Dominic downed what remained in his cup and set it beside Lady Sudley's. "I simply believe that a man should not be praised just because he does his duty."

"You have a rare modesty, Mr. St. Clair." Lady Sudley's smile returned. "However, it shall be as you wish. I would not repay your chivalry by making you uncomfortable." Rising, she clapped her hands. "Now, Clarissa, it is time for your embroidery lesson, and, Newton, your tutor asked me to send you to him as soon as we finished our midday repast."

When both Clarissa and Newton grumbled before following their mother into the house, Abigail chuckled.

"You would not find it so amusing," Dominic said,

offering his hand to help her from her chair, "if you were the one who had to study inside on such a lovely day."

"I spent many days sitting in a corner with a book that did not intrigue me as much as the chance to go with my uncle to his ship."

He did not release her hand as he led her across the terrace and out toward the enthusiastically blooming roses. "So you, too, know the siren song of the sea?"

"I liked being with my uncle. He always told me the most amazing stories about his voyages, and I never tired of them, even when I was no longer a child."

"Why did he and your aunt raise you?"

Abigail had been about to bend to enjoy the fragrance of a rose that was the color of freshly churned butter, but drew back. "My mother died shortly after I was born."

"From your birth?"

"I don't think so. I was almost six months old when she died."

"Then how?"

She was glad for his hand around hers as she delved back into painful memories. "I honestly don't know. Once or twice a year, when I was very young, I asked Aunt Velma about it. She always told me that my mother's death had been a tragic accident. Nothing more."

"But you don't believe that?"

"I want to believe it. I might have, if Aunt Velma had met my eyes when she told me that. Sometimes even a child knows that something is not quite right."

He said nothing as he turned toward the pond. She was glad, because she did not want to chance an ear overhearing this conversation. As raw as her emotions were around this unhealed wound, she feared she might speak the very word that would damn them.

Only when they were at the edge of the pond and walking toward the springhouse did he murmur, "So you never asked again?"

"Aunt Velma always acted as if she wanted to cry when I did, so it seemed best not to ask. I did sneak out of the house several times a year to plant flowers on my mother's grave. I wanted to know her and to know my father."

"But instead you were left with your aunt and uncle."

"Who loved me dearly. They had no children of their own, so they needed me as much as I needed them."

He laughed shortly as he stopped by the door to the small barn that held the spring. "Mayhap your childhood was a blessing. You were better off than you would have been if Fitzgerald had raised you."

"Dominic!"

"Spare me the lecture about your father's saintliness. You are the first to admit that you do not truly know him. Mayhap it is time for you to admit as well that he is not the paragon you considered him when he intruded into your life whenever it was convenient for him, bringing you trinkets from far-off places."

"He seldom brought me gifts." She glanced at him and away. "Don't look at me like that."

"Like what?"

"As if you had proven your point. Just because my father is not sentimental does not mean he has no affection for me. I am his daughter. He is my father. There is a loyalty there that cannot be ignored."

"Is there?" When she started to walk away, he stepped in front of her. He did not touch her, but she was held by the sorrow in his eyes. "*Chérie*, I have come to wish that your father could have been a respected enemy. A respected enemy is to be treasured almost as much as a friend."

"You are talking nonsense."

"Am I?" He took her hand and pressed it to the center of his chest. "Listen to my heart if you will not to your own. Even though we pledged it to be so, you and I will never be friends.''

"That is true." Her fingers trembled beneath his palm, and she wanted to sweep them across his broad chest.

"Are we enemies still?"

"I wish I knew how to answer that."

His smile sent something whirling like a sea storm through her center. "You know the answer, *chérie*. We are enemies because there is one who will separate us forever."

"My father?"

"He remains between us although he is far from here, in France. You have to accept that your father is not the man you believed him to be. You saw the guns in the hold. You know there are no Americans here, save for you and probably a few people from your government. What kind of man sells guns to his nation's enemies and—''

Putting her hand on his arm, she was shocked when he brushed if off. "And what? What makes you hate my father so much?"

"That is simple, for again you know the truth. Although you say nothing of it, I see it in your shattered eyes when you speak of your father. You comprehend no better than I do how a man could leave his daughter to his enemies." His fingers stroked her cheek. "*Chérie*, I can forgive him for his loyalties, even though he is a traitor to your country. I can forgive him for his brutality when we hailed his ship. I cannot forgive him for leaving you without protection."

"Nor can I." She looked to the east and France where her father was awaiting the trial that could lead to his death. "I try to believe there is a reason, but I cannot guess what it might be. It no longer matters, does it?"

"No, it does not." His thumbs beneath her chin tipped back her face. He smiled as his fingers spread across her cheeks beneath her bonnet. "So let us think of happier things."

"I do not trust that twinkle in your eyes, Dominic."

"You are a smart woman." He laughed and released her. "Come with me."

"Where?"

"I thought you might be interested in what I discovered when I returned to the springhouse this morning."

Abigail looked at the stone building. "You came back here? Why?"

"I saw something yesterday that intrigued me, but the time to explore it was not right."

"Because Newton would want to join in?"

"No more questions." He tugged on her hand. "You shall understand when I show you what I discovered."

Knowing how useless it was to pester him with questions, for he was as impervious to them as Lady Sudley had been to her children's complaints about their lessons, she went with him as he opened the door. She stepped into the cool shadows and listened to the soft whisper of the water in the pool in the center of the room.

"Take care," Dominic said as he drew her around the outer rim of the springhouse. "The floor is slick."

Abigail gasped with delight when she saw a simple sluice in front of her. The waters from the spring flowed through it and dropped down in a miniature waterfall into a second pool before vanishing beneath the floor. "Why hide this in the darkness?"

"It was not always so dark in here."

"What do you mean?"

"Come and I will show you."

Her curiosity sped her feet to keep up with his longer strides as he continued along the outer wall. When he stopped, she bumped into him. His laugh echoed oddly.

"Here, *chérie*," he said, taking her hands and placing them on the wall. "Wait right here."

"Where are you going?"

"Have patience."

"You are enjoying my impatience."

"As you have enjoyed mine."

Abigail wondered if he could see her blush through the deep shadows. She could not mistake the meaning of his words. He had been more patient with his ankle and with being away from his ship than with his desire for her.

She heard a thump, then a second one before Dominic called, "Abigail?"

"Where are you?"

"Up here."

"Up there?" She tried to see him, but saw only darkness. Then she realized that directly above her head there was a different shade of black about the size and shape of a settee.

"Take my hands, *chérie.*"

"Your hands?" She laughed. "I would if I could see them."

He reached down from wherever he was and grabbed her hands. "Hold tight!"

She laughed again as he pulled her up through a hole in the ceiling. When she sat on its edge, she glanced around. All she saw was more darkness.

"Move away, *chérie.*"

"To where?" She put out her hands but discovered nothing, not even a wall.

Dominic chuckled as his hands settled on her waist. He lifted her back from the hole, sitting her on something that was softer than the wood at the edge.

Putting out her fingers, she found the wall. She followed it up and realized that the ceiling in this space was not far above her head. The top of Dominic's would brush it.

A thump resonated through what must be a small storage room. "What was that?" she cried. "Dominic! Are you still here?"

"I am here."

"Where are you?"

"Here." His hands edged her face, turning it to the right.

"What is this place?"

"The perfect place, *chérie*." His fingers stroked her cheeks before sifting up through her hair. The caress of his breath lured her mouth toward his. As her lips found his, he leaned her back. She gasped with amazement when the softness enveloped her.

As he loosened the ribbons on her bonnet, tossing it aside, she whispered, "Clarissa said they were not allowed in here."

"Exactly." His laugh was low and rough. "No one will disturb us here. No maids bringing hot water to soak my ankle. No footmen bringing polished boots. No Lady Sudley making sure that we are comfortable." He slipped his arm beneath her as his strong hands pulled her against his hard body. "This is the best comfort I can imagine."

Her mouth was tilted under his before she could ask another question. Tenderly he kissed her. She could not fight the yearning his kiss invoked. As his mouth moved along her neck, she gasped with delight. He entangled his fingers in her hair, holding her closer as his fingers slipped up her back. He rolled above her, and she could not silence her moan of need.

She pulled his mouth down to hers, desperate for this pleasure that should never have been. She did not care about the loyalties that tried to pull them apart. All she wanted was this stolen moment, lighting the darkness with the sweet fires of their passion.

When he stroked her breast, a flash of ecstasy coursed through her as she softened beneath him. Everything in her world narrowed to his fingers caressing the tip of her breast and his mouth warmly moist against her neck. She enfolded him to her.

He pulled her over him and laughed, his breath caressing her, as he lowered the shoulder of her gown down her arm at the same time as he was unhooking its back. His finger trailed down her spine, an eager caress as he laved her skin with his fiery tongue. Sitting up, he put his hands on her hips to keep her kneeling on either side of his legs. Slowly his fingers glided up to the drooping front of her gown.

"This is no good," he whispered.

"No good?" She could barely speak the words because she was overmastered by this delight. Wasn't he sharing it? "Dominic, if—"

"Hush, *chérie*. How can I make love with you when I cannot see your face?"

Abigail squinted as sunlight crashed into the narrow space. He had opened a narrow door in the roof, she realized. A door edged with iron bars, so no one could enter or leave. So many questions battered her lips, but she did not voice them as she grasped his face and slanted her mouth across his.

With a husky laugh, he hooked his fingers in the front of her gown. His eyes glittered with anticipation as he lowered it along her, but his gaze did not shift from hers, even when he edged the gown off her.

"You look baffled, *chérie*," he whispered.

"I thought . . . You opened the window, so I thought you wanted to see—" She sighed in voiceless rapture as he cupped her breast.

"Your face, *chérie*. I want to see your face when I touch you, when you touch me, when we are one." His voice grew more ragged with every word. With a moan, he pulled her to him.

Her palms pressed to his back as he lowered her to the pallet and placed his mouth on the curves above her chemise. All conscious thought fled as she dissolved into a sea of delights. But not an icy sea, a heated one, for fire burned her skin where his tongue carved a line of ecstasy. With a hunger as voracious as his own, she discovered the shape of his ear as he continued to enthrall the most sensitive skin of her breast.

Quickly he removed her undergarments as she undid his waistcoat and shirt. She explored his muscular chest, delighting in giving him the pleasure he offered. When he ran his fingertips along her legs, he awoke sensations she had never guessed she could experience. Ripples flowed through her, pooling deep within her.

"You are the most beautiful woman on this earth," he whispered as she reached for the buttons on his breeches. He started to say more, but his words vanished into a gasp when she slid his breeches along him.

"And you are the most beautiful man."

His laugh thrilled her when he drew her atop him again. He held her hips to his, and she quivered with uncontrollable yearning as his hardness teased her. She wanted this. She wanted *him*.

A cataclysm built inside her as he caressed her boldly, seeking the secrets that soon would be all around him. She moved with the tempo of his touch as his kisses seared deep into her.

She needed no urging to touch him. Throwing aside every inhibition, she discovered how to bring him pleasure with her fingers and her lips. Each reaction echoed within her, offering him what she knew he had wanted since their eyes first met. Now she did, as well.

He murmured sweet, wordless endearments against her mouth as he brought them together. His pulsating heat captured her. She gazed up at him as he whispered her name. Eagerly she matched his motions as he led her to delights unknown.

She wrapped her arms around his shoulders and drew

his mouth to hers as she became lost in ecstasy. In one great crescendo of sensation, she shattered into prisms which revealed the very colors of her soul.

Abigail opened her eyes when kisses teased her eyelid. Smiling, she lifted her fingers to trace Dominic's lips.

"Happy?" he whispered.

"Is that an order, Captain St. Clair?"

He chuckled and watched her reaction when his laughter brushed her wherever their bodies touched. "How can anyone who tastes as sweet as you be so tart?"

"I could say the same thing of you."

As he grinned, she savored the vestiges of passion on his lips. She put her arm across his chest and snuggled close to him. She did not want the magic to end, for she wondered if she could ever be as happy again as she was at this moment.

"What is this place?" she asked.

"I would guess it was used by smugglers. Or it might be even older. Mayhap it is a priest hole."

"A what?"

Dominic smiled. "A place where English Catholics hid their priests from the fury of the Reformation, when to be discovered meant a heretic's death by fire."

"How horrible!" When he put his hand over hers, Abigail touched the ring on his left hand. "You never have told me why you wear this. All you told me was that the ring is a family heirloom. What is its odd design?"

"It was my father's wedding ring." He brushed her hair back from her forehead. "I am his only son, so when he died during the Terror, it came to me." Kissing her lightly, he traced the high arch of her cheekbones with his fingertip.

She batted his hand away and ordered, "Stop that!"

"Why?"

"Because I cannot think when you do that." She laughed as he lifted a single eyebrow. "All right, I *can* think, but only of one thing."

"Exactly."

At his satisfied tone, she shoved away his hand again. "You still have not answered me. What is this odd design?"

As he held up the ring to catch the sunlight, a distant loneliness softened his eyes. She wanted to ask what he was seeing in memory's mirror, but she waited for him to speak.

"You know of the Terror?" he asked.

"After the French Revolution?" She shuddered. "I have heard awful stories."

"Such as?"

"What anyone has heard of King Louis and his family being guillotined."

He nodded as he twisted a strand of her hair around his finger. "And have you heard of the others who died for no reason other than that they owned land or had a title or simply were declared an enemy by the new dictators?"

" 'Twas the people who ruled."

"*Chérie*, you are judging France's revolution through American eyes. It was nothing like your fight for freedom from English rule." His mouth tightened. "Madness infected a whole nation. Great ideals were prostituted to serve those who grasped for power. That is why we welcomed Napoleon."

She bit back the retort she would have made weeks ago. To think of Napoleon as the savior of France went against everything she believed, but she did not want to argue with Dominic. Not when they were lying in the warm afterglow of love. "And your family became victims of the Terror?"

"My father arranged for me to be taken by my mother

from Paris, ordering her to hide, so neither of us could
be found. She took me to Bordeaux, but she spoke often
of Château Tonnere du Grêlon. In English, Castle Thunderstone.''

"Thunderstone?" she gasped. "That is why you were
so surprised when I told you about Aunt Velma's stories."

He kissed her forehead. "Exactly, *chérie*. It was where
my father lived before he was swallowed by the shadows
of hate."

"Your father lived in a castle?"

"There are many who reside in a castle besides the
family that owns it. My mother is proud of her peasant
heritage and the years of service her family gave to the
duc's. Those who once lived in Château Tonnere du
Grêlon are scattered before the Terror's tempest."

"Have you looked for them? You might have other
family."

"To no avail. My mother can tell me little, save that
my father died bravely. I wear this ring to honor his
courage."

Taking his hand, she moved it so she could see the
design more clearly. The design was a slash of lightning
cutting through a rock. "Thunderstone," she whispered.
"Castle Thunderstone. That sounds so awe-inspiring."

"Whatever it was, it is gone. Nothing for me waits
there, so I have chosen my own life." He smiled. "And
it had been a very good one up until the day I found a
rare prize awaiting me on an American ship."

As her fingers combed through his hair, she whispered,
"And that caused your good life to change?"

"Need you ask, *chérie*? My life has been good, but it
has taken a turn for the better now." His smile melted
into her lips. When his arms tightened around her, she
knew he wanted to be done with talking so they could
savor this desire that refused to be quiescent again.

That pleased her, as well. She wanted this pleasure for

as long as it could be hers. Once they left this haven he had found among the eaves of the springhouse, they would be surrounded by the war again, forced to be enemies. Here, there was only joy. Here, there were better things to do than to argue about things that could not be changed. Here, she could delight in joy . . . and love. She loved Dominic St. Clair. That was one thing she doubted would change as long as they both lived.

But she knew how short a time that could be.

Chapter Fifteen

Abigail could not help staring. She had never seen so many glorious gowns. Even the richest shipbuilder in New Bedford would have looked like a poor relation amid the splendor in this London townhouse. Scents of sweet perfumes swirled around her like the dancers in the middle of the large ballroom. Light from the crystal chandeliers overhead bounced off the gems that were liberally scattered among the guests, perching in upswept hair or clinging to fingers. Even a simple walking stick in a gentleman's hand glistened with what was obviously gold.

And Abigail was elegant, too. The pearl white dress had been one of Clarissa's and hastily altered to fit her. It was finer than anything she had ever worn, because the fabric seemed to float about her, drifting about her ankles like a cloud with every motion. The one bit of color was provided by the pink rosebuds at the center of her bodice and on the lace at the hem of her short sleeves.

Lady Sudley had been disappointed that there had not been enough time to have matching rosebuds sewn onto Abigail's white slippers.

Hearing Dominic's laugh beneath the lilting melody played by the orchestra in a gallery above, she pulled her gaze from the ballroom to see his smile. "*Chérie*, you look like a young girl with a new doll."

"I feel like a doll. I cannot believe Abigail Fitzgerald is in a place like this."

He put his finger to her lips. "Take care what you say. Even your true name could be a betrayal here."

She nodded, chastised. She could not allow her excitement at this grandeur make her forget why they were here. "How long?" she whispered.

"How long until what?"

"Until we slip away to find your friend." She was careful not to speak Evan Somerset's name.

Dominic laughed as he adjusted his white gloves that matched his waistcoat and cravat beneath his black coat. His breeches took on a silver sheen in the candlelight. "Have you learned to read my thoughts before I utter them?"

"I have seen how you are eager to devise any excuse to slip out of the house. It takes very little imagination to guess why."

"I hope you are the only one with that imagination." He became somber. "When I take my leave, I will let you know."

"You? I thought—"

"It would best if you stayed here, *chérie*."

"I thought you trusted me," she said, not willing to be cut off.

"I do. That is why I am leaving you here to cover my absence with some tale that I am certain you can spin with ease." He sighed. "It is the harder task I am giving you, but where I will be going is no place for you."

She grasped his hand. "Do not forget I am a sailor's daughter. Where you will be going cannot be that different from places I have been before."

"True." He eyed her up and down. "So you know how much attention you would call to us if you arrived there looking as lovely as you do now."

With a smile, she plucked at the lapel on his coat, her fingers lingering against the front of his waistcoat. "So that is why you insisted on this dark coat. You will blend in with the shadows."

"I have come to like the shadows." His eyes narrowed, but the sparks of desire within them could not be concealed. "I will miss them, *chérie*, now that we are away from Sudley Hall."

"We will have to find new shadows."

His fingers swept along her face in a swift caress. "Or the bright sunshine, so I can see all of you quiver as I watch the pleasure on your face." He looked past her, and his tone changed. "Thank you so much, my lady, for inviting us to join you this evening."

Lady Sudley fluttered a befeathered fan in front of her face and smiled. Even though she was dressed much more grandly than the simpler frocks she had worn in the country, the lady's warm expression remained the same. "You are very kind, when you should be chiding me for failing to introduce you to my other guests, Mr. St. Clair."

Abigail saw how hard Dominic fought not to flinch when Lady Sudley spoke his name. As if it were of the least consequence, she said, "Lady Sudley, you had spoken to me on the way to London about meeting Mrs. Amsterdam, that she would be eager to talk with anyone from Canada. Would you be so kind as to introduce me to her now? Dominic has been anxious to speak with a friend he saw arrive a few minutes ago, but, dear heart that he is, he did not want to leave me alone." She continued to prattle, borrowing liberally from Clarissa's chatter, until Lady Sudley nodded.

"Thank you, *chérie*," Dominic whispered as he squeezed her hand before walking away.

She kept her sigh silent and put her best smile on her lips as Lady Sudley led her to meet the women grouped together on one side of the dance floor. Quickly Abigail learned all she needed to do was nod and smile. That kept her from having to explain her accent that identified her as an outsider.

As she edged from group to group, always keeping an eye on the door in hopes that Dominic would return soon, her arm was grasped. She started to pull it away, then smiled at Clarissa, who gave her a beseeching glance before looking back at the short, thick-waisted man beside her.

Startlingly white hair sprang from his head in every direction. He was dressed in elegant clothes, but his shoes squeaked as he took a step toward Abigail. She wondered if his shoes, like his waistcoat which strained across his wide belly, protested against the extra weight they had to contain.

"Abigail, this is Sir Harlan Morris," Clarissa said, relief easing the strain on her face. "Sir Harlan, my friend Abigail—"

"How nice to meet you," Abigail hurried to say before Clarissa could reveal too much. She wished Dominic had chosen a name other than his own when he had introduced himself to Clarissa and Newton. That he had been in great pain was his only excuse, one she understood well, but now she had to take great pains herself to prevent anyone from recalling that a French smuggler by that name commanded a ship in Napoleon's blockade.

"And you, miss." His eyes slitted as he appraised her openly. "I was just telling young Lady Clarissa here that—"

"Oh, excuse us," Clarissa said, interrupting him as hastily as Abigail had her. "I told Mama that I would bring Abigail to her as soon as I found her in the crowd. Have a pleasant evening, Sir Harlan."

Abigail was steered away from the bulbous man before she could do more than nod toward him. As Clarissa led her with rare speed through the ballroom, Abigail asked, "What is amiss?"

"That man!" She shuddered, an expression of distaste contorting her face. "He comes to London seeking a possible wife for his horrid son. I don't know why Mama and Papa invited him this evening."

"Just because they invited him here does not mean they would allow his son to call on you."

"I would think not!" Her eyes nearly popped from her head. "No decent person would allow that." She started to add more, then sighed as her name was called by one of the dowagers. "Abigail, you are so fortunate that you have found the man of your dreams, so you need not go through this Season having to be at the beck and call of every mother and father with a son they wish were wed."

Abigail chuckled softly as Clarissa went to speak with the dowager. Her smile vanished when her own name was called and she turned to see Sir Harlan coming toward her. A single glance at the door told her that Dominic had not yet returned. Forcing her smile back in place, she greeted Sir Harlan politely.

It was going to be a long evening.

Abigail hoped no one noticed how often she passed by the door that opened onto the stairs leading down to the front foyer. Like everything else in the Sudleys' London home, the staircase was perfection. Not a hint of dust nor a single gouge marred its beauty. Admiring it and the artwork edging the walls in the upper corridors would be her excuse for wandering in this direction so frequently.

Where could Dominic be? She had no idea how big London was, but it could not be that far by carriage to the river and to the port area she knew was called the Pool. He had suggested that he knew several people who could assist in getting both of them out of England. How long would it take to find one of them?

She remembered to smile each time a dowager walked by and to nod at the gentlemen. She was safe from their attentions because everyone believed that she was Dominic's wife.

Dominic's wife.

The warmth from deep within her unfurled like the softest flower petal. She was not sure how she had changed so completely in the past fortnight, but she could no longer imagine a life without Dominic in it. She wanted to savor his teasing laugh, his enticing eyes, his touch that led her to ecstasies she had never imagined.

Yet she knew too well that his life was his blasted ship. She had seen the life her aunt had, waiting always for the few short weeks when her uncle returned home before sailing again. This love of the sea was an alluring mistress no woman could compete with.

Dominic could take me with him on his ship.

She tried to ignore that thought which had taunted her when Dominic slept beside her, his cheek against her breast. More than once, she had almost asked him if he would consider letting her come with him when he rejoined his crew on *La Chanson*. She had not, because she feared he would give her dozens of logical reasons why she should not be on a French ship in the blockade against England. Then her dreams would be cold ashes.

Abigail gasped out an apology as she bumped into someone. She backpedaled, then looked up.

Two men stood in front of her. She had walked into

the taller man, whose hair was a sandy brown. Next to him stood a man who had no more hair than a chicken's egg. Both were dressed well, but not with the elegance of the *ton*. Yet neither wore the sedate gray livery of the Sudleys' household. She wondered who they were.

The taller man stepped forward and held out his hand. "Miss, forgive me for failing to watch where I was going."

She stared in disbelief. She could not mistake his accent. "You are an American!"

"Both me and Mr. Edwards." He smiled, the expression transforming his long, narrow face. "As you are, I would hazard a guess."

"What are you doing here in England?"

His smile did not waver, but his voice was cool. "Even in the midst of war, there is the need for diplomats to seek a peaceful ending to it."

"You should not ask Mr. Munroe anything further in that direction," Mr. Edwards said.

"Of course. I understand," she replied, although she did not.

"And, miss, may I ask why you are here? You clearly are an American, and I do not recall you among our small delegation."

"I am only recently arrived in London." Abigail wanted to tell the truth for as long as she could. *Where was Dominic?* This game of half-truths was one he excelled at.

"It is a pleasure to meet you, miss." Mr. Munroe glanced at his shorter companion. "One grows eager to hear the voices that bring home to mind."

"Yes." That she could agree with wholeheartedly.

"May we speak privately?" he asked, glancing about the room.

"Of what?"

"I have orders to bring information about any Americans in London to my superiors." He gave her a wry smile. "No need to look abashed, miss. You can ask anyone in this room, and they will tell you that what I am asking is commonplace when one is among one's enemies."

"Anyone else in this room would rightly consider any Americans their enemies, Mr. Munroe. I doubt that you or Mr. Edwards would be so foolish as to announce your citizenship here without great thought. Nor would I."

Mr. Edwards chuckled. "She is right, Munroe. You shall have to be honest with her."

The taller man glared at him, then nodded with clear reluctance. "Miss, we have heard that there are those who would do any American here great harm. We have a description of this man, but I do not want to speak of it here." His eyes brightened as he said, "How nice to see you again, my lady!"

Abigail looked behind her to see Clarissa walking toward them. The young woman's smile warmed as she held her hand out to Mr. Munroe. He bowed over it, and she giggled.

"Mr. Munroe," Clarissa said as she waved her fan in an imitation of her mother, "I see you have already met my friend Abigail—"

"Yes, we have met," Abigail hurried to interject before Clarissa could say more. Although Abigail was not an unusual name, the addition of Dominic's surname might betray them. "And you clearly know these gentlemen."

"They are friends of Father's." Clarissa started to say more, but was called away by another full-bosomed dowager. Without excusing herself, she rushed away.

"Miss?" asked Mr. Munroe with a half-bow and a motion toward the hallway.

When Abigail hesitated, Mr. Edwards murmured, " 'Tis for your own good, miss."

Abigail nodded. She could not mistake the sincerity in Mr. Edwards's voice. Although every instinct warned her about leaving the ballroom because she might miss Dominic's return, she feared that not having the information the men would share with her would be a greater mistake.

Mr. Edwards kept up a polite conversation, asking her how she was enjoying her visit to London, as they walked along the hallway past a room where men were playing cards. The smoke from their cheroots threatened to choke her. When she waved it aside, Mr. Edwards gave her a sympathetic smile.

Stepping ahead, Mr. Munroe opened a door and motioned for her to precede him into the room. Abigail went in, for she knew this room. She had taken tea with Lady Sudley here this afternoon while the carriage was unloaded and their bags unpacked.

The two men entered and closed the door. As she turned to ask them to explain, she stared at a third man who had been behind the door.

"You are alive!" she cried. "But what are you doing here? You should—" She moaned as something struck the back of her head. Everything vanished into oblivion.

Dominic walked along the cobbled street. He ignored the walkway, for it was broken in so many places that it was easier to use the street. Especially when he was being followed.

The man stalking him must not have guessed that Dominic was aware of him, because he clung to the shadows and paused when Dominic turned a corner, before slinking closer again. Dominic had taken note of him first in a tavern only one street back from the wharves. The man was not tall, but Dominic knew a smaller man could be as dangerous as a bigger one. A honed blade or a primed pistol evened the odds greatly.

If the man wanted to know what Dominic was doing

here near the Pool, the answer was simple. He was becoming more frustrated with every tavern he entered. As he opened the door in a building that looked ready to fall into the Thames, he did not look back. It opened again and closed as he walked toward where a keg and tankards were set on a low table amid another half-dozen tables where men hunched over their drinks. His stalker was close behind him.

Dominic sat at the table beside the keg and set a single coin in front of him. As he had guessed, the sight of gold brought the tavernkeeper himself. Good. He needed to speak with someone who might have the information he sought.

A full tankard was set on the table. "Join me," Dominic said quietly.

The tavernkeeper, a spare man with black hair falling into his black beard, filled another tankard with foamy beer and sat across from him. "This be no place fer fine gentlemen," he said. " 'Specially those foolish enough to flash their gold about."

"The coin is for you." Dominic smiled and put his hand on the gold piece as the man reached for it. "If you have the answers I need."

"Ye must want something real bad, gent. That be a fine coin."

"Yes. I am looking for someone."

"Figured that be so." The tavernkeeper tipped back his mug and swallowed deeply. "Who be ye lookin' fer?"

"An old friend. Evan Somerset. Do you know the name?"

The tavernkeeper put his mug on the table and frowned, although Dominic could barely discern the man's expression through the thick bush of hair. "Aye, I know the name. Used to be 'ere regularly."

"Used to be?" Dominic could not keep the irritation out of his voice. Where had Evan vanished to?

"Ain't been 'bout 'ere in a long time. Two years, mayhap three. Mayhap more." He took another reflective drink. "There be one who would know fer sure."

"Who?" Dominic drew his fingers halfway off the coin.

The tavernkeeper's eyes glittered with greed as he stared at it. "Red."

"Red who or what?"

"Just Red. Ye can find 'im at the Brass Fish. 'E knows everythin' that 'appens in Town. If'n yer friend is in London, Red'll tell ye where to find 'im."

Dominic let his fingers slide back a bit more. "Where is the Brass Fish?"

The tavernkeeper quickly gave him directions. Dominic picked up the coin and tossed it to the man. It vanished among the tavernkeeper's rags. Taking a sip from his own mug, Dominic grimaced. The beer was bitter. He shoved it aside and stood. "Thanks, friend."

"Any time, gent." He patted the front of his shirt where he had stored the coin.

Dominic edged past the other tables and slipped out the door. He walked back toward the center of the street.

"Gent?"

Turning, he rested his hand on a wooden post that once might have been for horses' reins but was so full of worm holes that it barely stood. "Yes?"

The man who had been following him stepped into the light that flowed into the street from another tavern. He held up his hands and turned them one way and then the other to show that he was not carrying a weapon.

"What do you want?" Dominic asked, motioning the man closer. "It cannot be that important if you have waited more than an hour to deliver your message."

" 'Tis important, gent." He grinned and held out a folded slip of paper. "*Now*, 'tis important."

Dominic took the paper. Unfolding it, he tilted it toward the light.

Captain St. Clair, come to the address below before midnight if you wish to retrieve Abigail Fitzgerald before she is turned over to the English authorities.

Midnight! It was close to that now. With a curse, he balled the paper and started to throw it away. He halted, not wanting to chance anyone else finding this damning note. Stuffing it beneath his waistcoat, he looked up. The messenger had vanished.

He swore again. His chance to learn who had given the messenger this letter had disappeared with the man.

Dominic sped along the street. He had no time to find Red and discover where Evan had taken himself off to, even though he would have liked to have his erstwhile partner with him right now. They had resolved issues this sticky before with easy success.

But never one that had so high a cost if he failed. That thought trailed him like the messenger had, nipping at his heels. A twinge caught at his ankle, but he ignored it. As soon as he reached an area where it was possible, he got a carriage to take him to the address not far from the old wall of London.

Dominic was not surprised to find lights blazing from all the windows of the house that was set between a milliner's and a bookstore on the cramped street. Those within would want to make sure no one was able to sneak up on them unseen.

Paying the coachman, Dominic strode to the door. He knocked. The door opened, and he knew he had been watched from the moment he stepped from the carriage. As he stepped into the entry hall, he heard distant church bells ringing midnight.

The woman who had opened the door was elderly.

Either she did not hear well enough to take note of his name as he spoke it or she was not surprised to see him. She motioned for him to follow her along the narrow hall that was surprisingly shadowed when the whole house was brightly lit.

At the single door across from the staircase, the woman opened it and stepped aside.

"No, Dominic!" he heard Abigail shriek. "Go! Get out of here!"

Dominic ran into the room, looking both ways to find her. His eyes locked with those of a man he had not expected to see again until he reached France. He gasped, "Fitzgerald!"

Chapter Sixteen

"I was wondering if you would come, St. Clair." Captain Fitzgerald smiled as he glanced at his daughter. "I feared I would not get to see you hang."

"Father!" Abigail cried. "Let him go. Let us both go. Please."

"Both of you?" Fitzgerald scowled when the two men flanking Abigail, each holding her arms, snickered. He raised his hand and struck her viciously.

She collapsed in pain to the floor. Reeling in the disbelief that hurt more than her aching head, she heard shouts and a fist striking someone. She pushed herself to her knees, grasping a chair as she tried to stand.

Dominic would not allow her to be abused. But he must not do something stupid like try to defend her. He must leave. Now!

She seized her father's arm and stood. "Stop this!"

she cried in horror when she saw Dominic on his knees, a knife at his throat.

"You are just like your mother!" her father sneered. "A whore who takes up with the first man who smiles in her direction." His voice rose with fury. "You are worse than she was, because you have allowed this French bastard to bed you. What value do you have for me now?"

"What value? What do you mean?" She swayed, but he did not keep her from falling. She sat on the chair. "Father, you are alive! I am alive. Let Dominic go, and—"

"*Dominic*, is it?" He raised his hand again.

She cowered away as she had never guessed she would from her father. In a whisper, she asked, "Father, what is wrong?"

He pushed past her to stare at Dominic. A pleased smile glittered cruelly on her father's lips. With a malevolent chuckle, he kicked Dominic viciously.

"No! Stop!" screamed Abigail. She raced forward, but was halted by Munroe. She struggled to escape, but it was impossible. He was too strong.

Dominic wheezed as he fought his way back to his knees. When Fitzgerald aimed his boot at him again, Dominic moved aside with the lightning reflexes Abigail had seen during the storm. He caught her father's foot. With a grunt, he twisted it.

Fitzgerald fell to the floor. Dominic's fist struck his nose, knocking him flat.

"That is for Abigail," Dominic snarled. "Now this one is for—"

A gun barrel appeared in front of his face.

Raising his hands in surrender, he smiled as Fitzgerald rose slowly. As Fitzgerald shook out his clothes, Dominic said nothing. He leaped to his feet, knocking the gun aside as Fitzgerald whirled to face Abigail, who was watching in horror.

"Don't hit her again, Fitzgerald!"

"She is mine! I will do with her as I wish."

"If you—" Before Dominic could take more than a step in Abigail's direction, pain seared across his skull.

Edwards chuckled as Dominic collapsed. Running his hand along the gun he held by the barrel, he tilted it toward Abigail. She fought against the hands holding her.

"You bastards!" she snarled.

Her father gripped her face. "Such language! Just think what your Aunt Velma would say if she knew her step-daughter was using such words."

"You mean her niece." Had Dominic's blow unsettled her father's mind? No, he had had this frightening glitter in his eyes from the moment she woke in this house to discover her father was in London and that Munroe and Edwards were part of the crew of his new ship.

He laughed. "I mean her *stepdaughter*. Don't tell me you never suspected that your dear uncle was your real father."

"Why should I suspect that?" She tried to edge past him to reach Dominic, but he stepped in front of her again, blocking her way.

"Because it is the truth. I had thought he would have bragged about bedding your mother before he married Velma."

Realizing he would not let her go to Dominic, she sank in the nearest chair. "Are you saying that Uncle Jareb and my mother were in love? If she loved him, then—"

"Be silent!" He struck her again. When she cried out in pain, he smiled. "You are a whore just as she was, but you may continue to have some value."

"Value? What do you mean?"

"Be silent while we deal with this French pirate."

"No! Don't hurt him." Erupting to her feet, she pushed past her father—no, he was her uncle. She pushed past *Captain Fitzgerald* and ran to where Dominic lay. When she saw he was still breathing, she knelt beside him, trying to shield him from the fury around them. "Stay back!" she cried as she pulled out the knife she had known Dominic would be wearing beneath his coat.

"Drop it!" Fitzgerald ordered.

"Let us go! Get on your ship and leave England. Forget you found us. You left me to Dominic once. It should not be difficult for you to do the same again."

He smiled coldly. "Don't be foolish." Taking the pistol from Edwards, he aimed it directly at Dominic's head. "Drop the knife, Abigail, or you will find you are resisting for no reason."

In horror, she gazed at the man who was proving again how little he cared about her. She wanted to demand that he tell her why he had insisted she sail with him on this voyage if he despised her so. But would she change the decision she had made when she left New Bedford? If she had not come on this voyage, she never would have met Dominic.

She could not let her father kill him. She must . . . All her thoughts disappeared into a crescendo of pain.

Arthur Fitzgerald picked up the knife that had skittered across the floor when Abigail dropped, senseless, to the floor beside St. Clair. Wiping it off, he smiled grimly at Munroe, who was putting the wooden bookend back onto a table.

"Bring the carriage. We shall leave now."

"Captain?"

He glared at Edwards. "What is it?"

"Them." He pointed to the Frenchman and Abigail, whose limbs were revealed by her dress that had risen nearly to her knees when she crumpled. "How . . . that is, what do you want us to do with them?"

"Secure St. Clair and stuff him in the boot. Treat Abigail with more care." He glanced at her and smiled coldly as he tossed the knife onto the table next to the bookends. "Munroe, you know what needs to be done."

"Yes, Captain," he said with a broad smile. He knew exactly what the captain intended for both his captives.

The carriage rolled along the road in front of the grand house. Set on a prominent position overlooking the small village of Morristown, the house commanded a view of the whole valley as it had when it was a feudal castle, first raised here nearly a millennium before. Wide windows had replaced the arrow slits, and any remnants of the outer wall had disappeared through the years.

Abigail had not looked out of the carriage at the twisting road which narrowed to the width of a single vehicle along the ridge. She had no interest in where she was going. All her thoughts were riveted on the jail where Dominic was. Asking Captain Fitzgerald about what would happen to Dominic had been useless. Captain Fitzgerald had refused to answer any question about Dominic or the *Republic* or his new ship.

She could think of nothing else. When they had stopped in the village at the base of the hill, it had been beside a grim, filthy prison. The rattle of the manacles that must have been snapped around Dominic's arms and legs before they left London resonated through her ears still. He had been stiff from the long hours of riding in the cramped boot. Her one attempt to speak with him had been for naught, for Captain Fitzgerald had clamped his hand over her mouth, silencing her. She had been able only to watch as Dominic vanished past the thick wall of the prison.

Captain Fitzgerald's words to the jailer continued to sicken her. "Make certain he is put in the deepest hole. It will give him a good idea of the hell awaiting French pirates when their necks are stretched." Then he had laughed with triumph.

Abigail leaned against the wall of the carriage, wanting to put as much distance as possible between her and the man she had believed was her father. She never would think that again. She did not want even to consider him as her uncle. He was a beast, hateful, vengeful, and cruel—the very thing she had so foolishly believed Dominic was.

The carriage slowed as it reached the house. It had been nearly a half mile from the gatehouse to the portico where guests were invited to climb the steps to an open veranda. Along the private road, the gardens had offered a somnolent beauty. Everything was tranquil, save for the pain in her heart.

A footman leaped forward to open the door of the carriage as it came to a stop. Stepping back, he placed a small stool in place so his master's guests would be able to alight with ease. He bowed and murmured, "Welcome, sir, miss."

Abigail did not look at the lovely flowers surrounding the veranda as she allowed Captain Fitzgerald to take her hand. Arguing now that she did not want to be here with him would gain her nothing but more abuse. Her gaze remained on the ground, because she was tired of seeing exultation on his face.

Captain Fitzgerald chuckled. "Why so glum, Abigail?"

"Are you as devoid of wit as you are of compassion?" she fired back, refusing to let him rejoice in her pain any longer. "What have I done to make you hate me so much? I did not die when the *Republic* sank, but that is no crime."

"I find it odd that only you and St. Clair survived."

"I jumped from the stern windows before the ship was detonated. Dominic tried to fight off your crew. The explosion sent him overboard. He was washed ashore."

"And no one else?"

"Dandy."

"Who?"

"My cat," she replied coolly.

He cursed. "No other person?"

"No one alive." She shivered as she recalled the seared corpses.

"How do you know that pirate did not kill them?"

"He could not have killed a sand flea in his condition!" Her laughter faded as she realized the truth had betrayed her.

"Traitor!" he muttered, and she knew he did not want anyone to overhear this conversation. "I have fed and clothed you! And what do you do to repay me? You nursed that bastard back to life!"

"And why should I be loyal to a father who provides guns to his country's enemies?"

"You are not my daughter!"

"So you have said."

"Don't be pert, girl." Closing the distance between them, he continued in the same taut whisper, "I should have known you would be just like her."

"What do you mean?"

He grasped her arms. "Your mother was a whore. A beautiful whore. She pretended to be in love with Jareb, but I wanted her. I . . . I convinced her to marry me."

Abigail's face paled. From his vicious scowl, she knew that she had not been the first to suffer his cruel hand. Somehow he had browbeat her mother into becoming his wife so she could not marry his brother.

His cold laugh froze her blood in her veins. "She failed to mention she was pregnant until the vows were exchanged. She intended to leave me when Jareb returned from his voyage."

"Why didn't you let her go?"

"She was mine!" he snarled. "You were not even weaned when she tried to run back to him. I took care

of her after I told her I would take care of her bastard."
He smiled. "And take care of you I have, daughter."

She stepped away from him. Was he mad? No, Captain
Fitzgerald was sane. Obsessive jealousy made him act
like this.

"You *took care* of my mother?"

Although she had not expected he would be honest,
his smile warned he was eager to brag. "It was an accident.
She fell onto the pier. Broke her neck." His smile broadened.

"Oh, sweet heavens," she gasped, realizing what that
smile meant. "You pushed her!"

"Don't be silly, Abigail." He patted her cheek. "That
would have been too risky. She might not have died."
Taking her arm, he continued up the stairs. "Now, you
be a good girl. It would be a pity if history repeated
itself."

She planted her feet, refusing to follow him willingly,
even though he might break her neck, too. "Where are
you taking me?"

"I thought you would be glad to know that I am fulfill-
ing a pledge I made to your mother before she died."

"A pledge to destroy my life?"

He laughed again. "I vowed that I would see that her
daughter was taken care of as she deserved."

Abigail did not give him the pleasure of asking again
what horror he had planned for her. She could not care
about her future when he had arranged to have Dominic
stand trial for piracy. She knew what the sentence would
be.

Death.

She did not dare to dream that Dominic would be exon-
erated. As soon as he opened his mouth, his French accent
would deem him guilty.

Her arm was taken in a tight grip, but she refused to
look again at Captain Fitzgerald. He was dressed in well-

made clothes for this call, and she still wore the elegant dress she had donned for the Sudleys' party. Why were they calling at this house when they should have been fleeing from England now that Captain Fitzgerald had gained his revenge on Dominic? She had no idea. Fitzgerald had not told her, and she refused to ask him, not wanting to let him gloat more.

At his tug on her arm, she walked forward. She could not fight Fitzgerald when her heart lay shattered within her. Her foot caught on the first step.

"Watch where you are going!" he snapped. "Didn't your aunt teach you a lady's graces?"

"My aunt taught me many things, but your belated interest in my education strikes me as ludicrous, *Father*." She made the name a vile epithet. "Of course, at this point, I find everything about your interest in me ludicrous."

"Be silent!" His face reddened with fury. "If you do not—"

"What will you do to me that is worse than what you have already done?" she asked, stopping in the middle of the long flight of steps edged with Grecian columns. "You have taken me away from my aunt who loves me. You condemn my mother and me, although we both wanted nothing more than to stay with the men we love. *I* have nothing to be ashamed of. *I* am not betraying our country by bringing guns to sell in England."

"You know nothing."

"I know what I saw in the *Republic*'s hold. Do you think that fact will be listened to when I state it at Dominic's trial?"

"You will not be testifying."

"No?"

"No." He smiled. "I have arranged for you to be busy with other concerns." When she did not answer, he asked, "Don't you want to know what?"

"All I care to know is that you have had the man I love arrested. What else can you do to hurt me?"

His eyes narrowed. "If you do not want to learn the answer to that, which I assure you will be to St. Clair's detriment, come with me now."

Abigail wanted to retort, but feared any protests would persuade him to find a way to arrange for Dominic's trial to be held without delay. She suspected he had had Dominic imprisoned because this was his way of controlling her. He would use her fear for Dominic whenever she balked. With a sigh of resignation, she knew she had no choice but to capitulate . . . for now. There must be something she could do. Until Dominic was sent to hang, she would not give up.

But why was her father, an American, wandering freely about England and turning his enemies over to English justice? Why had he brought guns here? Why had he left her on the *Republic* even though he spoke again and again of her value to him?

The boards of the porch creaked as they crossed them. The door swung open. She shivered with sudden fear. An invisible, odorless miasma oozed out of the house to encircle her in a clammy caress.

"Good afternoon, Captain, miss," said a butler who appeared out of the shadows beyond the door. His gray hair was drawn back sharply from his face and matched the pearl color of his immaculate breeches. His coat was a brilliant red. "May I take your cloaks?"

Captain Fitzgerald dropped his cloak quickly into the butler's hands. He turned to Abigail, but she moved to evade his fingers. She undid the ribbons at her throat. Removing her cape, she held it out to the butler. He took it as she gazed around the foyer instead of meeting Captain Fitzgerald's fury.

She noted the curved staircase with its marble risers and the richly polished furniture filling the broad hall, which seemed to run the depth of the house. It was even fancier than Lady Sudley's house in London.

A form moved in the shadows. Unlike the grace of the tall butler, this squat man waddled toward them. She frowned as she looked at him. She was certain she had seen him before. At the Sudleys' *soirée* last night? Mayhap, but she had met so many people, she could not put a name to his round face.

"You are here at last," he said, his voice sounding as if it echoed in the vast caverns of his body. Her head ached at the rumble. "Arthur, my friend, I am so delighted to see you unharmed after your trials on this voyage."

"It was a challenge, but one I bested." Captain Fitzgerald flashed a smile at Abigail, but she ignored him.

"I have heard you lost your ship and cargo to a French pirate. A true shame, for we anticipated the delivery of your cargo with eagerness."

"But I was able to retrieve my lost *Republic*'s most precious cargo. My daughter Abigail." He smiled when she looked at him as if he had lost all sense. He pulled her forward. "Abigail, this is Sir Harlan Morris. My good friend."

Sir Harlan Morris?

She dipped her head to him, but did not curtsy. If he was a friend of Captain Fitzgerald's, he was someone she must be wary of. Dominic had been right about Fitzgerald's treachery, as he had been right about so many other things. Panic clutched her. She was becoming further enmeshed in Captain Fitzgerald's web. She must discover a way to escape.

Sir Harlan chuckled. "So she *is* your daughter. I thought that might be so when we met last night at the Sudleys' assembly. Your description of her was excellent, my friend, so I felt quite confident about sending for your men to retrieve her."

"You?" Abigail gasped. "You sent for Munroe and Edwards?"

Instead of answering her, he put his hand beneath her chin and tipped her face up. She tried to pull away, but his fingers tightened on her cheeks. "Lovelier even than you described her, and a redhead as well. Delightful, Arthur."

A renewed surge of fear gripped Abigail when she heard Captain Fitzgerald chuckle with satisfaction. Before, that sound had forecast disaster for her.

Sir Harlan said, "Come to my study. We can speak in private there. I prefer this first meeting to be without too many curious eyes."

First meeting? Abigail frowned. What was the baronet talking about? Captain Fitzgerald's words had suggested the two men had spoken often, and she had been introduced to Sir Harlan last night.

When she stepped into the study, she saw that it opened into a lovely garden, but those doors were closed. Rich wood covered the walls, but was lost behind the multitude of paintings. Several were portraits. She identified one as a young Sir Harlan and guessed the woman next to him was his wife. A young boy stood beside the woman, who held a baby on her lap. Abigail recalled Clarissa's distasteful comments about the son Sir Harlan wished to find a wife for. She wondered which of the young men that was.

The exquisitely appointed furniture must have been carved by a master craftsman. This room was furnished with luxury, but she sensed a coldness that would never have been found even in Aunt Velma's front parlor, which was used only for weddings and funerals.

When Sir Harlan pointed to a chair, she sat, grateful. The lack of sleep last night was gnawing on her, threatening to steal her composure and leave her weeping. She held the chair's arms tightly while she listened to the two men talk with the ease of longtime friends. They sat opposite her in two heavy oak chairs. As she scanned the room, she tried to determine what horror Captain Fitzgerald intended to inflict on her.

Silent servants came into the room with trays. Abigail remained silent as they placed a bottle of brandy and a full tea on the table beside Sir Harlan. Brandy? Lady Sudley had never served anything but tea and cakes. When Sir Harlan glanced at her expectantly, she clasped her hands in her lap. She was not going to pretend she was glad to be here and offer to serve. She had no reason to distrust Sir Harlan other than his genial welcome to Captain Fitzgerald. That was enough.

The obese man looked at Fitzgerald, but the captain just shrugged. While pouring, Sir Harlan chattered on and on about events and people Abigail had never heard of. She watched Captain Fitzgerald nod and knew this was not his first trip to England. Nor was it his first meeting with Sir Harlan, so what had the baronet meant?

Staring into her cup, she wished she had had a chance to apologize to Dominic. He had been correct to warn her about Captain Fitzgerald, but she had not listened. She wanted to apologize for her foolish naïveté.

"How long are you staying?" asked Sir Harlan as he reached for a thickly iced cake.

"The rest of my cargo—"

Abigail's head snapped up. "Cargo? You brought more cargo to England?"

Captain Fitzgerald laughed. "Do you think that I have been doing nothing since the *Republic* was stolen? The French could not hold me when they had no proof of anything, so I came to England and arranged to purchase another ship. I have the *Torch* being unloaded in the Pool. It should be unloaded by the week's end. As soon as it is reloaded, I will be sailing for America. McCormick urged me to hurry. I need to have his cargo back to him before the end of October.''

Leaving for America? Such a short time ago, that had been her most precious wish, but she could not go when Dominic was imprisoned and faced death. She must persuade Captain Fitzgerald to change his mind. With a smile, she said, ''You will if you can elude the French blockade better than you did last time.''

Captain Fitzgerald bristled and snarled a curse.

Sir Harlan stirred brandy into his tea. ''Of course, your daughter will stay here, Arthur, while you tend to your business in London.''

Abigail sat straighter. If she remained here, she might be able to find help to free Dominic.

Captain Fitzgerald replied, with a sly glance at her, ''You are too kind. I had not envisioned that you would open your house to her now. I had anticipated I would have to take my daughter with me and bring her back on my next voyage.''

''Nonsense. Why endanger her?'' He laughed, his belly rocking. ''And how else will she be available for fittings? I shall arrange for a modiste to come here. The sooner the preparations are made, the sooner the wedding can be held.''

''Wedding?'' gasped Abigail. Clarissa's comment about Sir Harlan came back to her. ''*He comes to London seeking a possible wife for his horrid son.*''

Sir Harlan's cold blue eyes settled on her, but he spoke to Captain Fitzgerald. ''I assume by her question that you have not mentioned any of the details to her.''

Her fingers tightened on her cup as Fitzgerald said, ''She would have had difficulty keeping such news a secret, so I thought I would wait until we reached Morris Park.''

''So she knows nothing?''

''Nothing!''

Abigail refused to be left out any longer. "What are you talking about? Whose wedding?"

"Why, yours, my darling daughter."

She leaped to her feet. When she started to storm past him, Captain Fitzgerald caught her wrist so tightly she winced.

Standing, he ordered, "Calm yourself, Abigail. After all, you do not want to look like a hoyden when you meet your future husband."

"You are insane!" she cried. "If you think I would marry anyone *you* selected, especially his horrid son—"

"Horrid?" Sir Harlan pulled his bulk to his feet.

"That is what I heard in London. I shall not marry him."

"Silence!" Captain Fitzgerald pushed her back into her chair. Glaring at her, he added, "You will find, Sir Harlan, that she needs to be handled firmly. But you must be accustomed to that."

A strange sadness crossed the round man's face, but it hardened. "Yes, I am accustomed to that. Mayhap her strong will shall prove more effective with Clive than the last chit who ... Never mind."

"Clive?" she whispered, afraid to hear the answer to her question. "Is Clive your son?"

"Yes." Sir Harlan had resumed drinking his tea as if nothing were amiss.

"If you think I am going to marry an Englishman—"

Captain Fitzgerald snapped, "You know nothing, girl. Be silent. We have no interest in hearing from you."

She rose, her chin jutting with defiance. "You shall hear from me. Even if you were my father, Captain Fitzgerald, I would not marry whomever you have chosen."

Sir Harlan pushed himself to his feet. His round face rutted with bafflement. "She is not your daughter? Then who is she?" He scowled. "Are you trying to foist a diseased doxy on me to cheat me?"

"She *is* my daughter." Captain Fitzgerald gripped her arm and shook her as a smile strained his tight lips. "The child of my adulterous wife, but legally mine. She has been raised by my brother and his puritanical wife, so she has not shared the carnal ways of her mother."

"And her mother?"

"Dead."

Sir Harlan smiled. "Very good."

Furiously, Abigail snarled the French curse that Dominic had used so often. She was not sure what it meant, but she suspected Sir Harlan did when his face reddened. How dare he be pleased that her mother had died because she could not love the man who coveted her! She fought to escape Fitzgerald's hold.

He laughed at her fury. She was shoved into the chair again. Rubbing her aching arm, she started to stand. When Fitzgerald's hand rose, Sir Harlan grasped it.

"Do not strike her, Arthur," he ordered.

"What will a few bruises matter if they teach her to obey?" asked Captain Fitzgerald.

"I do not want to give him any ideas."

"Him?" she whispered.

Neither man answered her as they continued to argue.

"Sir Harlan," she asked when she could not tolerate their bickering any longer, "what is wrong with your son that he cannot find his own bride?"

Rage turned the baronet's face nearly purple. When he turned toward her, she pressed back against the chair. His hand rose and became a fist. She cringed, knowing that no one would halt him.

At a knock, Sir Harlan froze. He grabbed the bottle of brandy and filled an empty cup. He downed it quickly. His smile returned to his lips as, waving his hand, he said, "Open the door, Abigail."

Wanting to tell him she did not run errands for British baronets, she stood. To balk now would mean being beaten. She could see that in his eyes. She had to cooperate until she could find a way out of this house. Then she would seek out allies for Dominic. Had he had a chance to alert them before he was called back by the missive from Captain Fitzgerald?

As she went to the door, the heavy knocking became more insistent. She opened the door and stepped back with a frightened cry. Her eyes widened as she stared at a creature out of her worst nightmares.

The man lurking in the hallway was as tall as Dominic, but was twice his breadth. Blond hair, unwashed and greasy, hung along his face, which was obscured by several days' growth of beard. He hunched as he lurched toward her with a shuffling walk, as if his feet were too heavy to lift. His hands drooped at his side. From him came a shrill sound which hurt her ears. As her horror grew, she realized he was humming.

"Sir Harlan?" she called without turning. She did not dare to, because she was not sure what this hideous creature would do. Noticing two bulky men behind him, she wondered why they were there.

"Pretty." The blond man stopped humming as he reached out to touch her hair. "Pretty."

"Go away," she whispered. She tried to flee, but a chair blocked her escape. Was this how Captain Fitzgerald intended to break her to his will? She would lower herself to beg to escape this beast. "Help me. Don't let him near me! Please."

Captain Fitzgerald put his hand on her shoulder, but kept her between him and the huge man. "Watch your tongue, daughter. You are insulting Clive Morris, your betrothed."

"Betrothed? You want me to marry *him?*" With revulsion, she stared at the man's slack jaw and his vacuous eyes.

When she took a step sideways, his huge paws caught

her. His heavy hand patted her hair as if she were a favorite pet kitten. Over and over he repeated the same word. "Pretty. Pretty."

Appalled, she looked to one of the other men for help. None of them moved as they watched with what she did not want to believe was pleasure. She would have to escape alone. When she tried to pull away, Clive's arms tightened around her. His fingers moved from her hair to touch the ribbons on her bodice. She cried out in disgust.

His face altered with a fury that was stronger than any she had ever seen. She heard shouts of warning, but Clive's fist caught her on the cheek. She fell to the floor.

Sobbing, she paid no attention to the scuffle behind her. She hid her face against her arms and wept out all her pain. She cried for herself and for Dominic and for the love denied them by these men who had no idea of what love was.

The door closed. A sharp order from Sir Harlan made her look up at his rock-hard scowl. He held out his hand. "Get up, Abigail," he repeated.

Knowing she had no other choice, she put her fingers on his hand and let him assist her to her feet. Fearfully she looked about, but the monster was gone.

When Sir Harlan gripped her face, she groaned. His lips tightened with anger, but she could not be sure if he was furious at his son or at her. Glancing past her, he asked Captain Fitzgerald, "Does she always bruise this easily?"

"I don't know." He poured himself some brandy, but offered none to Abigail, who could have used its golden warmth to soothe her. "I have not been around her enough to know."

"Do you, Abigail?"

She drew herself out of Sir Harlan's pudgy arms. Going to the tea tray, she dipped a napkin into the hot water. She pressed it to the tender spot on her left cheekbone.

"I am afraid I bruise very, very easily, Sir Harlan. The legacy of being a redhead."

He cursed vividly. "How can I have my son marry a woman who has a blackened eye? What would the *ton* say?"

"A bit of rice powder will cover it, and she will be wearing a veil," Captain Fitzgerald said, refilling his cup. "Do not worry about it, Harlan."

"I shall not marry that—that thing!" Abigail cried.

"Yes, you will." Sir Harlan regained his composure and smiled. "You must never show anything but obedience to Clive. He needs to be treated with respect. Don't be like the other one."

"What other one?"

"Clive's last betrothed. She unfortunately met with an accident before the wedding."

"Accident? What kind of accident?"

"Her neck was broken. Most unfortunate, don't you think?"

"He did *that* to her?" She looked at Captain Fitzgerald and noted that his expression was studiously benign. He would not admit he had rid himself of his wife the same way. "If she was murdered, you—"

Sir Harlan put his finger directly in front of her face. "It was an *accident*, Abigail. To suggest otherwise might cause needless trouble. Cooperate, or you might find it as uncomfortable for you here. Do I make myself clear?"

"Yes, you do."

He turned and yanked a bell pull. "I think it would be best if you retired now, Abigail. You will join us for dinner."

"I would rather not." She touched her cheek.

"My son does not dine with us. He eats in his private rooms. I suggest you join us, my dear, rather than dine with him. Since Clive has seen your loveliness, I think it would be wise to limit your meetings." He cleared his throat. "Young men sometimes can be overcome with the longing for their bride before the wedding."

"You need not be delicate with me, Sir Harlan." Abigail smiled. This was exactly the opening she had been waiting for. "Mayhap Captain Fitzgerald failed to mention that I am no longer a maiden. I know about a man's desires."

As she had hoped, Sir Harlan flushed and rounded on Captain Fitzgerald. "Arthur, you said nothing of this!" Her dream of escape was dashed as he continued, "When? Is there any chance she could be pregnant?"

Captain Fitzgerald nervously pulled at his collar. " 'Tis possible. She and the Frenchman who is in your jail traveled across England from where the *Republic* went down."

"And you were this Frenchman's lover?" the baronet demanded, scowling at her.

She folded her arms in front of her and gave him her coolest smile. "Captain Dominic St. Clair is a very charming Frenchman, Sir Harlan."

He sniffed. "This causes a bit of a problem. The child must be Clive's. There must be no question of that. It would be a shame not to wed him to your daughter. Not only does he find her appealing, but she has attributes I would like to see in my grandchildren." He shrugged. "We will know within a few weeks. The wedding can be delayed until then."

Abigail hid her smile. A lot could happen in a few weeks. Only a few weeks ago, she had been sailing on the *Republic*, believing it was bound for the Caribbean. Since then, she had lived through disaster and found ecstasy. Surely in the same amount of time, she could devise a way to save both her and Dominic from their fates.

Chapter Seventeen

A silent servant led Abigail up the stairs to the room which would be hers while she waited for Sir Harlan to be satisfied that she was not pregnant. The woman had glanced at the mark on Abigail's cheek in shock, but said nothing.

Abigail kept her gaze on the floor tiles which peeked from beneath a carpet runner that covered the middle of the corridor. She wondered if it would be possible to pretend she was pregnant. No, that would be useless, because Sir Harlan would be determined that any child that was not his son's would not survive to be born. Even deep in her thoughts, she noticed more than one door opening furtively so an inquisitive servant could peer out at the woman chosen to marry Clive Morris.

The thought sent a shiver of disgust along her. No wonder Clarissa had been so appalled at the idea that her parents had invited Sir Harlan to their gathering. Although

Abigail was curious why Sir Harlan was so desperate for
a bride for this son and why Captain Fitzgerald had agreed
for her to be that bride, she tried not to think of the horror
of the creature's touch. Only Dominic had caressed her
like that. She did not want that monster to.

"Miss Fitzgerald, these will be your rooms," the maid
said.

"Thank you," she said in a toneless voice. To release
any emotion would free all her agony.

She fought the temptation to surrender to her grief
again. *Not in the hall*, the warning rang through her mind.
If someone saw her collapse in tears, Sir Harlan would
be informed posthaste. She did not want to give him any
more satisfaction at her pain.

The door closed behind her. Stiffly she crossed the
antechamber to find another room beyond. Standing in
the doorway, she leaned back against the door frame and
closed her eyes. Mayhap if she opened them slowly, she
would find this was just a nightmare. Then she could
awake in Dominic's arms in the grand bed at Sudley Hall
as his kisses swept away these horrible memories.

When her eyes opened, Abigail sighed. She had not
escaped. The bedchamber before her was decorated in
soft shades of rose and green. The high bed was topped
with an enticing pile of lacy pillows that matched the thin
curtains pulled back from French doors that led to a
balcony. Chairs were arranged comfortably, and another
door must open to a dressing room. It was lovely, perfect
for Sir Harlan's future daughter-in-law, but it was a prison.

Stumbling forward, Abigail dropped onto the bed. She
hid her face in the satin covers, wanting to call out to
Dominic to rescue her, but he was suffering his own hell
in that odious jail. Their adventure, which neither of them
had guessed awaited them when they set sail, had come
to an ignoble end. While he died at the end of a rope,
she would be ravaged by that half-witted beast.

Hands stroked her shoulders. She bit back a scream and looked up. A sigh of relief escaped her lips as she saw a black-haired woman standing behind her. The tall woman's simple gown and tightly drawn back hair labeled her a servant. She had many more freckles than Abigail.

"Who are you?" Abigail asked.

"My name is Tessie. I am here to help you."

A pulse of hope exploded through her, but she dampened it. Tessie was here to serve as her maid, not assist her in escaping.

"Miss Abigail, calm yourself." Tessie's voice was sedate, although her wide eyes belied that serenity.

"How can I be calm?" Abigail crossed to the double doors opening onto a small balcony overlooking the valley. "How can I be calm when I know Dominic is in prison and I am being condemned to torment here?"

"Dominic?" The maid's eyes grew even wider. "So it is true what is being whispered. You were with a French spy."

Abigail was no longer amazed how quickly gossip spread. "He is not a spy. He was just trying to get both of us out of England." She sighed, not wanting to tell the whole story again. "Why are they doing this to us?"

"Surely you heard about Sir Harlan seeking a bride for his want-witted son."

"Yes."

"Yours is not the first father to offer his daughter in exchange for the amount of money Sir Harlan has promised any father who gives his daughter as a bride for Clive."

She choked, "Money?"

"Five thousand pounds at the wedding and five thousand more when the bride gives birth to a son."

Abigail dropped onto a chair and stared at her clasped hands. Too late, she understood why Captain Fitzgerald had brought her on this voyage. Value . . . she had some value for him. How many times had he said that during the trip down from London? For the first time in her life, he had said. He could make money from her while he sold her to a madman and his idiot son. It was all the sweeter for him because now he had a final revenge against her mother, for he was destroying her daughter's life as well.

"Sir Harlan wants to be sure I'm not pregnant before he marries me to his son," she whispered.

Fury strained Tessie's kindly features. "So he really plans to wed you to that thing he calls his son?"

"Yes."

"What will you do?"

"What I must." She raised her head and clenched her fists on the arms of the chair. "He fears that I am pregnant with Dominic's child. I think he should be unsure about that for as long as possible."

"I will tell him nothing." She dropped to her knees beside Abigail's chair. "I know you have no reason to believe that, Miss Abigail, but you can trust me. That beast attacked my sister after taking a fancy to her." Her face grew hard. "Clive was a kindly lad, as gentle-hearted as a babe. 'Tis those men who watch over him. They have goaded him to become the beast he is. I do not want to see anyone else hurt like she was."

"And like his last betrothed was."

Tessie nodded. "That was horrible."

Abigail hesitated. If Sir Harlan had instructed Tessie to say these things, then she was about to betray herself. She needed an ally in this house. *And you did learn to trust Dominic*, her heart reminded her. "So you will help me hide the truth?"

"Aye, Miss Abigail. I will be silent. I do not like this at all." She clucked her tongue as she stood. "I do not like them making you marry poor Clive. Let me know what you need me to do, and I will. Sir Harlan will never learn the truth from me.''

"Thank you. I cannot tell you how grateful I am for your kindness.'' She squeezed Tessie's hand.

Tessie blushed, then said, "I have finished unpacking for you, Miss Abigail. You will be staying here while your father goes back to ready the *Torch* for sailing.''

"I know.''

Abigail rose and walked out onto the narrow balcony. She ran her fingers along the waist-high wall. Her heart contracted at the ultimate cruelty inflicted on her. With her room overlooking the village, her balcony offered her a view of the hideous prison where Dominic was being held. She wondered how much worse it was on the inside.

She would not be a victim of Captain Fitzgerald's greed. She repeated that vow again and again. She intended to prove to him and Sir Harlan that she would not dance when they pulled the strings. She would foil their plans.

The only thing she did not know was how.

Captain Fitzgerald left to oversee the loading of the *Torch* exactly on schedule. Abigail made a point of not telling him farewell. When he returned, she would be forced to marry Clive. When he returned, Dominic would be hanged. That much had been made clear during the intolerable dinner when Captain Fitzgerald and Sir Harlan had toasted one another over and over until they dropped in a drunken stupor by the table.

Captain Fitzgerald's departure did not lessen the horror of her days as one rolled into another until a week had passed. Abigail woke each morning, dreading the day to come. If she tried to hide in her rooms, a servant was sent to rout her out with a question about her health. Even Tessie's efforts to waylay the servant were unsuccessful.

Abigail knew Sir Harlan was seeking any sign that she was pregnant. With Tessie's help, she kept him guessing.

It was the afternoons she dreaded, for that was when she had to let Clive call on her. One afternoon, she had dared to protest going into the parlor to meet Sir Harlan's son and suffering another battering. The beating Sir Harlan had given her had been worse than his son's pawing.

As she stood by the parlor door to repeat the torment of pretending that Clive would be human today, Abigail saw Sir Harlan marching down the hallway from his study. He was as pompous as a rooster strutting in his yard and about as witless.

"Is it time for your visit with Clive already?" He chuckled, his belly bouncing beneath his waistcoat. "How the morning has flown!"

"It has not for me."

Again he laughed and patted her shoulder with feigned sympathy. She pulled away. She had no interest in his hypocrisy. Tessie had told her why Sir Harlan had gone to this elaborate plan to find a bride for his son. Sir Harlan's wife remained in London, detesting her husband's company as much as Abigail did. An older son had died without any legitimate issue. That left only Clive to give Sir Harlan the grandchild he needed to inherit his estates, which he did not want to give to his wife or brothers. He planned to gain himself a legitimate grandchild, even if it cost him ten thousand pounds and left Abigail as broken mentally as his son.

"Abigail, my dear, the wonderful glow of health you had when you arrived is fading." He tweaked her cheek. When she moaned as he pinched where her skin remained tender after her last session with Clive, his smile broadened. "You must get outside more. I have arranged for you to go into Morristown tomorrow morning for your next fittings for your wedding clothes."

"Morristown?" she repeated, shocked he was going

to let her leave the house. Then she realized he had guessed the truth that she would not flee and leave Dominic here to die. The very thing that gave her the strength to endure this could be the same thing that destroyed both her and Dominic.

"I will send my coachman with you. Orr will make sure nothing happens to you. Let the villagers see how lovely my future daughter-in-law is."

As the parlor door opened, Sir Harlan made a quick excuse to leave. Abigail had discovered that he could not abide being in his son's company. Not that she blamed Sir Harlan.

The larger of Clive's two guards, a coarse-speaking man named Fuller, smiled. "Right on time, aren't you, Miss Fitzgerald? Eager to see your sweetheart?"

"Yes," she answered honestly.

When he sputtered with astonishment, she pushed past him to see Clive standing by the fireplace at the far end of the room. It had been the truth. She wanted to see her sweetheart, for it had been more than a week since she last had had a chance to speak with Dominic. As she stared at the man she must marry, she thought of Dominic's warm embrace. The only thing she needed to fear when she was in his arms was that she would be driven mad by the exquisite ecstasy they shared.

Clive's high-pitched humming filled the room. Abigail fought to keep her face serene, for she had learned that Clive reacted savagely to any hint of fear. The sound of her footsteps must have entered Clive's slow mind. He peered at her like a huge bird trying to bring her into focus one eye at a time.

"Look who is here!" crowed Fuller. "It is your pretty, Clive."

Abigail sat in the closest chair. She had learned that was the easiest way to avoid Clive's horrible embrace that threatened to choke her. She whispered, "Good afternoon." She never said anything but that and "Farewell."

Wincing, she suffered Clive's patting on her head and the mumblings which occasionally contained a word or two she could understand. Almost every time, that word was "pretty." When she looked past him to Fuller and Greene, the other guard, she wished she could find some way to wipe the smiles from their faces. She recalled Tessie's words of how Clive had been a gentle creature until these two men had been hired.

She swallowed her cry of anguish as Clive's hand struck her shoulder harder than usual. That he did not understand he was hurting her did not lessen the number of bruises that discolored her shoulders and back beneath her gown. When he whirled away, she waited until he was busy with something on the other side of the room. Then she rose. She started for the door, but Fuller blocked her way.

"Ain't been no hour yet. You know what Sir Harlan wants. One hour for you here with your sweetheart."

Abigail took a deep breath. If she raised her voice, she chanced calling Clive's attention back to her. She must avoid that. "Mr. Fuller, Clive is not interested in me today. I suggest you move aside so I may leave."

"Ain't interested in you?" He chuckled. "I can remedy that."

Abigail watched in disbelief as he turned to Greene. They were as inhuman as Clive, and their madness was cruel.

She ran to the door, but strong hands jerked her back. She screamed, then clamped her lips closed. But it was too late.

Fuller swore as an answering shriek came from the other side of the room. "Now you have done it!" Fuller growled. "I should leave you here with him, but I do not want to clean up the pieces of you afterwards." Opening the door, he shoved her into the hallway as Clive screeched again. "Get the hell out of here. You had best think up an excuse for Sir Harlan. He will be furious that you upset his son."

Abigail bumped into a maid. The frightened woman stared as shouts and the sound of breaking furniture erupted from the parlor. As the maid scurried away, Abigail decided to do the same.

She was not more than a few steps up the stairs when Tessie appeared behind her. "Miss Abigail, *he* wants to speak with you as soon as you are done with . . ." She gulped and looked at the parlor door. She cringed when something crashed beyond it.

Leaning on the banister, Abigail sought what strength she could find. She could not guess why Sir Harlan wanted to speak to her now. Neither Fuller nor Greene had had time to carry their tales to their employer. By all the stars, how could she continue to fight against Sir Harlan and his minions who wished to destroy her?

"If you want," Tessie whispered, "I can tell him you are indisposed."

"No," she replied, although she was tempted to agree. She did not want Tessie to be punished by Sir Harlan, nor did she want the serving woman to come to his attention. If the baronet discovered Tessie was Abigail's ally, he would replace her posthaste. "Where is Sir Harlan?"

"In his study."

"All right." Putting her hand on Tessie's arm, she lowered her voice. "As soon as I am done, there is something you and I must discuss upstairs."

Tessie frowned. "Are you hurt? Did he—?" She shuddered again when something made of glass shattered within the parlor.

"I am fine." Abigail squared her shoulders. "Or I will be when I find a way . . ." She bit back the words that could betray her.

Tessie nodded, then ran up the stairs.

Going down them, Abigail walked along the hallway. She knocked on the study door and waited until Sir Harlan called to her to enter. As she opened the door, she asked, "You wanted to speak with me?" Her voice was cold, and she did not try to warm it. She hated Sir Harlan more than she did Clive. The younger man could not help himself. It was the father who was the true monster.

Sir Harlan stood. "Close the door."

When she neared the desk, Abigail could not keep from staring. Spread across it was a selection of jewelry unlike any she had ever seen. Stones of every color scintillated in necklaces, earbobs, and bracelets. Emeralds, sapphires, rubies, pearls, and other gems she could not name. They must have been worth hundreds of pounds.

"Do you think these are lovely?" Sir Harlan asked, his lips curling in a sly smile.

"They are splendid, but I would have guessed that your wife would have kept these to wear in London."

"I chose not to leave them with her." His smile became tight as he added, "She would lose them in a night of gambling with her cronies."

"So you keep them here in your study?"

"Only for a short time more. Soon they will be yours."

"Mine?" Her voice squeaked in shock.

"You shall be my son's wife." He gestured at the beautiful jewelry. "You are Arthur's daughter, so I know you will appreciate the rewards of being Clive's wife."

Walking away, Abigail sat in an overstuffed chair. "He is not my father. I have told you that."

"He is your uncle, then." Picking up a spectacular emerald necklace, he draped it over his hand and held it out toward her. "I know how much he appreciates the finest things in life."

"Put it away. I do not want it."

"No?" He laughed. "Then you are as foolish as Clive. Do you have any idea how valuable these are?"

"Yes."

"But you don't want them?"

Leaning forward, she said, "Sir Harlan, you have bought Captain Fitzgerald's loyalty. You have bought me in your son's bed, but you will never buy my soul. Mayhap I am a fool, but I will be my own fool, not yours." She stood and added, "Good day, sir."

"Wait!"

Knowing the price of ignoring his order, Abigail slowed and turned. Sir Harlan scooped up the jewelry and returned it to the box on his desk. After he put it on a bookshelf behind him, he locked the glass doors with a key that he placed in the top drawer of his desk. He rounded his desk.

"Don't forget," he growled, "that I can have your French pirate hanged whenever I wish. It is only because I am a good representative of the English government that I am granting him the privilege of a trial. Make me angry, my dear, and you will find how quickly I can forget that. Do you understand me?"

Folding her hands in front of her, she nodded. "I understand you completely. What *you* fail to understand is that, if you kill Dominic, you shall have no hold on me. Do you understand *me?* You will, I suspect, if you think on it long enough." She turned toward the door as he sputtered incoherently at her.

Abigail savored no satisfaction at her slight victory. If she did nothing, Sir Harlan would have his way. She would be forced to wed Clive, and Dominic would die. She was determined that Dominic would escape England alive. She had to find a way to help him, and prayed that he could help her. If not, she would spend the rest of her life in hell.

Chapter Eighteen

As she stepped from the fancy carriage, Abigail took note of everyone on the street that climbed the hill toward Sir Harlan's estate. This village could have been any of the ones she and Dominic had traveled through on their way to London. Similar shops clung to the narrow, twisting street, and the wagons and pedestrians were the same.

But no other village had been shadowed by the walls of a prison. Nor had she needed to be anxious in any other village that Sir Harlan had arranged for someone to spy on her. He certainly would have if he suspected where she was now and why.

Thanking the footman who had helped her out of the carriage, Abigail smiled and pressed a coin into his hand. "You gentlemen must be thirsty after the dusty ride down from the house." Her smile included the coachman. "Is there a place where you can find something to drink while I complete my errands?"

The footman hesitated. "We have orders to—"

From his seat at the top of the carriage, the coachee called, "Be silent, fool! Thank you, Miss Fitzgerald." He tipped his cap to her. "We are grateful."

"I shall be done in about two hours." She waved toward the shop with the sign that read MRS. RICHE — COUTURIÈRE.

"We will meet you right here, Miss Fitzgerald, in two hours." To the footman, he bellowed, "Climb aboard. We cannot block the street. Other ladies might be coming to see Mrs. Riche."

Sweeping aside the dust that rose in the carriage's wake, Abigail waited patiently for it to turn a corner. Nothing must betray her now. She forced herself to a sedate pace as she walked in the opposite direction. As she went along an alley, she pulled a plain cloak over her dress. She hoped the cape would make her less conspicuous. She had borrowed it and the coins from Tessie. Somehow she would repay the maid.

At the end of the alley, Abigail paused and stared at the jail. Crenellations marched across the top of the high walls. Tightening her grip on her bag, she forced her feet forward. She hoped that, once she entered this heinous place, she could escape again.

She walked through the narrow door and immediately was met in the filthy courtyard by a tall man. He was as disgustingly dirty as his surroundings. With every step, a ring of keys clanked at his hip. He smiled, his gaze slithering along her.

"What are you doing here, missy?" he asked.

"Are you a jailer?" She had not guessed the warden would look as hideous as the prison.

"I am Pritchard. If you have business here, you have it with me."

"I have to come to see Captain Dominic St. Clair." Silently she congratulated herself because her voice remained calm. "Will you be so kind as to tell me where I might find him?"

He held out his hand. "You will be needing an escort, missy."

Knowing she had no choice, she withdrew a coin from her bag. His smile grew broader as he pocketed it. "Right this way, missy. Good thing you are coming to see him now. 'Tweren't much to look at when we fished him out of the pits this morning."

When Abigail smiled, Pritchard choked back a gasp of surprise. She did not care what he thought. It appeared that Tessie's visit earlier today had been successful. Tessie had known how many coins it would take to get Dominic out of the common cell.

She wished she could have heard what Tessie had experienced here, so she could be prepared for what waited within. No matter; she would do what she must. She lifted her skirts over stinking puddles. As Pritchard held a door and motioned her inside, the stench in the dim corridors was even worse.

He led her down staircase after staircase until she was sure they must be nearing the gates of Hades. When he shoved aside a thick door, an odor, more pungent than a fisherman's hut in New Bedford, swelled out. She pulled from her bag a perfumed handkerchief Tessie had insisted she must have and pressed it to her nose.

The feeble light from the jailer's battered lantern braved the darkness only a few inches on either side of them. The walls glowed with intermittent splotches of whitewash. Scurrying sounds warned that large bugs or rats fled from the light.

A hand reached out of the darkness and grasped her skirt. She screamed as she was jerked against the bars of a narrow door. Fingers tangled in her hair to twist her face toward the cell. A colorless face peered through the woman's matted hair. She broke away from the desperate fingers only to be caught by another nightmarish creature. Other scrawny arms covered with sores reached out.

Pritchard chuckled when Abigail shrieked again. Then he stepped forward. Viciously he struck the bony arms stretching through the bars.

"Keep yer hands off her, slime," he snarled. A smile tilted his lips, revealing broken teeth.

Abigail willed her stomach not to revolt. There were children among the women in that cell. What could a child have done to deserve this? Tears welled into her eyes, not just for the children, but for Dominic, who had endured this torment for the past week. When she recalled how he delighted in the breeze blowing in his face, she knew the punishment must be doubly severe for him.

She looked at the turnkey. "Please take me to Captain St. Clair." As she slid away from the grasping fingers, others clutched the back of her skirt. She whirled to see another prison cell behind her. This one was filled with men as ragged as the women. More children peered through the bars, their slender arms unable to reach far.

Pritchard laughed again and lifted his lantern close to her face. As her hair caught the light, a man called out, "Put 'er in 'ere, turnkey. Treat 'er real nice, we will. Just for the night. Give 'er back to ye in the morning."

"No!" she cried as the man seized her arm. Her hands curled around the bars as she tried to push herself away. Rust cut her palms.

With a snicker, Pritchard said, "Seems like yer pennies have gotten ye 'bout as far as ye are going, missy."

Escaping to the middle of the corridor, she tried to straighten her gown. Her trembling fingers refused to work. "You have been paid to take me to Captain St. Clair."

"Seems to me any friend of that Frenchie pirate must be a criminal as well." He grinned. "Might be doing everyone a favor to lock ye away."

"You must be insane!" She glanced at the skeletal women. "You cannot put me in with them!"

"Not over there." Grasping her arm, he twisted her to face the cell where the men shouted lustful obscenities and crooked their fingers at her. "In here. How long do ye think ye could survive with them? Yer choice, missy. Ten shillings, or in ye go."

"Ten?" Her voice was faint in her ears.

"Ten," he repeated.

"Put 'er in 'ere, turnkey! We'll tend to 'er right nicely." The man who had grabbed her leered as his broad hand reached for her.

With fingers that shook so harshly she did not know if she could open her bag, Abigail withdrew the coins. Tessie had warned her to take at least a guinea with her. Now Abigail understood why. Pritchard chortled as she counted the coins into his hand. She would worry about how she would pay for another visit later. Right now, all she wanted was to escape this abyss.

Pritchard's clawlike fingers tightened on her arm as he hurried her up a flight of stairs. Shouts and curses followed them until he closed a door behind them at the top.

It was as if they had entered a different world. Although the doors still had bars in small windows covered with sliding panels, the passage was lit with candles every few feet along the wall. Some doors had the panels pushed aside. At them, the faces pressed to the bars did not look as cadaverous as the ones below. These were the fortunate ones whose friends and family could afford to bribe the guards.

Pritchard paused before a door that looked exactly the same as the others. Peering in, he called, "St. Clair!"

"Shut up, Pritchard!"

"Dominic," she whispered, not sure if, until now, she had believed she actually would see him again.

"St. Clair, ye've got company."

"Begone!" Dominic's voice set her heart thudding against her breastbone.

"Ahoy there, Cap'n! Prepare to be boarded." Pritchard guffawed.

Footsteps and the clank of metal came from beyond the door. The small panel slid aside. Dominic looked out the narrow opening and gasped, "Abigail!"

"Dominic." She wanted to say more. She had so much she wanted to tell him, but she could only whisper his name.

"Are ye goin' to stand here or go in?" Pritchard asked.

"Open the door, please," she said, her gaze still held by Dominic's. "Don't ask for more money. I have paid you all I can today."

Her suggestion of future bribes brought a smile to his lips. He sought along his key ring for the key for this door. "Back away, St. Clair. If ye try anything, yer pretty lady will be the one to suffer." He added to Abigail, "Ye have half an hour. That should give ye time to complete yer business."

Abigail knew she was blushing, but said nothing as he pulled out the key and the door swung back with the hushed whisper of well-oiled hinges. Pritchard's hand in the center of her back shoved her inside. She gasped when she heard the key jangling again in the lock.

"He will come back for you," Dominic said with a tight smile while he slid the panel closed so the turnkey could not spy on them.

"Are you sure?"

"How else will he get the bribe you will pay him to take you out of here?"

"Tessie's money did not buy much here, did it?"

"Tessie?"

"A friend." She did not explain further as she looked around the small room. A table, a rickety chair, and a bed frame heaped with straw were the only furnishings.

A slit allowed in some light and fresh air. She flinched when she heard Pritchard's laugh fading down the passage and wondered what it would cost her to get out of this prison.

Dominic cupped her chin and brushed her lips with a gentle kiss. She flung her arms around him. When she heard the clank of iron as he stepped closer, she pulled back in horror. Manacles weighed heavily on his ankles.

She could not look away. The chain between his ankles forced him to walk awkwardly and ensured he could not outrun any guard. Impotent fury filled her, but she forced it deep within her. Anger would not help him.

"I should thank both you and Tessie for this luxury," he said, startling her out of her shock.

"How are you faring?"

He curved his finger along her cheek. "As well as any man who has spent the past week rotting at the bottom of a black well." His voice grew raw with need. "How could I have forgotten in a single week how truly beautiful you are? I have thought so often of you, wondering if you are well, fearing what Fitzgerald would do to you."

Dominic frowned when Abigail turned away. Her face had closed up when he spoke her father's name. What had the bastard done to her now? He knew he should ask, but he did not want to waste a moment of this short time arguing. Instead, he yearned to relish her beauty and listen to the soft lilt of her voice, the very voice that had sifted through his dreams that had pulled him out of this living nightmare. Even more, he ached to pull her into his arms and savor her soft touch.

When she shrugged off her cloak and folded it over the chair, he clenched his hands at his sides, knowing that the torment he had suffered before was less than what he felt now when he saw her in a dress of golden silk that accented the highlights in her hair. The neckline scooped lower than what she had worn on the *Republic*.

Her slender profile teased him to pull her into his arms and love her as he had dreamed of doing during the week they had been separated.

He took a single step toward her, then froze when the chain on his ankles clanked. If he tried to hold her now, the clank of his manacles would provide the melody playing through their rapture. No, he would not taint their pleasure with that horror.

"Being in the pit downstairs was not so bad once I subdued those who thought they could subdue me," Dominic said when she turned to face him.

She shivered. "They are beasts."

He frowned. "How do you know?"

"Pritchard took me there."

"To get more money from you?"

When she nodded, his hands knotted more tightly into fists. He wanted his fingers around Pritchard's throat. "How much did it cost you to get here?"

"Eleven shillings."

He forced his anger aside. It would do her no good if he infuriated the turnkey. "Then sit down, Abigail. You have paid highly for this visit and this luxury. The least I can do is be a charming host. You will, of course, be polite and not mention the clank of these irons around my ankles."

"Dominic, stop it!" She grasped his forearms. "Please stop making this sound like a joke. I am trying to help you. Can't you be serious for one moment?"

"Why? If I take this seriously, I have to believe I will soon hang."

"Is there anything I can do for you?"

"Do you still need to ask?"

Abigail smiled shyly and lowered her eyes. "Anything else, I mean?"

"Can you come back again?"

She nodded. His intense tone warned that he already

was planning something. Mayhap it would be the very thing that could free him.

"I can come into the village as often as I wish, and I can come here as often as I wish," she replied. "As long as I pay the turnkey, of course."

"Of course," he repeated grimly. Stepping away from her, he paced the narrow room. At the clatter that matched each step, she shuddered. He scowled. "Do not waste your sympathy on me now, Abigail."

"I hate seeing you here."

He paused in front of her. His broad hands settled on her shoulders, then rose so his fingers spread along her face in a gentle caress. "I hate being here," he whispered. "I hate being away from you, *chérie*." He frowned as he tipped her arm toward him. "What is this?"

"Just a bruise."

"A bruise? There are several here. If Fitzgerald—"

"This is not his doing."

"Then whose?"

"It is just a bruise, Dominic." She forced a smile. "I have not been as cooperative as others would wish."

"That is no surprise, *chérie*, but no one should hurt you like this."

"I will be fine." She took a deep breath, then lied with a smile. "It shan't happen again."

He hesitated before nodding. "Then tell me where you are living."

Abigail was not so quick with this answer. Although no one in the prison might know of the abuse she was suffering, it must be known throughout the village where she was living. She did not want to burden Dominic further. He could not help her, and she feared he would do something foolish if she revealed why Captain Fitzgerald had brought her to England. She must answer his questions, so he would be satisfied and ask no one else.

Quietly she said, "I am a guest at the home of Sir Harlan Morris."

"Sir Harlan Morris? That traitorous mercenary?"

"You know of him?"

Dominic nodded. "Aye, as does any man who sails between the Continent and America. He has a fleet of ships, but he seldom engages in normal shipping. He prefers higher profits, so he works for whichever government will buy his loyalty."

"Then why isn't he in prison?"

"Because right now, I would guess, it is more convenient for the British government to have him working for them."

"That would explain why he and Captain Fitzgerald are friends."

"Captain Fitzgerald?" Dominic frowned. "Why are you calling your father that?"

Abigail quickly told him the truth that Captain Fitzgerald had delighted in divulging. Wrapping her arms around herself, she whispered, "I wish I could remember my mother."

"As I wish I could recall something of my father."

"I hope I can someday go to my aunt and tell her how wonderful she was to take in a child she could have hated. But she loved me as if I were her own. How I would like to thank her for that." She gazed up into his eyes. A sweet warmth seeped from her center. She leaned forward, and her hands swept up his arms to grasp his elbows. "Most of all, I wish to help you."

"What I need is information."

"I can try and get it for you."

Dominic smiled, but his expression chilled her. "Captain Fitzgerald is not the only one interested in seeing me dead."

"I know."

"The Americans and the English would send me to hang."

"I know."

"But you will still help me?"

"How can you ask me that? I thought you realized that I want to help you." Her voice rose with her pain. "I suffered the horror of coming here to see you, so I could help you. *Now* you accuse me of wanting to help those who wish to see you dead."

With a groan, he pulled her into his arms. "*Chérie*, forgive me for doubting you, but I had to ask."

"I know." She hid her face against his chest. Here was where she wanted to be. In his arms, where she could think of nothing but the joy of his touch.

Reaching up, she drew his mouth to hers. Their breaths mingled, growing strained, but he raised his head with a remorseful sigh. She reached for him again. Shaking his head, he said, "This is not the place for what is so sweet."

Abigail nodded. Anything she might say could convince him that she feared he was doomed. She would not believe that. There must be a way to save him.

"Have you heard when my trial is?" Dominic asked as he began pacing again.

"No one can tell me that. Or they will not tell me." Sighing, she sat on the bed, ignoring the prickly hay. Her shoulders sagged.

Dominic halted. The clatter of the chains echoed in the room as he looked at Abigail waiting on his bed. The fantasy that had kept him from madness was now real before him. *Non!* He would not hold her here. If he did not survive this, he wanted her to remember the joy they had shared at Sudley Hall, not a desperate coupling in a jail cell before he was sent to hang.

Sitting next to her on the straw, he put his arm around her. She quivered like a sail in a fickle wind. When she leaned her head against his shoulder, he raised her hand to his lips.

Softly he said, "We must contact *La Chanson de la Mer*. You will have to do that."

"Me?" She pulled away, her eyes wide with shock.

He smiled. "Can you travel whenever you want?"

Abigail thought of how she would have to be cooperative about spending time with Clive in order to be granted such a favor. Looking up into Dominic's eyes which glowed with enthusiasm, she knew she had no choice if she wished to help him. "I can find a way."

"Good." He looked about the room and cursed. "Do you have a coin or two?"

She opened her bag and placed two shillings in his hand.

Sliding open the panel and pounding on the door, Dominic got Pritchard's attention. "I want paper and ink and something to write with," he ordered.

Pritchard sneered, "And I want a carriage and four."

"I can pay."

"How much?"

"Two shillings if you bring them now."

Pritchard's eyes sparkled with greed. "I shall have them here in no time." He rushed away.

Dominic turned and asked Abigail about what was happening beyond the prison's walls. He was interested in news on any subject. Only then did Abigail realize how he had been cut off from the world here.

A knock intruded. Dominic passed the coins through the bars in exchange for the paper, quill, and ink. "Give her another fifteen minutes, Pritchard. You cheated her enough already."

"She just paid me to keep her away from yer friends. Yer old buddy Chapman was right interested in yer pretty lady."

Dominic's hushed voice did not hide his fury. "Bring her directly here next time."

"I will bring her any way I wish, St. Clair."

"Will you?" He leaned his elbow on the small window and smiled. "Take her any way but the most direct route here and I will find myself talking to Captain Josephy about how you do not pay him his share of your bribes."

Pritchard's face paled.

"Do we understand each other?" Dominic continued. "Take any other visitors I have any way you wish and charge what you wish to help them find their way out, but not Miss Fitzgerald."

"Ye are wasting the time she has left today," Pritchard answered, but the fear was bright in his eyes. "Fifteen minutes; then she must leave."

Dominic nodded and crossed the room to where Abigail was struggling not to smile. She should have realized Dominic St. Clair would end up being in command, even in jail. He spread the paper across the table and began to write. When she stood, intending to read over his shoulder, he said, "No, *chérie*, do not read it. You will be safer if you remain ignorant of what is in it."

"If you are writing in French, I cannot read it."

"Some words are similar enough." He folded the page, sealed it with wax, and pressed it in her hand. "See that it is delivered to Ogier on *La Chanson* or my friend Evan Somerset."

"How?"

"In London you can find a man named Red at the Brass Fish, a tavern near the Pool. I was on my way to speak with him when I received the message that brought me to Fitzgerald's house. Red can arrange for the note's delivery."

"In London? You want me to go back to London?"

He chuckled. "*Chérie*, I told you once that I would be

a fool not to know every man in England whose loyalty can be bought.''

Abigail shivered. Loyalty was no longer clear-cut. Sir Harlan had bought his son a bride not only with cash, but with guns which would be turned against Americans. ''I have learned that. But how—''

''Try.''

''I will, Dominic, but we are almost five hours from London.''

He frowned. ''Five hours?''

''By coach.''

''So far? Are you certain?''

She nodded. ''When you were brought here—''

''I slept.'' His lips twisted at the memory. ''Fitzgerald's men must have drugged the wine they gave me. I have had no idea where we are.'' He sighed. ''Can you get from here to London, *chérie?*''

''I will try. I will try as soon as possible.''

His hand curved along her face. ''Come back soon.''

''I will as soon as I have some information for you.''

Standing, he drew her to her feet and into his arms. ''Or sooner, *chérie*. Your smile brightens my eyes, wiping away the darkness of despair.''

Unsure how to reply to such surprising honesty without revealing the pity which he would despise, she nodded. ''I will.''

When he tilted her mouth beneath his, she welcomed his kiss. She sighed and pressed more closely to him as she rediscovered the tender torment of being close to him and not being able to share their passion. As his lips glided across her face, teasing, taunting, daring her to surrender, she clung to him. His fingers moved along her, cupping her breast. Against his mouth, she gasped when rapture threatened to overwhelm her.

''Abigail—''

The clink of keys in the lock brought a vicious oath

from Dominic. He released her, and she walked out after Pritchard had opened the door.

As she trailed Pritchard along the corridor, Abigail held the piece of paper tightly, knowing how important it was. She was not sure what Dominic was requesting in this letter, but it would be a way to flee England. With her help, he might be successful. Her steps faltered as she emerged onto the street. Dominic had told her more than once that there was no place for her in his life on the sea. She could not think of that now. Somehow he would escape. Somehow she would persuade him to take her with him. Such a life might not be easy, but with Dominic, it would be exciting.

Chapter Nineteen

Abigail's happiness vanished as soon as she entered Sir Harlan's house. She saw Fuller in the hallway. What was he doing here? Usually he loitered in the kitchen, bothering the maids.

Then, with a stomach-twisting pulse of disgust, she realized it must be time for her daily visit with Clive. *Not all prisons have bars on the windows and rats in the corners.* She shivered at that thought.

Fuller grasped her arm and pulled her close. Boothe tried to interfere, but Fuller growled at the butler, "Get out of the way, old man! Sir Harlan wants her and his son together each afternoon."

"Miss Abigail has just arrived back from Morristown," Boothe argued. "She must be fatigued."

"Yes," seconded Abigail, wanting to give Boothe a smile of gratitude, but knowing that she must not turn

Fuller's cruelty on her unexpected ally. "I am fatigued.
I will return to see Clive in half an hour."

Fuller smiled coldly. "In half an hour you will be
halfway through your visit with your darling Clive." He
forced her ahead of him toward the parlor. He pointed at
the butler. "Say a single word, Boothe, and you shall be
sorry."

He shoved her into the room and slammed the door.
Abigail snarled an impotent curse at the closed door, but
it did not relieve her frustration. With a sigh, she chose
a chair next to the hearth, so she would be as far from
the door as possible when Fuller returned with Clive.

She tried to hide her terror as the door opened. The
laughter from Clive's guards warned her it would be more
difficult than usual to keep him from hurting her. She did
not rise, for Clive could construe any motion as aggres-
sion.

Every attempt to hide her fear vanished as the trio
burst into the room. Fuller and his assistant Greene were
struggling to restrain Clive, but Clive's fist knocked
Greene off his feet.

Fuller screeched, "Get up, Greene! Help me!"

Jumping to her feet, Abigail said in a strained voice,
"Calm down. You are making him worse."

Fuller stamped toward her, leaving Greene to deal with
Clive. He put his finger directly in her face, but she batted
it away. With a growl, he stated, "Don't tell me how to
do my job."

"I shall not, if you do it!"

"No," he drawled. "You do it." Before she could
answer, he walked out, motioning for Greene to follow.

She gasped in horror. They were leaving her alone with
Clive! She ran to the door, but it closed before she could
reach it. A key twisted in the lock. She put her hand on
the latch, but she was torn away from the door.

The arm around her waist tightened until she could

hardly breathe, as Clive stroked her hair. He continued to be fascinated with its bright color. That added to her fear, but she gently pushed on his arm and said, "Let me go. You are hurting me." She repeated those two sentences over and over as she tried to breathe. She did not know what he would do if she collapsed. She must not let him kill her. If he did, Dominic would die, too, for Sir Harlan would have no reason to keep him alive.

When his grip loosened, she sucked in a deep breath. He released her, not moving until she reached again for the door. She edged away from his broad hands, and his puzzled gaze stalked her around the room. A vacant smile appeared on his face as he lumbered toward her.

Abigail gasped. She had been maneuvered easily into a corner. Had she and everyone else underestimated Clive's intelligence?

"Pretty," he mumbled as he stepped closer. "Pretty."

"No," she whispered. When she saw rage on his face, she added hastily, "Not pretty."

"Pretty." Childish petulance filled his voice. He reached for her. "Pretty. Mine."

Her eyes widened. She had never heard him use that word. Suddenly she understood why Fuller had locked her in here with Clive. By leaving her and Clive alone, Fuller hoped she would have to scream for his help. That would set Clive off more, and Fuller could come to her rescue to gain his employer's gratitude. Or would he even come to save her? She wondered if Clive's other bride-to-be had died because of Fuller's pride.

"Abigail," she said as she caught Clive's outstretched hand. Pressing it to her shoulder, she whispered, "Abigail." She put his hand on his chest. "Clive." Slowly she repeated the action endlessly until he began to mouth the words with her. She smiled, believing she was reaching the child within the man.

Suddenly he pulled his hand away. When he raised it,

she fought her instinct to cower. If she did, he might go
on another rampage. His heavy hand settled on her hair,
and he stroked it jarringly.

"Pretty. Pretty. Pretty Abig."

"Yes." Hoping she would not make the situation
worse, she put her hand on his shoulder. "Pretty Clive."

She struggled not to cringe when she heard a bizarre
sound; then she realized he was laughing.

He patted her head hard. "Pretty Abig. No pretty Clive.
Pretty Abig mine. Clive be good boy. Pretty Abig mine."

Abigail swallowed her shock. Never had she heard him
string so many words together. If she had not been about
to be forced to become his reluctant bride, she could have
felt pity for him. He had been shut away and ignored for
most of his life, until, like her, he had gained value in
his father's eyes.

"Do you want to see more pretties?" she asked.

"Pretty Abig?"

She shook her head, wondering how long she could
communicate with him before his frustration over-
whelmed him and set him off into a rage again. "No,"
she said, pointing to the doors to the garden. "Pretties
out there."

"Yes. Yes."

Abigail took his hand before he could shake his head
off his shoulders in his enthusiasm. He reminded her of
the toddler who lived next door to Aunt Velma, but Clive
was not a child. Keeping up a steady patter about the
"pretties" they would see, she led him out the doors.
She steered his uneven steps around the chairs on the
terrace and across the perfect grass. How it must infuriate
Sir Harlan, who insisted that everything be kept exactly
as he wanted it at this house, that he had a son with so
many imperfections.

When Clive paused by a tree, she ran his hand along
the bark. He laughed when it tickled his palm, and her

pity grew. She tried to guess how old Clive was. At least a decade older than she was, but he acted as if he had never touched a tree. She suspected he had not.

Tessie's comments about Sir Harlan's older son who had been the heir suggested that Clive's brother had died within the past few years. She glanced at Clive's delighted face. Until his brother's death, he may have been shut away in some windowless attic where he could not be seen by anyone.

"Pretty Abig." He pointed at the tree and struggled to find a word.

She laughed, but halted when his face twisted with rage. Instantly she understood. Too many people had laughed at him. Keeping a smile on her face, she ran her fingers along the bark and said, "Tree. Pretty tree." As she had before, she repeated the words over and over.

Again the sound like a rasp being drawn across rusty iron came from him. He touched the tree. "Pretty." Another new word seemed beyond his limited capabilities.

"More pretties?" she asked.

"Pretty." He held out his hand and smiled expectantly.

Abigail's eyes flooded with tears as she saw how he longed for affection. Not the lust his father yearned for him to have in order to obtain Sir Harlan another heir, but the longing for friendship. She put her hand in Clive's. When he closed his fingers too tightly, she loosened them with a gentle smile. He nodded, but she was unsure how much he understood.

Watching his face so she could gauge any change, she walked with him to where rosebushes were lush with bright red flowers. She simply said, "Pretty."

His thick fingers touched the bright blossoms, sending petals cascading to the ground. She saw the joy on his face. This was what Clive wanted. To be surrounded by "pretties" and escape from his prison. She wondered how Sir Harlan could be so indifferent to his son's needs.

She shivered as she folded her hands behind her back and watched Clive examine the flowers with a child's curiosity. Unlike Clive, she had been fortunate enough to have Aunt Velma and Uncle Jareb to love her. She had always adored her uncle, although she had never suspected he was her true father. She ached for such a giving love again. She turned to look toward Morristown. In the prison there, she had a precious love that might be as doomed as her uncle's ship.

Renewed pain cut through her as if she had touched the thorns on the vines. If she did not do as Sir Harlan ordered, he would see Dominic hanged. Her love would be gone, and she would be forced into Clive's bed.

She touched her bodice and heard the crackle of the page she had secured there. Dominic's letter to the man named Red at the Brass Fish had not been lost. Somehow she had to find a way to go to London and see Red. She smiled when she realized she might have just the way.

Anxious to do what she must to help Dominic and realizing that they must return to the house before Fuller discovered what was happening, Abigail urged Clive toward the garden doors. He grumbled, and she said, "We will see pretties again, Clive. All right?"

He stroked the soft petals he had gathered from the ground. She wondered how many promises had been made and forgotten by those who guarded him.

He reached for her hand. When he saw the petals in his hand, he looked from them to her.

She smiled. "Pretties for Clive."

"Clive good boy?"

"Yes," she said with sympathy. "Clive is a very good boy. Next time we will get more pretties."

"More?"

"Yes. Next time," she repeated firmly. She was beginning to understand how to deal with him. Once she set boundaries he could accept, he was docile. It was only when he was frustrated that he exploded into violence.

He babbled something she could not understand as they walked back to the house. When he paused as if expecting her to answer, she smiled. The only words she understood were their names and his favorite word.

When they entered the parlor, she paused. Fuller and Greene had already arrived. Fuller was looking about the room with a horrified expression. She shuddered as she realized he was looking for her corpse left behind by Clive.

"Lose something, Mr. Fuller?" she asked quietly.

He whirled, fear straining his hard features. When he saw her smile, he growled.

Clive lurched across the room with his drunken gait. Holding out his prize, he announced, "Pretties. Clive pretties."

Fuller knocked the petals from his hand. When Clive let out a screech, Fuller asked, "Clive want pretty? There is pretty. You want pretty? Abigail is pretty."

"Abig pretty?"

The guard could not hide his surprise at the name Clive had given her, but he glanced at Greene as he said eagerly, "Yes, Abig pretty. Clive good boy. Abig is for Clive."

"Abig mine?"

"Yes. Abig is for Clive. Touch pretty."

The guards chuckled as Clive dropped the last petals and turned to face Abigail. She stared at Clive's transformed face. The gentle Clive who had walked with her in the garden had vanished. She backed away as he came closer.

"Clive . . . Clive," she whispered, knowing too well the price of screaming out her fear.

"Pretty. Pretty." He grasped her and pulled her against him. He fondled her, then touched her hair. Suddenly he released her. "Pretty Abig?"

Not sure what else to say, she answered, "Pretty Clive?"

When Clive chuckled, Fuller cursed. Fuller crossed the room and grabbed Clive's arm.

"Don't hurt him!" Abigail cried when Fuller grappled Clive into his control with Greene's help.

Fuller snarled, "I don't know what you have done to him, but Sir Harlan will not be pleased. You can be damned sure that the next time—"

"What about next time?"

At the question, all of them but Clive glanced toward the door to the hall.

Sir Harlan walked into the room. "What about next time?" he demanded. Before anyone could answer, he added, "Get Clive out of here."

Fuller and Greene hastily led Clive out of the parlor and up the stairs toward his room. Abigail sat in a chair, closing her eyes as her shoulders sagged. Her small connection with Clive was the last thing Sir Harlan would have wanted.

"What in hell happened here?" Sir Harlan asked as he went to the sideboard to pour himself a brandy.

Deciding not to mince on the facts, she told him how Fuller had left her alone with Clive. "He hoped Clive would hurt me, or mayhap even kill me." She laughed icily. "That did not happen. Clive and I took a walk."

"You did what?" He stared at her as if he could not believe what he was hearing. She was sure he did not.

"We took a walk in the garden. Has he ever been in the garden before?"

He disregarded her question as he smiled with the frigid rage she recognized as dangerous. "Have you civilized him?"

"He wants only to be with his 'pretties.' " She picked up a flower petal. "He laughed with me today."

"He did what?" He knocked the petals from her hand

as viciously as Fuller had sent them flying from Clive's fingers. When she gaped in astonishment, he snapped, "I don't want him to be a gardener. I want him to father my grandchild. You will not see him again until the wedding. By then, with Fuller's tutorage, he shall not be interested in looking at flowers with you."

She came to her feet. "He is your son! Don't you care about him at all?"

"No." He chuckled when she swallowed the retort she had been about to make. "You didn't expect such honesty? 'Tis the truth. If my older son had not been killed in that duel, I would never have bothered to bring Clive from the home where he was with others like himself. Go to your room, Abigail. The very sight of you vexes me."

She went to the door. "Sir Harlan?"

"Leave me, girl!"

"After I say one thing." Before he could halt her with another order to leave, she said quietly, "There is a gentleness in your son which you will never know. Who is the lesser man?"

For once, he was the one shocked to silence. She left the room. As she climbed the stairs, she knew it was too late to try to reason with Sir Harlan. Clive's fate and hers had been assured by his father's hatred for both of them. Now she had to try to find a way to foil Sir Harlan's schemes before she and Dominic and Clive all became the victims of the baronet's malevolence.

Chapter Twenty

When Abigail left her room, she made sure she looked her very best. She kept her head high and tried not to smile, but she glanced in the mirror set amid the paintings along the railing leading to the stairs. Tessie had spent more than a half hour curling Abigail's red hair into ringlets which were pinned up on her head before dropping onto her shoulders. She did not want to ruin Tessie's work. In a high-waisted gown of her favorite mint shade, she was set for battle.

As her hand followed the curve of the banister, her fingers tightened on the wood. Two men waited in the foyer. Captain Fitzgerald! What was *he* doing back here so quickly? She had not planned on him being here tonight.

Abigail was aware of both men watching her, but she did not acknowledge either of them until she stepped down onto the marble floor. When Sir Harlan stepped forward with his officious smile, she raised her right hand formally to him.

Taking her fingers, Sir Harlan bowed over them. When he started to raise them to his lips, she pulled them back, not hiding her distaste. She did not offer her hand to Captain Fitzgerald.

"Good evening, Sir Harlan," she said quietly. She glanced away from him and added, "This is a surprise, Captain Fitzgerald."

The man she had believed was her father snickered as he sipped on a glass filled high with brandy. "Listen to her! Putting on airs as if she is a fine lady already. She shall change her tune after the wedding."

Sir Harlan flinched more visibly than Abigail did. "I do not wish to speak of such private matters here," the baronet said.

Captain Fitzgerald just laughed, and Abigail realized he was already intoxicated. She wondered how long the two men had been drinking while she had been upstairs getting ready for the evening. Then she noted that Sir Harlan was as sober as a parson. Tessie would have warned her if Captain Fitzgerald had arrived before she came to help Abigail dress. Captain Fitzgerald must have been drinking before he arrived.

She shuddered. She did not want to be here with Captain Fitzgerald or with Sir Harlan. The past fortnight had been an endless torment. Every day, she feared Sir Harlan would announce that Dominic's trial would be held that day. Life in the huge house had become even more uneasy. Sir Harlan refused to let her see Clive again. Several times, she had heard shouts from the wing where Clive had his rooms. She ached for the poor soul who was a victim as much as she was.

"Abigail?" asked Sir Harlan, offering his arm.

She disdained it by stepping back a half step. That set Captain Fitzgerald to laughing harder. With his face reddening, Sir Harlan led the way along the hallway.

Abigail walked beside him, but kept a forearm's length between them.

As they entered a large parlor that was fancier than the room where she had met with Clive last week, Abigail recalled the lessons she had learned when she had believed that Dominic was her enemy. If she remained in control of her own errant emotions, no one could guess that fear was the strongest one.

"May I say you look lovely this evening?" Sir Harlan gushed as she sat in a chair that was separated from the others by a pair of round tables.

"Thank you." When she added nothing else, the two men exchanged uneasy glances. She was pleased she could disconcert them, but she had already learned that any victories in this house for her would be small and infrequent.

Captain Fitzgerald almost collapsed as he was trying to sit. With a guffaw, he raised his glass. "To the fulfillment of your dreams, Sir Harlan, and the filling of my pockets."

"Of course, Arthur, you will not receive any remuneration until she marries Clive." Again the baronet appeared embarrassed.

Abigail stared at Sir Harlan in astonishment. Why was he coloring as red as her hair when he was getting what he wanted? Then she realized that he was not embarrassed, but furious. Again the question was why.

She had her answer when Captain Fitzgerald sat straighter and lost his drunken smile. Setting his glass hard on the table, he said, "You agreed that if the wedding was held before month's end you would pay me—"

Sir Harlan turned away from him, jerking around to face Abigail like a dog taking a scent. "Abigail, I have received exciting news today. I daresay I cannot wait a moment longer."

"Exciting?" She let sarcasm drip into her words.

"What could be more exciting than the life I am living here now?" When she noticed that her hands were trembling, she clasped them behind her back.

Captain Fitzgerald rounded on her. "You cannot think you can make us believe that you *want* to marry Clive Morris."

Sir Harlan's face deepened to a ruddy fury, but he reached under his coat and drew out a piece of light cream paper. "I received an invitation from Lady Sudley."

"Lady Sudley?" Abigail strained to keep her face serene. There must be no hint that she had been awaiting this answer to the note she had sent to Lady Sudley last week after visiting Dominic in the prison. That Sir Harlan was excited over the receipt of the letter suggested that Lady Sudley was willing to help her and Dominic.

"Yes. She has heard that you are to be married and wishes you to come to London."

Captain Fitzgerald grumbled, "And slip away with her help, no doubt."

"You do not know Lady Sudley, so you should not judge her so," Abigail returned, letting vexation creep into her voice. Why had he returned *now*? "She offered me shelter when I had none and welcomed me as if I were part of her family."

"Yes," seconded Sir Harlan, unfolding the page. "She knows Abigail's mother is dead, and she wishes to help Abigail with the selection of the perfect wedding gown." He smiled broadly. "And the dear lady is inviting me to join her family in Town as well."

"Do not trust Abigail in London." Captain Fitzgerald lurched to his feet, as unsteady as Clive. "She is a scheming shrew just like her mother."

Abigail shrugged. "I do not wish to go, Sir Harlan. I admit that I would greatly enjoy seeing the Sudleys again, but I have no interest in the perfect wedding gown for this ceremony."

The baronet bristled, and she knew her remarks had
been as effective as Captain Fitzgerald's at upsetting Sir
Harlan, who clearly could not wait to play court on the
Sudleys. "Of course, you will go and allow Lady Sudley
to help you. It would be beneath reproach to turn down
such a generous invitation. I shall hear no more of this."

"But, Sir Harlan—"

"Abigail, I said you shall go, and you shall."

She glanced at Captain Fitzgerald, who was beginning
to smile. Let him think she was browbeaten. If he was
enjoying that, he might not think again of his suspicions,
which were uncomfortably close to the truth.

"Sir Harlan—" she began again.

"If you are going to say anything but yes," the baronet
said in his most condescending tone, "then say nothing."

Clenching her hands at her sides, Abigail blinked as if
she were about to cry. She must not let them guess she
wanted to spin about with delight. She turned and walked
toward the door.

Sir Harlan called to her back, "We will leave at dawn
the day after tomorrow. Be ready."

She stiffened her shoulders, but did not reply. She
walked out. As she closed the door behind her, she heard
the baronet say, "And you can stay here, Arthur, to oversee the final details before the wedding."

Abigail put her hand over her mouth to silence her
giggle that the contemptible Captain Fitzgerald was having to deal with the matters that Sir Harlan wanted to put
aside in order to win the Sudleys' friendship. Mayhap it
was not so horrid that Captain Fitzgerald had returned
just now.

Climbing the stairs, she stroked the smooth banister.
Soon she would be out of Sir Harlan's house and seeking
a way not to return. Turning, she scanned the lower floor.
She wanted to shout her farewells now.

Another giggle tickled in her throat as she could hear,

in her memory's ear, her aunt's reprimand after a far younger Abigail had slid down the banister in the house overlooking New Bedford harbor. Each admonishment Abigail received had been accompanied by one of her aunt's warm hugs. So much love was shared in that house, but she had not appreciated the treasure she had possessed.

How proud Aunt Velma and Uncle Jareb would be to learn of Abigail's idea to contact Lady Sudley! It had been a risk, but, as her uncle had always said, nothing truly wonderful came without some risk.

She smiled. Dear Aunt Velma and Uncle Jareb. Not her uncle, but her father. She reconstructed his wind-sculpted face from memory. His red hair and stubborn chin were so much like hers that she wondered why she had never questioned her parentage. How Uncle Jareb would have admired Dominic if the war had not stood between them! Uncle Jareb always spoke with respect of the men who commanded ships facing the sea's many moods.

Her happiness faltered as she climbed the stairs. Captain Fitzgerald would not take a message from Abigail to Aunt Velma. Instead he would devise lies. She feared his tales would be aimed at hurting Aunt Velma because she had taken Abigail into her heart.

But that would not matter if she could find help in London and free Dominic so both of them could flee from England. Then Captain Fitzgerald could wallow in his lies, and she would be done with him.

She hurried to her rooms that were her only haven in his house. When she reached the door, it opened before she could put her fingers on the latch. She smiled at Tessie.

"Lady Sudley wrote to Sir Harlan inviting us to London," Abigail said as soon as she closed the door behind her.

Tessie's smile widened her cheeks. "How wonderful! And so quickly."

"We leave for London at dawn the day after tomorrow." She went to the French doors and flung them open. "Which gives me tomorrow to pay a visit to the modiste."

"Tomorrow?" Tessie's voice lost its good cheer. "Do you think that is wise, Miss Abigail? If you are discovered—"

"I shan't be. Sir Harlan is oblivious to anything but gaining Lord Sudley's patronage." She laughed. "He intends to leave Captain Fitzgerald here and put him in charge of overseeing what wedding plans still must be completed." Rubbing her hands together, she stared out at the prison. "This has to work. It may be our only chance."

"I hope you are right, Miss Abigail."

"I hope so, too. We shall not get a second chance."

Abigail's skin became gooseflesh as she entered the shadowed clamminess of the prison. The ugly prison courtyard was deserted. She had never seen any prisoners out here. When she heard a scratchy, too familiar voice, she turned. Pritchard must have been watching for her.

"Good day, Miss Fitzgerald," he said, holding out his hand for a bribe.

She placed the coins on his palm. When he counted them and grimaced, she wondered if he would believe how difficult it was for her to get even these few shillings. She was surrounded by wealth, but to obtain it she would have to sell her soul to Sir Harlan.

Shuffling his feet, Pritchard walked toward the stairs that led most directly to Dominic's room. She kept her cloak close to her. If anyone saw filth on it, her visits might be discovered and halted.

"Trial be coming around soon," Pritchard said.

"Unfortunately for you! Then you will not be able to beg for shillings from me."

He shrugged with a smile. "Others come to replace those who go to the gallows. Others have those who want to visit them. They shall pay as ye did." Grumbling, he added, "Mayhap better."

Abigail did not bother to answer. If she lowered her facade of cool regality, he would prey on her vulnerability. She kept her gaze focused on the corridor ahead of them as she climbed the final set of steps leading treacherously up to where Dominic was imprisoned. To see the ghostly faces staring through the bars in the desperate hope of a visitor would tempt her to tears.

At Dominic's door, Pritchard banged his ring of keys on the battered wood. "C'mon, Cap'n. Ahoy there. Ye be wanting company?"

The small panel slid open, and she saw Dominic's welcoming smile.

When Pritchard opened the door, Abigail did not wait for him to shove her into the cell. Skipping lightly past his loathsome fingers, she ignored his muttering as he relocked the door. She untied her bonnet and drew off her cloak. She dropped both on the chair before turning to Dominic.

He was too pale. She hoped that it was from lack of sunshine and decent food, and that he had not taken ill with some prison fever.

"You act surprised to see me," Abigail said. "Did you think I would go to London without visiting you before I left?"

"London?" He slammed the panel on the door closed and whirled her into his arms. "*Chérie*, you have managed the impossible!"

She laughed as she locked her fingers together behind his nape, trying to ignore the clatter of chains that emphasized every step he took. "Only partly. Sir Harlan and I leave for London on the morrow."

"Sir Harlan is escorting you there?" His brows lowered in a frown.

"I would rather it be he than Captain Fitzgerald."

"Fitzgerald is back here?"

She nodded. "I wish he had stayed away, but it might be better that he is not in London while I am there doing an errand or two that needs to be done."

He tugged her even closer. When he pressed his mouth over hers, she sensed his intense longing. Not only that, but some darker emotion he could not hide.

She pulled away slightly and whispered, "What is it, Dominic? Is something wrong?"

"Nothing should be wrong when soon we will be away from this chamber pot of an island."

"We? So you will take me with you?"

He hesitated. "*Chérie*, I did not mean—"

Abigail moved away to sit on the single chair. "Nothing has changed, has it? *La Chanson* is first in your heart."

Crossing the room, accompanied by the jangle of his manacles, he knelt and took her hands between his. "You don't understand, do you? I shall not put you in such danger again. Mayhap when the war is over . . ."

"Enough, Dominic." She stood. "This is not the time for arguing."

"When you return to your Aunt Velma, you will see I am right."

Her face became icy. "Mayhap."

He gripped her shoulders. "What is it? What is stealing the color from your face? Has Fitzgerald threatened you?"

She put her arms around him. She was tempted to tell him the truth about her betrothal to Clive Morris. But she must not. Dominic might squander his sole chance to escape in an effort to save her. The boundary between France and England might as well have had a brick wall along it. Few ships crossed the invisible frontier. If *La Chanson* did not return in time, Dominic would die. She would not let him know what she would suffer if they did not escape, because there was nothing he could do to halt it.

"I do not want to be without you," she whispered. That much was the truth.

His fingers touched the center of her chest. "You cannot be without me. My heart is here with yours. That part of me will be with you forever."

When he drew her back into his arms, she did not resist. The caress of his lips told her what she knew too well. He dreaded their parting as she did, but Captain Dominic St. Clair had taken to the sea to serve his country. He would not be waylaid from that obligation until it was completed, not even for her love. Yet it was that sense of duty that she admired, and he would not be the man she loved without it.

His fingers combed through her hair to send her hairpins cascading to the floor. As the red strands fell to her waist, he brushed them aside to unhook the back of her dress. "I love you, *chérie*. I want your love now."

"You love me?" she gasped, pulling away.

"*Oui, chérie.* How could you not know that?" He ran his fingers along her cheek. "My heart, before it left to join yours, told me that you might love me, too."

"I do love you, Dominic." She laughed, unable to contain her joy. "Although if you had told me when you boarded the *Republic* that I would fall in love with such a bold pirate, I would have called you a liar."

"A privateer, *chérie*."

"Mayhap, but you have stolen my heart."

As his lips moved along her neck, she let the remnants

of her unhappiness and fear of what awaited in the future flow from her mind. She wanted the joy he gave her. She wanted it, and she wanted him.

Tossing her cloak over the scratchy straw on the bed frame, he leaned her back on it. She held out her arms to him. Grinning, he murmured, "One moment." He sat beside her, drawing her up as he finished unhooking her gown.

She sighed with eager anticipation as his mouth etched moist fire into the skin above her chemise. When footfalls paused outside, she stiffened and grasped his shoulders.

"Pritchard will not disturb us," Dominic whispered as he leaned her back onto her cloak.

"How do you know?" She twisted her fingers into his hair that reached past his shoulders.

"Because I paid him well."

"*You* paid him? How?"

He took her hand and brushed her fingers against his ear.

"Your earring!" she gasped. "You gave him your earring? You were so proud of it."

He framed her face with his broad hands. "What good is it, *chérie*, when it is of the past? I want you, for you are the pleasure of this moment."

As his hands explored her in a thrilling voyage of rediscovery, she closed her eyes and delighted in the warmth of his touch. His lips soared along her skin, bringing every inch of it alive.

Although he hurried to undress her and then tossed his shirt atop her clothes, he slowly caressed her. His mouth explored her as eagerly as he had the first time she had given herself to him. She moaned against his mouth as his hands stroked the downiness of her inner legs, enticing her to press more tightly to him.

When she loosened the buttons on his breeches, she

realized why he had not removed them. With his ankles manacled, he could not take off his breeches. She began to laugh. "I think we have a problem."

"I do not find it particularly funny," he growled against her ear, sending a fiery shiver through her.

She looked up to see his lips twitching. "You, my dear Captain St. Clair, seem to be a prisoner of love."

"Me?"

She could not answer as he teased her with kisses that stripped all strength from her, but she tried to undo the buttons. She pushed his breeches down his legs, stroking him with each movement. The touch banished her laughter as she was consumed by a more potent joy.

He whispered against her neck, "I need your love to take with me when the trial—"

Her fingertips covered his lips. To hear him speak of the horror waiting beyond these walls would ruin her happiness. "No. Not now!"

The roguish sparkle returned to his eyes as he rolled her onto her back. Raising himself over her, he stated, "Yes, now, *chérie!*"

Her bare skin touched his, and it was as if she had become alight with fire. His light kisses scintillated along her. When she pressed on his shoulders, she leaned over him to taste his warm skin. It heated to a higher temperature to send the flame cascading through her. When her fingers flicked across him, she heard his quick intake of breath. A smile tilted her lips as he growled with the longing that would no longer be denied.

She cried out in surprise as he pushed her onto her back. His gaze refused to release hers as he smiled victoriously. Grasping one of her wrists, he pinned it to the straw. He did the same with the other and bent to place his mouth against her neck. When she writhed beneath him, he smiled.

"Let me go!" she gasped as she tried to escape the ecstasy which was speeding her toward madness.

"Never, my russet vixen," he rumbled in her ear. "You are my prisoner of love forever."

With a throaty moan, she shivered as his tongue teased the soft skin behind her ear. His tongue moved along her in its succulent spiral, and she forgot everything but its heat as he traced a path along her breast and into the downy hollow between them. Her breathy call of his name did not halt him as he moved to sample her most intimate delights. She became the flame.

She only realized he had relinquished his hold on her when she placed her arms around his shoulders. Guiding his mouth back to hers, she tangled her fingers in his hair. As he slid within her, she sighed against his mouth. Nothing had ever been so wondrous, so perfect, so glorious.

Hungrily she pressed to him, letting her need for him career out of control. His mouth was branded into her mouth by his uneven breath. That caress threw her into the powerful pulses of yearning. As rhythm ruled them, their craving gained strength. In a cataclysmic explosion, the fire melded her heart to his as it had yearned to be for so long.

When Abigail opened her eyes to see Dominic's sad smile, she did not speak. Holding up her lips for his kiss, she swallowed her sobs. To ruin their time together with tears was something she had vowed not to do.

He held her in silence. She knew he was no more willing than she to speak the truth about the fear within their hearts that they never would be able to share this ecstasy again. As his fingers traced an aimless path along her arm, she stared at the filthy ceiling.

"Hush, *chérie*," he whispered. Only then did she realize her sobs had escaped.

"I love you so very much, Dominic," she moaned through her grief.

"And so very well."

At his light tone, her lips demanded the chance to smile. That he could joke in the face of death proved to her that Captain Dominic St. Clair was not ready to cede himself to English justice. What exactly he had written in the note she take to London she still did not know, but she suspected he planned on being rescued in a most spectacular way if the crew of *La Chanson* could reach him in time.

Leaning on her elbow, she looked down into his smiling face. He tickled her side, and she laughed with a happiness she had not expected she ever could know again. Her amusement faded as she realized Dominic wanted his legacy to her to be a love laced with laughter.

He reached past her, and she watched in confusion as he drew off his ring. "Take this, *chérie*." He pressed it into her hand.

"But why?"

"In case all does not go as we hope when you are in London." When she looked at him in wide-eyed horror, he smoothed the furrows from her brow. "Take it back to Château Tonnere du Grêlon. Sometime, when there is peace between our nations again, return it to where my father's heart rests."

"Dominic, don't talk like this."

"If you can find any of the St. Clairs, tell them I died bravely in the service of my country." A tender smile lessened the harsh line of his mouth. "Tell them as well that you are the woman I have loved as I loved no other. Tell them you are the one who would have borne my name if I had not died too soon."

She dropped the ring on his broad chest. Sitting on the

edge of the bed, she hid her face in her hands. A pang sliced through her as she heard him speak of marriage. That was what she faced in Sir Harlan's house, but that marriage would be hellish.

"Chérie?"

"Don't ask, Dominic," she whispered. She could not tell him of the fate that Captain Fitzgerald had arranged for her.

"Chérie?" He drew her hands from her face and clasped them between his. "Do not weep for me. Do not weep for yourself. So many wander through life without finding this love we have discovered. Would you rather that we had not had this joy which cannot be taken from us?"

His easy acceptance of death should have strengthened her. If only she could share her pain with him ... No! For the thousandth time, she reminded herself of how she wanted to let him go to the gallows thinking he had saved her.

Rising, she said, "I must get dressed. Pritchard will be back soon. He never lets me have a second longer with you than I can pay for."

Dominic watched in silence as she hurriedly pulled on her clothes. As his gaze traced the slender lines of her body disappearing beneath her chemise and stockings, he wondered what else she was hiding from him. Something more than her fear for him. Something that held her in a captivity as horrifying as his. When she glanced at him and quickly away, he wanted to take her by the shoulders and shake her until she told him the truth.

During her first visit, he had guessed that her deepening terror was all for him. He had become less certain of that on her later visits. Her eyes shied from his each time he spoke of the future. Something was frightening her beyond the walls that kept him from seeing the rest of the world. His one attempt to get information from Pritchard had sent the turnkey into paroxysms of laughter. That had made him more certain that Abigail's fear went beyond seeing him hang. Something was sucking her down into horror.

With a half-bitten-off oath, he stood. He pulled his shirt on and sighed. If only he could tell her about how often he savored his fantasy of escaping to the free life of *La Chanson* with her by his side. She never had been on his ship, but he thought frequently of her by his side at the helm as they faced the tempests the sea threw at them. He doubted if she would believe that he ever had thought of her being there, for he had told her too often that he could not have both her and his ship. Even though he had been honest with her in the past, he could not tell her now that, after having been without *La Chanson* and without her, he missed Abigail far more than his ship.

He said nothing as he walked to her. Slowly he hooked her dress closed. After she twisted her hair up and settled her bonnet over it, he took her left hand. He placed his ring on her fourth finger and closed her fingers around it.

"Remember," he said. "If something happens to me, take this ring to my family in France. And make sure you tell them you are the woman I loved."

Gazing up at him, Abigail fought her sorrow as her tears blurred his strong face. "I shall try," she whispered. She knew that if he did not live to escape and take her with him, she would fail to keep this vow. Sir Harlan would never allow her to leave until she gave birth to a healthy child. Then another and another until he was assured of an heir who would reach its majority.

"I know you will." He bent to kiss her cheek.

The key rattling in the door kept her from replying. Picking up her bag, she went to the door. Pritchard snarled some insult at her, but she ignored him as she blindly went out into the hallway. She did not turn to look at

Dominic. Neither of them had spoken of her errand in
London, but he knew, as she did, that if she failed, the
next time she saw him might be when he was led to the
gallows.

Chapter Twenty-One

Abigail eased the box from the safe, careful not to bang Dominic's ring, which she wore on her finger with several layers of fabric wrapped around its back so it would not slide off. Glancing toward the door of the study, she saw Tessie watching her as she held one hand on the door. No one would enter without Tessie hearing them. They must not be discovered here. If Sir Harlan came in now, Abigail was not sure if his desire for a grandchild would outweigh his fury at her attempt to rob him.

She had no choice, if she wanted to help Dominic. Her visit yesterday to the prison had taken the last of Tessie's cache. Help in London would cost even more dearly, so Abigail had to have a way to buy it. The solution was so simple. Sir Harlan had this jewelry locked away here where it helped no one.

Now the jewels would be the way to buy a messenger to take Dominic's message to his ship. She hoped that if she gave one of the pieces to the man named Red at the Brass Fish, he would accept it in exchange for having the letter taken to *La Chanson de la Mer*.

In spite of knowing she must remain silent, Abigail gasped as she lifted the top of the velvet-lined box. Her fingers trembled as she took out an emerald necklace. By the door, Tessie pressed her hand over her mouth to keep her amazement silent, too.

Abigail started to put it back in the box. It was so lovely with its intricate pattern of stones blinking like feline eyes amid twistings of gold and pearls.

"Miss Abigail," hissed Tessie, "what are you doing?"

"It is too beautiful to steal."

The maid stormed across the room, her eyes narrowed with fury. "Are you mad? *He* is planning to steal your life from you. Your life and the man you love. What could be more beautiful than the life you could share with Captain St. Clair?"

Abigail's fingers tightened on the necklace until the faceted gems cut into her palm. "You are right."

"Then do not feel guilty for taking this one thing from *him* before he takes everything from you." Tessie's eyes filled with tears. "I hope it is the finest piece in there, for he stole the finest part of my life when he did nothing when his son killed my sister."

Coming around the desk, Abigail gave the maid a quick hug. "Thank you for all your help."

"Just foil his plans and you will have repaid me."

"Will you come to London with me?"

Tessie's eyes widened. "You want me to go with you?"

"Yes." She shoved the necklace into her reticule and grasped Tessie's hand. "I will need all the allies I can get there. I do not know if Lady Sudley will still be willing to help when I tell her the truth."

"That Captain St. Clair's ship was a part of the French blockade?"

Abigail nodded as she closed the box and went to place it back in the safe. "I can only hope her gratitude that he saved her children will make her anxious to help us."

Although she wished she could put the box beneath the rest of the boxes and papers in the safe, she did not want anyone to suspect anything had been disturbed. She replaced the key in the drawer and checked to be sure that nothing appeared amiss.

Tessie followed in silence as Abigail slipped past the door and into the hallway. Even though she had her back to the maid, she sensed Tessie's tension. She wanted to tell Tessie to pretend to be calm, but how could Abigail ask that when she was struggling to appear unruffled herself? She fought her feet which wanted to send her scurrying up the stairs.

In her rooms, Abigail sank into the closest chair and stared down at the reticule in her lap. Tessie rang for tea.

"Two cups," Abigail ordered.

"Two?"

"You look as peaked as I feel." Abigail managed a smile. "Mayhap we should order some of Sir Harlan's brandy, too."

"It will be better if I keep busy." Tessie rubbed her hands together. "I will finish packing for you."

Abigail drew out the necklace. "Hide this in the toe of one of my shoes. I doubt that anyone will look for it there." She hesitated, then asked, "Do you want to remain here instead of going to London? I cannot ask you to go if you do not want to. Sir Harlan would give you your leave and make sure you never worked anywhere else in England if he discovers you have been aiding me."

"Miss Abigail . . ."

Abigail smiled as she put her hand on her friend's arm. "Be honest, Tessie. I have asked so much of you already. Your loyalty, your savings, your help with a crime that could send both of us to the gallows along with Dominic."

"I will go with you." Her smile was as forced as Abigail's. "What does it matter if you and Captain St. Clair die alone or with me?"

"It matters to you."

Tessie's smile vanished. "What matters to me is seeing Sir Harlan denied his wishes for another heir so I have my vengeance on him."

Abigail was not sure how to answer that, or if there even was an answer.

"This is most unexpected." Lady Sudley set her teacup on the table and folded her hands in her lap. Her pose of serenity was ruined by dismay burning in her eyes.

Abigail had not tried to pick up her own cup, because her fingers were trembling too hard. "I know we should have told you the truth from the beginning, my lady, but with Dominic injured and being here in England and—"

"Say no more, Abigail." She sighed. "You had no reason to trust me then, nor do you have any more reason to trust me now."

"That is not true."

"You believe that because Captain St. Clair rescued my children from a highwayman I will set aside my loyalty to England and assist him in escaping and preying on English ships again?"

"No."

"No? Then what?"

Abigail swallowed harshly. She had known how difficult this interview with Lady Sudley would be in the exquisite parlor overlooking the gardens of the house set next to a park. The net of lies had closed around them, capturing them as completely as the prison bars did Dominic.

"Lady Sudley," she said, her voice dropping to a near

whisper, "I believed that you would help us because I know you are a woman of honor."

"A woman of honor would not consider betraying her country."

"But a woman of honor would not want to see a man slain simply because he stands in the way of Sir Harlan Morris obtaining a bride for his son and an heir."

Lady Sudley, for the first time since Abigail had met her, lost her cool tranquillity. Pressing her hand to her bodice, she stared at the closed door. "You are to marry *his* son? I had no idea. Why didn't you put that in your note?"

"I need to keep the situation quiet until I can be certain there is no way to free Dominic from his prison and from the gallows."

"So you would risk marrying that mindless beast in order to save Captain St. Clair?"

Abigail nodded, not wanting to waste even a moment to explain that Clive was not truly a beast, just a poor soul who was his father's way to obtain a victory over his wife. "I love Dominic."

"Ah, that always explains so much." Lady Sudley's stiff pose relaxed. "My dear child, you did not need to tell me that. I saw with my own two eyes how you and Captain St. Clair were so very deeply in love." Coming to her feet, she went to the closed door and opened it. She smiled as she faced Abigail. "I believe Lord Sudley will be able to keep Sir Harlan Morris occupied for as long as necessary."

Abigail laughed. "Sir Harlan wishes your patronage so much that he would be willing to do almost anything."

"Almost anything, save letting you break the betrothal."

"Yes." She dampened her lips. "Even if he were to agree, I fear it would mean Dominic's death, for Sir Harlan would have no further reason to let him live.

Captain Fitzgerald knows that if Dominic escapes, the French will have the proof they need to capture and hang any of the surviving crew of the *Republic*.''

''So it seems that your plan to seek out allies remains the best one.'' Lady Sudley suddenly gave a smile as mischievous as her children's. ''Then I suspect I have the very best way for you to achieve that.''

Abigail locked her hands together. ''So you will help us?''

''Yes, gladly.'' She crossed the room and put her hands on Abigail's shoulders. ''The debt we owe Captain St. Clair will not go away simply because he fights for our enemies. Nor can I forget one fact that you have so graciously not mentioned. My household failed to protect you, giving Captain Fitzgerald's men a chance to kidnap you from beneath our very noses. That failure has led you and Captain St. Clair to this predicament, and it must be rectified.''

''Thank you.''

''Do not thank us yet.'' Walking to the door, Lady Sudley stared at the closed one across the hall where her husband was in conference with Sir Harlan. ''If what you are trying fails, I am not sure that we can do anything more to help you.''

''I understand.''

''I am sure you do, but I am equally sure that I hope you never have to face the high cost of failure.''

That, too, Abigail could agree with, for then the nightmares that stalked her while she slept would become reality.

Abigail stepped out of the hired carriage on the twisting street near the Thames. By this time, the Sudleys' carriage with Tessie wearing Abigail's favorite cloak must be most of the way back to Mayfair. Abigail had slipped out of the carriage near the old city gate. How she would return to it so Tessie could stop riding around and around the park she was not quite certain. She hoped that inspiration would come by the time she had completed her errand.

The breeze from the river urged her to hurry. Her nose wrinkled as some disgusting odor surged around her, rising up from the waters. She wondered how Dominic survived in his stench-ridden prison cell.

As she walked along the wooden pier, she glanced at the ships edging the wharves. She must not wander too close to the *Torch*, for if one of her father's crew recognized her, everything would be for naught.

She ignored the men she passed as she hurried toward the tavern she knew was the Brass Fish. Several of the men near the walkway called out, but she pretended not to hear their lecherous suggestions. If they thought she was just another whore, they would soon forget her.

Opening the tavern door, Abigail glanced overhead at the sign, which creaked threateningly. She scurried beneath the fish, whose gold paint was peeling. As her eyes adjusted to the darkness inside, she tried not to choke on the odor of cheap whiskey. Carefully she picked her way around the unwashed tables.

On the far side of the room, the lone man in the tavern looked up, then leaned back on the keg beside him. With his knife, he continued to pare his nails. "Wrong door, darlin'. Get outta here."

"Are you Red?"

"Aye, that I be." He cocked an eyebrow and pushed aside the gray hair which once must have been the same color as hers. "And what be ye wanting, darlin'?"

"A friend of mine asked me to contact you."

"A friend?" He stood with the help of a crutch. As he crossed the shadowed room, she saw that his right leg had been sheared off in the middle of his thigh. His empty breeches leg flapped in tempo with his odd gait.

Swallowing her dismay at the sight, Abigail choked, "My friend needs a message delivered."

"Where and when?"

"Immediately." She hesitated as she added, "To Calais."

His eyes narrowed as he appraised her. "Expensive task your friend has given you."

Abigail was glad she was prepared. As if it were of the least importance, she said, "Money means little at this point. What we are discussing is if you can deliver this message for my friend."

"We can play these games all day," he answered with a sudden grin. "I have my price which ye must pay if ye want the message delivered, Miss Fitzgerald."

"How do you know me?" she gasped.

He lowered himself awkwardly to a stool and pushed one toward her with his dirty crutch. As she sat, he leaned his elbow on the table and withdrew his knife to continue cutting his nails. " 'Tis all about Town that Sir Harlan Morris found himself a lass to marry his witless son."

"I did not guess you were current with the Polite World's *on dits.*"

"*On dits*?" He grinned. "Did St. Clair teach ye that Frenchie talk?"

Abigail stiffened. Red knew about her and Dominic, so he must know she was here on Dominic's behalf. She must pretend that his words had not unsettled her. "He finds the way the English use French very amusing."

"Must say ye seem a bit smarter than I expected Sir Harlan's daughter-in-law to be." Red eyed her with new respect. "Didn't think no smart gal like ye would be marrying that mad lout."

"Sir—"

"Red be my name."

"All right, Red. Here is what I can pay." She pulled

the emerald necklace from her bag and dropped it to the table.

He snatched the necklace before it hit the dirty surface. Raising it so the gems caught the light, he whistled lowly. "These stones be real."

"Yes."

" 'Tis worth St. Clair's ransom."

She chuckled. "Exactly. In exchange for that, can you deliver this?" She set the sealed letter on the table, but kept her fingers on it. "Can you deliver it unopened?"

"Aye, 'tis possible." He scratched the stump of his leg. When he saw her flush at the intimate motion, his grin broadened. "Gal, do ye know what ye be letting yerself in fer with this game?"

"Aye," she answered. He rumbled with laughter at her imitation of his thick accent.

He dropped the knife onto the table, ignoring its clatter and how she flinched, but tightened his grip around the necklace. "All right, gal. Who be the one to get this letter?"

"Unopened."

"Unopened," he agreed. "Who be the one?"

"Ogier Broulier, first mate on *La Chanson de la Mer*."

Nodding with satisfaction, Red stated, "I suspected as much. That will cost ye more, darlin', than even this necklace. I need plenty of money to quiet tongues. I have no interest in hanging next to St. Clair."

"Nor do I. How can I know I can trust you?"

He laughed and rose. Hobbling to the keg, he drew two mugs of rum. He dropped one in front of her. When it splashed on the table, she stood, moving her arm away in distaste. If she came back to Lady Sudley's house smelling of cheap rum, there would be all kinds of questions she could not answer.

In an eye-blurring motion, Red grasped her hand and pinned it to the table. "Ye can trust me to make it easy for ye.'' He picked up the letter and stuffed it back in her bag.

"What? You will not have it delivered?"

"Ye can deliver it yerself."

Abigail wondered if the man had lost his mind along with his leg. "That is impossible. Ogier is not in London."

"But Evan Somerset is."

"Evan Somerset?" She sank to the bench, ignoring the stickiness on it. "You know where he is?"

"I know where ye can find every rat in London." He chuckled and released her arm. "Ye gave me the necklace, so I give ye his address."

"All right. Where is he?" As he began to spout the directions, she asked for something to write with and drew a map on the back of Dominic's letter. "Thank you," she said as she stood.

"Miss Fitzgerald?" Red called as she went toward the door.

"Yes?"

"Don't ye want to know why I am willin' to help ye?"

"I thought you were Dominic's friend."

His laugh brushed the rafters of the empty tavern. "He's a Frenchie. No friend of mine."

"Then why are you helping me?"

"St. Clair and ye have made yerselves Sir Harlan's enemies. That makes ye my allies." Standing, he slapped at where his leg had been. " 'Twas because of his tryin' to save money instead of buildin' a decent ship that I lost m'leg. 'Tis time he learned that he can't use people to line his pockets with more gold. Good luck to ye, Miss Fitzgerald. I hope ye and Cap'n St. Clair tweak the baronet's nose good for him."

"I hope so, too."

Red sat and took another drink. "Now I think ye should be on yer way. Don't need no ladies cluttering up m'place when they ain't doing no business with me."

"Thank you," she said, then reached for the door. She hoped she was one step closer to saving Dominic.

Abigail was amazed to discover that Red's directions led to a small French salon not far from Tottenham Court Road. She looked through one of the large windows, but saw no one within. Mayhap everyone was in the kitchen.

A bell rang as she opened the door. The scents of spices and chicken stock welcomed her. For a moment, she imagined herself in Aunt Velma's kitchen, although the garlic and basil here were much more pungent than in anything Aunt Velma had prepared.

She glanced around and saw another door on the far side of the room. A quartet of tables were topped with pale blue dishes and fresh flowers set in small, clear vases. More dishes were stacked in a corner cupboard beyond the salon's larger window.

The other door opened. A dark-haired woman smiled as she came into the salon, wiping her hands on the apron. She was obviously pregnant. "I am sorry," she said. "We are not open for service this early in the day. If you wish to come back later . . ."

"I am looking for Evan Somerset," Abigail replied, knowing that she might not be able to return if she went back to Lady Sudley's house with her errand not completed.

"He is in the kitchen. One moment." She went to the door and opened it. "Evan, you have a caller." Coming back to Abigail, she motioned toward a table. "Please be seated, miss."

"I should not." She batted at her cloak, which still stank of the tavern beside the Pool. "Your chairs are so lovely, and—" She looked past the woman as a man came through the door.

His hair was light brown, glistening golden where the

sun touched it. Of a height with Dominic, he was not quite as broad in the shoulders, suggesting that this man had not led the rough life Dominic loved on his ship.

"Good afternoon," he said. "I am Evan Somerset. This is my wife, Brienne." He put his arm around the dark-haired woman who regarded him with obvious love.

Abigail tried to smother the envy that raged through her. She wanted to be in Dominic's arms as he gazed at her with the affection in this woman's eyes, which were as dark as his. "My name is Abigail Fitzgerald. You do not know me, Mr. Somerset, but we have a mutual . . ." She hesitated, then said simply, "Friend. Dominic St. Clair."

"Dominic?" Mr. Somerset chuckled. "I was just talking with Brienne about him the other day. About our last trip to France. Remember, Brienne?"

His wife laughed. "How could I forget your outrageous tales of the adventures you shared with Dominic?" She motioned again for Abigail to sit, then dropped gracefully into a chair herself. "Have you heard the story of their escapades in Bordeaux?"

"No." Abigail sat and fought not to tap her fingers on the table. She did not want to talk about the past. She needed to find help for Dominic right now.

"Evan, you should tell her about it."

Abigail jumped to her feet. "No!" When the Somersets stared at her, she took a steadying breath and sat again. "Forgive me."

"What is wrong?" Mr. Somerset asked, his easy smile gone.

"I need your help. Dominic is in terrible trouble."

"What kind of trouble?" His face became serious, his eyes matching the intensity she had seen in Dominic's.

"He is in prison here in England and is about to be put on trial as a spy or as a captain of a ship on the

French blockade or something. He will be hanged. Mr. Somerset—''

''Evan,'' he corrected, then sat beside her at the table. ''Dominic is here in England now? Is he mad?''

''We were shipwrecked when my father's ship's crew blew up the *Republic* and—''

''Whoa!'' He raised his hands. ''Slow down and start at the beginning.'' As she did, he listened intently for a moment, then said, ''Brienne, I think Miss Fitzgerald could use something to drink to steady herself.''

''All set.'' Brienne placed a tray with a pot of tea and cups on the table.

Abigail tried to smile her thanks, but failed. She had not even noticed Brienne leaving the room. Taking the cup Brienne handed her, she continued with the complicated story of how her and Dominic's lives had intersected and then taken such a peculiar series of turns to bring them to where they were now.

''This is for you,'' she finished, drawing the letter out of her bag. She hesitated, then asked, ''Do you read French?''

''What I cannot figure out,'' he said with a taut smile, ''Brienne will help me with. She was born in France.''

Abigail handed him the letter. She tried to sip her tea as he broke the seal and began to read. It was impossible to swallow past her fear, so she set the cup back on the table.

She dared not breathe as Evan began to read aloud, translating from the French.

"My friend, I need your help. The woman who has had this message delivered to you is Abigail Fitzgerald. You must find her, either in London or at Sir Harlan Morris's estate, and get her out of England without delay. She has saved my life more

*than once, mayhap because she knew that by keeping
my heart beating it would long to become hers.''*

Evan chuckled. ''You French are such romantics,
Brienne.''

His wife ruffled his hair and smiled. ''And you love
it, don't you?''

''I cannot disagree with that.'' Bending over the sheet,
he ran his finger along the words and read,

> *''Arrange for her to be returned to her family in
> America, if you can. There she will be safe and
> begin her life anew. I thank you, my friend.''*

Evan put the sheet of paper down on the table.

Abigail gasped, ''There must be more.''

''Only his signature at the bottom.'' He handed her the
letter. ''See for yourself.''

Although she could not decipher the words written in
a bold scrawl, Dominic had been correct when he told
her that enough words were similar to English that she
would be able to pick out some of them. The letter said
nothing of asking Evan to contact his crew to help him
get out of prison.

She looked up when a hand settled on her arm.

Brienne Somerset gave her a sympathetic smile. ''He
clearly loves you very much, Miss Fitzgerald, because
all his thoughts are for you.''

''I will not leave him there in that prison to die.''
Abigail came to her feet again. Her voice rose, too. ''Until
he is free, I shall not leave England. You cannot force
me to do so.''

''Force you?'' The door from the kitchen opened again.
''Who is forcing you to do something against your will?''

Abigail's face grew hot as an elderly woman came into

the room. The woman's French accent was even stronger than Dominic's.

Brienne went to her and said, "*Grand-mère*, this is Abigail Fitzgerald, a friend of Evan's friend Dominic St. Clair."

"Forgive me for acting so out of hand," Abigail said, sitting when the old woman did. "It has not been an easy day. I fear I overreacted to what was so unexpected." She clenched her hands on the table. "If he thinks I shall leave him here to die, he—"

Mme. LeClerc gasped and grabbed Abigail's hand. "Where did you get this?" She ran her finger along Dominic's ring.

"Dominic gave it to me. He thought I could trade it along the docks for help in having his letter delivered to his ship, but I was told to come here and Evan Somerset would help me." She drew her hand away from Mme. LeClerc, unsettled by the fervor in the old woman's eyes.

The elderly woman's face became as gray as her hair. She stared at the ring. "May I see it more closely, Miss Fitzgerald?"

Abigail hesitated, then drew it off and placed it in Mme. LeClerc's trembling hand.

Mme. LeClerc unwound the material and tilted it to look inside. "I do not believe it!"

"Believe what?" Abigail asked, glancing at the Somersets, who seemed as baffled as she was.

"The design on the side." She ran her finger along the bolt of lightning. Looking up at Evan, she asked, "Do you recognize it?"

"The thunderstone design that is on Brienne's vase."

Abigail did not want to waste time on this conversation that seemed to be going nowhere. "Yes, it is a thunderstone. Dominic told me that. Is it a popular design in France for a wedding ring?"

"Not in the least. See here?" Mme. LeClerc pointed

to the etched letters that had been nearly worn away by Dominic's life on the sea. "Can you see the initials?"

"No." Abigail squinted, but still could not see anything along the polished gold.

"I can. My eyes may be old now, but they were much younger when I first saw this ring."

Brienne asked, "In France?"

"At Château Tonnere du Grêlon."

"Château Tonnere du Grêlon?" Abigail gasped. "Dominic said that was his father's home. You were there, too?"

Mme. LeClerc whispered, "I was there when the *duc* brought these rings home from Paris so he might marry his beloved Sophie. See inside? It is engraved *MML & SR*. Marc-Michel Levesque and Sophie Rameau."

"Levesque?" Abigail shook her head. "Impossible. Dominic said this was his father's wedding ring, and his father's name was St. Clair."

"It was Levesque." She turned to her wide-eyed granddaughter. "Do you remember me telling you that you were not the eldest; that you had a brother?"

"Yes." Brienne put her hands on her stomach as if to embrace her unborn baby.

"It seems that he did not die in Paris when the *duc* was beheaded on the guillotine. The little boy's nurse was a St. Clair from the village outside the château, if I recall correctly." She laughed. "Just as your nurse was a LeClerc, *ma petite*. I believe this Dominic is your lost brother, Brienne."

Abigail glanced from one face to another. Mme. LeClerc was still staring at the ring. The Somersets wore identical expressions of shock.

"I'll be damned," Evan said as a smile stole his amazement. "Dominic is a *duc*'s heir? I daresay the residents of Château Tonnere du Grêlon are in for a shock when they meet their new *duc*."

"My brother," Brienne breathed. "My brother is alive."

Abigail hated having to ruin their happiness, but she said, "Dominic shall not be alive much longer if a way is not found to free him from that prison. Once I am married—"

"Married?" Evan asked sharply. "I thought you and Dominic are lovers."

"It is not that simple." She sighed. "Please listen to what else I have to tell you, and then mayhap you can help me find a way to help him soon. If not, he will die."

Chapter Twenty-Two

Abigail rushed into Dominic's cell, then paused, looking back to be certain Pritchard had closed the door behind her and left. He *must* not be privy to what she had to share with Dominic. She slid the panel closed and leaned against the door, glad to be here. Her fears that she would not find a way to sneak away from the house had been for naught. Sir Harlan had returned home and immediately gotten into an argument with Captain Fitzgerald. That had given her the chance to come here.

Dominic swept her into his arms. His lips, eager for love, claimed hers. She clung to him, for just touching him helped her believe the nightmare was over.

When he raised his head, he whispered, "I missed you, *chérie*."

"I missed you, too." She brought his mouth back to hers.

His kiss was swift before he drew back to ask, "Did you talk to Red?"

"Yes."

"And?" he prompted when Abigail added nothing else.

"He sent me to your friend Evan Somerset."

"Evan is in London?"

She smiled. "He told me to tell you that you would not recognize him now that he is a happily married man with a child on the way."

"Married?" Dominic chuckled. "He was right. I cannot imagine him giving up his vagabond ways."

Abigail gripped his fingers more tightly. "Dominic, that is not all. We believe his wife, Brienne, is your sister." She drew off the ring and pressed it into his hand. "The symbol on this ring belongs to the *duc* who held Château Tonnere du Grêlon. Brienne Somerset is his older daughter. There was another sister, who may be alive somewhere in France." She closed his fingers over the ring. "And a son. You, Dominic."

"I have a sister?"

"Two." Putting her hand over his, she said, "Brienne believes that your father gave you to the care of your nurse, as she was given into the care of hers when your father died during the Terror. Your mother fled with your other sister, who was only a baby."

He slowly opened his fingers and stared at the ring. "I never guessed."

"That you had two sisters or that you are the heir of a *duc*." She laughed. "*Duc* Dominic Levesque."

"Levesque?"

"Your father's name. Your name, Dominic, when you claim Château Tonnere du Grêlon."

"It matters not." He handed her back the ring.

"What?" She frowned. This was not the excitement she had anticipated.

He sat her on the edge of the straw-topped bed. "*Chérie*, while you were in London, my long-delayed trial was held." He gave her an ironic smile. "You would have been furious at the quick disposal of my case which will lead to the quick disposal of me.''

''Dominic! Why are you jesting about this?''

''What other choice do I have?''

Abigail closed her eyes as her shoulders sagged beneath the weight that had been lifted so briefly by the glad tidings she was bringing to him. She could not answer his question.

''When?'' she whispered.

''By week's end. I had thought Fitzgerald would have me dragged from the trial to the gallows, but he did not protest the delay.''

She bit her lip to keep from speaking the truth. Dominic's trial must have been the last detail before the wedding that Sir Harlan had mentioned. No wonder he had been so eager to take her to London. Not only could he court the Sudleys' favor, but he kept her away during the trial.

And the reason the hanging was being delayed was just as simple to understand. Sir Harlan knew she would not marry Clive unless he had this threat to hold over her head.

A pulse of hope burst through her. Mayhap Sir Harlan would be willing to bargain with her instead of Captain Fitzgerald. If he would let Dominic go, she would not only marry Clive but help him obtain the Sudleys' investments in his business. She recoiled at the very idea, but as she looked up into Dominic's eyes, she knew she would pay any price to grant this man his life and his freedom upon the sea.

His finger beneath her chin steered her lips to his. Slowly, thoroughly, he kissed her, exploring each slippery surface of her mouth. With a moan, he pulled her into his arms. She gasped as his fingers found the curve of her breast. Pleasure scorched her, burning away all other thoughts.

She grasped his shoulders as the untamable tempest burst forth within her. She answered his hungry desire with her own craving. His legs pressed against hers as his arm tightened around her. When his tongue teased her lips, she combed her fingers through his hair. Each strand clung to her hands, enmeshing her in the bewitchment, as his tongue delved again into her mouth. Its touch sparked against her, setting her aflame with madness.

"My love, my Abigail," he whispered between fevered kisses.

Bringing her to her feet, he turned her so her back was to him. He slowly began to undo the long line of hooks along her back. He bent to place his lips against the warmth of her neck. When she sighed with eager delight, his fingers slipped beneath the loosened gown to stroke her breast.

She gave a soft cry of yearning as he placed a line of fiery kisses on her shoulder. His hands on her waist brought her to face him. As she raised her fingers to sift through his hair again, she jerked away and shrieked, "No!"

Dominic whirled at her cry of terror to see Fitzgerald standing in the doorway to the cell. Pritchard and two other men he did not know stood in the cell. Before he could do more, hands wrenched him away from Abigail. She screamed again as one of the men struck Dominic viciously. He careened backward into the wall. With an expression of surprise, he balanced there a moment before he slid down to the floor.

"Dominic!" The rest of her words were swallowed by her scream as she clawed at the men reaching for her. Ducking beneath their hands, she rushed to him. She took his face in her hands and whispered his name.

"I am all right, *chérie*," he mumbled. Wiping blood from his mouth, he rose. He took her hand and helped her to her feet so they could face Fitzgerald and his men together.

Abigail shivered so hard that he drew her even closer. He stared at the four men. Fitzgerald was obviously in command here. Dominic ignored the others as he met Fitzgerald's triumphant eyes. Fitzgerald's henchmen would not attack without an order from their master.

"Captain Fitzgerald—" Abigail began.

"No!" snarled Dominic. "Do not negotiate with him."

Fitzgerald laughed. "Listen to your lover, Abigail." His laugh echoed through the cell. "Sir Harlan will not be pleased with your whorish ways. I could have told him you would be just like your mother. Yet he is eager to have you marry his son."

"She is not going to marry that idiot!" Dominic exclaimed.

"No?" Fitzgerald's smile grew even more superior. "Ask her if you do not believe me."

Dominic whirled Abigail to look at him. He gripped her face and saw it had no more color than her drooping gown. "Tell me he is lying."

Abigail could not meet Dominic's eyes as she whispered, "I do not want to marry him, but—"

"Fitzgerald, you bastard! You would consign her—"

"No, Dominic!" she cried as he leaped forward, his fingers on Fitzgerald's throat.

The guards swarmed over Dominic, pulling him away from Fitzgerald. As they pressed him up against the wall, Fitzgerald crossed the cell. "You are even more idiotic than I thought, St. Clair."

"The name is Levesque."

"I do not care if it is the Prince Regent." Captain Fitzgerald snickered. "You are a fool to think you could have my daughter."

Abigail could not read the thoughts hidden behind Dominic's blank face, for he did not look at her. He must be hurt that she had not been honest with him, but surely he would understand that she had not wanted him to suffer more.

Captain Fitzgerald continued, "Now that we both know the truth about Abigail's future, I shall take my daughter and leave."

"You will not marry her to that beast!" He pulled away from his captors and started to lunge toward Fitzgerald. He halted when the hammers on four pistols drew back at the same time.

"No!" cried Abigail. "Don't shoot him!"

"Come here," ordered Captain Fitzgerald. "Obey, or I will let you watch as I deny the hangman his prey."

Forcing her feet forward, she shook off Dominic's hand that reached out to stop her. She could not let him die to protect her. As long as he lived, there was a chance he might escape.

Captain Fitzgerald grasped her arm. He smiled and placed his gun back under his coat. The other men kept theirs aimed at Dominic.

"Fitzgerald, don't marry her to Sir Harlan's son," Dominic said quietly. "You will have your vengeance on me. Do not make her suffer more."

"My vengeance on *you?*" Captain Fitzgerald laughed sharply. "You value yourself too highly. That you are dying is just a bonus. Abigail is all I have thought of." He flicked at the lace on her dress. "Her and the ten thousand pounds I will receive when she gives Sir Harlan's son a child."

Dominic shouted a curse as he jumped again toward Fitzgerald. Abigail's scream drowned out Dominic's groan as he fell to the floor beneath the hard butt of Pritchard's gun. He did not move.

Captain Fitzgerald pulled her out of the cell before she could be certain if Dominic lived or not. She clawed at him, but he struck her hard. Her head spun, and she nearly collapsed. He dragged her out of the prison and toward a carriage waiting on the road beyond it.

He shoved her into the carriage. She grasped the straps on the side as it started wildly along the street. Hiding her face in her hands, she tried to stop her head from careening about as crazily.

Her head was tilted up to face Captain Fitzgerald's fury. She tried to push away his hands, but he spat, "You fool!"

"You are the fool! If you think I will cooperate now, you—"

He chortled. "You will, daughter. If you do not do everything as I say, he shall be sent to the gallows post-haste."

Abigail started to retort, then recalled how she wanted to negotiate with Sir Harlan. Captain Fitzgerald could see only the sparkle of gold and his chance to have his final revenge on the woman who loved his brother more.

"I should have guessed this was where you were slinking off to when your maid said you were being fitted for your wedding gown," Captain Fitzgerald growled.

"Tessie believed what I told her." She must not let her sole ally in the house be punished or banished.

"Sir Harlan will not be happy that you have been playing the whore for that pirate." He leaned his arm on the window. "I do believe I shall suggest that, instead of delaying the wedding again because of your lusts, he lock you in your room to keep you chaste."

If she had not been so fearful for Dominic, she would have laughed at this odd conversation. Captain Fitzgerald knew as she did that Sir Harlan did not care what she had done before she became betrothed to his son. All he wanted was to be sure no one questioned that the child she would be forced to conceive was his legitimate grandson.

"I love Dominic," she said simply.

"Be silent!"

Abigail folded her hands in her lap, obeying only because she did not want anything she said or did to cause Dominic to be sent to the gallows more quickly.

The assertive knock on Abigail's bedchamber door identified the caller as Sir Harlan even before Tessie went to open it. Abigail turned on the chair by her dressing table where she had been getting ready for bed to see Sir Harlan waddle into her bedroom.

He carried something in his hands, but she ignored it as he said, "Good evening."

She nodded.

His bulbous face lengthened with a frown. "I hope you will be more gracious when we dine tomorrow evening. The minister is calling to meet you before the wedding."

She nodded.

"Do you have no curiosity when the wedding will be held?"

She simply stared at him. She would not let him use her words as weapons against her. Her attempt this afternoon to get him to listen to reason and free Dominic in exchange for what she could offer had failed utterly, and she had nothing left to say him.

"It shall be at the end of this week."

It took every bit of strength Abigail had not to react. Hearing Tessie's hushed sob, a sound that was quickly masked when Sir Harlan scowled at the maid, Abigail picked up her brush and continued to work on her hair as if nothing else concerned her.

"I want you to wear these tomorrow evening," ordered Sir Harlan as he dropped a jewelry box on the table.

Abigail again stiffened her shoulders so she would not flinch. She recognized the box, for she had taken it from the safe herself. Not daring to look at Tessie, she picked up the box. She kept her fingers from shaking as she raised the lid. "Oh, how lovely! But, Sir Harlan, I—"

"No arguments! You will wear the necklace and earrings."

"Necklace?" she asked, hoping her astonishment sounded unfeigned. "What necklace?"

He ripped the box from her hand and stared at the earbobs next to the indentation where the emerald necklace should have been. Slowly he closed the lid and placed it on the dressing table. "Tessie, leave us."

"Sir Harlan, it is late. I must help Miss—"

"Leave us, I said."

The very serenity of his words frightened Abigail, who added, "I will call you when I need you, Tessie. Thank you."

"Yes, Miss Abigail." She dropped to a quick curtsy that Sir Harlan expected from the servants, then left the room.

Knowing Tessie would not go far but was helpless to assist, Abigail rose. "Why do you want to speak to me alone?"

He stuck his nose close to hers. "Where is it?"

"It? If you mean the necklace, I have no idea." That was the truth. Although she was sure Red had sold the stones immediately, she did not know where they were now.

He shoved her back onto the chair. "You are the only other person who knows where I kept the key to the jewelry case."

"Someone else must possess that knowledge. Mayhap someone else in your family?"

"Are you suggesting Clive?" He laughed icily.

"Clive is not as witless as you pretend he is. If you would—"

"Be silent! We are not talking about your betrothed. We are talking about this necklace. Where is it?"

"I told you. I don't know."

"Did you take it?"

Abigail laughed as sharply as he had. "Why would *I* ake what would be mine when I marry Clive?"

He put his hand on her shoulder. Slowly his fingers drilled into her until she winced. "Mayhap you had some need for the money you could get for it. Captain Fitzgerald et me know that you have been visiting St. Clair in his prison."

"Dominic's name is Dominic Levesque." She wanted to add that Dominic could claim the title of *duc*, but Tessie had warned her that Sir Harlan would be furious to learn Dominic possessed a higher rank than he did.

"St. Clair or Levesque—I do not care what his name s. I want to know why you stole the necklace. Did you ry to bribe the guards to get him out of prison?"

"No."

"You didn't?" His malicious laugh filled the room. "Are you certain?"

"I am not lying."

"We shall have to see about that."

Abigail frowned as he went to the door. Sir Harlan ordered her not to move, but she slowly stood. His glare warned her to disobey no more of his commands.

Hearing his shout along the corridor, she cried, "No! Tessie knows nothing of any of this."

She watched in horror as Fuller herded Tessie into the room. She had not guessed the burly guard did more than keep Clive out of sight. When she saw what he carried n his hand, she moaned in horror. He handed the cudgel o Sir Harlan, who stroked it.

"Tell me when you wish to speak the truth, my dear," he baronet said. "If you do so quickly, you will save your maid a great deal of pain."

Before she could answer, he motioned to Fuller, who shoved Tessie to the floor. Sir Harlan raised the cudgel.

"All right!" Abigail cried.

"No, Miss Abigail!" shouted Tessie.

Sir Harlan asked quietly, "All right what, my dear?"

"I did take the necklace! Don't hurt her!" She lowered her eyes away from his triumphant smile. "I told you the truth. Let Tessie go."

He waved to Fuller to let Tessie stand.

The guard grumbled, unhappy that he had been denied the chance to beat Tessie into submission. When Tessie tried to rush to Abigail, he shoved her out of the room.

"Don't let him hurt her," Abigail whispered.

Sir Harlan tossed the stick onto the bed. "He will not, if you do as you should. Where is the necklace?"

"I don't know." She added quickly when he reached for the door to call Tessie back, "Honestly, Sir Harlan, I don't know where it is. I . . . I gave it away."

"You *gave away* a necklace worth hundreds of pounds?" he choked. His face became a choleric red as he ranted about her stupidity which made her no better than his witless son. When she did not react, he stopped his pacing and asked, "And whom did you give it to?"

"A man who did me a favor."

"Which was?"

"Delivering a message."

He growled, "It must have been a very important message."

"It was."

"Damn you!" he shouted. "I gave that necklace to my wife the day we were wed. You were to wear it when you marry Clive. Instead you used it to carry tales for a French pirate." Suddenly his rage became laughter. Patting her shoulder, he picked up the box. "In the long run, it matters little. Your attempt failed. By this time tomorrow, your gallant lover will be raven's meat on the gallows."

"Tomorrow?" She sat on the chair. "Tomorrow? I thought—that is, I was sure that—"

"That I would let your pirate live until you married Clive?" He smiled. "That had been my plan, my dear, until you were so stupid as to let me give you another to bring you to heel."

"Tessie," she whispered. Looking up at him, she knew she had underestimated his determination to get his son a bride. "You put her here as my maid, knowing she would help me because of her sister's death."

"Exactly."

The sound of his laughter remained when he walked out of the room. It taunted her with knowing that all she had done had been for naught. Now Dominic would die because he had tried to save her, and she was not sure how to halt the execution.

She put her head down on the dressing table and wept.

are son, and that someone to whom it would wou...

Chapter Twenty-Three

Dominic leaned his arm against the wall by the slit that let in the moonlight. He had been standing here since the sun vanished beyond the hills. The blood on his face had dried to a crust that tore each time he spoke. His last words had been fired at Pritchard when his supper had been brought and he had refused it with a curse.

The only reason he was still here instead of in the hellish pens below was the view out of this slit. He knew that Fitzgerald wanted Dominic to spend his final night alive staring at the house where Abigail would be forced into Sir Harlan's son's bed by week's end.

Pritchard had been glad to share every disgusting detail with him. Dominic had heard the rumors during his short time in London about the witless son of the pompous man who was hated by the French for betraying them as Fitzgerald had betrayed the Americans. He should have guessed that Sir Harlan would pay highly for a bride for his son, and that someone like Fitzgerald would be eager to obtain that money no matter the pain it caused.

His fingers curled into a fist. Curse Fitzgerald! Why hadn't he cut the cur's throat when he had the chance? If he had slain Fitzgerald when the *Republic* was captured, Abigail would not be facing this horror now.

Nor would she have ever forgiven Dominic for executing a man she then had believed was her father, a man who wanted to give her the chance she never had to know him. Now Abigail had learned the truth along with its cost.

There must be someone who would put a stop to this wedding. Evan Somerset! If he could contact his old partner, mayhap Evan would come to her rescue.

With a sigh, Dominic continued to stare at the house that was brightly lit against the night sky. He had no way to contact Evan. His father's ring would be more than enough to pay for the message to be carried to London, but he did not trust Pritchard.

A key rattled in the door, but Dominic did not turn. When it opened, he said, "Take the food away. I am not hungry."

"I guess there is a first time for everything."

Dominic spun at the laughter in the voice from his past. He grasped Evan by the shoulders, then pushed past him and closed the door.

"Don't worry about anyone discovering I am here, *mon ami*," Evan said with another chuckle. He held up a ring of keys.

"How did you get those?" Dominic walked back to his friend. "If I recall correctly, your skills as a pickpocket are much lacking."

"But my wife's skills as a cook are not."

Dominic frowned, puzzled. "Do you want to explain that? I thought your wife was the daughter of a *duc*."

"Brienne's life has been as unlike the child of a *duc*

as yours has been. She grew up working in the kitchen of the LeClercs' salon in London.'' He patted his stomach. ''I can assure you she is an excellent cook. She made some of her delicious chicken soup for the guards in this prison. She added a bit of something extra to it before I delivered it to the kitchen. Nothing too dangerous. Just a healthy serving of opium.''

''I think you made a wise choice in a wife, my friend.''

''She is very anxious to meet you.'' Evan arched a golden brow. ''Who would have guessed I would end up as your brother-in-law?''

''Not I.'' Looking down at the ring he wore when he saw Evan staring at it, he added, ''It seems as if there is much to be said between all of us. Can we talk about old times on our way out of here?''

Evan nodded, abruptly serious. ''I have sent word to *La Chanson* that I planned to come here tonight, and your ship should be offshore to pick you up around midnight. Apparently, your first mate has been loitering near the English coast waiting for your message. I suspect the news of how the *Republic* met her end has been shared in every seamen's haven.''

''You should know that I will not leave England without Abigail.''

''You may need to.'' He reached under his dark coat and drew out a piece of paper. ''This is the message your friend Red delivered to me at my wife's salon just before I left this morning.''

''Red? I thought he sent Abigail to you.'' Dominic frowned. ''Why would he do more than that?''

''It seems, from what little he was willing to tell me, that she was generous in her payment to him, so he felt obligated to contact Ogier on *La Chanson*.''

Dominic banked his curiosity about what Abigail had given the tavernkeeper to bring out this unexpected generosity. He ripped open the page and scanned the short message. "*Merde!*" Crumbling it into a ball, he threw it at the far wall. It bounced back at him like a taunt.

"What is it?" Evan asked.

"*La Chanson* is needed to be part of a raid on an English convoy of ships that is about to set sail from Plymouth. I am ordered to return to my ship and resume command as soon as I receive these orders. No excuse for any delay, for this may be the most important sea encounter since the horrible losses the French fleet suffered at Trafalgar."

"Dominic, if we steal her out of the house—"

"No delay, it reads. How can I disobey orders I have vowed to follow?" He swore again, even more viciously. "But if I do not free her from that house, Abigail will be forced to wed a monster."

"If you want, I can—"

Dominic held up his hands. "No, my friend. I cannot let you risk yourself. You are now a married man with a wife and a child about to be born. This is my battle alone." His smile became sad. "I do not wish my legacy to my sister to be that she is made a widow because of me."

"I was not planning on dying." Evan's grin reminded Dominic of other times when they had been in harrowing situations. But then, he had thought only of himself and of his ship. Then, his heart had not been pleading with him to forget everything but the woman within it, although he knew without hesitation that Abigail would have urged him to go and do his duty.

He went back to the window and looked up at the house. Mayhap he had done too good a job of persuading her that he cared most for his life upon the sea. She had come to believe what he no longer did. Now he knew that even the salt air would be flavorless if she were not there beside him to breathe it.

"Let's get out of here." He pounded his fist against

the wall, then pushed himself away from it. "While we are doing that, mayhap I will have some inspiration that will allow me to follow orders and save Abigail, too."

Evan put his hand on Dominic's arm. "You know that is impossible."

"*Oui*, but I must hope." Walking to the door, he opened it. Then he looked down at his legs and cursed. He had become so accustomed to the rattle of his chains that he had forgotten the manacles. "These will alert every man to my passage."

Holding up a ring of keys, his friend laughed. "Do you have any idea which among the guard's keys goes with those manacles?"

Dominic snatched Pritchard's ring and flipped through the keys. "Here it is." He smiled and held up a long one. He could not forget it, for he had promised himself when the manacles were placed about his ankles that he would find a way to escape. His smile fell into a frown. That pledge he had kept, as he must keep the one to serve France. How easy it had been to make that promise when he had not guessed the cost it would demand of him.

He twisted the key in one manacle, then the other. Picking them up, he tossed them into the hay. "Where is Pritchard sleeping?"

"Just outside your door."

"That is convenient for us."

"Very." Evan rubbed his hands together in anticipation.

Hoping his friend would be as enthusiastic at the end of this night's escapade as he was at the beginning, Dominic peered out the door. He saw Pritchard curled up by the wall. Motioning with his head, he had Evan grab the guard's arms as Dominic lifted the man by his legs. They quickly deposited Pritchard in the cell. Few things had ever been as satisfying for Dominic as locking the door, leaving Pritchard a prisoner in his own prison.

They had not gone more than a few steps when Dominic pressed his friend back into the shadows. Two guards stood only a few feet away, talking. They must not have gone in to have dinner yet.

"We need a diversion," Evan hissed.

"I know just the one." Gesturing for his friend to follow, Dominic hurried in the other direction and down the stairs that led into the pits. He had come this way only once, but each step of the journey from the pits to the cell above was engraved in his memory.

He heard Evan's muttered curses as the stench swelled up around them. Coughing, he wondered how he had survived down here as long as he had. He wiped his watering eyes and found the key to open the door to the women's cell as Evan ordered everyone to silence so the guards would not be alerted. Throwing open the door, he stepped back, then turned to the door on the other side. He unlocked it and jumped back as the men surged out.

Shouts sounded from behind them. Dominic tossed the keys into the mire on the cell floor and motioned for Evan to follow him.

"What are you going to do now?" Evan asked as they burst out into the prison yard. Fires leaped in one corner. The other prisoners were racing toward the prison gate, which was swinging shut. Guns fired, but no one slowed.

"What I must," said Dominic.

"That did not answer my question. I—" His voice rose into a shriek of pain as the guns fired a second time.

Dominic ran back to where his friend was sprawled on the ground, unconscious. He bent to lift Evan over his shoulder. Something struck him on the back of the head, and he collapsed, senseless, on top of his friend.

Chapter Twenty-Four

The clouds roiled as if in pain. Heat pressed down a[s] if trying to destroy the earth, but no rain fell. Not eve[n] the distant rumble of thunder promised a letup from th[e] discomfort.

Abigail turned her back on the glass which reflecte[d] the bride dressed in her elegant gown. She wished sh[e] could shred the dress and put an end to this. Going ou[t] onto the balcony, she looked at the prison in the valle[y] below.

It was quiet now. It had not been quiet the night befor[e] Dominic was to be executed. She had been lying in he[r] bed, not able to sleep, when the guns had fired, and sh[e] had jumped out of bed. Her first hope that Dominic ha[d] found a way to rescue her vanished when she saw th[e] flames rising from the prison and the screams of thos[e] within its walls. Tessie had brought her the news of a[n] attempted escape that had been foiled.

She guessed that Dominic must be involved somehow, but she could not get more information. Sir Harlan refused to let even a whisper about it be repeated in his house. Sending Tessie into the village was impossible, because the maid was now as much a prisoner within these walls as Abigail was. Dominic must still be alive, or Sir Harlan would have wasted no time in telling her every grim detail of his death.

A pang cut through her with the speed of her breaking heart. Within a few hours, it would no longer matter. She would be the wife of Clive Morris. Then, before the night was over, she would be forced to welcome him into her bed. She feared what would happen, for she was certain Fuller would have put Clive in the foulest possible mood.

"It is time, Miss Abigail."

As she heard Tessie's sad voice, Abigail came back into the room. She closed the shutters on the doors. The darkness matched the shadows in her soul. Staring at the thin stripes of light against the wall, she thought of the bars on Dominic's window in the prison. That hers were not made of iron did not make any difference.

Tessie put her hands on Abigail's shoulders. "Miss Abigail, is there anything I can do to stop this?"

"If you do, you will be killed. Sir Harlan has made that very clear."

"If you wish—"

"No, Tessie. Do not say that. I will need you after the ceremony more than ever."

"He may not let me stay here."

"I know." She closed her eyes in resignation.

When a knock sounded on the door, Abigail went to answer it herself. Captain Fitzgerald stood on the other side. Although he was dressed in the elegant clothes he had worn during their first call on Sir Harlan, he wove drunkenly on his feet when he stepped forward to offer her his arm. She did not need to smell his thick breath

to know that he had started celebrating his good fortun
already.

"You look lovely, Abigail." He laughed and plucke
at the sleeve of her pale pink gown. "The same colo
your mother wore the day we were wed."

"Mayhap because she expected the same grief that
do from my wedding. Do you think so?"

He flushed with fury at her question. "Watch you
tongue, girl."

"No, *you* watch your back. If you think you are goin
to be less of a target because Dominic Levesque is nc
commanding *La Chanson*, you are a fool. His crew wil
be looking for you in whatever ship you sail." She smile
and raised her chin. "I suspect the *Torch* is doomed t
live up to her name when *La Chanson* finds her at sea
Although you did not have a chance to see the *Republi*
meet her end, I am sure Dominic's crew will offer
repetition for you when they sink you and your ship."

Silence fell on the room like a wool cloak as Captai
Fitzgerald's face became a ghostly shade. He could nc
deny her words, because she was correct. *La Chanso*
wanted revenge against Arthur Fitzgerald, and they woul
not rest until they had it.

Grumbling something, Captain Fitzgerald gave Abiga
no chance to add anything else as he grabbed her arr
and forced her to walk with him toward the stairs. H
almost stumbled more than once, but her hope that h
would pass out so she could flee was futile.

None of the servants stood in the foyer. Boothe mus
be busy in the garden, greeting the few guests invited t
the wedding.

When they walked through the parlor door where Abi
gail had taken Clive into the gardens, Sir Harlan bustle
forward. He was carrying a bottle of wine and staggere
even more than Captain Fitzgerald did. He shoved a smal
bouquet of flowers into her hands. "Your daughter make

a beautiful bride, Fitzgerald. Any man would be happy to bed her." He put his arm around her shoulders and leered at her. "Even Clive will find it hard to resist such a prettily wrapped package."

Abigail edged away from him.

"Where do you want her?" Captain Fitzgerald asked.

"By the roses. The ceremony will take place there." Sir Harlan glanced toward the house. "Where are Fuller and Greene? They should have been here by now."

"Mayhap it is for the best. If he sees her too soon, he may not wish to wait for the ceremony to be completed."

"I arranged with the minister for the shortest possible one."

Captain Fitzgerald chuckled drunkenly. " 'Tis always an advantage to have the man's living in your pocket."

"Always an advantage." Sir Harlan looked across the garden. "This must be done quickly. I want it over before anyone beyond the house knows it has started."

"Go and see what is keeping them."

Sir Harlan took a step toward the house, then shuddered with disgust and called for a footman.

Abigail wrapped her arms around herself. It was clear from Sir Harlan's hesitation as well as his words that Clive would be in a truly beastly mood. That had been arranged, so there would be no chance of his heeding anything she might say.

She listened to Sir Harlan and Captain Fitzgerald debate all the details as if she were as witless as Clive. For once, she did not interrupt them. Every minute they argued was another in which she had to hope something would halt this wedding.

"Oh, no!" she whispered when she heard the unmistakable rumble of thunder far off in the distance.

Abigail yanked her arm out of Captain Fitzgerald's grip and turned to flee into the house. She must be inside, far from the rage of the thunder and lightning.

"Where do you think you are going?" demanded Sir Harlan, seizing her arm.

"The storm . . . I cannot stay."

Captain Fitzgerald laughed. "Just like her mother. Afraid of a thunderstorm." His gaze drilled her. "She might not have fallen to her death if she had not panicked at the storm that night."

"That night," she whispered. Memory opened, spilling out the truth she had tried to hide for most of her life. She had been a baby, but she could remember Aunt Velma's heart-rending shrieks as thunder boomed overhead. Her screams had risen to hysteria with each flash of lightning that cut through the darkness.

A strange calm flowed over Abigail as she met Captain Fitzgerald's eyes. She had not been foolish to fear the storms. She had had a reason to be frightened, for she had lost her beloved mother in the midst of a storm.

"You might want to learn to fear the lightning, Captain Fitzgerald. *La Chanson* would enjoy watching you sink as the light bounced off the waves."

He snarled a curse at her, but added nothing else as several people, including the minister, entered the garden.

Sir Harlan tugged on her arm. Abigail pulled away. He caught her by the shoulder, his fingers digging into her skin. When she moaned, he drew her veil over her face. Did he want to keep up the fallacy of tradition, or did he fear that someone would see her despair and come to her rescue?

She walked by his side, but refused to let him touch her again. Gazing at the four guests, who were all male, she guessed they were Sir Harlan's business acquaintances. She was sure they did not want their women here when Clive Morris was released from his captivity.

Abigail stiffened when she heard bets being placed among the guests. Would she even survive the ceremony? The bets were heavy that she would, but not the night.

Sir Harlan growled something at the men, but they just laughed. No one mentioned the oddity of a wedding in which the bride waited at the altar and the bridegroom was brought to her.

As soon as she stood by the minister, who refused to meet her eyes, Sir Harlan signaled for the groom. She did not watch as she scanned the garden from the rose arbor where she stood. The arbor was set to one side of the garden, but was too far from the wall. She could not run away before she would be caught and returned to the wedding.

She noted the odd glitter in Clive's eyes as he was led from another doorway. Fuller had not forgotten his promise to prepare the groom for what followed the vows he would not understand. She fought her instinct to cringe away as Clive halted next to her. Someone lifted her hand and placed it in his.

"Pretty Abig?" he whispered.

She stared at him. He remembered her. Who had told him to be quiet? Or did he realize the import of this ceremony? She was not sure what he knew and what he did not.

When she looked at him through the mesh of her veil, he gave her his lopsided grin. Someone had brushed his hair and trimmed his long beard. For a moment, a swell of hope teased her. Then she knew it was useless. Fuller would convince Clive to rape her.

"Good day, Clive," she answered. She did not know what he had been told, so she dared not say anything else.

The minister cleared his throat as Sir Harlan flashed him an impatient look. He began the service in a near whisper. The thunder came closer as lightning sliced open the clouds.

Abigail did not listen to the words as Clive's fingers moved along her arm. He tugged on her hand as he had when they had walked in the garden. Planting her feet, she feared what would happen if the groom dragged his bride away in the middle of the ceremony.

"Do you, Miss Abigail Fitzgerald . . ." The minister's voice became an odd choking sound as he looked past her. His face was as gray as the clouds thickening overhead.

Abigail whirled to see a half-dozen men edging into the garden. They wore masks over their faces, and each one held a cocked pistol in his hand. Not one spoke. The leader, who was dressed in tattered breeches and a simple linen shirt, held out a bag to one of the guests. He needed no words as he gestured with his gun.

Slowly the guest removed his rings and placed them in the bag. The thief leaned forward, saying something too low for Abigail to hear. The guest heard it and flinched. The thief pressed the gun to the man's skull. The guest replied, but his words were no more than a whisper.

Abigail watched in silence as the man approached Sir Harlan. When she saw blond hair falling from beneath the mask, she knew her hopes had again been in vain. Dominic had not come to save her. This was just a group of blackguards who had seen the wedding as an opportunity to profit.

Fingers grabbed her arm. She tried to shake them off. She could not let Clive sense her fear, for it might make him berserk and then the gunmen might fire.

The hand on Abigail's arm refused to be ignored. She glanced backward to see another of the masked men. She drew in a breath to scream, then stared at the slow wink behind the mask. She almost spoke Dominic's name aloud. How had he gotten out of the prison, when Sir Harlan had been told that all the prisoners had been recaptured?

When he tugged on her hand, she understood what he wanted. With the guests' attention on the thieves, no one would notice the bride fleeing.

Only Clive would.

Leaning toward Clive, she turned him to face her. She pushed her flowers into his hands. "Pretty," she whispered. "Pretty. For Clive."

Like a child, Clive beamed with happiness. He glanced from the flowers to her. "Pretty? For Clive?"

"For Clive. I told you I would get you pretties. Clive stay here. Abig get more pretties."

"Abig. Pretty," he repeated. His big hands stroked the flowers with the gentleness she had seen on their previous visit to these gardens.

Sympathy filled her. When Dominic pulled on her, she knew she had no time for anything but to escape. She would not be given a second chance. The wedding and the consummation would be held immediately under Sir Harlan's observation.

Dominic drew her behind the rose arbor. When he tugged her toward the house, she shook her head. She took his hand and led him through the flower gardens she had explored with Clive. They wrapped around the back of the house and toward the rear wall. If the gate in it was locked, she was sure they could find a way to climb over the wall.

Thunder rang overhead quickly after a flash of lightning.

"That was close," he whispered.

"Too close."

"Will you be all right?"

She nodded. "I am not going to cower here so they can catch us again. And I don't plan on letting the lightning sear me before I find out how you got out of prison."

" 'Tis a good tale." With a chuckle, he pulled her into the shadows creeping from beneath a tree as the storm loomed over them.

Dominic pushed her behind him as they approached a gate. Suddenly he pressed her against the wall and raised his gun. Holding her breath, she watched the moving bush. When he cursed and chuckled, she relaxed as a small bird popped out of the flowers and peered at them with curiosity.

"Scared?" she teased.

"You would think so, wouldn't you?" He pulled on her hand as he reached for the latch on the gate.

It opened, and Abigail hurried through. When he stood beside her, she said, "And I thought I would never see you frightened, Captain St. Clair . . . I mean Levesque."

"That is because I never have had so much to lose as now. I do not intend to lose you again." Taking her hand, he motioned with his head toward the valley. "Let's go, *chérie*. We are not safe yet. I am not sure how long Ogier and the others can keep your wedding guests entertained."

"Ogier? Ogier Broulier? Evan was able to get a message to him?"

"That, *chérie*, is also a tale I cannot wait to tell you."

She flung off her long veil as they ran along the path leading down into Morristown. "Where is *La Chanson?*"

"Not far. There is a river beyond the village that leads quickly to sea. We have a jolly boat waiting there to take us out to the ship."

"You are an incorrigible pirate!"

"You suspected otherwise?" He whirled her into his arms. "I stole my enemy's ship and your heart. I bested England by denying them a victim at their gallows." His eyes raked her with the heat of his desire. "*Ventre bleu*, my love, you are the prettiest bride I have ever seen!"

When he kissed her, her fingers rose to the back of his neck where his kerchief still was tied. The yearning that she thought would never be satisfied again ached through her.

"Come," he added softly. His black eyes glistened like the polished facets on a nugget of coal. "Let's get back to *La Chanson*. I want to consummate our wedding."

"We are not married."

"Save this dress, *chérie*. I want to see you in it when we stand before a priest in Calais." He grinned as he drew her along the rugged path. "But now, I want to see you out of it."

"You *are* incorrigible!"

"And you love it!"

She put her arm around his waist as they hurried along the path. "I love you, *mon cher*."

With a chuckle at her atrocious accent, Dominic increased their pace. She understood and tried to keep up, for someone soon would notice that the bride had vanished. Dominic whispered that the crew from *La Chanson* had orders to flee the wedding at that point, leaving their booty to confuse Sir Harlan's guests.

Abigail's soft slippers slid as she ran on the stones. When her breath sounded loud in her ears, she hoped they were nearing the village. She always had ridden in a carriage into Morristown, so she could not judge how far it was on foot.

"Halt!"

Abigail cried, "It is Captain Fitzgerald." She looked back and bumped into Dominic.

He caught her and pushed her behind him. She realized Captain Fitzgerald somehow had managed to get ahead of them on the road. He must have noticed them leaving and taken a more direct route.

Dominic raised his gun. "I do not want to kill you in front of her, Fitzgerald," he said quietly, "but I will, if you do not get out of our way."

Captain Fitzgerald gestured with his own pistol. "Release her or I shall put a bullet through her."

"And risk losing your five thousand pounds?"

"If I cannot have the money, she is useless." He waved the gun. "Release her or I shall put a ball through you, and then one through her."

"No!" Abigail cried as Dominic shifted. "Don't sur-

render to him! Don't send me back to ..." Her words
faded as she saw a shadow lurching toward them.
"Clive," she whispered. He must have followed, wanting
the pretties she had promised him.

When she heard Captain Fitzgerald repeat his orders,
she realized both he and Dominic were so intent on each
other that they had not noticed Clive coming toward them
like an oversized puppy.

Captain Fitzgerald aimed his gun at Dominic. Abigail
screamed, but its sound was swallowed by a crash of
thunder and Clive's roar. He raised his hands and ran at
Captain Fitzgerald.

"No, Clive!" she shouted, but it was too late.

Captain Fitzgerald whirled and raised his gun. It fired,
drowning out the thunder.

Her shout became a moan of sorrow as she ran to where
Clive fell to the ground. He gave a soft whimper, and
she could not tell if he spoke her name or simply "pretty."

Dominic pulled on her hand. "Come on, before Fitzgerald can reload."

"But Clive—"

"He is dead, *chérie.*"

Realizing he was right, she could not see through the
tears blinding her. She stumbled along the path with him,
but they had gone only a few steps when she heard Sir
Harlan screech some wordless threat. A second shot
resounded through the afternoon.

"Damn! They all are insane!" muttered Dominic
through clenched teeth. Lightning struck a hilltop on the
far side of the village. "Let's go. If he got Fitzgerald
with that shot, Morris will want you next."

A ball whirred past Abigail's ear. She gathered up her
dress and ran. Was it only Sir Harlan after them or all
the guests?

Only when small pebbles beneath her feet threatened
to trip her did she realize they had reached the stream.

She gasped as Dominic scooped her up and placed her in a waiting boat that had been hidden in the shadows of the trees. He bent to push it into the river. The sharp retort of a gun sounded.

Dominic dropped to one knee. Abigail screamed as blood flowed from his shoulder. Putting his fingers over the hole, he glanced back toward the man approaching them. Sir Harlan grinned victoriously as he aimed a second handgun directly at Dominic.

"That is how I like seeing a French pirate. Groveling," he chortled with evil mirth. "Beg for your life before I end it."

"I will not!" Dominic snapped, but his voice was weak.

Abigail started to speak, but something was shoved into her hands. Dominic's pistol! He could not rise to fire it, but she was facing Sir Harlan. She could kill him.

No, she wanted to scream. She had never killed anyone. She had not been able to slay Dominic when she discovered him wounded. If she had not been able to smash his head with a rock when she had hated him so deeply, she feared she could not fire the pistol, even though she despised Sir Harlan more than she ever had Dominic.

"Try," Dominic whispered beneath Sir Harlan's continued ranting.

His single word strengthened her as nothing else had. Slowly she rose to her knees. Aiming at the center of the round man's chest, she called, "Put down your gun, Sir Harlan, or I will kill you!"

"You?" He laughed and lowered his weapon. "Go ahead. Shoot, Abigail. Then I will end your miserable lover's existence." His voice became darker as he growled, "Then I shall show you how I punish the woman who murdered my son."

"I did not kill Clive!"

Dominic muttered through clenched teeth, "Aim low."

Repositioning the gun, she drew back the hammer. Her

fingers shook. She tried to fire it, but her fingers refused to obey.

Sir Harlan laughed again as rain struck them. "All done? Good. Then I shall show you how it is done. Say farewell to your lover." He raised his gun again.

"No!" she cried. The gun in her hand leaped as it fired. The boat rocked as Dominic fell into it and shoved it into the stream. His hand pulled her down as a barrage of shots followed hers. Cowering in the wet bottom, she clung to Dominic's arm. She sought his pulse and counted each heartbeat which showed her that he still lived.

The boat hit a rock and stopped. "No!" she cried. She reached for an oar.

A hand halted her. She shrieked.

"Let me help you, mademoiselle."

At the heavy French accent, Abigail looked up to see a blond man. The leader of the thieves!

"Ogier? Ogier Broulier?" she whispered.

He nodded as he bent to check his wounded captain.

Dominic grinned at her as he waved his first mate aside. "I am alive, and I want to stay that way. Let's get the hell out of here. *La Chanson* waits for us."

Dominic's words brought soft cheers from the men who stepped out from among the trees. Quickly they scrambled into the small boat.

"Where is Evan?" demanded Dominic.

"Evan?" Abigail asked. "Evan Somerset?"

"There!" Ogier pointed to a man racing through the trees, pulling a woman as fast as she could run.

"Tessie!" cried Abigail. She turned to Evan, who was helping Tessie into the boat. "Thank you, Dominic."

"Did you think I would forget your friend and mine?" he teased with all the charm which had won her heart. "Are you coming with us, Evan?"

Evan shook his head. "That life is yours, *mon ami*. My life is in London in a tiny salon with a woman who loves me as much as Miss Fitzgerald loves you. Although I cannot guess why any woman as clearly intelligent as Miss Fitzgerald would give her heart to an old sea-crab like you."

"Odd," Dominic said with a laugh, extending his hand to shake Evan's. "I was wondering much the same about my sister. I shall have to set her to rights as soon as possible."

"Yes." Evan's face became serious. "Come to see Brienne as soon as you can get to London safely, Dominic. She wishes to meet you."

"Even though I left you with a hole in your leg from our escape out of Sir Harlan Morris's prison?"

Abigail noticed the bandage around Evan's leg for the first time. "Can you get back to London, Evan?"

"I still have a few tricks." He laughed and kissed her cheek. "Brienne hopes you will pay us another call again soon, too, Miss Fitzgerald."

"Abigail."

"Abigail," he repeated and stepped back as the men shoved the boat off the rock and out into the deeper waters of the stream. "Soon!" he called before disappearing among the trees.

"I think you do have quite a tale to tell me," Abigail said as the men began to row the boat quickly toward the sea. She pulled up the hem of her skirt enough to rip a strip from her petticoat. As she wrapped it around Dominic's wounded shoulder, she smiled. "I am better prepared this time."

"I hope this is the last time I need your nursing, *chérie*," he murmured. He winced as she shifted his shoulder while winding the material behind him. "You are going to stay with me, aren't you?"

Glancing at the men rowing the boat, she saw they all were smiling. Her life with Dominic always would be a public one as they shared close quarters with his crew. As if no one but she and Dominic were in the small boat, she bent forward and kissed him.

"Of course, *mon cher* pirate."

Epilogue

Abigail held her face up to the sea breeze. She had forgotten how exciting the tang of salt could be when it spiced each breath. Beneath her feet, the deck danced with the music of the waves.

La Chanson de la Mer.

The sea's song . . . At last she understood why Dominic had named his ship that. The ship seemed to be a part of the melody, never ending, ever changing.

"I thought I would find you here."

She smiled up at Dominic. "At last I understand why you missed this ship so much. It is like flying to stand here by the rail and taste the wind."

He sat on a crate and drew her down beside him. "I feared that I would go mad in that prison when I did not think I would be able to return here."

"But you did."

"*Oui.*"

"And it is a tale worth telling?"

He chuckled. "At the time, it seemed as if it would be a tale with a tragic ending. When Evan was shot in the leg, I went back to get him. I did not see a guard coming up behind me. He must have struck me on the back of the head with a gun. Both of us were senseless, and no one disturbed us while the guards who had not been incapacitated by Brienne's opium-laced soup were trying to recapture all the prisoners we had released."

"You never do anything simply, Dominic."

"Never. By the time I regained my senses, most of the courtyard was on fire. I dragged Evan out of there, and we hid in the woods until we could sneak to the river and find our way to *La Chanson.*"

Abigail hesitated, then said, "I have heard you disobeyed orders from your government to come back and get me."

"*Oui.*"

"But won't you be in trouble for that?" She put her hand over his heart. "I did not hope for you to escape the gallows in England just so you could hang in France."

Standing, he went to lean on the rail. "*Chérie*, I could not leave you there to marry another man."

She went to him. "But—"

"I also know that *La Chanson* is the swiftest ship on the seven seas. We will reach the rendezvous point with time to spare." He laughed. "As well, I know that the ships did not sail out of Plymouth as was planned."

"How do you know?"

"Haven't you learned that I know every man in England who will trade some information for gold . . . or his life?"

She frowned for a moment, then laughed. "Was that what Ogier was talking to Sir Harlan's guest about?"

"That guest was one of the premier shippers in England, a thief in his own right just as Sir Harlan was. It is a shame that he decided not to be a part of the trap to be sprung on the French.''

"So you will be a hero instead of being punished for disobeying orders.''

Dominic chuckled. "You sound almost disappointed, *chérie*. I hope you will change your mind while we are bound for France and some leave for the crew and a refurbishment for *La Chanson*. That will give me time to ask questions about the whereabouts of my younger sister.'' He drew off his ring. "Mayhap this ring, which revealed the truth to Brienne's grandmother, will help me locate my other sister.''

"I hope so. She must be somewhere looking for you, too.''

Taking her hand, he placed his thunderstone ring on her palm. "Keep this safe for me, *chérie*. When I have found my sister, I want you to keep this as my promise of love.''

"I do not need it, for I can see it in your eyes.''

He lifted her left hand and slipped the oversized ring onto her fourth finger. Looking down into her joy-filled eyes, he said, "I certainly do not need it, for I have everything I want right here, *chérie*. My ship, which is a song upon the sea, and the woman I love, who gives meaning to the melody of life.''

She did not doubt him. Dominic had proven to her that he could make miracles come true. After all they had suffered, it had required only the smallest miracle for her to love a French pirate for the rest of her life. Gazing up into his eyes as his lips lowered toward hers, she whispered, "So do I.''

Dear Reader,

I fell in love with Reg the first time he walked through my imagination, and when I 'met' Abbie, I knew I'd found the perfect match for this hero.

Reg isn't th elast of the lovable Worthington brothers, however. Look for the youngest son Cam's story, RUN-AWAY RANCH, in January 2001. A former rake turned parish vicar, Cam can't leave his wild ways behind and ends up banished to Texas, where a troubled young woman with a shady past teaches him about love, honor, and trusting the leading of one's heart.

I love to hear from fans. Write to me on the web at CynthiaSterling@aol.com or P.O. Box 816 Pine, CO 80470.

Cynthia Sterling

If you liked LAST CHANCE RANCH, be sure to look for Cynthia Sterling's next release in the Titled Texans series, RUNAWAY RANCH, available wherever books are sold in January 2001.

Outspoken and unconventional, Cam Worthington, the youngest son of the Earl of Devonshire, has come to Texas as a new member of the clergy in the hopes of changing people's lives for the better. He gets the chance right away when a sudden thunderstorm finds him stranded in a barn, facing a farmer with a shotgun, a nervous young woman named Caroline Allen, and a preacher ready to perform a hasty marriage ceremony—with Cam as the elected groom. . . .

COMING IN NOVEMBER FROM
ZEBRA BALLAD ROMANCES

___EMILY'S WISH, Wishing Well #2
   by Joy Reed   0-8217-6713-5 $5.50US/$7.50CAN
Intent upon escaping her troubled past, Miss Emily Pearce flees into the night,
only to come upon Honeywell House. Rescued from uncertainty by celebrated
author, Sir Terrence O'Reilly, Emily becomes the heroine of the greatest love
story of all—their own.

___A KNIGHT'S PASSION, The Kinsmen #2
   by Candice Kohl   0-8217-6714-3 $5.50US/$7.50CAN
Ordered by the King to wed two cousins from the borderlands of Wales, Raven
and Peter met their match in Lady Pamela and Roxanne. Thrown into marriage
by royal decree, the brothers soon find that what began as punishment can end
in love.

___ADDIE AND THE LAIRD, Bogus Brides
   by Linda Lea Castle   0-8217-6715-1 $5.50US/$7.50CAN
Seeking a fresh start in a virgin territory, the Green sisters leave for the charter
town of MacTavish. There is only one thing that stands between the sisters
and a new life ... they have one month to wed if they are to remain in
MacTavish. Will the necessity to leave lead to the discovery of love?

___ROSE, The Acadians #2
   by Cherie Claire   0-8217-6716-X $5.50US/$7.50CAN
Warm, vibrant, and exceedingly lovely, Rose Gallant vowed to keep alive her
family's dream of finding her long-lost father, but her heart dreams of finding
true love. Amid the untamed forests and moss-strewn swamps of Louisiana
Territory, Rose discovers the fulfillment of love.

Call toll free **1-888-345-BOOK** to order by phone or use this
coupon to order by mail. ALL BOOKS AVAILABLE NOVEMBER 1, 2000.

Name _____

Address _____

City _____ State _____ Zip _____

Please send me the books I have checked above.

I am enclosing	$ _____
Plus postage and handling*	$ _____
Sales tax (in NY and TN)	$ _____
Total amount enclosed	$ _____

*Add $2.50 for the first book and $.50 for each additional book.
Send check or money order (no cash or CODS) to:
Kensington Publishing Corp., Dept. C.O., 850 Third Avenue, New York, NY 10022
Prices and numbers subject to change without notice. Valid only in the U.S.
All orders subject to availabilty. NO ADVANCE ORDERS.
Visit our website at www.kensingtonbooks.com.

Put a Little Romance in Your Life With

Hannah Howell

__**Highland Destiny** 0-8217-5921-3	**$5.99US/$7.50CAN**
__**Highland Honor** 0-8217-6095-5	**$5.99US/$7.50CAN**
__**Highland Promise** 0-8217-6254-0	**$5.99US/$7.50CAN**
__**My Valiant Knight** 0-8217-5186-7	**$5.50US/$7.00CAN**
—**A Taste of Fire** 0-8217-5804-7	**$5.99US/$7.50CAN**
__**Wild Roses** 0-8217-5677-X	**$5.99US/$7.50CAN**

Call toll free **1-888-345-BOOK** to order by phone, use this coupon to order by mail, or order online at **www.kensingtonbooks.com**.

Name _____
Address _____
City _____ State _____ Zip _____
Please send me the books I have checked above.

I am enclosing	$_____
Plus postage and handling*	$_____
Sales tax (in New York and Tennessee only)	$_____
Total amount enclosed	$_____

*Add $2.50 for the first book and $.50 for each additional book.
Send check or money order (no cash or CODs) to:
Kensington Publishing Corp., Dept C.O., 850 Third Avenue, 16th Floor, New York, NY 10022
Prices and numbers subject to change without notice.
All orders subject to availability.
Visit our website at **www.kensingtonbooks.com**.

Celebrate Romance With Two of Today's Hottest Authors

Meagan McKinney

__In the Dark	$6.99US/$8.99CAN	0-8217-6341-5
__The Fortune Hunter	$6.50US/$8.00CAN	0-8217-6037-8
__Gentle from the Night	$5.99US/$7.50CAN	0-8217-5803-9
__A Man to Slay Dragons	$5.99US/$6.99CAN	0-8217-5345-2
__My Wicked Enchantress	$5.99US/$7.50CAN	0-8217-5661-3
__No Choice But Surrender	$5.99US/$7.50CAN	0-8217-5859-4

Meryl Sawyer

__Thunder Island	$6.99US/$8.99CAN	0-8217-6378-4
__Half Moon Bay	$6.50US/$8.00CAN	0-8217-6144-7
__The Hideaway	$5.99US/$7.50CAN	0-8217-5780-6
__Tempting Fate	$6.50US/$8.00CAN	0-8217-5858-6
__Unforgettable	$6.50US/$8.00CAN	0-8217-5564-1

Call toll free **1-888-345-BOOK** to order by phone, use this coupon to order by mail, or order online at **www.kensingtonbooks.com**.

Name _____

Address _____

City _____ State _____ Zip _____

Please send me the books I have checked above.

I am enclosing	$_____
Plus postage and handling*	$_____
Sales tax (in New York and Tennessee only)	$_____
Total amount enclosed	$_____

*Add $2.50 for the first book and $.50 for each additional book.

Send check or money order (no cash or CODs) to:

Kensington Publishing Corp., Dept. C.O., 850 Third Avenue, New York, NY 10022

Prices and numbers subject to change without notice.

All orders subject to availability.

Visit our website at **www.kensingtonbooks.com**.